CHANCTONBURY

CHANCTONBURY

Natasha Murray

Best Wishes
Abi

Natasha Murray

First published in Great Britain in 2014

Published by Natasha Murray ISBN 978-0-9927828-0-1

1

The line between becoming a victim and finding the strength to be a survivor is fine. No matter what happens, the past cannot be changed. If there is regret then there is hope but if the past is buried then the future will be troubled. There are those that prey on distressed souls and lie in wait. Within a hill, crowned with a ring of beech trees in the South Downs, someone listens for those cries for help and should they stray his way, he may embrace them. To the brave that walk around the circle of trees seven times, he offers to them a bowl of soup or if he is feeling particularly generous, grants them their dearest wish. But being good can be tiresome.

Sarah Brunning watched a raindrop weave its way down the windscreen of her car; she wondered if it would make it to the bottom or whether it would be sucked into a larger stream? Eagerly she waited to see if it would make it. A gust of wind blew the rain drop from the windscreen; she hadn't expected that.

Sarah had been waiting outside the primary school for half an hour, her interview was at 10:30am and she still had another ten minutes to wait before she went in. She breathed in deeply, trying to settle her nerves, this was her first interview since she'd returned from Afghanistan and her first attempt, as her counsellor had put it, to 'start leading a normal life.' She wondered, what normal meant, she doubted if she would ever feel like a normal person again.

She tried to remember how she'd spent her life before Afghanistan, she'd been normal then and had spent several years at university, received a first class honours in English and then went on to do teacher training, before volunteering to teach English in the hills of a quiet village, a few miles north of Kabul. Sarah was bilingual and she'd chosen to go to Kabul as her mother, originally from Afghanistan, had taught Sarah from a baby to speak her native language, Dari. There was another reason too. Sarah sighed, she was only twenty three and her university days seemed to be just distant memories.

She'd no brothers or sisters and often felt lonely so after a particularly dull thirteenth birthday, just after her father had died, Sarah had decided that she would try and track down her relatives on her mother's side as her father had none that they knew of. As the years passed, she found that she couldn't stop thinking about her distant family. She was concerned, however, that if she did find them, she might not be welcomed as her mother had disgraced her family and had run off with an English man. Sarah hoped they would warm to her. It would make her feel much happier about herself if she knew more about her roots.

When she finished her teacher training course, she felt that it was the perfect time to begin her search. She wasn't in a relationship, had no mortgage and some of her university friends had gone off travelling too. After much research, Sarah decided that she would join a Christian missionary group, who as well as providing medical services to poorer countries, offered to teach English to those that wished to improve their chances of finding a professional career. She discovered that English teachers were needed in villages near to where her mother was born and with her ability to speak Dari; this made her an ideal applicant and gave her the opportunity to find out more about her relatives.

After a quick look at herself in the sun visor mirror, she smoothed down her dark brown hair that she'd tied back in a ponytail and looked at her eyeliner to make sure it hadn't smudged. Her brown eyes stared back at her, she looked a little tired but that was to be expected, she hadn't slept well lately and she was thankful that her make-up covered up the dark rings under her eyes. Sarah looked at the time, it was 10:25am, time to walk up the path of the school and show the headmistress, Mrs Richards, that she still was that confident, clever and fun loving individual that had set off from Heathrow on her way to Kabul, a whole year ago to the day.

As she locked the car door, she was glad that the rain had stopped as she hadn't brought an umbrella with her. She opened the school gate; the playground was littered with leaves, which blew at will, looking almost as if they were alive. They scuttled across the hop scotch and got caught in rubber tyres laid out around the playground; the wind gusted and caught them again, sending them flying through the air in different directions. Sarah walked briskly on to avoid getting caught in the next gust of wind.

Sarah waited for several minutes before the receptionist appeared. She seemed surprised that she was there for an interview; she looked through her diary as if the appointments logged there were a mystery to her.

"Oh yes," she said after a few moments. "Sarah Brunning, there you are, to see Brenda at 10:30am? If you wouldn't mind taking a seat, I'll tell her you're here."

Sarah looked behind her and saw a row of classroom chairs against the reception wall; obediently she perched on the chair at the end and waited. She passed the time by looking at the colourful paintings decorating the walls. She loved being at school as a child and even now this small primary school in a quiet Sussex village, felt like a warm and exciting place to be. Did all schools smell of powder paint and school dinners? She was feeling much calmer now, her decision to apply for the primary school teacher's post seemed to be a good one; it was a step in the right direction and would stop her mother worrying about her.

Mrs Richards came into the reception hall to greet her. She didn't shake her hand; she seemed much too grand to bother with such pleasantries. "So you're Sarah Brunning," she stated. "Follow me please," she added, heading back to her office.

Sarah surveyed Mrs Richards' back as she followed her. She was a tall woman in her late fifties, Sarah guessed. Her hair was dyed black but she'd a white streak on the right hand side running through and she'd rolled her hair up into a French Pleat. She wore a tailored tweed jacket, a matching calf length skirt and her shoes were flat. Sarah anxiously looked down at her own attire; she was wearing high heels and a black trouser suit. She felt that her outfit was inappropriate, more suited to an executive in the city and she wished that she'd worn a skirt instead.

She was shown into a small untidy office and was surprised to see piles of folders and documents stacked around the room. The desk top was barely visible, it was covered with cups, papers, a first aid box and several plastic boxes filled with pens.

Sarah moved from a chair a supermarket bag containing bean bags onto a milk bottle crate on the floor next to it and sat down whilst Mrs Richards sifted through a stack of papers on her desk for what Sarah decided was her application form.

Mrs Richards put on her glasses "There we go," she announced, when she finally found the documents she was looking for. "Sarah Brunning," she read out as she sat in her chair. "So you want to join us then? I see you've had experience of teaching adults to speak English in Afghanistan. Whatever made you want to go there?"

"My mother is from there and I thought, as I speak Dari, I could make a contribution. There are many business people in Afghanistan that need to be able to speak English in order to pursue a professional career," Sarah replied. "I did realise when I joined the organisation, that there would be dangers but I honestly thought that as I was trying to assist the Afghan people, I would be welcomed and left to carry out my job." She could feel her voice shaking.

"You'll find working with children a lot more challenging than working with adults and I have to say that I'm a little concerned that you have noted that you are receiving counselling. We do like our teachers here to be reliable. It is very difficult getting supply teachers in and it is very unsettling for the children. I have a reference from the school where you did your training, they were very complementary. Teacher training is one thing, actually teaching children for real is a whole different kettle of fish."

Sarah could feel the colour rising in her cheeks; it was almost as if Mrs Richards was writing her off. Was it such a crime to be receiving counselling? Many people did. Did seeing a doctor make her incompetent or an irresponsible person? On her application form, when asked to elaborate on her condition, she'd decided not to put down too much detail about her ordeal and had jotted down her side effects. These being, night terrors and a phobia of being in the dark; these she found most difficult to cope with. On reflection, she wished that she'd left this off her application form as she was determined to conquer these problems. Her confidence too, needed to be worked on but she thought it better to not mention that. "I'm fine now, really," she began. "I'm sure that by the end of this year, I will be back to my old self," she continued trying to sound confident and was determined not to let Mrs Richards belittle her. "I can't remember the last time I had a day off sick. I thoroughly enjoy teaching children of all ages and am looking forward to being back in the classroom again."

Mrs Richards straightened her back and looked speculatively over the top of her glasses at Sarah. "What brought on the down turn in your mental health? You are young and have very little to worry about. Are you on medication?"

Sarah was beginning to get annoyed and wondered why Mrs Richards had actually selected her to come for an interview at all. "I'm not on any medication and any personal issues I may have had are private and will not have an effect on my ability to teach. I would also be able to contribute to the school in other ways; I'm artistic and have very good organisational skills and am happy to assist with any events held here."

Mrs Richards drew a deep breath. "If you've quite finished! So you don't think the fact that you were kidnapped and kept in solitary confinement for six months has affected you. I'm sorry but I think you are a little naive if you think you are going to be better any time soon – a thing like that would leave scars and perhaps affect one's brain for good. I need someone I can rely on, someone who is strong and is able to put the children at this school first. I'm not sure that you have what it takes."

For a moment Sarah sat there in stunned silence, she felt surprised that Mrs Richards knew about her kidnapping, she hadn't mentioned it on her application form. She felt emotionally exposed. It had been five months since she'd returned to England, the media attention had died down long ago and she hoped that nobody would remember her name.

When she'd been kidnapped, there had been very little media coverage as any western attention she received would have pushed up her captors' ransom demand. This was a clever game plan by the Government and was one of the main reasons she'd been set free as she'd become almost worthless to her captors. Mrs Richards' treatment was inexcusable, Sarah really had no idea why she was there at all. This strange woman had no intention of hiring her and seemed to be taking great pleasure in trying to humiliate her.

Sarah stood up slowly and walked towards the door; she opened it and looking back at Mrs Richards, said calmly. "I wish you all the best in finding a suitable candidate for this vacancy. I'm not a victim and never will be. I am resilient and have always had a fighting spirit. I wouldn't ever consider working for you, not even if you were to go down on your knees, I pity your staff and think it might be an idea if you took a long deep look at yourself!"

Cold air filled Sarah's lungs. It was a relief to be outside the school and such a pity that the headmistress had turned out to be a bit of a weirdo. She looked back at the children in the class rooms, the windows were steamed up but she could still see them happily writing and drawing in their work books.

As she drove out of the village and headed for the dual carriage way that would take her to her home in Horsham, she wondered what she would do next, maybe it was a bit too soon to find a job. Perhaps she needed a few more months to recover. The wind was picking up now, leaves scuttled across the road as if they were shielding vermin making her feel anxious, she didn't want to run over a live animal even if it were a rat and just thinking about rats triggered off memories of being locked up.

Sarah thought back to early spring that year, when she'd been imprisoned; she hadn't been tortured or raped but just kept in isolation and treated as an infidel. Her days in captivity had passed slowly for her. She feared that she may be executed and the endless waiting for something fatal to happen had been too torturous and painful to endure. On some days she wished that they would shoot her, put her out of her misery and end her suffering.

She'd been kept up in the mountains, in an outbuilding behind a small house and treated as if she was unclean. Food and water were pushed into the shed and a bucket provided for waste which she tipped out of a window each day and then watched hungry dogs below clean up for her. This window was her one link with the world outside and she spent a lot of time just staring at the hills. She could tell what time of day it was from the sun's position in the sky. Sometimes, she would watch the clouds as they floated by and they became a comfort to her. The sun, moon and clouds are the same, wherever you go. On good days the clouds formed themselves in to dragons, dogs and people. Sometimes she saw nothing and the isolation and loneliness became so unbearable that she would cry like a baby.

As the summer progressed the days became extremely hot. Sarah dreaded the nights even more, sometimes she had moonlight but most nights there was only darkness and for some reason on those nights she couldn't breathe properly as the air around her was stifling. The window although it had no glass in it, did not let any cool air through and she longed for someone to open the door and let some air in but no one ever did. There was a thin mattress on the floor to sleep on but she couldn't because of the heat. As she lay awake, she listened out for the rats to start running across the floor, she wasn't sure where they came from but her cell soon became congested with them and she screamed when they climbed on her.

The insects were also a nuisance and they flew in through the open window and feasted on her as soon as she did fall asleep. She was pretty sure that she'd nearly died several times from various fevers brought on by the insect bites and when her temperature was high she saw someone standing by her bed. She didn't know who he was, all she knew was that he was to be feared and she was afraid of him. When her fever had gone she realised that there had been no one there. Perhaps she was naive to think that those six months in captivity wouldn't cause her problems in later life.

Sarah couldn't face going home; her mother was at work in a nursing home in Horsham and wouldn't be back until after lunch. She didn't like being in the house by herself, she much preferred to be out walking or being with friends. Her circle of friends had shrunk since her return from Afghanistan; most of them were too busy to meet up, had found jobs or had moved away. Sarah smiled, at least she still had George to talk to, her old roommate from university. If she was feeling a bit down, she would chat to him on Facebook and he was always very supportive.

A walk she decided would clear her head, she'd her training shoes and a coat in the boot and she knew just where to go. She was quite near to the turn off for the Chanctonbury Ring; this would be a good place to think things through. She'd spent many hours up amongst the beech trees, just thinking. The trees were a bit ragged now, since the 1987 hurricane but it was a beautiful place to be on a clear day, she could see for miles and it felt as if she was on top of the world when she looked across the South Downs.

The roundabout that Sarah needed to turn right at was just ahead, there was a small queue of traffic waiting there. Sarah drew up behind a red Volvo; she read the sticker on its rear window, 'Volvo Lovers on Board' and thought it strange to want to declare such a thing. She looked up ahead and wondered what the holdup was, it was mid-morning and this stretch of road was usually quiet. She wondered if a car had broken down.

As Sarah waited, she stared aimlessly into the woodland that lined her side of the dual carriage way. At first all Sarah could see was a tangle of branches but as she looked deeper into the thicket, she could make out tattered dwellings, made from tarpaulin and scraps of hardboard. She wondered who lived there and how long the settlement had existed, she hadn't noticed it before. The land was probably owned by the Council and the travellers, she decided, had gone unnoticed during the summer months when the vegetation was abundant. Sarah didn't think that there was a homeless problem in the south and hoped that she wouldn't see children there.

The traffic ahead was beginning to move, she put her car into first gear and crept forward. Out of the corner of her eye, she saw a man making his way out from the settlement, he slipped through a gap in the bushes and appeared on the grass verge, a few metres ahead of her and he looked down the dual carriage for a chance to cross. Sarah's heart leapt with fear, her heart pounded as instantly she recognised the man before her and she prayed that he wouldn't look into her car and recognise her.

2

Evie Merryweather waited outside Horsham train station for her bus. It had been difficult to find a spot that was out of the wind and her cheeks and fingers were tingling with the cold. She'd been waiting under the bus shelter for over half an hour and wished she'd worn something warmer than her mac as it was far too thin; she vowed that she would buy herself a new winter coat next time she visited the charity shop in Fulham, around the corner from where she lived.

The 23 bus arrived and she climbed on, paid her fare and found a double seat to herself. She sat down by the window; it was so much easier to scan the countryside if you were by the window and not in an aisle seat. Evie placed her handbag on her lap and her shopping bag next to her on the bus seat, hoping that nobody would ask her to move it. She liked to have her bag by her; it was almost as if Albert was sitting next to her, not just his ashes.

As the bus began to move, Evie looked out anxiously at the people walking along the street, the wind strength was picking up, their hair was blowing in all directions and they didn't look happy to be outside. Evie patted her curly grey hair, she'd only just had it washed and set and she really didn't want her hair do to be destroyed on the second day.

Evie sighed; she wasn't sure if had been a good idea to come out today as Tuesday wasn't one of her most favourite days of the week. The last Tuesday, she'd set out on one of 'expeditions' as she called them, she'd fallen over and all of her eighty two years had flashed before her. She was glad that she'd only bruised her arm and hadn't actually broken anything. This she decided was because she was physically fit; she'd her weekly tennis sessions to thank for that. Today was her only free day, her cooking class had been cancelled and the rest of the week was booked up as Edward, her son, was coming down from his home in Cambridge to visit her. Albert would have been proud of his son, she wished bitterly that she'd told him that she was pregnant but he'd gone off to war and she didn't get a chance to tell him.

Edward was a dear boy, an academic and a tutor at Trinity College but he'd never married. She wondered why that was; Edward always managed to skirt around the subject, whenever she brought it up. She feared that he was getting too old to marry; he'd become set in his ways and didn't seem interested in meeting anyone. Edward's flat mate Jon was single too, he was a lovely boy, always holding dinner parties or off dancing somewhere, she'd spent many a happy Christmas Day up in Cambridge with them both; he was an excellent cook.

Evie sighed again and looked down at the shopping bag, maybe today would be the day that she would find a place to scatter Albert's ashes, she knew that he'd loved Sussex as this was where he'd been born and she'd spent many trips looking for the perfect place. Many a time, she'd reached a peak with a view or the ideal bubbling brook but there had always been something or someone there to blight her task and she'd returned home again with his ashes secretly stowed away at the bottom of her bag in a biscuit tin. The tin was quite battered and had a picture of a steam train on the lid; Albert had adored steam trains. The truth be told, she knew in her heart, that she was always very much relieved to take Albert home again. She looked out of the window and hoped that the weather would improve; she really wanted to scatter his ashes on a sunny day, not on a cold and windy Tuesday in October.

The bus continued on its way to Worthing, Evie thought that she might as well go on with her journey and have a look in the shops at Worthing, have lunch and then wander up the pier if the wind was not too strong and then return home. She put her hand in her pocket looking for her silk head scarf and felt relieved that it was there. A fleeting thought passed through her mind; she could release Albert's ashes into the Channel but this idea passed quickly, Albert was never one for swimming in the sea, he was scared of it and believed that there were creatures lurking beneath the waves, which would drag him down to the wrecks below. Evie had laughed at his phobia and teased him when they walked hand in hand in the sunshine along the beach at Goring all those years ago. She smiled, they had been happy days but both had little idea that a war would break out and that all their dreams would be shattered.

Evie looked around the bus to see who was travelling with her. There was an elderly couple sat on the front side seats and an Asian gentleman with a rucksack next to him at the back of the bus, she wondered where he was going to. Perhaps, she thought, he was travelling the world and had made his way down from Scotland. Evie hadn't been that far north and wondered if Albert had, she'd only been dating him for a year before he went off to war during the autumn of 1940 and there were things she hadn't asked him. It had been so hard to say goodbye. He'd planted a kiss on her forehead, reminded her that he loved her and would be back soon and they would marry. They planned to wed after Christmas when the war ended and she'd waited patiently for him to return. It was just before Christmas when Evie realised that she was pregnant. The war didn't end that quickly and Albert didn't come back.

She'd struggled to bring Edward up by herself, she was only eighteen when he was born and she was practically a child herself. Her parents had disowned her when they found out that she'd decided to keep her baby and not give him up for adoption. Desperately, Evie had turned to her old neighbour and best friend, Milly. Her friend had married and gone to live in Dorset. She had twin boys Christopher and Charlie who had just started school. Milly had been only too happy to have Evie and Edward to stay with her on her farm. When the war started, her husband Peter, had volunteered to join the RAF as he had always dreamed of becoming a pilot. He left his boys and the dairy farm in Milly's capable hands.

Evie and Milly took turns to supervise the children and look after the farm; Evie thought back to those times with fond memories but also remembered the pain they had all suffered too. Milly's husband had been killed in action and she'd supported her as she grieved. So many young men had died and left grieving widows or in her case a grieving partner behind. She could say that word 'partner' easily now; it was perfectly acceptable to live with a partner these days, without feeling accountable. She could, however, not shake off the guilty feelings she had, that had come from having a child out of wedlock.

At the beginning of the war, Evie had kept in contact with Albert's sister Lilly and asked her to send any news about him. Evie sent many letters to Albert but he didn't reply. Lilly wrote occasionally but only talked about the Canadians in Worthing and annoyingly, did not mention Albert. Eventually Lilly's letters stopped and Evie lost contact with her as well.

Evie sighed again, she wished so much that she could talk to Albert; she was tired of being alone in the world. Her parents had both died in the Blitz and she didn't get the chance to make up with them. She saw Daisy her neighbour daily and yes she had her Edward but she longed to have a husband, someone she could love and share her life with. The years had gone by but she could never commit to anyone and thought that it was because she'd never really got over losing Albert. She kept herself busy but always felt that there must be something more to life and the words that it was better to have 'loved and lost than never to have loved at all' stuck in her throat. How could anyone have said anything so silly?

The bus pulled up in Washington and the bus driver rose up from his cab, to address the passengers. "I'm sorry to announce this," he began. "I'm going to have to terminate the bus here, there's a light showing on my dashboard and I think that I've got an engine fault. There'll be another bus along soon, so, if you want me to transfer you to the next bus, then please wait here."

Evie wasn't sure what to do, she looked across the road at the recreation ground, a handful of boys were kicking a ball to each other and she wished she had their energy. Watching them made her feel thirsty and she thought it might be an idea if she had a cup of tea in Washington and then she would return home. Evie picked up her bags and when she stepped out onto the pavement, the wind blew her breath away, it was getting stronger. She struggled to tie on her head scarf and she wished she'd done this in the bus.

As she walked along the country lane, she looked eagerly for a suitable cafe, she was very particular about where she had her tea, she didn't like cafes that served all day breakfasts, they seemed to attract the wrong sort of people and the windows were always far too steamed up to see what was going on outside. Evie picked up her pace, she was glad to leave the bus behind her and be in the fresh air, it was obvious that her day was not going to be a good one but she would try and make the best of it. She wondered what the village of Washington would be like. She was sure she was going the right way as she'd seen a sign pointing in the direction she was going from the bus. Evie passed by The Frankland Arms on her right and continued up a hill, hoping that the village would appear soon as she was beginning to feel cold. She looked at the hedgerows as she walked along, they were barren and the thorny bushes looked menacing and unforgiving.

Ahead of her she saw an animal lying in the road, she knew immediately that it was a fox. She remembered her mother's dark brown fox stole with its shrunken head. As a child, Evie had always found the scarf to be hideous and frightening and she'd refused to go anywhere near her mother when she wore it. There were of course, she remembered, the foxes that used to skirt around the edges of Milly's farm waiting for the right moment to sneak in and cause havoc.

Evie shivered as she approached the fox and she looked at the creature with a morbid fascination. It hadn't been dead long and looked as if it was sleeping. Evie felt sad for it and thought that it must have been hit by a car. As she passed it, she noticed, something move in the hedgerow. She stopped and turned back to look and saw two eyes peering out from below a bush. Evie stepped on the verge for a closer look and saw another fox staring back at her; it was much smaller than the dead one and didn't seem to be phased by her presence. She bent down, to get a closer look and realised that it was a fox cub. She suspected that it might have come out in daylight to find its mother.

Evie stood up again and was not sure what to do, if she walked away then the fox cub would perish, it didn't look old enough to look after itself and if she did try and pick it up then perhaps it would bite her or run off. Evie looked back down the road and remembered seeing a pub. If she walked back to it, someone there could ring the RSPCA and then it could be taken to a refuge. She started to walk back down the hill and then stopped; if she left the fox cub then it might run into the road and get run over too. Evie looked at her hands, she was wearing leather gloves and the cub didn't look vicious. She decided that she would take a chance and try and pick it up and put in her shopping bag with Albert. A car tore past her and made up her mind.

Carefully, Evie approached the cub and ever so gently, she scooped it up and placed it in her bag. The cub didn't resist and seemed to be very frail and didn't put up a fight. Evie headed towards the Frankland Arms with urgency, she didn't want the cub to suffer any more than it needed to.

The pub was surprisingly busy for a Tuesday lunch time and Evie was impressed by its interior; it had a cosy feel to it. She wouldn't have normally walked into a pub by herself but this was an emergency. A young girl was serving a couple at the bar; Evie looked around, hoping that she would see someone older that would know where to find the number of the RSPCA. She stood away from the bar deciding what to do; perhaps she thought, she should walk up to the village and find the police station; they would be able to help her.

"Are you lost?" asked a man who was sitting at a table in the far corner.

Evie turned round, to see who was talking to her. She hadn't noticed him when she walked into the pub and was quite relieved to see that he was as old as she was and looked quite respectable. "No, I'm not," replied Evie. "Do you know who the proprietor of this establishment is?" she asked.

"Yes I do, but they're out at the moment, they shouldn't be long. You're not from Washington, are you? I know everyone that lives here. Just popped in for lunch, have you?"

"No, not exactly, I was just on my way to the village for refreshment and I came across this poor fox on the road," continued Evie looking in her shopping bag.

"Oh yes, I saw it on the road on my way down here. You haven't got it in your shopping bag, have you?" he asked but he'd a mischievous smile on his face.

"Of course, I haven't!" Evie was quite appalled that he would even think that she would do such a thing. "It's a different one. I've found a live fox cub by the dead fox and I was hoping to find someone that would ring the RSPCA." Evie walked over to him and opened her bag to show him the frightened cub.

The man got up to get a better look and noticed that it was lying curled up on a biscuit tin. "That's just a scrap of a thing, he won't last long. I know just the woman to help him," he said getting a mobile phone out of his pocket. He squinted as he looked at the list of contacts on the screen and then after selecting a name put the mobile to his ear. "Ah Helen, you're in. It's me, Tom," he said running his fingers through his white hair. "I've got a sick fox cub here that needs your help. Can I bring it over to you; it's not looking too bright? No it's not injured, probably just needs some milk and warming up. I'll be over in a moment. Ok, thanks Helen. Bye." Tom looked at his phone to make sure he'd disconnected and then replaced it in his pocket. "Shall I drive or are you going to?"

"Oh!" exclaimed Evie surprised, she was lost for words for once; she hadn't expected to find help so quickly and certainly didn't expect to be getting in a car with a perfect stranger. "I don't drive, I came here by bus. It's very kind of you but you really shouldn't put yourself out, I'm sure you are very busy and..."

Tom cut in. "Oh, it's no bother, Helen lives on The Street, she's a foster mother to all sorts of wild animals and your fox cub will be in very good hands. It's not out my way, I live up there myself and I was just about to leave. You did say you were going there too," Tom added.

"If you put it like that, how can I refuse," replied Evie. "That's very kind of you, Tom."

Feeling self-conscious, Evie followed Tom out to his car and was shocked to find that it was a two seated sports car. It was British racing green and was well looked after. She'd planned to sit on the back seat as she felt Albert wouldn't have approved if she sat in the front with a strange man. Tom held the passenger door open for her; she climbed in and pulled across her seat belt but had difficulty plugging it in. Tom assisted her and she blushed as she placed her handbag by her feet and the shopping bag on her lap and then laughed at her incompetence. "It's been a long time since I've been in a car like this," she said nervously and then realised that she'd never been in a sports car at all.

"She's a beauty, isn't she? replied Tom, starting the engine. "I've had her for twenty years and she's not given me any trouble. You said that you came by bus, are you visiting someone?"

"No... I'm looking for a beauty spot, somewhere peaceful, somewhere with history or with a good view."

"Oh...you've picked a bit of a wild day for sightseeing. Have you been to the Chanctonbury Ring? That's a nice place to go on a summer's day – you can see for miles up there.

"I've heard of it." Evie said looking down at the fox club to make sure it was still breathing. "Is it far from here?"

"If you came up from Horsham, then you might have seen the Ring from the bus."

"Oh, no, I didn't but I do remember Albert talking about it. The hill is enchanted, I think, that's what

Albert said. He went up there with his father when he was a child."

"I wouldn't say that exactly," laughed Tom. "There are tales about the Ring but they're all nonsense, I just like to walk the dog up there. My Barney likes a bit of a run, he's a retired greyhound but he still has his moments. Who's Albert, is he your husband?" asked Tom as he turned into The Street.

"Albert died in the war," replied Evie looking down at the sleeve of her coat for any signs of dog hair. "I still miss him."

"Yes I know how you feel, my Martha died five years ago and it doesn't get any easier. I still think she's somewhere in the house, when I get home."

They drove up a narrow road, it was steep and there wasn't much traffic. The Street was lined with small terraced cottages and as they reached the crest of the hill, Evie saw a red telephone box on her right, the Asian man, she'd seen on the bus was inside with his backpack on his back. He wasn't on the phone but looking at a map, the telephone box was shielding him from the wind. They pulled up outside one of the cottages and as Evie climbed out of the sports car, she looked along the road for a cafe but was disappointed.

Tom led Evie up the path of a white cottage and a young girl opened the door. Evie expected Helen to be much older. She welcomed them in, she was a large woman with fair hair and a rosy complexion and Evie thought her to be no more than thirty. Helen led them to the back of the house, through the back garden and into a Swiss chalet style outhouse that she'd turned into a small animal hospital. Cages were stacked along the wall containing a variety of wild animals in various stages of recovery. In the centre of the chalet was a table with a baby's changing mat on top. Evie placed her bag on the table and Helen, after putting on thick gloves, reached inside the bag and lifted out the cub. "Ah," she said, looking at Evie and Tom "He's quite young, he can't be more than twelve weeks old. He has probably only just left the den. Where did you find him?" she asked.

"By a dead fox, just past the pub. Do you think that was his mother?" Evie looked at the cub lying on the changing mat; it looked like it had given up on living

"More than likely," replied Helen. "He was probably just learning to hunt. It's lucky you brought him to me; he wouldn't have survived another day. He looks quite healthy, probably just needs some food and a couple of hours under a heat lamp. I'll soon have him on his feet again."

"That's very kind of you Helen, you are marvellous," exclaimed Tom, "We'll show ourselves out and let you get on. I'll give you a ring later to see how he's getting on."

"No, it's no trouble. It's a shame about these poor old foxes; so many are getting killed on the road these days. It's a good job they've banned hunting or they could have ended up as being an endangered species."

Evie and Tom let themselves out of Helen's cottage and walked back onto The Street.

"Well, I'd better be going, thank you Tom for all your help." Evie announced looking down the hill as she drew her mac collar across her; the wind was relentless.

"It's not really the weather for sightseeing; you look like you're freezing, would you like a nice cup of tea before you go?" Tom suggested. "My house is just around the corner, it won't be any trouble."

"No, I'm fine," replied Evie. "I can't take up any more of your time."

"Don't be daft, you look cold through to the bone and I've nothing better to do. I won't take no for an answer," insisted Tom.

"Well, I could really do with a cup of tea and if you are really sure?"

"There, that's settled then, come with me, Barney would be glad of the company."

Evie followed Tom along the street and hoped that she wasn't being a nuisance; it would be a welcome relief to get out of the wind and have something hot to drink. It wasn't like her to accept assistance from anyone but Tom was so kind and seemed trustworthy. She looked down at Albert and hoped that he didn't mind.

3

Michael McGrath stood in a deserted wooded copse and surveyed his camp with pride; to the untrained eye it could not be seen. His chances of remaining undetected were high, his only concern were the dog walkers; for some unknown reason they didn't keep to the paths and tracks and always seemed hell bent on walking across untamed woodland. It was because of them he'd picked a particularly steep slope to build his shelter on, beneath the roots of a fallen tree as he doubted if anyone would want to come that way. An abundance of green moss snaked its way along the tree's black rotting trunk. Many of the trees around him had been up rooted or had been damaged and black spiky stumps littered the woodland floor like decaying teeth; could the wind be that brutal he wondered?

Michael looked towards the path above him and hoped that the public who wandered up the steep paths weaving their way to the summit would not be tempted to climb down the bank. Anxiously he looked around him for people, earlier he'd only seen one woman solemnly walking past but she hadn't seen him. It was generally quiet during the day but the evenings and weekends were a nightmare for him. It was the dogs that he feared most, not only did they not mind their own business but they were also prone to barking, which he now found strangely alarming. It reminded him of the nights when he had to sleep out in Helmand. Sometimes, gun fire had woken him; sometimes it was dogs barking nearby. Both sounds merged in to one, each jolted him awake and made his heart beat almost to bursting point. The dogs would have to be careful of the rabbit snares he'd left out!

Michael felt his chin, he didn't like having a beard, it didn't suit him and it made his skin itchy. His brown hair was getting long too and he noticed grey hair had begun to appear, which was a surprise to him as he was only thirty six. He much preferred to shave his hair off completely but he really didn't have much choice as his dwindling money supply was reserved for the most essential items and razors was not one of them. Considering his circumstances, he decided, a beard provided him with the perfect disguise.

Michael looked at his watch, it was midday. He'd been so preoccupied with building his shelter that he'd forgotten to eat breakfast. He walked over to his rucksack and pulled out some crackers, some rabbit meat, then sat on a fallen branch and ate slowly. His mind kept telling him to eat quickly, he was almost starving. He knew that he must remain in control as his mind liked to play tricks on him of the cruelest kind. His only hope of staying sane was to be regimented when carrying out his daily tasks, making camp, catching food, eating, drinking, sleeping and travelling by night. Eighteen years in the army had taught him to be disciplined but it hadn't taught him how to deal with civilian life.

He thought about his army career; being in the military was all he'd ever wanted to do and being forced to leave hadn't been in his plans. Michael rubbed his head and looked about himself uneasily; he knew that he needed to be on his guard night and day. Being a highly skilled martial artist too, had taught him to always be on the lookout for trouble and to always be prepared for a surprise. He could only spend a few nights in his camp and then he would have to move on. Michael swallowed the last of his cracker, leant forward and put his face in his hands. He was tired and hungry and he'd no idea what he should do to resolve his problem.

A loud crack of a twig breaking made him jump; he leapt to his feet and looked around him. He couldn't see anybody and he sighed with relief, he knew he was being hunted but he also felt that someone else was watching him, waiting for him, waiting for him to drop his guard. He would have to be more careful and decided that he would crawl into his shelter and try and think of a plan. He surveyed his surroundings one more time and finally decided that it would be safe to enter his shelter; it would be a relief to escape from the public's view. The best way to remain underground was to keep moving and never leave a trail. He didn't like this wood; it was eerie and merciless and he would be glad to leave it.

Michael could only lie in his shelter and there was just enough room for him to turn over. He lay on his sleeping bag and used his rucksack as a pillow. He'd lined the base of his shelter with plastic and dry leaves but all his possessions felt damp. The British climate didn't suit him, he much preferred being abroad; he could cope much better in desert-like conditions. He missed his comrades, he missed being with the army. They were his family and it hurt that they had abandoned him when he needed them most. His thoughts turned to his sister

Helen, she and her daughter Brighton were all he had left in the world. He felt one of his pockets, his mobile was there, she was only a call away but he dared not turn it on and call as he was sure that his calls would be monitored. Helen had been through too much and didn't need him bothering her. She would only tell him to turn himself in and explain to the authorities what had happened - she would also say that he needed help.

He hadn't turned to drink and drugs like some ex-soldiers had, he just needed time to sort out his head and find a job. It was too late now, he knew that if he got caught, then he would be charged and thrown into prison for something he was pretty sure he hadn't done. Michael exhaled slowly, he needed to flee and start a new life. He could see himself working in the fields, picking olives or herding animals in a warm sunny place away from everyone, away from the foolishness that surrounded him in England. Yes, he said to himself, he would steal a boat and go across the Channel to France. He could see the Channel from the top of the next hill. Michael closed his eyes, he would try and sleep and wait for night to fall and then if the sky was clear, he would empty his traps and head for the coast; the sea was tantalising close. He tried to relax and wait for sleep to steal over him. He hadn't slept properly for months, probably years and longed to drift in to a deep sleep, with no dreams and wake up rested.

It was not always the same dream that haunted him and quite often he found he could influence a satisfactory ending. His dreams were not always about war, mutilation and loss but were often set in calm and surreal settings, where bizarre things happened. These dreams he could not control and they usually ended with a barbaric twist. Quite often he dreamt about a small Afghan boy, playing in a street. The boy was pretending to be a soldier, blissfully unaware of any potential dangers - snipers often killed civilians in error. The boy was confident that the friendly soldiers that occupied his village would protect him from the ruthless Taliban. Michael didn't remember ever seeing this boy in real life and thought that perhaps he represented the hopes of the villagers that the forces were trying to protect. He expected in his dream to see the boy shot down and he would watch him fall to the floor with his eyes wide open, disappointed that Michael hadn't been able to protect him. This dream haunted him.

Near the end of Michael's service, the years of seeing terrible things had taken its toll on him, he'd become disillusioned and it was not always clear to him that he was assisting a country and then could not bear the resentment the villagers finally displayed as the war went on. He'd joined the army to swiftly resolve disputes and rebuild countries not to make things worse.

Sleep didn't come to Michael; his mind raced and ran over and over the events of the past three months. He needed to remember every detail, every tiny thing that had happened. There had to be some clue, some small detail he'd overlooked that would make all the difference, prove his innocence and free him from his fragile existence.

The nightmare had begun at the end of July on a hot summer's night; Michael had been staying with Helen and her two children Aaron and Brighton at her house in South London. Helen was a kind soul and didn't mind him staying with her until he found a job and a place to live. He had savings and was able to pay his way. She was a single mum and worked hard to keep food on the table; she really didn't deserve to suffer such a tragedy.

That particular July night, Michael had been unable to sleep, he was restless and felt too confined in Helen's small house to think clearly and so he'd gone off into the night to walk and think things through. He'd walked the streets for hours, his mind tormented and turning over and over unable to find out exactly what was bothering him. He knew he needed help but was not quite sure who he should see. He didn't want to go to a doctor; he didn't want to be given a diagnosis of depression as that would only hinder his job search.

His mobile phone rang out into the night, the ring tone echoing in the deserted streets; it had made him jump and snapped him out of his frantic musing. He'd looked at the caller on the screen and wondered with alarm why Helen would be calling him at that time of night; she knew that he often went out for a walk in the early hours of the morning. Hesitantly, he took the call and put the phone to his ear, only to hear her screaming and crying - the house was on fire, she was trapped in her bedroom and could hear the children calling out for help. Michael ran back to the house, hoping he was not too late, a rescue plan forming in his head as he ran. He wondered how and where the fire had started; he or Helen didn't smoke. He wondered why Helen had called him and not the fire brigade first and why their mobile batteries had died before they could ring them?

Michael opened his eyes; he didn't want to remember any more from that night. Helen had jumped from the upstairs window, breaking both her ankles and the fire had taken hold of the whole house and there was not much they could do to save any of their possessions.

Whilst Helen recovered in hospital, Michael had taken Aaron and Brighton down to her friend's mobile home in Littlehampton. Helen didn't want the children to see the contractors clearing the house, she wanted it restored and the charred ruins erased from their memories. Looking after an eight year boy and six year old girl was a challenge for Michael but fortunately they both enjoyed going down to the beach; the sea seemed to wash away their pain. Michael was surprised how resilient the children were and how easily they mended. He wished life was that simple and those weeks with the children were perhaps, the most peaceful weeks of his life. He could still see the beams of sunshine fanning out from behind the clouds and stretching into the sea that was as calm as a millpond with Brighton wandering along the sand, looking for sea creatures and shells.

At the end of August, Michael and the children set off from Littlehampton and headed back home. The house had been refurbished and Helen had been let out of hospital and was able to get around with the use of crutches. Brighton, being the youngest was very excited about seeing her mother again but Aaron seemed strangely subdued and hadn't spoken since breakfast. Michael had passed Aaron's silence off as nervousness; perhaps he was apprehensive about seeing the house again.

As Michael drove along the motorway, he looked in his rear view mirror at him, he was a strange boy, quiet and emotionless and he was never quite sure how he felt. The evening before, Michael had been shocked when Aaron had approached him in the kitchen and accused him of not giving him any pocket money. Michael had been surprised, Helen hadn't mentioned anything about pocket money and although Michael didn't have much, he was more than happy to buy them the odd magazine or sweets when he could. Aaron was only eight, yet the way he spoke to him was so adult like; he made him feel uncomfortable.

Michael looked in the rear view mirror and saw Aaron staring directly at him; it was almost as if he knew what he was thinking. He looked away as he was not willing to meet Aaron's stone-cold gaze again and shuddered, he knew something was not right, his head ached and the car felt stuffy, Michael opened all the windows wide and decided that he would come off the motorway and find somewhere to have lunch. If Aaron had a problem then he would rather sort it out with him before they got back home. Michael indicated to turn off the motorway and then followed the road around to a country lane. As he drove along, he looked out for a pub or restaurant where they could stop and have lunch.

Ahead of him he could see that there was a zoo and he thought that this might be an ideal place to stop. Michael turned into the entrance and was just about to let them know what his plan was when Brighton had let out a piercing scream. Michael stopped the car and looked behind him, to see what the matter was; her mouth was open and her eyes were wide with fear, she seemed unable to speak and just pointed in Aaron's direction. Michael looked at Aaron's seat, he'd gone. He looked frantically around the car park for him but his attention was drawn away by a rattling sound from within the car and was then amazed to see a large snake on Aaron's seat. Panic filled Michael, he was not sure what to do, he didn't want Brighton to get bitten and wondered how the snake had got in the car.

"Aaron just turned in to a snake," whispered Brighton in a small and terrified voice.

Michael looked hesitantly at the snake and watched it as it slowly began to slide towards the open window. He put his fingers to his lips to tell Brighton to be quiet and not to move. The snake wound its way up the door handle and then just as it reached the open window, its head turned towards him. Michael looked at its eyes; they were the same cold menacing eyes he'd seen earlier. He knew immediately that Brighton was right; Aaron had somehow turned himself in to a rattlesnake.

The snake slid out of the car and wound its way across the tarmac. Michael was relieved and was grateful that it hadn't attacked Brighton. He became alarmed that it seemed to be heading towards the people waiting at the ticket kiosks. Quickly, he jumped out of the car and telling Brighton to wait, whilst he went after Aaron, ran towards the queue of people. Unnoticed, the snake passed the people winding its way through their feet and slid into the zoo. Michael ran past the queue of people, the lady in the kiosk didn't see him go by but those waiting jeered as he knocked into them. Michael apologised and ran on, the snake, was just ahead and had stopped briefly to read the direction boards and then took a sharp right turn towards the reptile house. Michael couldn't believe what he was seeing and he wondered what he would tell Helen.

Michael ran into the reptile house and scanned the room, it was busy with people staring mesmerised into the vivariums. There was no sign of Aaron, he was obviously going to ground and a reptile house was the ideal place to hide. He ran from room to room and finally found the snake house and he knew that this was where Aaron would be hiding. He looked into each tank in turn, frantically trying to find a rattlesnake. In the central area of the reptile house there was an open enclosure with a small waterfall at its centre. Various snakes were wrapped along branches or coiled up basking beneath heat lamps within the enclosure. The waterfall ran over a couple of rocks and filled a small pool. At the side of the pool was an overflow vent and floating on the pond was the grill that covered the outlet. Michael looked at the open outlet; it was just big enough for a snake to slide into. He concluded that Aaron must have escaped down there and might now be in the sewers or wherever the water filtered off to.

Michael ran out of the reptile house and viewed the landscape, wondering what to do next; he knew he would have to get back to Brighton soon; he didn't want her wandering off too. Below him, in the distance Michael saw a lake surrounded by a beach. Children were playing in the water and some were building sandcastles in the sand. The sunshine danced on the lake, making it difficult to look directly at the water. Maybe, thought Michael, the excess water from the reptiles' pool might flow through to the lake; it was just a hunch. He decided to have a quick look to see if he could see Aaron. Perhaps it had all been just a bad day dream and he would find Aaron playing by the water.

Michael made his way down to the lake and as he approached he noticed a small boy on the water's edge screaming. He was pointing to something on the shore. Michael began to run, it had to be Aaron that was causing the child to scream. Michael was right the boy was pointing at a snake poised ready to strike. Without thinking Michael reached out and grabbed the snake by the neck, it writhed angrily in his hands, hissing and rattling its tail. He gritted his teeth; he didn't want to lose hold. He squeezed its throat as hard as he could, trying his best to squeeze the life out of its body. He looked around him for help but nobody seemed concerned, only the boy it was about to attack watched on anxiously. When Michael looked back at the snake he found he had his hands around Aaron's neck. He immediately let go, he didn't want to hurt him. Aaron smiled darkly at him and then immediately turned back in to a snake and slid off into the undergrowth. He stood there stunned. He couldn't believe what had just happened.

As Michael drew up in front of the house, he could see Helen at the living room window looking out for them. He smiled weakly back full of regret and anxiety; he really didn't know what to tell her and was not sure how she would react. Brighton had cried all the way home and her face was hot and tear stained. He looked around at her. "Come on Brighton, stop crying," he'd said. "Your Mum won't want to see you in that state; she's been looking forward to seeing you again. You've got a new bedroom to see too."

Michael hoped that Helen might have had a phone call from someone that had found Aaron and he would be able to go and pick him up but he knew that this would be unlikely. He got out of the car and lifted Brighton out of her car seat; she struggled out of his arms and ran up the garden path to find her mother. Michael sighed; the next few moments were going to be dreadful. Helen opened the door with difficulty as she was on crutches, she looked pale and had lost a lot of weight but she smiled as Brighton hurled herself towards her, she couldn't pick her up but hugged her with one arm and just managed to stay up-right. "Well someone's pleased to see me. Oh you've been crying. What's the matter, darling?" she asked Brighton.

Michael listened as Brighton launched in to the day's events but not once did she mention Aaron. It transpired that they had stopped at a zoo and he'd gone in by himself leaving her alone in the car and then come back after ages and not let her go and see the animals. Michael was intrigued, how could she have forgotten that Aaron had turned in to a snake and had then disappeared? Michael looked at Brighton, she was only little and had probably been so shocked that this important part of her story had been forgotten.

Helen had frowned at Michael and asked him if this had happened. Michael felt desperate; he really wanted Brighton to tell her mother about Aaron but all he'd said to his sister was that it didn't exactly happen like that and that Aaron was missing. What Michael heard next took his breath away. "I know," Helen had whispered, quietly trying not to cry and let Brighton hear. "We're all missing him; they just couldn't get to him in time. If only I'd checked the battery in the smoke alarm."

That afternoon, Michael had spent in his room trying to make sense of what had happened. His room was simply furnished with only a bed, an empty wardrobe and a bedside cabinet. All that he owned was what he had in his backpack, his army kit had perished and everything of value had gone. He was shaking and he didn't want Helen and Brighton see him in that state but his confusion and pain were nothing to what he would feel later on that night.

Michael had gone down into the kitchen to prepare a meal; he'd managed to steady his nerves. It was just before six o'clock and he knew that Brighton would be hungry and he really didn't want Helen to be cooking; she needed to let her ankles heal properly. She'd smiled as he walked past and he knew that she'd forgiven him for upsetting Brighton. He'd found ingredients for a Bolognese and when the meal was ready; he'd taken it in on trays to them and settled down to watch the television. They'd been watching the news much to the annoyance of Brighton who hated it and Helen had tried to stop her from changing the channel. As they wrestled a report came on about a recent murder and asked for the public to come forward if they'd noticed anything suspicious. Michael hadn't taken much notice at first but when he heard the name of the zoo that they'd visited and saw the face of the child that had been strangled, he nearly choked on his meal; it was the same boy that he'd saved from being bitten by the snake.

Michael froze and listened to every word the news reader said. A four year old boy, named Ben George had been found strangled to death only yards away from where his family had been sitting. Apparently nobody had witnessed the murder but there had been a man seen loitering by the lake and the police urgently wanted to speak to him. A photo fit picture appeared on the screen and he was dismayed to see that it was a fairly good likeness of himself. Helen looked directly at him and said nothing, he could see in her eyes that she knew the sketch was of him.

That night Helen slept with Brighton and locked the bedroom door. Michael knew instinctively that she thought he was guilty and he was distraught. After pacing up and down in his room for a few hours, he thought it would be best if he left; he knew Helen would not believe his story and he could not bear to hurt her any more.

4

From the south a ferocious wind blew continuously across the Downs, challenging any obstacle in its path to remain upright; it danced merrily along the hill tops taking pleasure in its gaining strength.

After emerging from the steep woodland path, Amy Warren had battled to walk along the South Downs Link; she'd leant into the wind and forced her way onwards, until finally she found refuge at the centre of the Chanctonbury Ring, where peculiarly, the wind was absent. She hadn't been on this hill before and despite its reputation for being haunted, she was pleasantly surprised. Not only did she feel a sense of peace within the ring of trees but the crying feeling inside her had ceased. She felt guilty; she should have been shopping and didn't really know why she'd decided to go for a walk instead. She'd followed her instincts and had been led to a place of tranquillity.

In a way Amy felt like she was rebelling. If she went to get the weekly groceries then she knew she wouldn't be able to concentrate on this task and had, in a moment of madness, turned the car around to look for a place to think things through. She needed to be away from everyone and the Ring seemed to be calling to her. Amy loved being up high and had often walked along the

Downs Link as a teenager just so she could be alone. Things had been different since she'd met Ted and her life had been put on hold. All her dreams and what she enjoyed doing in her life had slipped away in to the shadows of her past.

Amy found a place to sit on the hillside; she'd a carrier bag with her and used this to sit on as the ground was wet. She looked at the landscape around her; she could see for miles; a patchwork quilt of fields and woodland spread out below. The houses that she'd passed earlier were now in miniature and seemed so far away that she felt like she was on top of the world looking down upon her kingdom. Amy breathed in the fresh air, appreciating a moment to herself. Her busy schedule didn't allow her to think; Ted saw to that, he didn't allow her to have any free time.

She'd been with Ted for nearly five years, he was a taxi driver and although he worked many shifts, he always seemed to be popping in to see if she was ok and he constantly rang her to find out what she was doing. She'd moved into Ted's top floor flat in Findon only weeks after meeting him and regretted this. For the first year of their relationship she'd found his fussing endearing but slowly as the years had passed, she realised that she was being smothered. She could understand his harassment if Ted found it difficult to be parted from her but the plain fact was that he didn't trust her. That gave Amy the most pain as she gave Ted no cause for concern. She looked at and cared for nobody else, was in all honesty a good person and had no desire to stray.

Thinking back, Ted's mistrust started on the first day they met. She'd met him after work on a rainy evening. Amy always walked home from Horsham station but that particular evening it was raining hard and she'd no coat. She'd also had a heated discussion with her boss and was feeling sorry for herself and not wanting to get drenched had decided to take a taxi.

Amy had poured her heart out to Ted on the way home and found him very charming and easy to talk to. That night after a few drinks, they had ended up in bed together. Usually, Amy liked to get to know someone properly before sleeping with them and she thought that perhaps for this reason Ted regarded her as easy and as much as he said he loved her, seemed to think that she was a loose woman.

Initially their relationship had been exciting and tender, Amy had given up her job at Treadmill Marketing agency willingly and had moved into Ted's flat and kept it clean; waiting each day, in excited anticipation for him to return home. Ted had been keen for her to give up her job too, he didn't like the people she worked with and told her that he didn't think women should work and that he enjoyed looking after her.

Gradually their relationship began to change; he became less loving and more paranoid about her behaviour. She'd been sent to 'Coventry' on many occasions for talking to unsuitable men, in a flirtatious manner. She was always completely shocked by Ted's jealous outbursts as the men she'd been talking to were cashiers in shops or friends of Ted's that she found she was obliged to speak to, if they bumped into them. His friends were the last men on earth she would be interested in. She always made sure she didn't have eye contact with them and as far as she was aware she'd spoken to them in a civil manner and hadn't flirted with them in any way. Amy always felt so helpless and was mortified that Ted thought of her as a woman with loose morals.

In the space of a year, Amy had gone from being an outgoing, bubbly lively person, to a lonely and frightened door mat. Ted gradually wore her down, he criticised how she cooked and cleaned and went in to detail for several hours about the right way to do the housework. After a while, Amy had suggested going back to work but Ted just laughed and said that if she couldn't cope at home then she wouldn't be able to cope in the outside world.

She felt that emotionally, she'd been put through the mill the past five years and had in her darkest hour contemplated suicide. She knew that she should have left Ted a long time ago but she'd no job, had lost all her confidence and had been diagnosed with having depression. Sometimes she felt like she was going mad as to the outside world, Ted was the most sociable and most likeable character anyone was likely to meet. One night, she had a dream that she was standing on a white bridge over a stream in a beautiful and fruitful garden. An old woman had approached her and smiling had said.

"Why do you say all these bad things about Ted? Ted is such a charming man and you are a wicked person to think and say such things."

Amy had woken up distressed that night and had cried silently, Ted lay next to her and slept on, unaware of the pain she was suffering.

She knew that if she tried to speak to him about their relationship, then he would twist her words, everything would be turned on its head, he would get really cross and although he never hit her, would almost be on the verge of doing so and Amy would end up apologising to diffuse the row. In some ways it would have been easier for her if he'd hit her, that way there would be bruises and broken bones, evidence of his cruelty and she could go to a woman's refuge. Emotional pain and the misery she'd endured had cut her deep but the scars were invisible.

She looked about her and wondered why she was up on the hill, she'd intended to go shopping and follow the schedule that Ted had instilled in her but something in her head had stopped her from continuing onto Worthing. She decided that it was the memory of the letter she'd left on the sideboard for him that had thrown her off course.

The events of the past few months had been life changing for her and had given her back her confidence and self-belief. She no longer needed medication; she knew that she was not defective and was in fact a decent human being and that she should be treated as such. The letter highlighted this and also mentioned that she'd been asked to support West Sussex police with their murder investigations. She knew Ted would be furious that she'd gone behind his back and got herself a part time job but there was part of her that hoped that he would be pleased for her and that he would change his attitude and perhaps treat her like he did when they'd first met.

Amy thought back to when she saw her first ghost. To start with, she thought the sighting was a result of the anti-depressants she'd been taking but when they continued long after she'd stop taking the pills, she realised that she had a psychic gift. The first spirits she saw were animals and her first sighting had been on a summer's evening at dusk when she'd been in the car with Ted. She'd seen a white cat waiting to cross the road and it looked as if it was going to run out in front of them. As they got closer, Amy realised that the cat was lying on its side in the gutter and didn't appear to be moving. She knew they hadn't hit it and was sure that she'd seen the cat alive, only moments earlier and yet there it was lying dead. Amy pointed out the cat to Ted as they passed by but he said that he hadn't seen it. Amy looked behind her and wondered if they should go back and see if it was hurt but it had gone. There hadn't been time for it to run off. She was sure that she'd seen it but if this had been a one off incident, then she would have thought no more about it.

From that day on, every time Amy went out, she could see hazy images of animals and occasionally people lurking in the shadows, all vying for her attention, hoping that she would allow them to show her their demise so that she could help them. At first she thought she was going mad and Ted thought that she should go back on the anti-depressants and get psychiatric help but after a while she taught herself not to look too hard and the troubled dead remained locked away in the darkness.

Amy shivered; her peaceful moment was being tampered with. Although there was nobody around, she couldn't help feeling that she wasn't alone. She tried not to think about the spirits at the Chanctonbury Ring but there were too many to ignore. The most prominent spirit was that of a beautiful girl, she looked to be no more than sixteen; she'd been up on the hills for centuries from early Roman times. She was wearing a tunic and fine woollen cloak wrapped around her. The cloak was fastened with an ornate pin that glistened. The girl was wandering through the copse behind her and she could sense that she was upset about something but she knew if she looked back then she would see and she would ask her for help.

She also noticed that there was a spirit of a young man climbing up the hill; he had on his head a grey wig and wore an eighteenth century frock coat, he was carrying a spade and a beech sapling that he planned to plant on the summit. He too appeared to be distressed.

On the other side of the hill was a more ancient presence, an old man in ragged clothes, he was in a bad mood and was poking a stick into the ground, turning the rocks over and appeared to be hunting for something. Amy tried to concentrate on her own problems but it was proving difficult as the hill seemed to be abundant with ancient spirits.

Her first major psychic vision happened one lunchtime; she'd been watching the news with Ted and a report came up about a little girl that had gone missing in Worthing. The girl was only seven years old and her parents made a live appeal asking for anybody to come forward if they could give any information about her. They had shown a picture of the child, a girl with her blond hair tied back in a ponytail. She wore blue jeans and a pale blue cardigan with thin white stripes running through and a white T-shirt. A film clip showed a deserted beach where she was last seen. Amy looked carefully at the beach, it looked familiar, she felt that she'd been there before and had stood near to the breaker.

It was a hot Sunday; she could see herself standing on the beach looking at the sea and at all the people. She felt herself to be a lot smaller, almost as if she was a child and she could feel the anxiety building inside her. She knew she was lost, she'd been walking along the beach, towards the pier with her parents and had stopped to look at a dog running along in the waves and wanted to show them it but both her mum and dad had gone. The girl had decided to carry on walking along the beach towards the pier and catch them up. She'd walked for ages, passing under the pier, hoping that she might see them but they were nowhere to be seen so she decided to stop and wait for her parents to find her.

The girl had been waiting by the breaker for a long time, the tide was coming in and she really wasn't sure what to do. She knew that she shouldn't talk to strangers but she was becoming desperate and really needed to ask a grown up to help her. Through the girl's eyes Amy had looked at the people on the beach, there were many people around but all looked too busy or unapproachable. The girl looked for a woman that had children; she saw a family packing up all their beach things into bags but they were all arguing and would probably not be nice people to talk to. Just as she was about to cry, she saw the man with the dog she'd been watching earlier walking towards her, it was almost as if he knew she needed his help. He stopped and smiled at her. "You're lost aren't you?" he said, putting out his hand, inviting her to take hold. "Come with me, I'll take you home."

Amy had come out of her day dream and knew instinctively that the girl on the television had been murdered by this man. For some reason, she'd the feeling that the man was named Bernard; she wasn't sure of his surname but she knew that he lived alone in a basement flat in Hove with his dog. She felt compelled to ring the police and give them a description of the murderer and of his dog too and was sure that they would be able to trace them.

She'd waited until Ted had gone out. She knew he would laugh at her and prevent her from calling and although she felt guilty for going behind his back, she knew that what she'd seen was important and she would be able to describe what Bernard looked like and what he was wearing in detail. Amy had got through to the police easily and she was a little worried that they might think she was a crackpot and dismiss her sighting. Amy spoke to a very kind police officer who didn't laugh at her and had taken down, in detail, everything Amy had seen in her vision. The police officer thanked her for her assistance.

Sadly, a few days later the girl's body had been discovered in a shallow grave on the edge of a field and dog hair had been found on her clothes. A man named Bernard Thorne had been arrested and charged with murder. Amy had shuddered when she'd seen his face on the television; he was exactly as she'd described him. She was too scared to tell Ted about it.

Over the next few weeks, she found herself watching the local news or trawling through the local papers looking for reports about any offences that looked to be unsolved. She found that she would read a word or see something in a picture that would trigger off a vision and had been able to help the police with more than ten cases. For some reason her ability was restricted to local cases and if the victim had been murdered. She really wanted to help globally, especially with the notorious Madeline McCann case but regretfully she saw nothing. Amy had come to realise that she'd a connection with the dead and hoped desperately that she would see something that would help the police find the victim alive and not just help them find a murderer or a body.

One morning, thankfully when Ted was working, she had a call from the police, from a man named Inspector Brandon. She'd wondered why he was calling and was surprised when he thanked her for all her assistance and although it was not often publicised, he would like her to register as one of their listed psychics and might call her in for any particular cases that the Sussex Police were investigating and would generously reimburse her for any expenses incurred. Amy was shocked and didn't know what to say, she took his number and said that she would have a think about it and call him back. She was puzzled why she was being offered payment for something she'd been giving for free.

She again thought about the letter that she'd left for Ted, explaining how she felt, about her life and about what she'd been doing for the police for the past few months and wondered what his reaction would be. He would be home for his lunch soon and she knew it would only be moments before her mobile would ring. She knew it would have been better to speak to him directly but she was afraid that he would be angry and then would twist everything she said. She hadn't mentioned that she'd spoken to Inspector Brandon as she knew that Ted would believe she was having an affair with him.

Amy stood up with difficulty, her jeans were too tight. She would have to diet and lose some weight; she couldn't afford to buy new clothes. She shook the water off the bag, folded it up and placed it back in her pocket. Her pocket had a rip in the lining. She hated her black anorak; it was one of Ted's old ones and hung on her like a sack. If she took the job, she could save a little money then she would treat herself to a new one. She would also get her hair coloured, she'd tied it back as most of her blond hair had turned grey and she looked as if she was fifty rather than forty two.

Amy now regretted leaving the letter, it would only cause untold trouble, he would be angry that she'd been going behind his back and had contacted the police. She wondered if she'd time to remove it and started to walk down the hill towards her car but then stopped, she was too frightened to go home. She would go back to the summit, out of the wind and plan what she would say to Ted when he rang. She would tell him that she was sorry and that she was in need of medication and that way he might feel sorry for her and his anger would subside more quickly.

5

Stunned, confused and full of fear, Sarah had parked her car in the car park at the foot of the Chanctonbury Ring and had sat there thinking about the man she'd seen crossing the road. She'd seen him before but only briefly; his face had stuck in her mind. His skin was dark and pitted, his profile was unmistakable; she would recognise him anywhere. She couldn't believe her bad luck and wondered if she should contact the police but felt unable to as she was shaking and she didn't think she would be able to get her words out.

She thought back to the day of her release, a day she didn't think would ever come. It had been early morning and this very man had dragged her from her prison and out into the sunlight. At that point, Sarah thought that she was going to be executed and through tears, she'd looked into his eyes and had begged him for mercy. He'd frowned, tutted and then forced a black hood over her head, dragged her through the house and bundled her into a car.

Sarah sighed, she really needed to get some fresh air and think; she walked around to her boot and as she leaned in looking for her trainers, the wind whipped around her. She took off her jacket pulled on a blue hooded sweatshirt and then put on her waterproof coat.

She sat on the rim of the boot and pulled off her heels, then put on a trainer and standing on one foot, rooted through her boot to find the other one. She made a mental note to tidy up her boot that week. As she put on her remaining shoe, she realised that she was shivering violently; the wind was wild but not cold and she knew she was shaking with nerves. She felt cross as well and couldn't understand why he was in Sussex. Was he looking for her or was there another reason he was living rough at the Washington roundabout? Perhaps she thought, he was planning to harm others.

She shut the boot, locked the car and headed towards the car park entrance that led to the road. Sarah looked right to see if any cars were approaching and screamed. Her kidnapper was there, standing motionless by the car park entrance, staring at her. Sarah's heart was beating so fast and loudly, she could feel it in her ears. Tears started to run down her face, she couldn't breathe properly and was unable to move or say anything.

"I'm sorry," he said in broken English. "I didn't mean to frighten you. I'm just waiting for a friend."

It suddenly dawned on Sarah that perhaps this was a pure coincidence and that although she recognised him, he wouldn't necessarily recognise her. She was wearing Western clothes, she'd put on weight and her hair was lighter now that it was clean. In her head she knew she should walk back to the car and drive away but she was shaking so much, she felt that she wouldn't be able to drive properly. She shook her head and tried to smile as she brushed away the tears.

"No, I'm sorry..." she replied quietly unable to finish her sentence as she walked away from him, trying not to meet his eyes.

Fearfully, she headed towards the style that led to the winding path to the Downs Link and away from her nightmare. She cursed to herself for not going home and looked up to heaven to ask why this was happening to her. She wondered what were the chances of her bumping into one of her kidnappers, at the foot of the Sussex Downs, on a Tuesday lunchtime. The chances had to be a million to one. She might have understood if she'd been in Afghanistan but this reunion was beyond belief.

"Wait.... you stop please? I know you." Sarah heard the man call out to her and she stopped involuntarily for a second or two. She could feel an icy chill spread over her. It took all of her strength to move forward as she tried to pretend she hadn't heard him. His words had blown away in the wind, she'd imagined them.

More urgently now, Sarah pressed on up the hill, longing to escape from his view. She felt so relieved as she made it around the first bend, away from her foe and stopped for a second to catch her breath. Again tears were streaming down her face; she didn't really understand why she was crying. She was free and she didn't need to worry, soon she would be up on the ridge of the Downs and would leave him far behind.

"Why do you run from me?" called out the man. "I will not hurt you. I need your help."

Sarah whipped around and gasped. She saw the man approaching her; he was smiling and seemed oblivious to the pain she was enduring. She said nothing, she'd been shocked into silence again and couldn't believe that he'd the audacity to ask her for help.

She looked at him incredulously and marched on, determined to ignore him and escape from his company. Trying to think rationally, Sarah decided that she should call the police, she felt in her pockets for her mobile but then realised that she'd left it in the pocket of her suit jacket and she'd left that in her car. Sarah was starting to feel hysteria setting in, perhaps this man wanted to kill her. She started to run; the path was muddy and difficult to climb at running speed. She was beginning to make progress, the gap between her assailant and she was increasing all the time. She leapt onto some rocks to avoid a mud pool but stood on a loose stone and slipped; she twisted her ankle and then landed on her hands and knees. Quickly, she got back up, her ankle ached a little but this didn't stop her flight. She looked over her shoulder and could see the man was still following her, he would soon be with her if she didn't pick up the pace. After a while, every step she took hurt her right ankle, the journey was becoming torturous. She could go no further and knew that she would have to face him. Defiantly, Sarah waited for him to catch her up.

When he reached her, he explained again that he didn't want to hurt her and that she mustn't be scared. His name was Nabeel Azizi, he'd fled from Afghanistan and had come to England to seek asylum. Every word Nabeel uttered irritated her and she found herself yelling at him, screaming at him, reminding him of all the atrocities she'd endured, the pain that she felt and the nightmares that taunted her. She could see by his eyes that he didn't understand her and that made her feel infuriated. Sarah was livid with Nabeel; he was standing there so casually in front of her as if he was innocent. He and his criminal associates hadn't only spoilt her life but they'd changed it beyond all recognition. She didn't care about his pathetic story and if she had a gun, she would have almost certainly have pulled the trigger.

***

Michael opened his eyes. He could hear someone yelling nearby and he rolled over onto his stomach, moving a few dried leaves so that he could see through the branches he'd pulled over the entrance of his shelter. He could hear a woman from the paths below shouting at someone. He couldn't see her but was concerned by her tone - she obviously didn't want to be with the person she was shouting at. Michael hoped that they would settle their differences and go. He listened carefully and became increasingly alarmed and wondered if the woman was being attacked. He knew he should act and try and help her but he really didn't want to get involved and blow his cover. The woman sounded hysterical, he could bear it no longer and reluctantly, struggled out of his camp. He decided that he would find a spot where he could view the couple unseen and then intervene if there was any violence. He crept down the slope and stopped by a jagged tree stump and peered round. He wasn't sure what he could do if the man attacked the woman, he felt weak from hunger.

He could see the couple on the path below, the woman was quite young and had dark brown hair, maybe black and had olive skin; she didn't appear to be hurt. She'd stopped shouting and was slowly making her way up the hill. She seemed to be limping. Michael looked at the man. He too was walking up the hill following the girl; he was keeping his distance but there was something malevolent about his presence, it was almost as if he was stalking her. Michael cursed; he sensed that it wouldn't be too long before this woman would be attacked. It was almost as if he'd seen this scene play out before, in his dreams or perhaps in a film. He worked himself around the tree to stay hidden. He decided that when the couple were on the path above his camp he would go back and get his rucksack and follow them. He really didn't want to get involved, he wasn't sure if he could trust himself. The incident at the zoo had shaken him; he didn't want another tragedy to take place.

***

Evie climbed out of Tom's sports car and felt the wind tear at her coat. She didn't mind as she was wearing one of Tom's daughter's coats and a pair of borrowed socks and walking boots. She'd enjoyed her cup of tea and cake with Tom, he was such a pleasant man, so easy to talk to and so kind. He'd persuaded her to walk with him up to the Chanctonbury Ring. Barney needed a good walk and Tom had promised to take her back to Horsham station afterwards. The coat she was wearing had a removable fleece lining and was much more suited to the weather conditions. Tom got Barney out from behind the seats of his car and clipped the lead onto his collar. He said that there were some big dogs in the cottage at the foot of the hill and he didn't want him running up to them. Barney despite his age, still considered himself to be the dominant male and he didn't want him upsetting the bear like dogs that lived there. Barney pulled at the lead eager to head off for his walk; Tom had difficulty holding him. They were just about to set off when Tom noticed Evie's handbag and shopping bag. "Do you want to leave your bags in the boot? It's quite a walk to the top, and they might weigh you down."

Evie looked down at her bags. "Goodness me no, I'll be fine, your car might be stolen or broken in to and then I'll lose everything."

"Ok, then but you don't get that kind of thing going on around here. My Martha used to be very attached to her handbag too, it's a mystery to me what you girls keep in them."

Evie smiled but inwardly, she knew that Tom would be surprised, if he knew what she had in her shopping bag.

They passed the cottage but the dogs Barney liked to visit were not there, so Tom let him off the lead and he pelted off, up the hill. Evie and Tom followed.

"It's strange," said Evie, I feel like I have been here before. Perhaps Albert or my father brought me here."

"It's quite unusual for a lady, like yourself to be wondering about alone, looking for beauty spots. Did you ever think of remarrying?" asked Tom.

"Dear me no," exclaimed Evie. "Nobody was interested in a single mother in war days. Later on a few men from the tennis club asked me out but they all seemed to be married or more interested in themselves, than in me. So, no Tom, I never thought about getting married again, Albert would have been most upset."

"You obviously cared for your husband very much but I'm sure that he wouldn't have wanted you to have remained alone for all these years."

"Well we swore to each other when he went to war that we would wait for each other, whatever happened," replied Evie struggling to climb up a particularly muddy part of the path. Tom held out his hand to assist her and gratefully she accepted.

***

In place of the ring of trees and copse, Amy could see Cornelia Tiberius stood on the top of the stairs of a temple and through her eyes looked towards the east across the Downs, the sun was high in the sky and was attempting to break through the rain clouds; the wind blew in gusts and tugged hungrily at her cloak. Nervously, Cornelia looked about her as really she shouldn't leave the building without permission. She felt dizzy and needed some air. She stood near to a column so that she could sink into the shadows if need be but thankfully there was no one around. From her view point, she could see for miles, it was good to be outside but she didn't feel well, she could feel cold sweat on her face and she'd pains in her stomach.

The temple had been her home for the past two years and she was forbidden to leave its grounds. When she was twelve, because she'd a pretty face, she'd been selected to become a novice vestal virgin and had been overjoyed at the news and her parents had given her away. At first Cornelia had been very excited, it was an honour to be chosen to become one and she would be treated as an empress for the next thirty years. In reality, although the villagers treated her like a goddess; behind closed doors, it was another matter.

She looked across the Downs and longed to run freely through the grass and play with her friends in the fields around the farms again. She wondered what had become of them, she felt like a prisoner with only her bad tempered teacher, Alexa for company. Cornelia knew that she wasn't a good novice; she'd let the fire in the temple go out many times and had been whipped by the priest as a punishment. Her back stung when she lay down to sleep, she suspected that she may have an infection. She wondered if it was this that was making her feel ill but it didn't explain the cramps in her swelling stomach. Nervously, Cornelia looked back into the temple, from where she was standing, she could see the fire near the altar, it was still burning; she felt relieved, she would add more wood in a moment.

The novelty of becoming a vestal virgin had long gone. She loathed ritualism, her whole life had been dedicated to assisting her mother with daily rituals carried out in her home and now she was assisting Alexa with the rituals in the temple; all so that the Gods would look favourably on them all. She knew she was a wicked girl but she wanted so much for Alexa to be pleased with her and she really didn't want to be beaten by the priest again.

Cornelia always felt nervous when the priest came to the temple; she couldn't look him in the eyes and was sure that he was overzealous when he punished her. A few months ago at the end of a particularly vicious flaying, she'd lay slumped over a table naked and bleeding with tears streaming down her face. He'd told her to hold still and parting her legs had rammed something hard into her, he grunted as he lunged his body forward until finally he groaned and pulled himself out of her. She didn't move, she was petrified, in pain and was barely conscious. The last thing she remembered before she passed out was feeling hot liquid running between her thighs, she thought it might be blood.

She knew that she was bad and deserved to be punished but suspected that in some way she'd been violated and made impure. She wondered if she should tell Alexa but she wasn't sure if she would be sympathetic, she already thought that Cornelia was an imbecile. If Alexa told on her, she feared that she would be sent to trial and if found to be impure, be buried alive and bring dishonour to her family. She couldn't bear the humiliation.

Cornelia's head was beginning to spin, she hadn't eaten properly for days and her stomach pains were unbearable. She hung onto the column to steady herself but her legs felt too weak to hold her up and gently she slid down to the floor. Through half closed eyes, she could see the sky in black and white. Feebly she called out for help but knew that nobody would hear her. Unhindered and jubilant, the wind flew past Cornelia, into the temple and extinguished the fire.

Upset by what she'd seen, Amy got up and looked behind her, only the woodland within the ring of trees stared back at her; she'd almost expected to see a temple and Cornelia lying at the top of the marble steps, dying from septicaemia with a still born child between her legs. She wished there was something she could do to help her as she'd died such a tragic death.

When Amy had first seen Cornelia walking through the copse she'd tried not to hear her story but sitting alone within the ring of trees, she'd found Cornelia's anguish too hard to ignore. The poor, innocent girl hadn't realised that she'd been raped or that she was carrying a child. For many centuries, Cornelia had wandered about on the hill, looking for someone to forgive her and to free her from her miserable half-life.

Amy had read about psychics being able to talk to the dead and when they managed to get the lost souls to realise that they'd died then they could leave their half-life and find peace. Since Amy had familiarised herself with Cornelia's story, she sensed that she'd moved back into the shadows, almost afraid to hear the truth. It felt like her cries for help and her story replayed over and over, like a needle stuck in a record caught in an untouchable dimension. If she called to her, Amy wondered if she might be able to tell her why she died and release her. She stared into the shadows and shutting her eyes, tried to visualise Cornelia in her mind, she'd no idea if this would work. The hill seemed so still and quiet, not even the birds were singing. The air around her became icy; she could sense that a spirit was standing close to her. Just as Amy was about to speak, her mobile phone went off in her pocket, ruining her chance to help her. Amy opened her eyes. She was alone again and trembling; she pulled her phone from out of her pocket, she knew who was calling - it was Ted.

Amy watched the phone ring in her hand; she knew if she didn't answer right away, Ted would be enraged. Her thumb hovered over the receive button but she couldn't press it as a burning sensation hit the palm of her hand and automatically she threw the phone into the air and watched it as it crashed landed on a tree root. She clenched her teeth; she expected the phone to shatter. The screen was cracked and the ringing had stopped. She bent down to pick it up but it was too hot to touch. The phone melted into a river of oozing plastic and glass and spread like sauce over the root. Amy looked down at the bubbling mess in disbelief.

6

Nabeel Azizi didn't want to lose sight of Sarah; he couldn't understand why she was so angry with him. He'd seen her in her car and had recognised her instantly. When he'd crossed the road, he'd watched her car turn right at the roundabout and had come across her again on his way to meet a friend. Her hysterical screaming when she saw him had been unnecessary; she'd only been held captive for a few months and had then been released unharmed; she was lucky to be alive. When his faction had realised that she was unlikely to bring in any revenue, then they had been all for killing her and dumping her body. It had been he that had saved her life, he'd convinced everyone to spare her, he'd taken a risk for her and now she owed him her life.

He had grown tired of fighting, tired of war and of always being in hiding or being misled by a power crazed leader; these were some of the reasons that he'd decided to flee Afghanistan. He'd borrowed from a friend enough money to get him a safe passage to England as he believed here the British Government would be sympathetic to an ex Taliban soldier and would grant him asylum. Nabeel had travelled for many weeks, either walking or getting a ride on cargo lorries, heading for the port and after a turbulent sea crossing, entered England at

Newhaven. On a wet and miserable day, he'd been smuggled in with two others beneath a lorry, the spray from the tarmac soaking them through as the lorry made its way to their drop off point.

Nabeel looked at the muddy track ahead of him and felt miserable. England wasn't what he'd expected it to be, he didn't know who to ask for help, his English was poor and he knew no one with any influence. The reality was hard to bear; he'd ended up having to fend for himself, in a country that he hated with no means to move to a more suitable climate. He'd met up with other travellers and they had made their home in woodlands beside the motorways and like him they just wanted to lead a peaceful life.

He had been waiting by the car park for a friend from his campsite. They were going to scout the land for food, they hoped they might be able to catch and slaughter a sheep. Nabeel's fingers traced the edges of a small knife in his pocket. He was skilled in butchery, his father, who had been murdered, blown up by a US missile, had taught him many useful life skills. Nabeel suspected today would be a fruitful day and he knew that his prayers for assistance would soon be granted. It was almost as if Sarah had been sent to him, she could aid him, she could speak his language and could help him to seek asylum and provide him with a roof over his head.

Sarah was determined to get to the Chanctonbury Ring; with any luck her stalker would grow tired of following her, if anything he would understand that she was furious with him, perhaps it would finally get through his thick skull that she wasn't interested in helping him and he would leave her alone. She also hoped that she might find somebody she could ask to borrow their phone so she could call the police. Her ankle was sore but she was determined to make it through the damp woodland and up onto the Downs.

After another agonising twenty minutes, Sarah emerged from the woods and made her way onto the chalky path that she knew to be the Downs Link and she looked towards the gate at the brow of the hill. As she proceeded, she looked over her shoulder, he was still following her but there was a fair distance between them. She looked along the wide track; there were usually herds of walkers making their way along the ridge. Today, there were none. Sarah limped on, if she made it up to the Chanctonbury Ring, then perhaps she might find others up there and could ask for help; it was a popular place for dog walkers. Sarah looked behind her, he was getting closer.

Michael waited on the edge of the wooded hill; it felt good to leave his camp behind him. He wasn't superstitious but there was definitely something unnatural, perhaps evil lurking there. He could see the young woman, making her way up towards the hill with the ring of trees and wondered why she didn't go back; her ankle was obviously painful; she had to be afraid of the man that was following her. Undetected, Michael watched the man walk by; he was frowning and looked angry. Michael decided that he would continue his surveillance. It would be a lot harder to track them both without being seen.

A squealing and scratching noise behind him, made him turn his head, he was really feeling on edge. He needn't have worried as one of his snares he'd laid earlier, had just been activated. Michael looked at the rabbit caught in the snare, it had worked beautifully, the rabbit, lay there dead, twitching; waiting to be collected. Michael dismantled the trap, got out his knife, quickly gutted the rabbit, put it in a plastic bag and dropped it and the snare into his rucksack; he would cook the rabbit later. After cleaning his knife and putting it back in its holder he saw the man go through the gate. Pulling his hood up, he set off after the young woman and her predator. Michael looked behind him to make sure no one was about and almost jumped out of his skin as a greyhound streaked past him.

Tom looked down at Evie walking alongside him, she was a friendly woman, perhaps a little older than him and yet she'd managed to climb the hill with ease. Martha had never liked going for walks with him. She'd been a wonderful wife and mother and he missed her dearly but she wasn't one for long walks. He now had Barney for company, who he walked every afternoon and he'd never thought of looking for anyone else.

Over the past five years since his wife's death, he'd made himself busy and had a weekly routine so that he didn't have time to dwell on Martha not being there any more. Mondays he cleaned the cottage, this didn't come naturally to him but he knew it had to be done. Tuesdays he had lunch at the Frankland Arms. Wednesdays he did gardening for Mrs Jacobs, who had become too old to maintain her rambling cottage garden; he always got a nice bit of cake there. Thursdays he rang his daughter and afterwards read his car manuals or a thriller. Friday evenings he joined his friends for the pub quiz and at the weekends, he worked on his beloved car, tinkering with her engine and polished her up ready for a Sunday drive.

The few hours he'd spent with Evie had made him realise that he missed the company of a woman. They'd chatted about their lives all the way through the woods and before he realised it they were walking along the Downs Link. Barney as usual, had raced on to the gate at the crest of the hill and was waiting patiently for himself and Evie to catch him up. Tom knew that once the gate was opened Barney would then race up to the Chanctonbury Ring. It was then that Tom noticed a man with a rucksack run across the path from the edge of the woods towards the gate. Barney stood up and started barking at him as he approached. Tom thought this unusual, as generally he greeted strangers with a wagging tale, hoping that he might get petted or be given food. The man stopped in his tracks.

Michael looked anxiously at the dog; it was quite obvious that he'd upset him in some way. Slowly, he edged forward; he really didn't like dogs and thought that this one could sense his fear. He couldn't stand the sound of the dog barking either; the noise jarred him and made him put his hands over his ears so he didn't go into shock. Since returning from war, loud noises seemed to upset him so much that he sometimes felt like passing out with anxiety. Michael looked at the dog's eyes and teeth and fully expected it to attack him. The sound of someone whistling made him look back down the track and he saw an old couple walking towards the gate, the old man whistled again, this caught the dog's attention and reluctantly Barney sloped off towards them. Michael was relieved that the dog had been silenced and he quickly went through the gate and decided to skirt around the foot of the tree crowned hill and then make his way to the top on the far side and wait in the ring of trees and see what transpired. He didn't like being out in daylight on public view and longed for the evening to come, so he could hide in the shadows and then make his way to Worthing.

"Are you all right Evie?" asked Tom. "Do you want to rest a while, before we go up to Chucklebury? The wind is quite bracing and unusually seems to be coming from the south."

"I'm fine," replied Evie. "What did you call the Ring – Chucklebury?" she asked viewing the information plaque by the gate. It says here that Charles Goring planted the ring of beech trees in 1760 and there are the remains of an Iron Age fort and a Roman temple here too."

"Oh, that's something my mother used to call it," replied Tom, stroking Barney's head. "Now she was a cheerful woman, born in Sussex and never left Sussex, I scattered her and Martha's ashes up there," added Tom, pointing to the Ring.

"Did you?" asked Evie surprised by Tom's revelation.

"Yes, caused a bit of a commotion with her sister and my daughter thought it was a daft idea but Mum and Martha always loved Chucklebury," continued Tom

"I feel I can tell you my secret Tom. Not even my son knows what I've been doing but I know you will understand and you won't write me off as a mad old woman."

"You're not a secret agent are you? He joked and then wished he hadn't said that when he saw Evie's confused face. "Only joking my lovely, go on."

"Well, I've been travelling all over Southern England, trying to find the perfect spot to do something I should have done long ago."

"What's that then" asked Tom gently. He could see that this was a difficult subject for Evie to talk about.

"I..... I have here in my shopping bag, I know it is wrong and I really shouldn't be carrying them about like this but it was very difficult, all those years ago to have someone that you loved so dearly and then to have lost them so suddenly, even before you had lived together. I tried to tell my son but he is quite needy emotionally and I don't think he would have been much help."

"Evie, just tell me, I won't judge you. Just tell me what you have in your bag."

She looked sadly down at her shopping bag. "Albert's ashes," she said quietly.

"Well that's not so bad is it?" replied Tom cheerfully. "We'll soon find the perfect place for him. Follow me; there is no finer place in England than the Chanctonbury Ring. My mother and Martha will be pleased to share their resting place with him. I'm sure of it."

Evie smiled, she was quite sure that Tom would pass her off as a raving lunatic and run for his life but as chance had it, he'd been the perfect gentleman and all her pain inside seemed to lift as she followed him through the gate. Barney shot off at breakneck speed and Evie and Tom leaned into the wind and fought their way up to the top of the hill.

Elated and safe inside the wind free ring of trees, Evie surveyed the land around her, she could see for miles and the atmosphere had a serenity about it. She was sure that Albert would approve. She wished she had a photo of Albert as in her dreams she could see his face clearly but when she tried to remember him in the cold light of day, she found that she couldn't see it that well.

"How many years have you been looking for a special place?" asked Tom.

"Oh, I don't know, probably, at least sixty," she replied quietly. There were quite a few people up at the Ring and she really didn't want them to know her business. "Perhaps I could come up here on another day, when there are not so many people around."

"We'll wait a while," suggested Tom. "I come up here quite a lot and usually there's no one else here."

***

Charles wiped his brow with a clean handkerchief, digging into the chalk hill was hard work, he'd given up counting how many beech trees, he'd planted - this was his last tree. He was proud of his achievement and surveyed the young saplings surrounding the wooded copse with pride. Although they were no taller than him, he smiled with satisfaction and wondered how many generations to come would thank him for his efforts. His work would be seen for miles around and neighbouring land owners would revere his management of the Wiston Estate. Charles sat down next to the sapling to view his extensive estate and took from his velvet waistcoat a small silver hip flask. Carefully, he removed the top and took a nip of brandy to celebrate. It was a fine day and his men were out in the lower fields, herding the sheep ready to drive them to market. Many lambs had been born in the spring of 1760 and he was sure that the estate accounts would show a healthy profit at the end of the year.

Charles brushed some soil from his knee and looked at his trees again and then became concerned that there was space for another tree further along in the Ring. He was surprised that he hadn't seen this earlier and then sighed despondently. This seemed to happen every time he brought a tree up the hill, to plant. Each tree he planted, he thought it to be the last one. It was almost as if the ring of trees were purposely deceiving him. He felt as he if had climbed the hill a thousand times and every time, he'd done the same thing, exactly as he had today and then almost on cue an old man, with bedraggled grey hair around his face, wearing ragged clothes passed him by. He held a long stick and poked the grass with it as he passed Charles and muttered to himself.

"Where is it?" the old man asked himself, oblivious to Charles's presence. "It's got to be here somewhere. Stupid oaf!" he cursed. "Hiding all we had, somewhere up here. No brains, my brother."

Charles watched the old man head off around the hill and watched him stop and push back a bush with urgency, hoping to find his lost treasure. Charles stood up and picking up his spade, he knew that he would go after the old man as this was his land and trespassers were strictly forbidden. He began to follow him and then before his very eyes, he vanished into thin air. He looked at the flask in his hand and thought perhaps the brandy had turned sour and had affected his vision. A tear ran down his face, he knew he was caught in an endless cycle with no way out and he wondered what he'd done to deserve this. His plight was too hard to bear. "Who will end this nightmare?" he called out to the Downs. His words were not heard and spiralled upwards into the clouds and floated away.

***

Amy looked at her phone, it was beginning to soak into the earth and she thought that the battery must have exploded. Her attention was distracted temporarily by a young man making his way up the hill, carrying a sapling and a spade, she'd seen him earlier and knew that this spirit was destined to tread the same path over and over. He didn't seem too distressed but she knew that once he sensed her presence things would be different.

Amy was doing everything possible to avoid thinking about her own situation. She couldn't face going home at the moment. Not only would Ted be annoyed by her letter she'd left but he would also be fuming that she'd cancelled his call; he would be too dangerous to face now. She imagined that he would be out in his cab trying to hunt her down. Luckily, he wouldn't think of looking for her on the Downs Link, he didn't know that she liked hill walking.

Amy thought about the friends that she once had. Her best friend, Carol, lived in New Zealand and she'd also kept in contact with Laura, a friend from college but hadn't e-mailed either of them or rung them for the last two years as Ted couldn't understand why she would need to keep friends with anybody, when she had him. Laura lived in Brighton with her husband, Paul and had three children. Amy wondered if she would put her up for the night. She felt guilty asking but she would be grateful to spend the night on the floor rather than facing Ted.

She shivered, the weather was taking a turn for the worse, the clouds were blackening and the wind was blowing at gale force. The trees were beginning to lean now and it was only a matter of moments before a storm hit them. Amy decided to rush back to her car and drive to Brighton, she knew where Laura lived. With urgency, she turned to walk down the hill and almost walked into somebody.

"Excuse me, I'm sorry to bother you but I urgently need a phone. You wouldn't have one I could borrow do you? It's an emergency, I need to call the police," asked Sarah, quickly looking over her shoulder again; her follower had almost reached the top of the hill and he didn't look happy with her.

7

Amy shook her head, "I'm sorry," she replied. "My phone's broken, I dropped it and the battery must have exploded. What's the matter, why do you need the police?"

"Oh, my God, he's nearly here," whispered Sarah urgently, looking behind her.

Angry black clouds covered the sky and large droplets of rain began to fall, the wind now at fever pitch whipped the rain into the faces of its victims. Amy and Sarah retreated into the Ring to try and find shelter and to prolong the impending encounter with Nabeel. Evie and Tom joined them. The central wooded area gave them a little shelter from the wind but the rain, undeterred, pelted down on them.

"Is he your boyfriend?" asked Amy. "Did you have a row?"

"No... yes, I know him, he's no friend, he's been following me. I'm really scared," replied Sarah.

"Stay with me," suggested Amy. "He might leave you alone if he thinks you're with someone." Amy moved in front of Sarah, to try and block Nabeel's view but this didn't stop him; he walked boldly into the Ring and glared at Sarah. Rain streamed down his face and his clothes were soaked through, his thin jacket was no protection against the foul weather.

"Why do you run from me Sarah?" Nabeel yelled. "I, Nabeel, come to this country for help and everyone rejects me. I am sick of it here, sick of its stinking weather and sick of the greedy people that live here. You must help me to get away from this hole. You have a car and a home I can use, I need you to do this for me, it is your duty. You are in debt to me." Nabeel lunged forward and grabbed Sarah's arm, Sarah winced in pain.

"Oh, I don't think so, young man," said Tom, interrupting him. "Take your hands off of her; she's obviously not happy to be handled so roughly and owes you nothing."

Evie stood back. She was uneasy with the situation; Tom was too old to take on this man and she feared that he may get hurt.

"Leave her alone," called Amy, "She doesn't want to go with you. Go back to where you crawled from."

Nabeel sneered at Tom and Amy and taking no notice of their words dragged her out of the Ring and down the bank towards the car park. "Let go you pig!" she screamed and then kicked him in the leg forgetting that this was her bad ankle and then winced in pain. Enraged, Nabeel slapped her face. Without hesitation, Tom and Amy ran down the bank and tried to pull Nabeel off her but being tall and muscular, he easily brushed them aside. Anxiously Evie, with a growling Barney by her, walked to the edge of the Ring; she was afraid and didn't want the situation to become worse.

Sarah was determined to break Nabeel's hold on her arm. Although he was much taller than her and had a vice-like grip, she wasn't going to let him abduct her. She could no longer tolerate being bullied. "Leave me alone you bastard," she screamed and struggled vigorously to free herself. Nabeel took no notice and continued to drag her along.

Michael was hiding behind a bush on the hill side. He hadn't made it to the summit as there were too many people around and they would have spotted him. He was glad that he had stayed where he was as the situation with the young woman and her stalker had escalated. Swiftly, using the element of surprise, he sprang out from his hiding place and despite his weakened condition and the wild weather conditions managed to round kick Nabeel in the face. Nabeel hadn't expected this and released his grip on Sarah as he rubbed his face. She hobbled, as fast as she could back up to the others, her ankle now barely able to support her weight. Michael immediately and with little effort, grabbed Nabeel's right hand and twisted his hand around, he stepped behind him and with his free hand rolled the top of Nabeel's arm over and pushed Nabeel to the ground until his face was down on the floor. He locked Nabeel's arm behind his back and pulled his hand firmly towards his wrist so that he flinched with pain. Nabeel cursed him in his own tongue but couldn't move out of the arm lock as he was in so much pain. Michael recognised the language and knew that he was from Afghanistan.

"I will break your arm if you move," Michael said fiercely. "Now listen carefully, I am going to release you in a moment and you will carry on down the hill, like nothing has happened. If you try anything then I will kill you. Do you understand?" Nabeel nodded, his face now muddy from the earth.

The rain lashed down relentlessly on the two sodden figures almost obscuring everyone's view of them from the Ring. "Do you think he needs our help?" Amy asked.

"What's he going to do with him? Now he's got him in an arm lock. We should go and get help."

"I'll call the police," said Tom. "I'm sorry Evie, this sort of thing doesn't usually happen up here. He got out his mobile phone and then looked at the screen. "I don't believe it!" he said looking at it with a puzzled expression. "There's no signal! I usually have at least three bars up here. Perhaps it's this storm." Tom walked away from the others to the far edge of the ring of trees, shielding his phone from the rain to see if he could get a signal. He put his phone back in his pocket; it was no use as it wasn't going to work. He sighed, he felt that he needed to sort out the dispute and he stared out towards the coast for inspiration. He also felt embarrassed that on his very first outing with a woman he'd almost got into a fight and for some reason, he didn't know why, he really wanted to impress Evie.

The horizon looked peculiar; it wasn't as it should be, the clouds in the distance were as black as night and were moving towards them rapidly. Tom squinted, the horizon line was distorted and then he realised with horror that the clouds were dragging, a huge wave along with it. He blinked not believing his eyes, the wave was enormous and he could see it mercilessly swamping the landscape, nothing stood in its way; its destructive force was like nothing he'd seen before. "Oh no....Oh for the love of God!" he yelled out as he ran back to the others. “There’s a wave coming,” he called breathlessly. “I can’t believe it, it’s huge. I’ve never seen anything like it. Call those two up here,” he said pointing to Michael and Nabeel. “Thank goodness we’re up here. We’ve got a fighting chance to survive if we hang onto a tree or something with deep roots.”

Michael stepped back from Nabeel and let him get back to his feet. He fully expected Nabeel to lash out but he was ready for him. Instinctively Michael knew that he’d been or still was a soldier and was unlikely to do as he was told. Nabeel shook his head and then cursing began to walk down the hill. Michael looked up at the others, he would wait for him to disappear first and then find shelter and wait out the storm. The girl that he’d helped was waving frantically at him; he didn’t want to go up to her as she’d probably want to call the police. If the police arrived, they would discover that he was a fugitive and he would be taken him into custody. Michael looked away and hoped that he wouldn’t be recognised.

Nabeel was, as he predicted, trouble, he suspected that he may wait for the girl in the woods below. He looked back up the hill again, everyone were now frantically beckoning to him; he looked harder at them through the rain, they seemed to be calling him up and then all of a sudden, they turned and ran away from the edge. Michael wondered what was going on, he looked back at Nabeel who had stopped his descent down the hill and was now shouting out something but his words were lost in the wind. Nabeel turned around and started to run back up the hill towards him. Michael thought that he’d changed his mind and was coming back to fight. He made himself ready for his attack but then realised why he was running. Through the rain and the wind, Michael could see a moving sea of creatures escaping from the woodland below. Thousands of animals had taken flight and like an oil spill they spread across the hill, weaving their way upwards towards the Chanctonbury Ring.

Panic stricken, Michael turned and ran up the hill too, wondering what had caused this and then to his dismay, he realised why these creatures were charging; they were running for their lives trying to find a high point and a place of safety. As he ran he could see a wall of water flying towards them at speed. Michael raced up the bank and with only moments to spare grabbed onto one of the beech trees and clung on to it to save his life.

He closed his eyes and holding his breath braced himself for impact, he wasn't sure if he would have the strength to hang onto the tree, the water hit the hill with force sounding like thunder, he heard the others scream and then he waited, anxiously for the water to hit him. He couldn't believe what was happening, hadn't he been through enough? What was it? A flood or something worse? This kind of thing only happened to others in distant lands. Michael didn't want to die; he clenched his teeth together, ready to be submerged. He wanted to see Helen and Brighton again and his dad. He sadly reflected that he hadn't spoken to his dad for over a year; that was too long. He wanted to clear his name; he didn't want to die being thought of as a murderer. He knew he wasn't well and he wondered if there was something psychologically wrong with him.

The wave hit the hill and for a moment he saw nothing but a wall of water around him. He was sure it was going to hit him but the wave split in two and crashed around the hill's flanks and Michael was so thankful that he hadn't drowned. Only the spray from the water soaked him through and looking back down the hill it swept away most of the vermin that had fled. The lucky survivors swarmed around his ankles as they headed towards the woodland within the ring of trees. Michael looked for Nabeel, the waves had knocked him down and he hung on to the bush that Michael had hid in and he screamed as rats desperately clung onto him as the water swept over their bodies.

Evie had held tightly on to Tom's arm not willing to take her chances on her own. She felt bewildered and shocked. Tom hung on to a small sapling, hoping that it would be strong enough to withstand the force of the water. With his other hand, he had held onto Barney's collar. Barney shook nervously suspecting that something out of the ordinary was about to happen.

Sarah and Amy had taken cover in a bush, wishing that they'd found something more substantial to shield them from the approaching bank of water. They had both screamed when they saw the tidal wave hit the hill and then watched in amazement as the water had split in two around it. Only the spray from the waves had rained down on them.

The reality of what had just happened to them all was slowly beginning to sink in. They watched the black cloud and the wave continue on its journey and then witnessed the land around them fill with water. The rain wasn't as intense now but continued to pour down on them in celebration.

Tom looked down at Barney, he was still trembling but wasn't hurt, and he shook himself to remove some of the water caught in his fur. Evie released her grip from Tom's arm and looked about her in awe.

"Oh my goodness," she exclaimed. "What's happened? Why has this happened? Your poor dog Tom, he's shaking. I think we all are," she added as Sarah and Amy stood up and stared fearfully at each other.

"He's all right," replied Tom. "He just doesn't like having a bath," he said lightly trying to ease the mood a little. He patted Barney's head to try and calm him. "I've never seen anything like it; I knew the wind was blowing the wrong way today. Let's go to the edge and see what's happened. Look the rain's easing up; things can't be all that bad."

From the edge of the hill top, water spanned around them in all directions as far as the eye could see. The land they stood on and the ring of trees was just a small island in a vast ocean. The wind had dropped and the clouds above were breaking up, allowing sun beams to burst through.

"Well I never," said Tom, staring out in disbelief. "The water's like a mill pond, nothing caught up in it, no signs of life or anyone dead. It's like we're the only ones left alive in the world."

"Oh no.... my poor mum!" exclaimed Sarah. "Do you think Horsham has been flooded?"

"I don't know," replied Tom. "I've seen flooding here before but nothing like this. All I can make out are some hills in the distance but that's it. The weather people said it would be windy today but they certainly didn't mention anything about there being a tsunami."

"Oh no...." cried Sarah. "She's probably been drowned," she sobbed.

"She'll be fine," said Amy putting her arm around her. "It's probably just local flooding." Amy tried to sound convincing but in her heart she knew that she was probably giving her false hope. Another thought entered Amy's head and she tried not to take any notice of her wicked thought and then felt very guilty for thinking such a bad thing. Secretly, she hoped that Ted had perished.

"Do you think those two men that were fighting got washed away?" asked Evie, looking over towards the area where they'd last seen them.

"I don't know, Evie," replied Tom. "I'd forgotten all about them." Tom pointed to two figures swimming in the water.

Nabeel had almost drowned and Michael had dived in to save him and then swam to shore and towed him along as he seemed unable to swim. When they climbed out of the water and onto dry land Nabeel followed Michael silently, showing no signs of aggression; he seemed to be in shock. "Are you all ok, is anyone injured?" asked Michael. He knew that he wouldn't be able to keep his distance now and his organisation skills had kicked in instinctively; as an ex-soldier he knew he should protect the people stranded on this hill top; it was second nature to him and his survival skills might just save their lives. He decided to keep his hood up and just hoped nobody would recognise him.

Everyone shook their head. Amy looked at Nabeel "What's he doing here?" she asked frowning.

"He won't be any trouble," Michael added. He didn't trust Nabeel entirely and would keep an eye on him but looking at his sorry state, he thought it was unlikely that he would try anything in the immediate future. "You all need to get dry and keep warm. I'll try and light a fire and the smoke from the fire might attract the helicopters when they send a search party out looking for survivors. We need to collect as much firewood as we can," he said beckoning to everyone to assist him.

The search for dry branches was a difficult task; almost everything had been drenched by the rain and sea water. Eventually after several failures, Michael and Tom managed to get a small smoky fire going on the edge of the woodland.

Tom took off his waterproof jacket so that he and Evie could sit down by the fire; he still had his tweed jacket on under his coat. Amy tore her carrier bag in half to share with Sarah, who had stopped crying and they too sat down, exhausted and tried to warm themselves around the fire. Nabeel kept away from the main group. He looked out at the water and mumbled to himself about his misfortune. Michael continued to collect more fire wood; he needed a stock pile so that the fire wouldn't go out during the night. He wasn't sure how far the flood reached, he marvelled at how unexpected nature was and how lucky they all were to be up on that hill at that time. He wondered how many thousands of people had been lost, sucked down into the water like rag dolls, lost forever, their hopes and fears washed away for eternity and he wondered why he and his new companions had been spared.

8

The afternoon had passed slowly; above them a handful of silent birds were circulating high up in the clear blue sky. Concerned, the last rays of autumn sunshine shone down on the six survivors. It tried to warm them and dry their clothes as if wanting to apologise for the tragedy that had occurred.

There was an eerie silence at the Chanctonbury Ring, nobody had anything further to say and all were just waiting for something good to happen. They'd been stranded in a strangely beautiful setting but all felt intimidated by it and unwelcome; every part of their lives had been put in to disarray.

Amy watched everyone with fascination, it had been such a long time since she'd been with other people and she'd almost forgotten the art of conversation. She was glad that nobody wanted to speak, she'd run out of things to say. Earlier, they'd talked about their lives and their relatives, she suspected that there was more to tell; she'd only fleetingly run over her life. Nabeel, who had decided to join them around the fire, had remained silent and the man that fought with him and had taken it upon himself to become their leader didn't talk much about himself. Amy sensed that he'd a troubled soul and was a very private person; he hadn't even told them his name.

He reminded her of her brother, they'd similar character traits and mannerisms. Amy hadn't thought of her brother in a long time, and she felt guilty that she'd been so preoccupied with her own life that she'd almost forgotten him.

Simon had died in a car crash at the age of eighteen; she'd been asked to identify his body and remembered looking at his battered face with dismay. They'd both been brought up in a children's home and he'd turned out to be a bit of a wild teenager. He'd no driving licence and had been stopped more than once in a stolen car; she'd begged him to stop stealing cars but he hadn't listened. The funeral had been a simple one with herself and just a couple of friends attending. Their house mother had come too but she'd remained aloof and seemed glad to leave the graveside. Amy had felt so lonely after he'd gone; she had nobody she could turn to for support. Since the funeral, she'd only been once to see his grave, the graveyard had always made her feel uneasy. She could now picture the graveyard in Worthing under water and Simon's gravestone in the far corner with a large fish swimming past.

She felt thankfully that the dead were keeping their distance but she had a feeling that they were waiting for night to fall and would then seek her out. She looked up at the sky the birds had gone, it was almost as if time had frozen. She didn't know how they'd be rescued; she thought that they would probably send out helicopters to search for survivors and they would be winched to safety but there was no sign of them. There were no boats either and it felt like they'd been waiting forever for help. She was getting stiff sitting on the ground, she needed to stretch her leg and find somewhere for a wee; she'd been putting it off for ages. "I've got to spend a penny," said Amy, clambering to her feet and breaking the silence. "It's all this water everywhere; it gets to you after a while."

"I do too," replied Sarah. "Wait for me," she said standing up.

"Do you want to go?" Tom asked Evie. "You girls always like to go together."

"Oh goodness no, I couldn't possibly go outside," she replied firmly. Tom smiled; Evie was a funny old thing.

Amy and Sarah disappeared into the wooded area; Amy looked behind her to make sure nobody was following them. "I'm feeling really bad," she said in a quiet voice. "You know I told you all about my partner Ted and how I feared he might have drowned."

"I remember," replied Sarah.

"Well the truth is," she continued faltering a bit. "The truth is... we haven't been getting on very well lately; in fact things have been really crap for ages and earlier I wished that he'd drowned. How terrible is that?"

"I understand," replied Sarah stopping by a small bush. "I think a similar thought went through my head when I realised Nabeel was still alive. When I was in Afghanistan, that man held me hostage in a shack. For months and months I was kept isolated and in squalid conditions. If anyone should have died, it should have been him," she added bitterly.

"Oh that's awful, I didn't realise. No wonder you wanted to call the police, I thought he was an old boyfriend. A right pair we are!"

"No we're not! You seem like a nice person Amy. Sometimes people can drive you in to doing or thinking the most unfortunate things. Nabeel who is sitting around our fire is an evil man and has the front to ask me to help him. I can't bear to even look at him"

Amy left Sarah where she was to relieve herself and found a quiet spot out of view. As she squatted an intriguing idea entered her head, the Chanctonbury Ring was renowned for unusual happenings and sightings of the Devil. If she were to walk around the ring of trees seven times, as folklore suggested to summon the Devil, rather than accepting a bowl of soup, she would ask for her dearest wish to be granted and have Nabeel and Ted exterminated. He would probably feel inclined to grant this wish as this would be a most sinister request. Amy stood up and as she fastened up her jeans, she laughed at herself. Normally, she wouldn't wish anyone harm and thought that she was beginning to lose her mind; she shivered guilt ridden for having such a malicious imagination.

As she turned to go back to the camp, she could sense that something was staring at her, she could hear breathing and whipped her head around to see who or what it might be. She couldn't see anything but felt like something was going to pounce on her, she could see its sharp claws in her mind and her heart began to beat with loud thuds in her chest. She had to make herself move away from whatever it was and then ran as fast as she could towards the others. She believed if she stayed a second longer she would be dragged down into the unknown, a dark place that was calling out her name. She cursed herself for thinking such bad things earlier and blindly she ran towards the fire and then almost ran into Sarah.

"Are you all right?" Sarah asked. "You look like you've seen a ghost."

"There's something behind me, something evil and dangerous," panted Amy.

Sarah looked back into the woodland but could see nothing following her.

"I can't see anything, perhaps it was a rat," she suggested but Amy shook her head as they joined the others.

"No it was bigger than that, I know what it was now, I think it was a cat, a big cat like the one in Jungle Book."

Tom laughed. "Don't you worry yourself Amy, if there had been a cat nearby, Barney would have been after it like a shot." Wouldn't you boy?" he said stroking his head. Barney's tail wagged happily, not quite understanding what was being said but hoping that this was a sign that he was going to be fed. "You're hungry aren't you?" Tom continued. "It's your dinner time. Sorry boy, you might have to wait a few more hours."

"Oh poor thing," said Evie, "I've got some mints in my bag. Would he like one?"

"That's very kind of you, I'm sure he and all of us wouldn't mind one, we're all getting hungry and probably thirsty too. All this water around us is no good to drink, it's too salty," said Tom looking bleakly at the expanse of water before them.

"Oh, I have water and biscuits with me too, would anyone like some?" Evie asked, delving into her handbag and then retrieved not only a small bottle of water but half a packet of shortcake and some soft mints."

"We mustn't get dehydrated." Michael said looking on approvingly as everyone passed the bottle around and took a sip of water. The biscuit was also welcome; he hadn't had sugar for weeks. "If only we knew what was going to happen, we could have collected rainwater to drink. It was raining so hard we would have had enough to last for days."

"You don't think we'll be here that long do you?" Evie asked Michael. "Only my son will be coming to stay with me tomorrow." It was then that she noticed her shopping bag containing Albert's ashes was missing. She looked frantically around her to see where she'd left it. The last time she remembered seeing it was when she'd lodged it between her feet when the wave had hit the hill.

"What's the matter?" Tom asked, seeing her worried expression.

"My bag, it's gone, Albert he's..., it's gone," she said rising to her feet. "I think I've left it in there she said, pointing to the woodland at the centre of the Ring."

"I'll come with you," Tom offered as he got up. "My knees have seized up, I could do with a walk," he added bending them a little to try and relieve the stiffness. Barney wagged his tail eagerly, thinking that perhaps it was feeding time at last and that the biscuit he'd just eaten had been an appetiser. There was no more food forthcoming and that was a disappointment; despondently he followed Tom and Evie into the woods.

They quickly found the spot where they'd sheltered from the wave but the shopping bag containing Albert's ashes was nowhere to be seen.

"I'm sorry Evie," Tom said gently. "I think they might have been washed away. Perhaps it's for the best, a sea burial is quite a romantic ending don't you think?"

"Yes, I suppose you're right Tom but I wish I could have said goodbye," replied Evie, she wanted to cry but was too embarrassed. She looked around her, there was an ethereal feel to these woods, almost as if they were calling to all the lost souls to gather there and be remembered. She knew that Albert would have loved it up there on the top of the hill but she wasn't so sure about him being buried at sea. She imagined the bag sinking to the bottom of the sea, lost forever amongst the wrecked houses and sea creatures he'd feared. A small sob escaped her and she tried her hardest to stop the tears, she didn't want to cry. Tom put his arms around her, she allowed him to hold her and didn't try and pull away; there was something very reassuring about being in his arms. For the first time for a very long time, she felt cared for and she wished that she'd known Tom all her life.

"Come on," he said after a few minutes. "We'd better get back to the others." Tom took her hand and he squeezed it gently, he felt sorry for her and didn't want her to be upset. He hoped that eventually he could persuade her to stay with him when the sea receded. "They might think we've been attacked by Bagheera. ...Between you and me, I think Amy might have a screw loose."

Evie dried her eyes on her handkerchief and she smiled; Tom was such a lovely man.

***

Sleepily, she washed her black paw, with her big pink rasping tongue, removing all traces of the blood from an earlier kill. The effort of washing was physically draining and she knew that she would sleep soon and perhaps not wake up again. Her hip ached where the bullet had entered and although she'd licked the area many times and stopped the bleeding, she hadn't managed to stem the infection that raged within her body. For years, unseen by humans, she'd passed silently through meadows, farms and woodland, her huge, black, silky body slipping through the rape and wheat unnoticed. There were plenty of deer and livestock around to fill her and lots of clean water to drink. She'd learnt to keep away from people and cars - their habits and ways were a mystery to her.

On one hot summer's afternoon in August, she'd been lying in the shade on the hillside at the Chanctonbury Ring, waiting for the sun to go down so that she could hunt. She dozed dreamily, occasionally opening her eyes to check for humans, when she noticed a young woman riding a large white horse further down the hill. She'd seen them many times before at the same time and had let them ride by unharmed. On this particular day, however, for some reason she felt an irresistible urge to chase them and take the horse down.

Her eyes now wide open, she watched the horse intently, its tail swished away the flies and this irritated her immensely; she forgot that it was being ridden by a human. Perhaps it was the heat that made her blow caution to the wind or it could have been her primeval hunting spirit enticing her out of hiding to hunt just for the sake of it. She could bear it no longer, keeping low to the ground, she moved closer to the edge of the shade she'd been lying in, waiting tentatively for that right moment to attack. Then like a black bolt, she sped down the hill and approaching from behind the horse, she leapt in the air with claws out ready to hook them into the horse's loins and pull it down. Her aim was perfect and she waited to land on the horses back. To her surprise, her claws gripped nothing but air and she found herself falling through both the horse and rider and she tumbled on the ground and flipped over several times. With frustration she roared. Although still visible, annoyingly both the horse and rider were nothing more than an apparition, a ghostly duo from another time. The young woman blissfully unaware of the panther's presence kicked the horse on and they cantered off leaving the panther behind them and then disappeared into thin air. The panther's tail twitched with frustration.

Angrily she made her way towards her hideaway but as she walked, she became aware of another human presence and instinctively she knew she needed to get away, she was exposed and in danger. The sound of gunshot from a Beretta confirmed this, the bullet narrowly missing her head. A lively young man wearing a hunting jacket was out rabbiting for beer money, had seen her and wanting her head for a trophy had taken a shot at her. Panic stricken, she dashed towards the ring of trees for sanctuary and just as she reached the beech trees, a shot hit her on the hip. Pain seared through her body and made her tremble. She waited for what seemed like an eternity for her attacker to enter the woodland and knew if he did try and find her then this would be the end for her. Nobody came.

From beneath the knitted branches of a bush, the panther heard intruders approaching and her amber eyes settled on a grey dog weaving its way through undergrowth, she growled at the beast as it passed by; Barney took no notice and continued his mission to unearth a tasty morsel or two from the moist earth. She was hungry but too weak to pounce; the dog's lively presence irritated her and she roared angrily. Barney froze to the spot and then barked furiously at the bush where he'd heard the roar.

"What's the matter?" Tom asked Barney. "You've seen something you don't like? He's got a bit of an imagination this dog. I bet you anything there's nothing there. Look, I'll show you," said Tom, walking over to the bush. Then, with one sweep of his arm, he lifted the mass of branches to show Barney that there was nothing underneath. "Oh my word!" he exclaimed. Evie looked at his concerned face. "Would you believe it? There's some sort of wild cat here."

"Run Tom, Amy was right," called Evie urgently.

"No, don't be alarmed Evie, there's not much left of it. It's been dead a while. I can't imagine why Amy thought she was being chased by it." Barney cowered behind Tom. "It's all right, you silly thing, it can't hurt you now." Tom said soothingly to him.

Evie came closer to look. "Oh it's such a shame," she exclaimed. "Such a beautiful animal. Do you think it escaped from a zoo?"

"May be. It might have been a pet and got too big. People keep the strangest things. I knew a man that kept an alligator once and it got so big and dangerous that he ended up dumping it in the Adur. I think there's been sightings and the odd dog has been dragged in the river.

Why he didn't call someone in to take it off him I don't know."

The panther growled at the people disturbing her peace and couldn't understand why they ignored her; did they not realise they were in danger? Earlier, she'd managed to scare a woman away but these two humans stood over her, they looked puzzled and were not alarmed by her threatening growls and roars. With effort the panther got to her feet and slipped away to find some peace, they didn't notice her leave and continued to look beneath the bush as if she was still there.

"This is a very strange day," said Evie wistfully, looking at the decomposing cat. "I've seen things and felt feelings that I've never dreamed of."

"It's going to be an interesting night too," whispered Tom. "Legend has it that all those that have attempted to sleep up here have been scared silly and have had to leave before morning. Unnatural things go on up here Evie. I just hope we're rescued soon."

9

Swiftly, the night as black as a raven's back, dissolved the day and swept over the sea, sucking up the light and left in its wake a thick white mist around the Chanctonbury Ring. The sea spirits, beneath their shroud, whispered softly in the heads of the survivors and asked them to step away from the fire that burned so brightly and to come and find them. A full moon was due to appear and the night promised to be a memorable one. Within the fiery core beneath the Chanctonbury Ring a black heart beat increasingly faster, eagerly waiting for midnight to strike and for more of the entertainment to begin.

Michael looked anxiously at his dwindling supply of wood and hoped that there would be enough to see them through the night. His main concern was that everyone should keep warm. The autumn nights were turning colder and he didn't want anyone to die of hyperthermia, he felt obliged to preserve what might be the last surviving members of Sussex. Evie and Tom were huddled together like two roosting birds and the girls were warming their hands near to the flames. He'd caught another rabbit and a rat and had cooked them over the fire. Only he'd eaten the rat, much to everyone's disgust. There were plenty of rats with them on top of the hill that had managed to out run the wave but Michael hadn't mentioned this, as Sarah seemed particularly disgusted by them. Talk had turned back to the discovery of the panther and about Amy declaring that she had psychic ability. This, apparently, was why she thought the panther had chased her.

"So you can only see troubled spirits?" Tom asked Amy. "My Martha's scattered up here. Do you see her?"

Amy looked thoughtful, "She's up here but I sense sadness though. She was ill for months and feels she was a burden to you. She knows you loved her but there's something she's hiding from me, I can find out if you like. Your mother's here too, but she's resting in peace."

"Goodness! No, we'll leave Martha alone, she's been through enough," exclaimed Tom; he wished he hadn't asked her about his wife; he hadn't expected her to be so accurate. "You're right, Mum's scattered up here too. You should be on the telly."

"Really," replied Amy. "No I'm not that good, I'm just learning. This is all new to me but I think I'm more in tune now; especially after what's happened here today. I'm still trying to understand why this is all happening to me. There's one thing I don't understand, though, thousands of people must have died in this tsunami and yet the waters around us are empty, there's not a soul within them. Maybe they don't know they're dead yet."

"I hope you're right," said Sarah. "I can't believe that my mother might be dead. The nursing home she worked in was at the top of a steep hill, there's a chance she's ok."

"I will pray to God for you, that she is safe," announced Nabeel breaking his silence. "We should also pray that your country cares enough about us to send out a search party."

"I'm just thankful that we are all alive and uninjured," replied Michael annoyed by Nabeel's words. "I'm sure that when it gets light, we'll be found. Think of all those poor people that have died."

"The earth has been cleansed," replied Nabeel. "I'm sure that Sarah's mother has been saved but it is only right that this has happened, the western world has become tainted by greed and corruption and yes, it is only right that the unworthy should die."

Everyone was shocked into silence for a moment.

"Then what the fuck are you doing here?" replied Michael angrily, his face red with fury.

Nabeel laughed. "I have a right, I am tired of war and am just trying to find a quiet place to live, mind my own business and then when I am established, I can enlighten and transform the sinners that live in the West. It is a miracle that I am alive and I am living proof that God wishes me to continue on this path."

"We're not all sinners," replied Amy. "Most of us are decent law abiding people.

"You may think you are," Nabeel was now enjoying the attention. "You have no idea. I have seen with my own eyes, the drunkards and the half-naked woman on your streets. Men, women and children so corrupt, that they offer themselves up for sexual services and then wonder why they become diseased and suffer. You all crave money and cars and have no idea how much you take from this planet. You have all forgotten God and deserve to be washed away."

"You don't know what you are talking about," replied Michael trying to keep calm. "I've served in Afghanistan and have seen the cruelty you display to each other. I have witnessed evil acts."

"There is no cruelty, there are laws and standards to maintain, we are passionate people and we do not take kindly when outsiders interfere with natural shifts of power. You are a soldier and are nothing, just a murderous puppet," snarled Nabeel, staring into Michael's eyes.

Michael breathed in deeply, he knew that Nabeel was trying to wind him up and he had to stop himself from taking the bait completely. He looked away from Nabeel and started intently into the fire, trying to think of soothing scenes in his mind.

Tom interrupted his thought process. "Come on now, you two, we are going to have to agree to disagree on this one. I think we're all a bit upset tonight. Perhaps we should all lie down and try to sleep, things will look better in the morning. Are you warm enough Evie?" he asked. She was looking very startled by what had just been said and was perhaps not used to men swearing.

"I'm ok but I'd rather not sleep, in case someone comes and I miss them. Wouldn't that be awful to wake up and find that everyone has gone and you're the only one left on this island?"

"You lie down and rest, I'll stay awake and make sure you're safe. Nobody is going anywhere without you. Here rest your head on my leg."

Evie was tired, Tom's words soothed her and she thought that a short nap would help. She longed to be lying in her feather bed in her London flat but just to lie down and shut her eyes for a moment would be a luxury. Gently, she lay down on the mac herself and Tom had been sharing and placed her head on his knee, she'd considered using her handbag but decided that although she felt a little embarrassed, Tom's knee would be a softer option. As she drifted off into a deep sleep, she forgot that she was outside, it was almost as if she was a child again sleeping in her mother and father's house in Goring, with fresh air blowing in from the Channel, smelling of seaweed and salt.

Nabeel got up and stretched, "I've got to see a man about a dog," he said, walking off. The moon, now high in the sky, lit his way.

Sarah watched Nabeel disappear into the darkness she was shocked by the hatred she felt towards him, he was an animal. Amy could sense her dislike for him and thought that she should share with the others what this man had done to her.

"Sarah, tell us what happened to you when you were in Afghanistan," urged Amy. "That man needs locking up; you wouldn't believe what happened to her."

Hesitantly, Sarah relayed her kidnapping story to everyone and didn't spare any detail and by the end she could feel herself shaking, she could feel the darkness she dreaded clawing at her and she tried her best not to look around, she'd cried enough that day and didn't want everyone to see her have a panic attack. Tom and Michael shook their heads with disapproval, Amy rubbed Sarah's arm to comfort her and wondered where Nabeel was, he'd been gone for over half an hour. "Nabeel has been a long time. Do you think he heard us talking about him and has decided to keep away?" asked Amy.

"I don't know," replied Michael, he should stay by the fire, the temperature is dropping. He can't be lost, the moon is shining; you can see quite well. We'll give him another ten minutes and then go and look for him. He's not our most favourite person at the moment but you wouldn't want him to die from hyperthermia would you?"

"No," said Amy but she knew that most didn't really care that much about Nabeel's wellbeing.

Ten minutes passed slowly, Nabeel didn't return. "Right," announced Michael fishing out a torch from his bag. "I'd better go and find him. I won't be long; he's probably just decided to go it alone. You'd think he'd have more sense. Like it or not, we've all got to stick together." Michael said heading off into the Ring.

Michael was used to sleeping out and usually the darkness didn't bother him but being alone in the woods, the trees seemed to be whispering, almost laughing at his foolishness for straying away from the fire. He hoped he would find Nabeel soon, although he wasn't sure what he was going to say. As he walked nearer to the centre of the Ring, he could feel his heart beating harder, he scanned the woods all around with his torch light, flicking from one side to the other and then finally he spotted Nabeel standing a little way ahead of him. Nabeel was smiling inanely, almost as if he'd been waiting for him. There was something about his countenance that was unnerving and he didn't seem to be aware that Michael was approaching. Nabeel stood there motionless and he seemed to be staring right through him. He stared harder at Nabeel and thought he could see two small horns protruding from each side of his head and he wondered if he was in fact staring at the Devil himself. Michael blinked; he didn't trust his eyes. He turned around to see if there was anyone behind him and then directed his torch back at Nabeel again, Nabeel had gone. "Nabeel," called Michael "I don't know what you're playing at. Look, I don't want to fight," said Michael, pivoting on the spot looking for him, fully expecting him to attack. Again Michael flicked his torch light around the woodland trying to find him but the trees stared innocently back at him not willing to give away their secrets. Michael could barely breathe with fear. He decided that he would go back to the fire; if Nabeel was trying to scare him then he was succeeding.

It was obvious that Nabeel had developed a grudge towards him, since he'd taken him down to the ground earlier. He half expected him to retaliate: there was something very sinister about his expression. Michael was no coward but he didn't relish the prospect of being attacked by a mad man and so turned on his heels and began to run, Nabeel could freeze to death for all he cared.

The fire called to Michael, it called out his name and chastised him for leaving it in the first place. Ahead, Michael could see the flames dancing; he'd almost reached the edge of the woodland, he could feel the panic inside him subsiding he could see the others sitting around the fire. He decided that his eyes had been playing tricks on him and he'd become delusional. Michael slowed down to a walking pace; he didn't want the others to think he was afraid.

Out of the darkness, like a frenzied animal, Nabeel pounced on him from behind. Michael yelled and dropped his torch and tried to remove Nabeel's arm that was locked around his throat. With all his strength, he elbowed Nabeel in the ribs and stamped hard onto a foot but this had no effect on his assailant. Michael called out for help, hoping that someone would come to his rescue. It was then that he saw out of the corner of his eye, a knife in Nabeel's hand, the blade glistened in the moonlight. Without thinking Michael managed to deflect the knife away from his body by blocking the blow with his left fist into Nabeel's wrist just as he tried to stab him in the side. Bending forward and backing into Nabeel's body, Michael managed to unbalance Nabeel and by twisting his own body around, Nabeel loosened his grip. Immediately Michael pushed the hand that held him around the throat away and broke free. He punched Nabeel in the stomach which winded him and then stepped in and managed to remove the knife from Nabeel's hand. He watched Nabeel collapse onto one knee; he wasn't sure what to do next. Surely he would stop his childish vendetta.

Michael looked behind to see the others cautiously approaching, Evie was rubbing her eyes and all looked alarmed and anxious. Michael stared at Nabeel, he could see no evidence of horns or the manic smile on his face and he wondered what his next move might be. Nabeel shook his head as if defeated and then sprang up in attack mode ready to strike again. Michael stood his ground, his guard up, ready for him, he looked at the knife in his hand tempting him to spill blood so he threw it away; he wasn't planning on killing anyone tonight.

Nabeel was giving nothing away; he wasn't sure if he was going to be kicked or punched. Either way, Michael trusted his self-defence skills enough to know that he wouldn't get hit. At the last moment, Michael realised that Nabeel was going to head butt him, he moved out of his way and avoided him. He sensed that all were witnessing Nabeel's attack on him and was glad that he'd an audience, if anything bad happened, he wouldn't at least be blamed for another death. Nabeel spun around and threw a punch. Michael blocked this and shoved Nabeel in the chest, expecting him to push him out of harm's way but to his surprise, he shot up in the air, high above all their heads and screaming, came hurtling down onto a broken sapling and was speared through the stomach. He died instantly; his body twitched like a dead rabbit and his blank eyes, wide open stared accusingly at his murderer.

Sarah and Amy both screamed, Evie looked away and Tom shook his head disbelievingly. "What did you want to go and do that for?" he asked Michael.

Michael was shocked; he couldn't believe what had just happened. "Didn't you see that," he stammered. "How could I have possibly thrown him up in the air like that? He was massive; I could never have lifted him up like that. I just pushed him out the way and anyway, he attacked me!"

"I don't know how you did it," replied Tom. "But it's clear that you're some sort of ninja expert and now someone has been killed. Poor man, it's a crying shame. Couldn't you have restrained him in some way? We could have tied him up and turned him over to the authorities in the morning. You've done an awful thing and I can see in your eyes that you've done something like this before. We know nothing about you, not even your name, there's something very odd about you. Come back to the fire with me Evie and have some water; you really shouldn't have witnessed this."

Michael stood alone and stared incredulously at Nabeel's broken body; he really hadn't intended on killing him and couldn't believe that anyone could think that he was a murderer. Dark forces were playing a hand in all this; he knew he couldn't have thrown such a large man that high into the air - not even in his wildest dreams. He was now wanted for two murders and had witnesses at both crime scenes; things didn't look good for him.

Amy looked back at the Ring; somebody had heard her crazy wish earlier and she felt guilty as if in some way she was responsible for Nabeel's death. Something really strange had just happened; there was no way that anyone could have thrown a man that size in the air. She walked back to the fire and sat down with Sarah and they both glanced at each other uneasily as the reality of what had just occurred sunk in. Sarah too had wished that Nabeel had died in the flood and now he was dead. Amy wondered if Ted had met his end too.

Aaron watched the proceedings with approval and then, smiling to himself, slithered away to join his master.

10

The silence was almost tangible as Sarah, Evie, Tom and Amy, stared, deep in thought, into the dying flames of the camp fire. The sea fog around them shimmered in the moonlight and they could hear the water as it lapped gently on the hill side, enjoying the new terrain and using the cover of darkness, deviously it etched out a new shoreline for itself.

"This is unbearable!" exclaimed Sarah. "What do you think is happening here? Are we all going mad and going to end up killing each other like in a horror movie? I can't believe that Nabeel is dead. If I hadn't have seen it with my own eyes, I wouldn't have believed it. I don't think his death was murder; it was just a tragic accident. We all saw Nabeel, he was the attacker; that poor man was trying to defend himself. He only pushed Nabeel and then something weird happened and he shot up into the air like a kite. We shouldn't have been so hard on him; he'll freeze to death out there alone. God knows what will happen next or what's in the woods waiting to strike; this place is giving me the creeps."

"Don't upset yourself Sarah," replied Evie. "I'm sure everyone will be fine. It will be light in a few hours and the rescue teams will be out looking for us. I'm sure Nabeel's death was a mistake and no one is to blame."

Evie looked across to Tom for reassurance but he didn't look convinced.

Michael had been sitting behind one of the beech trees not far from the others, trying to keep warm and had been listening to their conversation and thought that if he explained his situation to everyone they might understand. "I have nothing to hide," he announced emerging from his hiding place. Barney barked at him, surprised by his sudden appearance and then growled at him "My name is Michael and yes, I'm pretty sure that something peculiar is going on here, I really didn't mean to kill Nabeel. I'm not a bad person and was just defending myself; I just seem to be attracting trouble at the moment."

"You might say that," replied Tom. "My Barney knows a wrong'en when he sees one. He's a good judge of character, he is."

"That's not fair," complained Michael. "You can't let a dog judge me! Why did I stop Nabeel taking Sarah off and why did I build a fire and cook for you all, if I didn't mean well?"

"Hum... you say that," continued Tom. "What's your story, Michael? It looks like you haven't washed for weeks and you look like a vagrant. Not many people have a spare dead rabbit in their bag to eat; there's something about you that's wrong, you have desperation in your eyes. You look like you're a man on the run to me."

Michael was silent for a moment as he took in Tom's summary of himself, he'd seen straight through him. "Look," Michael said slowly. "I'm having a hard time at the moment but really, I don't mean anyone any harm. We've all hit hard times at some point in our lives and ..." Michael stopped mid-sentence as he felt the ground shake. "Did you feel that?" he asked as another tremor shook the ground.

All nodded and stood up and stared at the ground tentatively, looking to see if they could see it moving.

"It could be an earthquake," suggested Amy. "After today, anything is possible."

"I don't know" said Tom. I don't remember there being an earthquake ever in these parts. The ground is under a lot of stress with all this water on it, it's bound to want to shift about a bit."

The ground responding to their theories shook more violently, sending shockwaves through them, the land around them groaned out loud, complaining at the sea for causing its suffocation and castellation.

"What's going to happen now?" gasped Amy, looking for somewhere to run but there was nowhere to go.

"Don't panic," Michael called out, trying to keep everyone calm. "As Tom says, there's probably a geological reason for this."

The ground continued to vibrate and didn't give any indication of ceasing. The silence was again broken by the sound of branches ripping and roots tearing and these noises grew in intensity as slowly the hill began to split in two. The old beech trees screamed out as their roots were torn up. In slow motion, the ground tore open; the fire, burning embers and branches dropped down into the growing crevasse. For a moment the darkness engulfed them all, like a blanket until the moonlight could fight its way back through.

"Quickly," Michael shouted, looking at the widening gap and at the beech trees beginning to topple over. “Hang onto a large tree, the hill is splitting up, quickly before we get swallowed up.”

Down at the bottom of the crevasse a dark soul laughed at the humans above trying to make sense of their pathetic world.

Tom, Evie and Michael found a beech tree each and clung to it hoping that they too wouldn’t be dragged down into the fissure. Sarah and Amy, on the other side of the ravine, did the same. The ancient beech trees were now leaning at forty five degrees and their huge roots sprung up from the ground, laden with earth, their top most branches stretched out across the sea. Defiantly, they fought the temptation to plunge themselves into a watery grave.

Accepting that their end had come, the trees toppled over; their trunks thudded onto the ground and most of their branches disappeared beneath the water with all hope lost. “This is like Hell on earth.” Amy called out; she was sitting on the trunk of the tree, her legs astride it. She looked across the gorge to the others to make sure they were all right and saw that everyone was still attached to their respective trees. It was then that she spotted Barney, perched precariously on the edge of her side of the ravine. He was looking apprehensively at Tom on the other side and she could tell by the dog’s behaviour that he was eager to join him; he looked as if he might leap across the gap at any moment.

“Look Sarah,” she called but she was face down clutching her tree; she seemed to be petrified and far too scared to look around. “Barney,” Amy called. “Come on, come here boy.” He didn’t take any notice; she could hear Tom calling out to him, firmly telling him to stay where he was. The dog ran anxiously up and down the ragged edge, desperately looking for a place to jump across.

Evie closed her eyes; she couldn't bear to watch any longer. She knew that the gap was much too wide now to even attempt to jump and hoped that Barney would have more sense. This was the most extraordinary day, it was almost beyond belief, so much had happened and she feared that this may not be the end of their ordeal. She could hear Tom begging with his dog to stay where he was. The tree she was on had stopped moving and the ground had stopped shaking. She'd managed to right herself and sat awkwardly on the trunk of the tree with her feet resting on the ground. She had her handbag tucked carefully under her arm, she didn't want to lose that; losing Albert had been bad enough.

An explosion made Evie open her eyes rapidly and she screamed as a flame from the bottom of the gorge surged up into the air and then vanished. For a moment the night was like day. "What was that?" she immediately asked.

"One hell of an explosion! An ember from the fire must have ignited some trapped gas," Tom replied. "Can you see Barney?"

"No," said Evie looking towards the edge of the gorge - the dog had gone.

"He's probably hiding," called Michael, his ears still ringing from the explosion as he climbed towards Evie and Tom. They all called out his name and waited hopefully but he didn't appear.

"No, he's a goner," said Tom sadly. "What a way to go, poor old boy."

Evie looked at Tom sorrowfully, she could think of nothing to say that didn't sound like a cliché. In the end she said nothing at all and then found herself reaching across to him and patting his hand sympathetically.

"It's all right Evie," sighed Tom. "Barney was an old dog. ...I can't believe it, he didn't deserve to go like that. When he was young, he won many races and was one of the best racing dogs around; he's had a good life. I think he had a happy retirement with me. The explosion was over that quickly, he wouldn't have suffered much."

Michael remained silent; he knew that anything he said would just irritate him. For some reason Tom really disliked him and had labelled him as a criminal. Michael felt so tired he could barely keep his eyes open, he needed to sleep he needed to find a way to sort out his life, he needed a new start. His heart was still thudding in his chest after the explosion; he knew that this wasn't normal, loud bangs should not send him into shock. He looked across the sea for inspiration - his lonely world was becoming insufferable.

Sarah breathed in and out slowly, trying to get oxygen through her trembling body. She hoped that no one was watching her; she didn't want to look foolish and was embarrassed that she'd cried in front of everybody so much. Carefully, she turned herself over, so she was looking directly up at the night sky; the stars blinked unsympathetically down on her. She didn't want to look at the dark gorge or what might be lurking in the shadows around her; she wanted to see the first signs of morning and wanted to see daylight. She drew her teeth together to try and stop herself from shaking; she couldn't believe how pathetic she'd become. The spirit of adventure and love for life had been truly beaten out of her by past events. She hated her life; if only she could be more like her mother, she was an amazing woman. Even after losing her father, her mother had remained positive and thankful that she'd known him and that their years together had been happy. She worked long hours in the nursing home and loved being a carer; she was the most positive and courageous person she'd ever met. Sarah longed to see her again and then realised that she wouldn't. Tears began to work their way out of her eyes and she sighed, cross that she was crying again and wished that she could put this episode in her life far behind her.

Amy could hear Sarah sobbing, she wished she could say everything would work out but she knew that it was hard to console someone when they were grieving. Sarah, she decided, had clearly given up hope that her mother was alive. She remembered the pain she'd felt when she lost her brother and how long it had taken to accept that she would never see him again. She really wanted to help her and looked out across the sea for inspiration. Then an idea came to her, if she called on the spirits in the shadows to come to her, maybe they could search in their world and see if Sarah's mother was there. She tried to concentrate on the spirit she'd seen earlier. In her mind she could see Cornelia's face, her dark eyes, dove white pale skin and her fair hair drawn back from her face with a cascade of soft long curls falling from the back of her head down her back. For a moment she could sense her approaching but then felt her fear, Amy shuddered there was another spirit nearby, Cornelia slid back into the shadows cowering away, hoping she wouldn't be noticed by this entity.

Amy was surprised that she hadn't noticed his presence before; she could sense a dark and evil mass oozing from the depths of the gorge, defiant and swollen with pride, boasting to all that came too close, that for millennia, he alone had planted seeds of madness in the minds of others. He specialised in murder, chaos and devastation and watched coldly on as his evil plans twisted and turned and then escalated, taking on a life of their own. He was the master of the most sinister creations. Amy shook her head to escape from this spirit's dark world; she didn't want to know any more.

Barney eyed his surroundings suspiciously; he sensed that he was in a new place now and that Tom was no longer his master. He could smell burning, not the fire at his cottage but a smell of something unfamiliar. The stench revolted him; he could smell old meat charring. Instinctively he knew that he should keep away from the source, lest the hands that stretched out so wretchedly, should pull him in and force him to join them. He couldn't see clearly enough to estimate how big the dark space he was in measured. He was warm and glad to be out of the cold but he couldn't remember how he'd got there. He knew that his hunger would always be with him and that nobody cared enough to show him some kindness. His ears pricked up, his master was calling him to stand by his side. Reluctantly he trotted off to join him, realising that a failure to obey would be his undoing. He couldn't see him but knew he'd reached his appointed position and wagged his tail hoping for some recognition but none came.

His new master seemed in high spirits and was satisfied with his achievements so far that night; he revelled in his ability to flout the rules of his tenancy agreement that had been set in stone since man had walked on the earth. Little by little, he'd planted seeds of malice into the hearts of men causing untold damage. Like a viral worm, he would eventually infest the very fabric that held mankind together and then the balance between good and evil would be readdressed. Until that day, he amused himself by taunting a few unsuspecting victims, playing with their minds and lives, a highly interesting and wicked game to while away the hours. Legend had it, that on this hill, he was supposed to show benevolence. He smirked and congratulated himself for being so inventive. Yes he would embrace the strangers that had stumbled across his doorstep and go out of his way to accommodate his victim's wishes but they should be very careful for what they wished for; they might just get more than they bargained.

11

Thin streaks of orange in the dark sky signified that the sun would soon rise. The hours had slipped away quietly and without incident. No one had been able to sleep properly, all were tired and miserable and the thought of spending another night at the Chanctonbury Ring was almost too awful to entertain. Their hope that they would be rescued seemed to be just a dream. Some wondered if they should swim out away from their new acquaintances to save themselves but then the thought of being alone and perhaps dying alone was too much to bear. The need to huddle together as a group and find solace had become essential and inescapable. Michael closed his eyes and hoped that he would drift off to sleep instead of brooding.

Each was lost in their own thoughts, their fraught minds asking themselves questions over and over; desperately trying to find answers. Looking at the now blood red sky and watching the clouds fleeting past, some thought that there might be a heaven. Sarah grinned, she could see the top of the sun sliding up past the horizon; it was morning.

Others however, concluded that they had been riding their own decaying merry-go-round for far too long and were unable to jump off; the horses that they rode on were black and gnarled with age. If only the merry-go-round would stop and they could take stock of their lives and understand them or at the very least find peace. Their plight forced them to ask what reality was and what was their purpose on this most physical of planets. The sharp rocks at their feet, told them that humans bleed and the soft earth that promised them a future and to cushion them from harm, had lied and was barren. Feeling crestfallen and weary, Evie passed Tom the bottle of water; he looked tired too.

They wondered what it was they all sought, was it to find happiness or just to laugh again? Would their rescue bring this and would they be happy forever more? The merry-go-round had become a rollercoaster ride and the desire to leap into the green grass called freedom was overwhelming but the grass was out of reach and the black horses drove the merry-go-round forward and much faster making their heads spin.

Tom had tried to sleep sitting up; he was cold and his joints ached. It was impossible to get comfortable on the beech tree. There was some dry land around the trees but he wasn't sure how stable the ground was and he thought it would be too wet to lie on. From time to time during the night he'd nodded off, his head dropping onto his chest and then he would wake himself up just as he was about to slump forward. He looked at Michael; he'd managed to sleep sat on a sloping grassy bank near to his tree, hugging his knees. This looked a bit too difficult for him to achieve, he wasn't as young as he used to be. He looked at Evie, she too sat upright on her beech tree but she seemed to have mastered the art of vertical sleep, she occasionally closed her eyes and cat napped. Mystifyingly, she seemed to do this without falling forward.

Tom felt helpless, he couldn't bear to see Evie or any of the others suffer. He wished he could do something about their predicament. With renewed hope, he fished about in his pockets, looking for his phone; if he could just get a signal he could ring for help. Finally after searching several pockets, he found his mobile and looked at the screen, it was still on but there was no signal and the battery was low. It wouldn't be long before it died.

Tom thought of his daughter; he smiled to himself, Ruth although happy that her aged dad had a mobile phone, always laughed at him for having such an antiquated model. He didn't mind her teasing; she was a sweet girl, called him every night and popped in most weekends to see him. She had made his ring tone the tune 'The Teddy Bears Picnic' and he hadn't the faintest idea how to change it. This had raised a few eyebrows in the Frankland Arms. His heart pounded for a moment as he struggled to recall what day it was and then he remembered that it was Wednesday; his daughter would be safe and sound in Manchester, visiting a friend. He was then worried about her again and realised that she must be sick with worry, the South Downs tsunami would have been headline news and she must be desperate to hear if he was alive.

Tom looked down at his phone again to see if he'd any missed calls and then almost dropped it as it started to ring. The familiar ring tone rang out, waking everyone from their daydreams. Tom looked to see who was calling; he hoped it would be his daughter. He stared at the words 'withheld number' written across the screen and then quickly pressed the receive button and hoped that it would be a real person to talk to and not just one of those recorded messages. “Hello, Tom Barns here....hello?” he said cautiously.

At first the line was just white noise and crackled but gradually he could hear a man speaking. He’d a deep rasping voice but what the man was saying was unrecognisable; it was nobody that he knew but he thought that he might be able to get them help. “Hello, who’s calling? Do I know you? Can you hear me?”

“Yes ....” replied the caller. “I am your worst nightmare, if you want to stay alive go deep into the hill and save yourselves.”

“Pardon?” he replied, concerned. “Who is this?”

“Save yourselves.”

The call ended, Tom looked uncertainly down at the phone in his hand it was glowing red and then became too hot to handle. He quickly put the phone down in front of him on the tree trunk. The damp wood began to sizzle beneath it and then hissed as the phone heated up to melting point and then began to dissolve. “Well, I never!” he exclaimed, staring down at what was his phone. Everyone looked on in astonishment.

“How odd, I didn’t think a mobile could get overheated” said Tom.

“Who called?” asked Evie eagerly.

“Someone said, I don’t know who it was, that if we wanted to stay alive then we need to go into the hill and save ourselves. I don’t think he was joking, he seemed adamant about it. How very strange. How would he know about this hill? Perhaps it was someone from the army and there’s an escape route or do you think there’s some kind of bunker down there? What on earth has happened to my phone?” Disbelieving Tom looked down at the sticky mess oozing down the sides of the tree trunk.

"That happened to my phone too," called Amy from across the gorge. "Did he say he was from a rescue team?"

"Not exactly..., it was a very bad line and all I told you is what was said. He did say that he was our worst nightmare." He looked at Evie's expression and wished he hadn't said that. "Maybe I misheard that bit, there was shocking interference on the line." He knew he hadn't. "Somebody knows we're here. It's all very odd, perhaps we should go and look in the gorge; he was talking about saving ourselves. That statement is a bit worrying, it sounds like we're on our own and that our salvation is in our own hands."

"I'll go and look," said Michael stretching his back, he was eager to do something positive, just sitting around looking at each other and waiting for help was evidently not going to work. Carefully, he climbed up the tree root of Tom's tree and peered over the edge of the gorge, not expecting to see much.

Sarah watched Michael climbing up the roots with concern; she could see earth and debris dropping down and was convinced that the whole tree would be swallowed up at any moment. "Be careful," called Sarah, "That tree doesn't look very safe." Michael nodded and worked his way back from the edge.

"Your side of the gorge looks a bit more stable, have a look and tell us what you see."

"Ok," said Sarah, gently slipping down for her tree; her ankle felt much better. It was good to be doing something rather than just waiting for something to happen. The ground was firm and there was a large tree root that she planned to hold onto when she reached the edge, she wasn't sure if she would see much in the dawn light. Carefully, she made her way to the ravine and then holding onto a substantial root cautiously, trying not to lose her footing, she peered over the edge. It was getting brighter by the minute but she had to stare for a while, whilst her eyes became accustomed to the dark depths of the ravine. What she saw surprised her; she had fully expected just to see earth and rocks. Below, she could see a lake at the bottom of the ravine but above the water line were galleries on either side of the gorge with stone stairs leading down to a walk way. The floors of the galleries were covered with flagstone. On each side of the ravine, was a wooden door set within a stone arch. Sarah looked towards the others triumphantly.

"There's stairs, leading to doors down here. There's a door on your side and one on our side. Maybe Tom was right, perhaps they lead to nuclear bunkers. Or they might lead to ancient passages out of here. It's a bit of a drop onto the top stair but I'm sure we could all do it."

Evie glanced towards the gorge apprehensively; she was getting a bit old for climbing but the thought of finding civilization again filled her with optimism. There might even be a toilet behind one of the doors; she desperately needed to powder her nose.

"You need to go two large steps left of Evie's tree to put yourselves over the stairs," called Sarah as she worked her way along the edge to find the top of their stairs. "Come on Amy, I've got a good feeling about this."

Tentatively, Amy joined Sarah. Her heart was screaming at her not to go into the gorge, she sensed that Cornelia was alarmed too and was begging her not to go near the doors. As she reached the edge, she could almost smell evil discharging from below. There was something seriously wrong but she feared that everyone would laugh at her if she said out loud what she was thinking.

Sarah sensed Amy's reluctance to move forward. "It will be fine, there seems to be a solid structure under the hill, so we'll be quite safe. Let's hoped its water tight and these doors are unlocked, otherwise it will be very disappointing."

Amy helped Sarah over the edge of the ravine and on to the top step and then with Sarah's assistance, dropped down too. The air was colder below the surface. Amy shivered and rubbed her arms to try and warm herself. Michael was already on the stairs on his side and was helping Evie down.

"It's a bit spooky," Sarah whispered to Amy, her breath was white and wispy in the half light. "It's going to be a job to get back up," she continued, looking up at the tree roots above. "Come on, let's try the door, there might be a phone in there."

Michael, Tom and Evie stood in front of their door and looked at the round brass handle apprehensively; there was no lock on the door.

"These doors seem quite ancient," said Tom stroking the wood, they're probably made with oak; medieval I would say. Sussex used to be covered in oak trees. Right then, let's see what's behind here," he said grasping the handle and then sprang back, whipping his hand away. "Blimey, that was hot!"

"How can it be?" replied Michael. "It's cold and damp down here."

"I'm telling you, that handle was red hot. You try it, if you don't believe me."

Michael, carefully, using one finger touched the door handle and drew back his finger quickly. "You're right, it's red hot."

"There you go!" exclaimed Tom. "See, I'm not just having hot flushes."

"Let me try too, my hands are freezing" requested Evie. Michael stepped aside to let her try.

"Have you touched the handle yet?" Michael called out to Sarah and Amy.

"No, Sarah replied. "Why what's the matter?"

"Have a go but be careful it might burn you," he warned.

Tentatively, Evie stretched out her hand towards the handle, Sarah and Amy both did the same. They were surprised to find that it was cold - as cold as ice. This they reported.

"Try and turn the handle then," called Tom.

Evie turned it clockwise but it didn't budge, then instinctively she turned it anticlockwise and it began to move but it felt stiff.

Amy tried to turn her handle and found that it too would only move if turned anticlockwise.

"It's very old and rusty," announced Evie. "But it's beginning to give."

Tom stepped forward to help. He placed his hand over Evie's, trying not to touch the metal, he didn't want to get burnt and together they turned the handle fully to the left. With his shoulder, Tom pushed the door open.

Amy was struggling to turn the handle so Sarah helped her and then finally the door loosened in its frame; the doors hadn't been opened in a very long time. They creaked as they began to open and then a shaft of white light shone through the gap almost blinding them, calling to them, firing up their curiosity and then finally drawing them into the light. The doors suddenly swung freely inwards dragging those that dared to turn their handles with them, threw them into the light and then slammed shut behind them without giving them a chance to reconsider their actions.

"Oh...," Evie gasped. "Where are we?" she asked Tom, shielding her eyes from the white light as she tried to make sense of her surroundings. She looked over her shoulder to where she thought him to be but she couldn't see him.

Michael stood alone in the gorge, bewildered and confused, he touched the door handle, forgetting that previously he'd found it too hot to hold, he was eager to follow Evie and Tom and find out what lay behind the door but to his dismay discovered again that the handle was too hot to touch. He felt that he'd been abandoned and cheated out of his chance to escape.

He didn't deserve to be deserted. Was he such a bad person that he now deserved to be left in isolation? For months he'd travelled alone, shunning the world and mentally fighting with his inner most feelings but since meeting up with these people his life had changed for the better - he needed company. It wasn't wise for him to be left alone, his mind played tricks on him and bad things happened.

With urgency, Michael pulled his hand inside his coat sleeve and through the material, tried to turn the handle anti clockwise, trying his hardest to open up the door and escape from his solitary world. Merciless and unforgiving, the door remained closed and barred Michael's way. He finally gave up when he felt his hand burning as the material in his coat sleeve melted.

Exhausted, Michael fell against the door and slid down onto the ground, infuriated and miserable and he wondered why he was being punished.

12

Evie closed her eyes tightly; the white light around her was too bright to open them but she wasn't afraid. The scent of rose water, furniture polish and a cake baking filled Evie's lungs and almost took her breath away. She felt completely relaxed and the sweet familiar smells intoxicated her. Her head felt light and she knew that when she was able to open her eyes she would recognise her surrounding immediately and would feel comfort from what she saw. She'd breathed in the same scent many years ago and was surprised how well she remembered them. It was like someone passing you on the bus wearing a perfume that reminded you of someone you knew or a place you had been to as if it was only yesterday.

The white light around her subsided and slowly she opened her eyes and marvelled at her surroundings. It had been over sixty years since she'd been in her bedroom in Goring and it was just as she remembered it. This was her parents' second home and she'd spent many long hot summers here, escaping from the hustle and bustle of London.

When war was declared, her mother and herself had moved down to this house and her father came to stay with them at weekends. Her bed was in the corner opposite the window. The brass bed frame was tarnished; it had been in the family for generations. She noticed that the bed had clean, white linen, sheets and pillowcases, a light blue blanket and a patchwork quilt folded back neatly at the foot of her bed. The bed was crying out to be slept in, there was nothing like feeling fresh sheets against her skin. Evie's attention turned to her window; it was half open and the pale blue silk curtains billowed in the sea breeze. Outside, on the green at the edge of the shore, she could see the cool, green grass swishing in the wind.

Evie walked over to her dressing table; her fingers ran over the trinket pots she'd collected as a girl and her gilt backed hairbrush and mirror, embossed with flowers placed side by side. She'd spent many hours brushing through her long wavy auburn locks until the hair brush ran through her hair without getting caught up. Her mother used to brush her hair when she was small and would grumble at Evie for allowing her hair to get so knotted. She sighed, that seemed like a lifetime ago.

It was warm in her room, very summer-like so she pulled back her hood and unzipped her jacket. She was surprised to see a long lock of hair fall in front of her shoulder, not grey but the same auburn colour as it was when she was young. She felt the rest of her hair, it was the same length; her short curly grey hair had been replaced by a mass of auburn curls. Evie sat down heavily on the blue velvet cushion on the stool in front of the dressing table and stared unbelievingly into the mirror. A young girl stared back at her and smiled. She inhaled with surprise and touched her face to check that her eyes were not deceiving her. Her skin felt smooth, taut and unlike her own. As a teenager she'd beautiful skin, she'd tried to look after it and had moisturised every night but over time her skin had dried and crinkled, giving in to the inevitable problems that came with old age. Her eyes too, looked brighter and more open than she remembered and her whole body looked more upright and filled out; she'd a much better body shape then.

Evie covered her eyes with her hands and then looked again, hoping that a miracle had happened, it would be lovely to be young, she'd often wished that she could have her life over again. So much of it had been wasted grieving over Albert and she found that her life had slipped away without her realising it. She moved her hands away from her eyes, nothing had changed she really was young again, aged about seventeen or eighteen. Evie pinched her arm; it felt sore - this wasn't a dream.

She looked over her shoulder at her clock on the wall, hoping that it would tell her more than the time. Its shiny brass pendulum swung innocently on, as if nothing noteworthy had happened. The white rimmed clock ignored her and ticked away time, eager to make it to the next hour. It was twenty past seven in the morning; it was hard to make assumptions but she thought that it might be morning, yet her bed hadn't been slept in which was odd, she'd never stayed out all night and she wouldn't have made her bed herself; only her mother could make up her bed so neatly.

Her thoughts turned to her mother and a chill ran down her spine. The smell of baking meant that she would be down in the kitchen busy with her early morning chores. She often got up early to bake bread and cakes for the day and it then occurred to Evie that if she left her room and went downstairs she would see her again. The last time she'd seen both her parents was just before Christmas in 1940. This was the day that she told them that she was pregnant and it was also the day she was asked to leave. She'd given them her address and wrote to them, pleading with them not to cut her out of their lives but she didn't hear back and then finally gave up writing. She didn't know if she could face her now.

Both her parents had died in a bombing raid in their London home. Her mother had gone up there to pack some furniture up to be put into storage. The house had been flattened during the raid and they'd both been crushed to death by rubble in the cellar.

She'd got a letter from an aunt a few months after they were buried letting her know that they had perished and had asked if she minded her keeping a silver ladle found in the ruins; Evie found this very odd. May, her aunt didn't ask after Edward, he was such a sweet baby, only a few months old then and thought perhaps that her mother hadn't told her about her pregnancy. Evie had embarrassed her family and Edward's birth had been kept as a sordid secret. If Albert had come back alive from the war then things would have been different, they would have married and her parents would have welcomed her back.

Evie thought fondly of Albert, she could see his face in her mind; he was laughing. He was much taller than her and very attentive. In her daydream, he brushed back his fair wavy hair from his face and his dark blue eyes twinkled in the sunshine. He was looking at her adoringly; she'd blushed. Albert had been the love of her life. A thrill of pleasure ran through her, if she really was a teenager again then there may be a chance that she would be able to see him. Evie looked down at her waterproof jacket, her muddy walking boots and tweed skirt, if she was going to see him again, she would have to change.

She walked across the white washed floorboards to her wardrobe in the far corner of her room and flung the doors open and gasped. A row of ghastly summer dresses and cardigans her mother had made for her hung there. It was such a sad collection, that she wondered how Albert had ever fallen for her. After a few moments raking through her wardrobe, she managed to find a short sleeved, belted dress in pale yellow. She took off her muddy clothes and hid them in the bottom of her wardrobe under a couple of blankets and prayed that her mother wouldn't find them. She slipped on the dress and stood in front of the mirror again to check that she looked respectable and then after brushing her hair walked over towards the door with the intention of slipping out of the house unnoticed.

She'd only taken a few steps when a thought entered her head, she was not really sure what year it was, let alone what day. What if Albert had already gone off to war? What if she bumped into her mother and she questioned her? She needed to be more prepared and tiptoed onto the landing and looked down into the hall hoping to see the newspapers on the side table. If the newspapers were still there, then she would be able to see the date on them. The papers had gone from the hall. Despondent and confused, Evie sat down on her bed to think. A wave of nausea washed over her. She hoped it wasn't morning sickness; she was probably just hungry, she couldn't remember the last time she'd eaten a decent meal.

Evie was starting to panic and hoped that her mother wouldn't come upstairs and question her. She was bound to look guilty if she did and she really didn't want to see her again, it had taken her many years to get over being disowned and thinking about it, she'd not ever forgiven her mother for being so callous. She could never do such a thing to her son Edward. She wondered if he was alive, if she'd been thrown back in time then Edward may not have yet been born. He could however still be in 2013 and grieving for her, thinking that she was missing, presumed dead and lost at sea. A tear ran down her face, she was worried that he would be in pain; she didn't want him to suffer like she had.

She needed to find what the date was, there had to be a way. She guessed the war had started as there was a large piece of cardboard leaning against the wall below her window ready to put up to black out the light from her lamp at night. If she walked down the street she could ask someone but she really didn't want to draw attention to herself. Then she remembered her diary, she'd written in it every day, recording her day to day life, her hopes, her fears and her secrets. She'd taken it with her when she moved down to Dorset to have Edward. Evie looked over towards the wardrobe, where she used to stow it; she used to wrap it in a scarf and then hide it on the top shelf, so her mother didn't find it. Swiftly, Evie ran to the wardrobe, she was quicker on her feet than she used to be and she rummaged through the clothes on the top shelf looking for it - the diary wasn't there.

The first day she'd written in her diary, she'd left it on her bed only to find that her mother had quizzed her about her entry the following evening. Humiliated, by this event, Evie hid her diary from prying eyes.

Exasperated, she stood back from the wardrobe with her hands on her hips and stared into it, wondering where else it might be. If she'd been given a diary that had a lock, then she could have kept it in her bedside cabinet and needn't have been so secretive.

The clock ticked on loudly, almost as if it was laughing at her as she struggled to remember her past. She'd other hiding places in her room; one was behind her dressing table, another under her mattress and one under the wardrobe. After fruitlessly searching in all these places, Evie finally found her diary, stuck under the seat of her dressing table stool but didn't remember ever leaving it there. This was however her hiding place for her love letters from Albert and she remembered hiding them in the lining of the fabric underneath the seat; she took these out too and looked fondly at them. She wasn't sure what happened to them, she'd tucked them away and had not been able to find them again. Seeing them made her heart miss a beat as she looked at his handwriting - these letters had meant so much to her and she felt cross with herself for misplacing them.

Evie flicked through her diary to the last entry and looked at the following blank page and then breathed in deeply when she saw the date; it was Wednesday 9th October 1940, the day before Albert went off to war. That was the day she'd decided to sleep with him and the day Edward had been conceived. Evie's mind was racing again as she tried to recall what had happened on the morning of that day. It was a school day and she'd gone to school as usual and then she'd slipped out late in the evening to meet up with him. It occurred to her that if she didn't carry out the exact same actions, then her future would not be the same, Edward would not exist and she could in fact change the whole course of her own personal history.

The thought of sleeping with Albert concerned her, things were so different now, how could she possibly sleep with someone that was now only a memory? Her recollection of making love with Albert had always been remembered as a magical moment for her; Albert had been so gentle and passionate and she'd always recalled that night fondly. The truth was though; in reality the physical act of making love had shocked her. She'd not been prepared and had no idea what was involved. Since that day, she'd never slept with anyone else or had the desire to do so.

Evie walked over to the window, she was confused, it would be wrong to sleep with him a second time and desperately sad to see him again, knowing that he would never make it home. Evie sat down on the bed again and cried, if she didn't sleep with Albert then she wouldn't have Edward. Albert seemed to be almost like a stranger to her now after all these years. She wondered what she'd done to deserve to be put in such a corner.

Evie threw her diary to the side and wondered what she should do next; she looked desperately around her room, hoping that she would get answers. She thought if she put on her muddy clothes and shut her eyes, then perhaps she would wake up and find herself up on the Chanctonbury Ring. Then she remembered Tom, he'd been behind her when she'd gone through the old door, she wondered where he'd gone to. She suspected that he might be in the Frankland Arms wondering what had happened to her. She needed his advice about her quandary and decided that she would slip out of the house get her bike out and go and find him. She'd kept her bike leaning against the wall at the side of the house so it would be quite easy to wheel it out into the street without being seen. Her mother would be getting breakfast ready at the back of the house and would call her in ten minutes time at eight o'clock.

With her heart pounding, Evie put on a yellow cardigan and then tiptoed down the stairs and looked desperately around for her shoes, fortunately her school shoes were in the hall. They were just as she remembered them, hideous black monstrosities that pinched her toes, she was tempted to go back upstairs and get her walking boots but they would have looked ridiculous. Reluctantly, Evie picked them up and as she opened the front door. She looked affectionately up at the stain glass panel with a picture of a bird in the centre and then slipped out into the morning sunshine. Carefully she pulled the door closed and it was then that she saw through the glass panels her mother walking from the kitchen towards the hall. In a blind panic Evie ran along the path that led to the side passage where her bike was stored and prayed that she hadn't seen her. She held her breath and then to her dismay, heard the front door open again.

13

Michael climbed back up to the beech trees and lay on the edge of the ravine. The lack of food had taken its toll; he was exhausted both physically and mentally. He didn't care that the ground could give way at any moment and that he might fall into the watery abyss below and be swallowed whole. He stared up at the blue sky for consolation and watched as an odd black cloud flew across it. He tried to find one that took on the shape of something that looked familiar so he didn't feel so alone. Most of the clouds however, looked to him like wild beasts with distorted features and gaping jaws. The sky offered no comfort to him, there was no escaping the fact that he was on his own again; left with his own thoughts and fears. For all he knew, he could be the last man left alive in the whole of England and he felt the pain again of being an outsider, abandoned and defective; this was perhaps the lowest he'd ever felt in his whole life.

He needed to talk to someone, anyone, just somebody that would tell him that it would all be ok and that in fact he was dreaming and this situation he found himself in was just a nightmare. He didn't care about being tracked by the police any more; in fact he would welcome any human onto his pathetic excuse of an island, just to hear another human voice. He then remembered his mobile and wondered if he should plug his emergency battery in and ring Helen. He felt guilty that he hadn't told the others that he had a phone and felt guilty for being so selfish.

Michael sat up and looked around for his backpack, he was sure that he'd brought it up with him when he climbed back up and he thought he'd left it beside him but it had disappeared. He looked down into the ravine to see if it had fallen back down there. Loose earth and leaves spilled down onto the paving stones of the gallery below but it wasn't to be seen. He stood up and looked around him. The contents of his bag were all he had left in the world and he didn't like being without them. After a few minutes of searching, he spotted it floating in the sea several meters out from the shore, just beyond the tops of the beech trees. He couldn't understand how it could have floated out, he hadn't left it anywhere near the water's edge. Michael paced up and down the shoreline. Although the coating of the bag was waterproof it wouldn't be long before water would seep into it and it would sink. It was surprising that it was floating at all; the bag was very heavy to carry.

There was nothing for it, he would have to swim out and collect it. Michael took off his boots and socks and looked down at his feet and then at his backpack; it was no good, he didn't want to get his clothes wet and decided that it would be better to take everything off, swim out and return to dry clothes. The air was cold but the autumn sunshine promised him that he wouldn't freeze. Quickly Michael took the rest of his clothes off and naked, he slipped into the icy water and began swimming towards his bag. The water was colder than he expected and the bag seemed to be further out than he remembered but he was determined to retrieve it and with clenched teeth, swam on.

As he got nearer, he noticed that his bag was attached to something and it seemed to be hovering a couple of centimetres above the water line. Michael looked behind him, he'd a distinct feeling that someone was watching him from the shore; he could feel a pair of eyes boring into his back. There was no one there but as he reached his bag and turned his head away, he was almost sure that he saw someone move behind the roots of one of the beech trees. Michael shivered as the hairs on the back of his neck stood up.

Trembling, he stretched out his hand to reclaim his bag and then recoiled in horror; it was attached to a corpse, face down in the water. Without physically touching the body's arm or hand, he pulled the strap free. This movement unbalanced the floating body and it flipped over revealing the copse's identity; it was Nabeel. His eyes were wide open and he stared up lifelessly at the sky. Michael looked on incredulously and then felt anger rising within him; somebody was trying to mess with his mind. There was no way that Nabeel would have been able to pull himself off the tree stump where he'd died, put his backpack on and then swim out to sea. There had to be someone else on the island playing depraved games with him. Michael pulled his bag away from Nabeel who again flipped over and then face down, floated away from him. Disgusted and with relief, Michael began to swim on his back, with his bag on his stomach, towards the shore, determined to find the prankster and give him a piece of his mind.

He wasn't sure if the bag was becoming heavier as he swam or if he was so weak now that swimming was becoming more difficult. His body ached and he knew that it would take his very last ounce of strength to get back to dry land. He kept looking over his shoulder, to see if he was getting any nearer to the shore but his progress was slow. The Chanctonbury Ring laughed at him for wanting to return to its shores and for believing that it would offer him sanctuary.

Michael's hands and feet were numb with cold and he was beginning to feel hypothermic; he felt sleepy. He stopped swimming and trod water to rest for a moment and to try and build up some energy to swim the last few meters. He cursed out loud as without any warning, a dark thorny tendril coiled itself around his ankle and then yanked him down below the surface of the water. Mercilessly it dragged him towards the bottom. He let go of his backpack and left it floating on the lonely sea and then it too began to sink.

Panic stricken, he brought his foot up and saw the vine around his ankle and then desperately tried to shake it off but whatever it was, it had glued itself to his skin. He tried to use his arms to swim upwards but they were useless and the vine continued to drag him downwards. His only hope was to dig his nails into the creeper that held him, in the hope it would loosen its grip but to his dismay it didn't make any difference. Michael was terrified, his last breath was almost spent and he knew that at any moment his empty lungs would force him to breathe in the sea water and he would drown.

It was strange, if anyone had asked him earlier when he lay by the beech trees looking up at the sky, if he cared if he died, his answer would have been that he welcomed death. Now that he was faced with the prospect of dying, he knew that he wasn't ready. He couldn't leave the world being thought of as a murderer; he needed to find out if he was innocent.

Michael's head began to spin as he fought to hold his breath for the last few seconds. He closed his eyes, not wanting to see his final resting place and then unwillingly, he expelled his very last breath of air from his lungs and then waited to taste saline water as he inhaled. He could feel himself drifting off to sleep and if this was drowning then it wasn't that bad. He felt the vine slip off his ankle and then what surprised him most was that he'd breathed in air and not water; confused he took in more air; although he felt out of breath, he was actually breathing properly.

Slowly he opened his eyes; he was not in the sea but in a room he didn't recognise. He was on his hands and knees and was leaning over Sarah. Her eyes were closed but she was not asleep; she seemed to be in a lot of pain and cried out. He looked at her with fascination and wondered if she was in a trance. Aghast he realised that she was naked and then looking down at himself saw that he was too. He was also shocked to find that he was erect and was inside her and his body was wet with sweat. Confused and embarrassed, Michael pulled out of her and lay down next to her looking desperately around for something to cover himself. Sarah sighed, opened her eyes and turned on her side to face him. "It's happened again, hasn't it" she asked. "You've forgotten everything?" A tear rolled down her face.

Michael closed his eyes and opened them again. His head was spinning; he'd no idea where he was and thought that he was drowning and hallucinating as he died. He took in another deep breath of warm air; his breathing had returned to normal and he seemed to be alive still. He was in a tiny room, the walls were made of dry earth and it was almost cell like. There was a door and only one window; the last rays of sunshine shone through the closed shutters, lighting up one side of the room. Not far from the door there was a stove with pots and pans stacked beside it. Michael felt the bed; it was just a thin mattress, covered by a thick red blanket. There was little else in the room apart from a pile of clothing on the floor under the window.

"Am I dead?" he asked, doing his best to cover himself with the cover they were lying on. "It's so hot in here, am I in Hell?"

Sarah sighed and looked up at the ceiling, realising that for the next few hours, she would be asked hundreds of questions. She'd been through Michael's inexplicable memory losses, so many times. She was so tired of it; his memory had failed him at least six times over the two years that they had been together. She needed him to accept what she had to tell him and hoped that Michael would be able to cope with his lot and provide for them all. "No Michael you've not drowned, you're here with me and Jawid, you'll be fine when I tell you everything," she replied.

"What do you mean? How do you know that I was drowning? Who is Jawid?" Michael was confounded that Sarah had read his very thoughts.

"This is our home," Sarah continued. "We live in a village outside Kabul and Jawid thinks that we are his parents. When we went through the doors at the Chanctonbury Ring, we both walked into this room," she said handing him a shawl. Thankfully, Michael took it and covered himself up; he wondered how Sarah remained so relaxed lying naked next to him.

"I don't understand? Only moments ago I was there swimming back to shore with my bag and then something pulled me down." Michael said. "I nearly drowned! I didn't go through a door; it wouldn't let me."

"Yes I know, you always say that. I didn't see what happened on your side of the ravine, all I know is that Amy and I were pulled into the white light behind the door and I ended up here with you. I don't know what happened to Amy, I hope she's all right. It's been almost two years ago, since we walked into this room together and we've coped. We're poor but we get by, we have enough water to drink and just enough food, some weeks are better than others. We love each other Michael and now I'm carrying your child." Sarah said and patted her swollen stomach.

Unbelievingly, Michael looked at her, he didn't know how he hadn't noticed before but she was quite evidently pregnant; she looked so beautiful lying next to him on the carpeted bed roll but although she looked cross with him, he could tell that she was content with her life. Michael's mind was reeling, two years could not have passed by without him realising it. He was speechless as he tried to take everything in, he knew that mentally he'd not been too well but to lose two years of his life was beyond belief. Distraught, Michael stared at Sarah; he didn't know what or who to believe any more.

One thing he knew for sure was that he was very thankful not to have drowned and to have been given a second chance. At least in Afghanistan, the police would not be after him. It then occurred to him that he was an English man in a small village; he would look out of place, be conspicuous and his life may be in danger. Michael was cross and laughed incredulously. "You're joking with me, right? I can't have been here for two years. What have I been doing? Today for example, where have I been? Why haven't we been to the British embassy to ask for help?"

Sarah looked concerned. "We did think of doing that but we have no form of identification and we have Jawid to think about, we can't take him with us and we certainly can't leave him here. Michael, you work in the vineyard in the fields at the foot of our village, as do most of the men here and we are fortunate that the land owner allows us to draw water from his well. We have a few chickens and I exchange eggs for bread and rice."

"You can't expect me to believe you. A vineyard owner is unlikely to take on someone like me to work in a vineyard. I know very little Pashtu or Dari and nothing about tending the land."

"The villagers do not realise you are English, you speak enough Dari to get by and I've been helping you with the language. You've managed well working in the vineyard; the people of the village call you 'آرام یکی': 'the quiet one'. You work hard and are respected for that. Look at yourself in this mirror Michael, you will see that I am speaking the truth," she said, handing him a small hand mirror from her bedside.

The mirror was old and broken in one corner, when Michael held it up to his face he exhaled with surprise. His dark hair was as he remembered it but his beard had gone. His face was brown from the sun and had filled out a little. He then looked at his arms and chest. They too, were a deep brown and he could no longer see his ribs. His hands had callous and dirt from the fields caught in the cracks in his fingers. It were his hands that told him the truth, these showed him evidence of years of hard toil, honest labour and of freedom he'd wished for but could not remember. Michael's revelation was interrupted by someone coughing.

"Jawid," Sarah called. "Are you awake? I heard you cough, do you want some water?" Sarah sat up and slipped a long black shirt over her head.

Startled, Michael looked over to the bundle of clothes along the far wall and was amazed to see a small boy, aged about five or six climb out of them and watched him rub his eyes and walk towards them. He had dark hair, too and big brown eyes; he was wearing a white tunic and leggings. He carried a soft toy under his arm; it was a dog that had been made from scraps of material. Jawid stood in front of them and said that he did want a drink. Michael looked at the boy intently and was alarmed to find that this was the very same child he'd seen in his dreams; he recognised him immediately. This was the same boy he'd watched in his dreams get shot down in cross gunfire. He remembered him staring at him with accusing and judgmental eyes as he died in a pool of blood.

Sarah looked at Michael anxiously, "You have the same reaction each time," she remarked. "This is Jawid, you worry that you have seen him before when you were a soldier and that his life may be in danger," said Sarah getting up to get Jawid some water. "He hasn't been well, he's got a cough. Normally at this time, he would be playing outside with the others. There are no soldiers here in our village and the Taliban do not bother us. Life has returned to normal although there's no government support and very little health care. The people here subsist and look after each other."

"What day is it? And what year is it?" Michael asked, he was exhausted and he wanted to see outside but wasn't sure if he could take any more shocks. Seeing his surroundings would certainly be a reality check. Michael found next to his bed a beige tunic, which he presumed must be his. It was worn and dusty and looked as if someone might have discarded it when they climbed into bed. Embarrassed to be naked in front of both Sarah and Jawid, Michael pulled the tunic over his head and stood up.

"It's Wednesday and this is the autumn of 2015, it's exceptionally hot today but normally at this time of year the days are a lot colder. The past two years we've had drought and we have only been able to survive because of the water in the well. Where there is no water, the villages have emptied and the people have gone into Kabul or over into Pakistan to look for work."

"Mama," Jawid called as he waited for his water. "Can I go out to play? I feel a lot better now."

Sarah smiled and felt his head, "Yes she said, your fever has gone, you look a lot better but stay near the house."

Jawid drank some water and then threw his dog on to his bed and ran towards the door; he pulled it open, letting the evening sunshine in and ran out into the street, calling for his friends.

"Come with me," suggested Sarah, wrapping a headscarf around her head and offering her hand to him. "Let me show you our new world."

Without thinking, Michael took her hand and let her lead him out of the room and out into the sunshine. It was the fresh air that surprised him most; he'd forgotten how pure and clean it was in Afghanistan. They stood in front of their tiny, dust coloured house at the bottom of a hill. The roof tops of the other dwellings sprang up from the hill side above them and in front of them were vineyards as far as the eye could see on the plains below, with rows and rows of vines in the dry fields. The silence was absolute; there wasn't even the sound of distant gunfire.

Michael could see Jawid out of the corner of his eye, sitting in a tree near to the house. He called out to another boy passing him and then jumped down to join his friend, happy to find somebody to play with. Michael looked on sadly, knowing that quite soon, Jawid would lose his life.

14

Mrs Merryweather opened the door to sweep the doorstep and Evie waited by the side of the house for what seemed like ages whilst she carried out this task. She'd practically held her breath the whole time, with her heart thumping in her chest, hoping and praying that her mother wouldn't find a reason to walk her way. She was very relieved when she heard the front door close and knew that she only had minutes to escape, before she noticed that she was absent. As quietly as she could, Evie wheeled her bicycle down the front path and out on to the street. She remembered not to let the wooden gate bang behind her, the metal catch always clattered as it closed and she knew her mother would hear it if she let this happen. She was amazed that she remembered this after all the years that had past.

Quickly, Evie jumped onto her bicycle and peddled furiously along her street, hoping that nobody she'd once known would wave or call out to her. It was only when she reached the next street, that she realised that she hadn't been on her bike since she was a teenager and was pleased that she hadn't forgotten how to ride one. Happily, enjoying the experience, she pedalled harder, calling out with joy. The wind was in her face and her long hair blew behind her, she'd forgotten what it was like to be young and carefree.

Evie cycled along a tree line street, away from the shore that had become defaced and ugly since the barbed wire barricades had been deposited. As she cycled to Washington, she became aware that she was leaving her safety zone and she began to feel anxious and vulnerable. Most people, in Sussex during the Second World War, hadn't travelled far from their homes or workplace as they wanted to be close to their families and to the air raid shelters. Evie's parents had built an Anderson shelter at the foot of their back garden and they had spent many anxious nights in there, waiting for an air raid to finish. Thankfully, no bombs had fallen on their house as the Germans had been targeting warships, the docks and military bases. Every day, the threat of air attack or invasion hung over them all like a black, malevolent cloud.

Evie breathed in the cool morning air and wished she'd put on a coat; although the sun was shining, she was starting to feel chilled. As she cycled, she looked around the street she'd turned into; the houses were quiet at the moment but she knew that soon children would burst out of the front doors ready to walk or run to school. She looked along the street, she hadn't seen or heard a car since she set off, all she could hear were birds singing. Life seemed to be so much slower in 1940.

Evie wasn't sure how to get to Washington, she was pretty sure if she headed north, then she might see a sign; she'd no idea how long it would take her to get there. As a child, she'd once walked with her father from their house, across the fields and they had ended up in Sullington not far from Washington village. As they had walked through the fields and climbed up on to the Downs, he'd told her the names of the birds and the trees and the plants that they saw and she'd looked up at her father in wonderment. He was such a quiet and unassuming man and she'd been enthralled by his endless knowledge about nature. That day seemed to be a life time away.

If there was anyone that she wished she could see again, then that would have been her father. If she was to remain in 1940, (she wasn't sure of anything anymore), then she hoped she would see him at the weekend. Her father who was too old to be enlisted, much to their horror, preferred to stay at their house in London, near to his workplace and seemed unfazed by the bombing attacks each night.

The thing that hurt her most and above all, was that he'd stood by her mother when she'd been thrown out. She remembered looking at him to see if he really believed what her mother had been telling her but he couldn't look her in the eyes. The memory of that day had always haunted her and she'd always wished that dreadful day hadn't taken place.

Evie thought that it was strange that she'd been given one of her dearest wishes, a chance to change certain things in her past and yet her wish had become almost too much to bear. She'd loved Albert dearly, and their son Edward too, and she'd mourned for Albert's loss every day of her life. Now she thought about it, she wouldn't have changed anything. Her only real regret was that she hadn't got over losing him and had carried his remains around with her for far too long. She knew that people lost their partners every day and then went on to find new ones, she couldn't understand why she hadn't stopped grieving for him and moved on.

The truth was that she hadn't really known what had happened to Albert. He hadn't written to her, he hadn't come back from the war; he was one of many that disappeared and were never seen again. He was an unnamed soldier lost in battle and left to decay in the battlefields or buried in unmarked mass graves. The ashes she'd carried around all her life were just ash from her friend's grate in the farmhouse kitchen. These old wood ashes had weighed her down, mapped her life's course and become an unbearable burden.

Another unthinkable thought immerged in Evie's head; had Albert deserted her? She didn't like to think it but she thought that he might have slept with her and then forgotten all about her. She was starting to feel cross and tears burned in her eyes as this thought became a real possibility. He'd left her all alone with a baby to bring up and she'd lived with a secret suspicion in her heart that he hadn't loved her at all. The pain of rejection burned deeply into her very being.

The only good thing in her life was her dear Edward that she loved so very much and she knew that she had to take action and secure his future. She peddled harder, determined to get to Tom. She wasn't sure what he could do to help her but she would be grateful just to speak to someone; someone that cared about her.

Evie left the houses and pavements behind her and cycled as fast as she could towards Findon, the dry leaves in the gutter and decaying leaflets from Hitler, offering peace, swirled up angrily around her as she cycled through them, mocking her naivety.

As Findon village came in to view, to her dismay, she heard an air raid siren in the village start up and she knew she should take cover. She pulled on the brakes to stop, they squeaked as the bike slowed down. She frantically looked around for a place to run and to shelter from the planes. She'd stopped by a five bar gate that led into a field and noticed a haystack on one side of the field. Without hesitation, Evie left her bike on the grass verge and seeing that the gate was padlocked, started to climb it with the plan to run and hide, behind the haystack; so if any bombs were dropped, the haystack might shield her from the blast. Evie swung her leg over the top of the gate and it was then that she saw him running towards her.

"Evelyn," he called. She gasped with surprise and her heart stopped for a moment, she hadn't been called by her full name for a very long time. In fact, only Albert and her mother had ever called her Evelyn. Evie's eyes widened with surprise, she didn't know if she was pleased or horrified to see Albert. His wavy blond hair had been cut short ready to join his regiment and the smile she remembered wasn't there. This was his last day in England and she would never see him again.

"Wait, where are you going?"

Unable to speak, Evie pointed to the haystack, jumped off the gate and ran as fast as she could, across the field to hide from the Germans and possibly Albert too. Albert, grasping the top of the gate leaped over and ran to join her.

Heaving for breath, Evie shot in the haystack. Several bales of hay in the base had been removed, leaving enough room to crawl into a space big enough to sit up in. Albert crawled in after her. Evie immediately felt uncomfortable, the smell of cigarette smoke on his clothes was overwhelming and he was sitting too close to her; she could feel his breath on her face. Confused by her reaction to him, Evie sighed and tucked her knees under her chin, something she hadn't done in a long while. The siren stopped and the silence waited patiently to be broken by the drone of war planes.

"What's the matter?" Albert asked. "Why aren't you in your school uniform? Why aren't you at school? Are you ill?"

Evie wasn't sure what to say and struggled to think of an explanation. "I... I was coming to see you," she finally blurted out, remembering that Albert lived in Findon. His mother and father owned the grocery store in the village. "I couldn't bear to go to school knowing that I might never see you again," she lied.

Albert smiled. "You silly old thing, you know I was coming down to meet you later. You were lucky I bumped into you; you wouldn't have found me at the shop today. I was just on my way to see Granny before I go to war. You mustn't worry, Evelyn, the war will be over soon and I'll come back and we can get married."

"What if you don't come back, you might get killed on the very first day?" she replied, trying not to meet his gaze. She was feeling very uncomfortable being so close to him; it was almost as if he were a stranger to her.

"Evelyn, that's an awful thing to say! I don't know what's got in to you; we've talked about this before. I'm eighteen now and need to do my duty. Our freedom and our future depend on all those that are willing and able to fight. It's our only hope. You don't want us to be invaded do you?"

"No, I don't," sighed Evie. "You will write to me every day. You won't forget me?"

"Of course I will," he replied laughing. "I've sent you letters before, haven't I? Why wouldn't I write to you whilst I'm away? I need to know you will be there for me when I'm away; I would be lost without you. You are the dearest thing."

It was then that Evie realised that Albert really did love her and that he must have died in the first couple of weeks of arriving on the battlefield. How evil and destructive war was, she thought. Why would anyone ever want to take lives to gain land and to rule over others? She really couldn't understand man sometimes.

Albert lay next to her looking adoringly up at her, Evie remembered that look of desire in his face and in the past she'd allowed him to kiss her when he looked so love struck. Today however, she was confused, she'd loved Albert all her life, her memories of him had lit the room on lonely nights in but seeing him in the flesh after all the years of just remembering him wasn't the same; he seemed tarnished and unfamiliar.

"Albert," she said, trying to divert his attention from what he was intending. "If you don't come back from war, you would want me to find someone else and get on with my life, wouldn't you?"

Albert seemed shocked and a little hurt. "Why do you say that?" he asked. "Of course I will come back to you, I've promised."

"I know you've said that but things happen..."

"What do you mean things happen? What are you trying to tell me Evelyn? Is there someone else?"

"No...no there's no one else, truly, I meant what if something happened to you." Evie looked anxiously at Albert, he was becoming cross.

"Look," he said irritably. "I'm not going to ask you to become a nun am I? Just make sure you find anybody other than Wilf Green." Wilf was Albert's best friend. "He's turning in to a bit of a cad," he added.

Thankfully, Albert's mood seemed to soften and Evie felt a bit more relaxed.

"I do love you," she announced to pacify him further, she didn't want them to fight but these words didn't ring true. Her heart was tangled with confusion and for some reason it was telling her that she preferred Tom to Albert. Evie almost drew blood in her lip as this startling fact dawned on her.

"Then come to me tonight and spend the night with me, we'll have the house to ourselves. My parents are going to take Granny to hospital for her operation and are going to stay with her until it's done. My brother is going to run the shop whilst they're away. I know we shouldn't and it would be proper to wait until we're married but like you say if I didn't return at least we would have spent one night together."

"I don't know," said Evie trying to remember what she'd said all those years ago. "I'll have to slip out, at the dead of night and hope my mother doesn't notice. She will call the police if she sees me missing."

"Relax," said Albert smiling. I'll wait for you in the delivery van at the end of your street and then drop you back before your mother gets up. Come on Evelyn, be a sport."

"What if I get pregnant? What if you don't come back and you find that I have been thrown out because I was pregnant? Evie could feel resentment building and hoped he wouldn't notice how bitter, she was becoming.

"You won't get pregnant," replied Albert. "That kind of thing takes years to achieve," he said pulling Evie towards him, so that she lay next to him.

Evie allowed him to do this and all the while thought how immature and child like he was. He kissed her face and her neck slowly working his way to her mouth. Evie tried to relax, tried to remember how it had been on that night when he'd picked her up in the delivery van and taken her back to his parents' house. She'd been so excited and felt so grown up. Evie kissed him back and tears burned in her eyes; being intimate with Albert, wasn't the same as she remembered, she was fond of him but felt no lust, passion or love for him. She was over him and ready to move on with her life.

Albert was becoming more and more passionate and she knew if she let him continue then she wouldn't have to meet him that night. He'd found his way to her bra and tenderly cupped her breasts. She tried her best to make out she was enjoying the experience and breathed heavily as his fingers worked their way down her body. She felt almost as if she was acting and at any moment someone would call cut and the episode would end. She tried to imagine she was anywhere else but in a haystack that smelt of old grass and mildew. She could hear the familiar drone of the planes approaching and wished that they would aim for the haystack and drop their bombs, so that it would be over in one explosion, sending her back to her time, so her life could continue as it used to be but without the lifelong grief that had dominated every waking moment.

After a few minutes, Albert withdrew panting and she knew that the thing that she'd been dreading was over. He lay back down next to her laughing and although she felt sore and tearful she was glad that Edward had been created.

"That was amazing! He announced, feeling his pockets for a cigarette. "That was better than I expected. What did you think?"

Evie was at a loss at what to say. Sex for her was, like before, very uncomfortable, disappointing and now marred by the fact that she didn't love him. She'd spent the last few minutes of the ordeal remembering her mother's reaction when she told her that she was pregnant. She'd told her that she'd sinned, had spoilt herself and no decent man would ever want to marry her. She would have to stay with a distant relative and then give the baby away or leave. The actual act of making love was distasteful and had consequences. How could anyone really enjoy what she'd endured and want to do it a second time – were women mad? "You were marvellous," she said gently, trying not to cry.

15

It took a moment for Amy to realise that she was no longer holding onto the door handle of the old wooden door in the ravine at the Chanctonbury Ring. Instead, she had in her hand the handle of another door and was standing in what seemed to be a long dark hall, lit only by moonlight that poured in through a huge stain glass window at the end of the hall. She could smell musk and furniture polish and that made her think that she was in a very large old house. Paintings of people from the past and tapestries adorned the walls.

She looked down at her clothes to find that she was wearing a flowery shirt buttoned up to under her chin, a long dark skirt and over these she had on a long white pinafore apron that had been tied around her ample waist. On her head was a weird hat. She took it off immediately, feeling self-conscious and saw that it was a mob cap. Amy looked up and down the hall, if someone saw her wearing this ridiculous outfit, they would think she'd lost her mind and would laugh.

She looked at her hands, she was shaking and wasn't sure where or even who she was. She hoped that Sarah might appear as they had both been dragged by the Chanctonbury Ring's door into the white light at the same time. Sarah wasn't in the hall. Amy stared at the door in front of her and wondered if it would open into the ravine, she hesitated and thought better of opening it as she might make things worse. She wondered who had dressed her in such a bizarre costume and left her alone to flounder. Had she got herself drunk and someone had cruelly decided to play a trick on her? She really didn't know what to think.

The hall was so dark and oppressive that the walls almost screamed out to her in anguish, reflecting her own feelings. Traces of past lives in the wooden panelling were trying to claw their way out, desperate for recognition. She was too tired and confused to hear any more tales of woe. Her psychic ability seemed to be growing in magnitude all the time, she could feel the house she was in bearing down on her as it bristled, eager to shed its ghostly barnacles.

"Oh my God," she whispered to herself. "What is going on here? Where am I?"

"You're in Oakhill House, Miss Warren."

Amy screamed out with surprise and spun around to see a tall thin man next to her. He was in his twenties, although his manner was that of a much older man. The skin on his face was marked with acne scars, his dark hair was greased back and he wore a valet's costume, he held a lighted candle in front of him on what looked to be an ash tray with a handle."

"I'm sorry," she said embarrassed by her outburst.

"I'm sorry, Mr Firkin!" repeated the man.

Amy paused shocked by the man's rudeness and found herself repeating what he'd just said. "I'm sorry, Mr Firkin, I didn't see you coming up the hall."

"Clearly not," he replied. "May I ask what you are doing here? You're only allowed in the servants' quarters or in the kitchen. If you would be so kind as to remove yourself from the master's bedroom door and take yourself off to your room. You should be sleeping not creeping around the house at night."

"I'm sorry," Amy repeated; she needed to work out what was happening, she didn't want to engage in conversation or argue with somebody half her age that considered himself far above her. She wondered how he knew her name and why he'd called her Miss Warren; she hadn't been addressed by her surname since she was at school. "I'm lost," said Amy, it was all she could think to say. "Where's my room?"

"I know, you haven't been here long Miss Warren but it is high time you memorised the layout of the house. Come with me, I will show you to your room. We simply can't have this carry on; the master is indisposed and needs peace."

Silently, Amy followed the arrogant man along a rabbit warren of corridors, upstairs and past rows and rows of closed doors. It was no wonder that she was lost if that is what had happened to her. She decided that whoever the master was, then he must be worth a lot to own such a large house. Finally, they reached a room at the top of the house and the young man opened the door for her.

"Now stay there and don't you come out until the morning," he barked.

Amy was taken aback; she didn't like being spoken to in such a manner but thought it better not to retaliate. She needed time to think and try and work out what had happened to her, she much preferred to be back at the Chanctonbury Ring lost at sea, than where she was now. Something wasn't right she could sense that there was going to be a trouble ahead.

Her bedroom had no curtains and moonlight threw down just enough light so that she could see. The bed under the small dusty window hadn't been slept in; there was a white night dress in her size laid out across the bed. She felt her body; she'd put on at least two stone since arriving at Oakhill House. She found this most odd and wondered who had chosen her clothes for her. On the left wall was a small wooden table with a jug and large bowl on top of it. Amy wasn't sure if it was for decoration or if she was supposed to use it. On the opposite wall was a small dark wooden wardrobe with a large hat box on top. The last piece of furniture and the most disturbing was a child's chair in the corner, too small for her to sit on and this made her shudder; the owner of the chair had died long ago but was still around in the house. She knew that the child who had once owned the chair wasn't happy that it had been taken from the nursery and placed in the servants' quarters.

Amy walked over to the window. She looked out onto the moonlit land surrounding the house and tried to make out the landscape. She decided that her room was at the front of the house as she could see a long gravel drive which stretched away into the darkness. She could see lights in the distance but could see no other houses nearby, nothing to show her where she was or what year it was. On each side of the drive were ponds, she could see the moon's reflection in the water. She shivered again as there were spirits buried in the grounds that had suffered a violent end and needed to vindicate themselves.

Amy had no desire to go outside; she was relieved to be in a room with a bed to lie on and she felt unbelievably fatigued and in need of sleep. After leaving the chair in the corridor, with shaking hands she undressed herself and pulled on the white night dress, it fitted her perfectly; she really couldn't believe how much weight she was carrying. It would take months, perhaps years for her to have got so big.

Amy hung her clothes over the end of her bed and finally climbed in. She pulled the covers under her chin and stared up at the ceiling trying to make sense of the madness, perhaps her own madness, she really didn't know. If she slept for a few moments, she thought that she would wake up feeling refreshed and knowing what to do. She hoped that she would wake in familiar surroundings, see Ted as he was when she first met him and laugh at herself for getting in to such a state.

As she drifted off to sleep, she could see Ted, he was laughing at her for being so pathetic and then in her dream his face darkened and she knew he was beginning one of his bad-tempered episodes. Roughly, he held her arm so she couldn't get off a bus he'd dragged her on to. There would be no reasoning with him, she was to blame for a mishap; she was never quite sure what she'd done wrong and there was no way of pacifying him until the ill wind had blown its course. She called for him to let her get off and walk but he wouldn't and the bus drove on relentlessly at breakneck speed. No, she decided, Ted was the last person she wanted to see and yet she felt guilty for thinking that. Something else bothered her about him, she hadn't thought about it for a long time as she'd been so caught up in the misery of living with him.

She woke for a moment and thought that perhaps, she'd been sent to a sanatorium by a government body. As she dreamed, she called out to anyone that would listen, telling them that she shouldn't be there. Guilt ridden, she looked away from all those that turned their heads her way. She knew she was there for a reason as she'd protected and harboured someone that had done terrible things and was now being punished for it. Amy tried to push this dream away - it was all so very disturbing.

A loud rapping on her bedroom door woke Amy from a deep sleep, her heart pounded with the shock. "Are you up Miss Warren?" It was that annoying Mr Firkin again. "Breakfast is being served in the kitchen and you're already five minutes late. If you could make yourself ready, it is most urgent that you join us immediately. Can't get the right class of people these days!" he said sarcastically as he walked away.

Amy opened her eyes wide and she looked around the room trying to remember where she was and it took a little while for her to recall the events of the night. She knew that when she went down to breakfast she wouldn't hold back in giving Mr Firkin a piece of her mind; he was the rudest man she'd ever met.

Quickly, she dressed herself and she reluctantly put on the white pinafore over her skirt and blouse but decided not to wear the cap and left it on the bed. She brushed her short wavy hair with a brush that she'd found by the jug and bowl, her hair was shorter than she remembered it being; there were no grey streaks. She was grateful that her hair felt clean, though she did feel unwashed and she longed to have a hot bath and brush her teeth. As she rushed downstairs, she'd no idea where she was going but presumed that the kitchen in a manor house would be in the basement. As she ran, she noticed an open door and could see a bedroom which had an adjoining bathroom. She stopped in the doorway and seeing that there was no one in the room ran across it past a four poster bed and into the bathroom; she desperately needed to go to the toilet.

It wasn't too difficult to find the kitchen, she could smell bacon cooking and she then realised how hungry she was. Gasping for breath from running and with a red face, Amy burst into the kitchen ready to tell Mr Firkin what she thought of him. She was surprised to see that there were at least twenty five people seated around a long table in the centre of the kitchen. The conversation stopped and they all turned and smiled at her, as if they knew her. Amy found herself apologising for being late and then seeing a space free at the table climbed over the bench and took her place. She felt embarrassed for making such a dramatic entrance.

The kitchen looked like it was in a Victorian museum, brass pots and pans hung from the white tiled walls; there was a fire at the far end of the kitchen and a large black range opposite to where she sat. The floor was covered in red tiles and there was a white butler's sink beneath a steamed up window.

She looked down the table trying not to meet anyone's gaze to see if she knew anybody and could make sense of what was happening to her. There were women, dressed similarly to her and there were men and women of different ages that were wearing finer clothes. Mr Firkin, in his valet's costume, headed the table and

Amy was glad that she wasn't sat near to him as she didn't want to be told off again.

She hadn't been very good at history but she thought it peculiar that the finer people were sat with servants. Her mind was racing. How had she ended up going back in time? What had happened to her at the Chanctonbury Ring? She could see her hands shaking again so put them on her lap, hoping nobody could see her discomfort and as she did, she nearly brushed away her plate, cup and saucer laid out in front of her, causing some to stare again.

Two maids that had been sitting at the end of the table got up and went over to the oven and pulled out trays of bacon baguettes and placed them along the centre of the table. They then brought them trays with pots of tea and coffee for everyone. There was plenty to go around and Amy ate two bacon rolls with ease, her anxiety flushed away as the euphoria of eating took over and she surprised herself by having three spoons of sugar in her tea as if she did it every day. The taste of the sugary tea was familiar to her. Normally however, she drank her tea without sugar; it was no wonder she'd gained so much weight.

Discreetly, she took another bacon roll and as she ate it she looked again at the people around her. Opposite to her, there was a young woman that looked vaguely familiar, she'd dark hair, rolled back into a bun, she was wearing a dark blue dress, and it had a high neckline and tapered in at the waist. She wore a thin white shawl over her shoulders. Somebody called her Vicki and that name seemed familiar too. Amy found herself staring at her and then she saw her smile; she recognised her smile too but wasn't sure where she'd seen her before. Amy sighed silently, the woman in the blue dress recognised her but she wasn't sure how to respond, she wasn't sure if a servant was allowed to speak to the upper classes.

Her attention drifted from the table. There was someone standing in the corner of the kitchen that she could sense was in desperate need of her to take notice. A young girl, who was almost transparent, wearing only a white night dress, similar to the one she'd worn that night, looked at her with dark sad eyes. She was one of the many spirits in the house that dwelled within the walls of Oakhill House. The girl looked to be very young, perhaps no older than fifteen, her face was tear stained and her eyes haunted and swollen as if she'd been crying for a long time. Her dark hair was wet and hung limply around her face. She held in her arms a small bundle. Seeing Amy was watching, the girl pulled back the cloth to reveal a new born baby. She covered up the baby and then looked imploringly at Amy to try and understand what she wanted. Amy frowned, there were too many people around her to concentrate and find out why she needed help. She thought it might be better to leave the kitchen and call her to come to her, like she had with Cornelia at the Chanctonbury Ring. She was surprised that she saw the girl so clearly and that nobody else was aware of her. Her psychic powers seemed to be getting stronger by the hour. She stood up and started to climb over the bench to leave the table, when she realised that Mr Firkin was calling out to her, he'd risen to his feet and was stood at the head of the table, the young spirit was just to the left of him, making it very difficult for Amy to focus just on her.

"Miss Warren, if I can have your attention please, then we can begin!"

Amy looked along the table; everyone was staring and she felt a wave of anxiety wash over her. She wondered what they were expecting her to do. Were they all going to jump up from the table and start their day's work? Amy had no idea what she was meant to be doing. She looked back at the ghostly image of the girl silently pleading with her for help and thought it strange that she'd made herself so visible in such a busy place – her need must indeed be great.

"Let us begin," continued Mr Firkin tapping his teaspoon on the side of his cup. "Thank you for all joining me this morning. As you must be aware, though late comers may not be," he said with an air of importance. "Our Master, Lord Grey met an untimely ending last night and was found dead at approximately five this morning. As we all know, he hasn't been in the best of health recently and has been bedridden. I'm sorry to say that some of you may be shocked to know that he didn't die of natural causes – Lord Grey was murdered in his bed last night and his gold pocket watch has gone missing! This dastardly deed wasn't committed by an intruder but by somebody sat at this very table!" he declared.

Amy looked on bemused and then with concern at the rows of suspects seated at the table; it was hard to detect any signs of agitation or guilt. She then tried to concentrate on the deceased Lord Grey and could sense him being in the heart of the house. She shivered; he'd a dark soul and he didn't want to be discovered. The Lord Grey, she could sense, had died hundreds of years ago, not that night. Amy was confused.

"I'm determined to get to the bottom of this," he continued. "I was up for the most of the night and can confirm that nobody broke into the house. That is not to say that the house was quiet. No indeed not. Last night proved to be a very eventful one. There are some here that had a motive to kill Lord Grey and I would be interested to hear what you all think. For example Lady Grey, I notice that you are not weeping for your late husband and do not seem surprised by my announcement. Now that Lord Grey has passed away, you have become a very wealthy woman. It is no secret that you despised him."

Everyone looked towards an old woman dressed in black; she reminded Amy of Queen Victoria. "It was no secret that you wanted to sell Oakhill House and move abroad but it has been noted that Lord Grey has said on many occasions that he would rather die than lose his house."

Mr Firkin was then interrupted by a young man, wearing a maroon jacket with long tails; he wore cream breeches and long black boots. "Oh yes," he replied. "I think Lady Grey killed my stepfather. Only the other day I saw her in his room tampering with his medication. She has never forgiven him for taking me from the streets and turning me in to a gentleman and I am eternally grateful for his charity. Lady Grey had been asked to summon his solicitors and she discovered that he was planning to leave everything to me."

"That is preposterous!" Lady Grey retorted. "How dare you suggest such a thing! I think that you may find that there has been some skulduggery within these walls. Sir, I loved my husband and I will grieve for him when I feel fit!"

"Do any of you have any more theories?" asked Mr Firkin looking at everyone's puzzled faces.

"It was Mr Land, the gardener," announced one of the maids that had served them at breakfast. "I saw him in the house last night. What business would he have coming into the house at the dead of night when he should have been in his cottage at the end of the drive? We are all aware that Mr Land resented the changes that have been made to the gardens around Oakhill House and has become a broken man since he was asked to dig up the rose garden. Stranger things have driven a man to murder."

Amy saw an elderly man seated to the left of Mr Firkin rise to his feet. He wore a green waistcoat over a white shirt and brown cord trousers, from his pocket he took a white handkerchief and wiped his brow.

"I ain't no murderer, Miss. Yes, I think what they are doing to the gardens is plain outrageous but I ain't no murderer. I was in the house last night, looking for my bleeding dog. He's always sneaking in ere, looking for kitchen scraps. I didn't go near the Master's room; I swear on my dog's life that I didn't kill no one."

"I think I know who the murderer is," replied the lady that Amy thought she recognised. "I'm sorry Amy," she said looking at her, apologetically. "I was taking an afternoon walk around the gardens yesterday and happened to be passing Lord Grey's bedroom window and saw something that took my breath away. You were lying next to him on his bed and you were kissing. Do you have no shame! What was it that drove you to murder? Everyone here knows you have been sick every morning and are more than likely pregnant. I think you killed Lord Grey because he wouldn't acknowledge your relationship and he didn't want to support you and your child. I think you went to him in the middle of the night, whilst he was sleeping to steal something of value and he caught you taking his pocket watch from his bedside table. When he accused you of theft and threatened to send you to prison for this offence, you flew into a rage and suffocated him with a pillow. Am I not right Mr Firkin? Was Lord Grey not smothered to death?"

Amy looked at Mr Firkin, incredulously with her mouth open, and then at the woman accusing her of some fictional deed.

Mr Firkin nodded and smiled triumphantly. "Yes, Lord Grey was suffocated. I'm quite sure that if your belongings are searched, Miss Warren, then the pocket watch will be discovered."

Amy gasped out loud at the severity of the accusation; she could feel her cheeks burning with embarrassment and knew then that everyone would think that she looked guilty. "I caught you by Lord Grey's bedroom last night Miss Warren," he continued. "I believe that Miss Barlow's account is precisely what happened. Well done Miss Barlow for your attention to detail. Do you have anything to confess, Amy Warren, before the law enforcers are summoned?"

Tears ran down Amy's cheeks; she shook her head in disbelief as the loud tick from the gold watch hidden in her skirt pocket rang out loudly for all to hear.

16

At sunrise, reluctantly, Michael walked over to the vineyard to start work. That night, he'd only slept fitfully; his mind wouldn't allow him to rest as he tried to make sense of what had happened. Sarah had insisted before they'd slept that he must go to work in the morning as he'd a family to feed. He looked at her swollen stomach and pleading eyes and knew that he'd no choice in the matter. He'd no idea about gardening or how to tend grape vines but Sarah had assured him that there was nothing to it and that all he had to do was take a knife and basket from the store and go into the fields and harvest the last of the grapes.

Michael walked slowly up to the tool store and watched what the others were doing. After one of the men nodded good morning to him, Michael summoned up the courage and went into the tool store, took a knife and a dusty basket and stood away from the other land workers; nobody stared at him or seemed to mind him being there. He was thankful that no one approached him or called to him. He could hear the men talking together as they collected the baskets and he found that he could understand what they were saying. One of the older men was going to marry a twelve year old girl in a few days time and they congratulated him and talked about the wedding arrangements. Their spirits were high as they walked out into the vineyard and they called out laughing and joking with each other as they cut the grapes from the vines. Michael followed the land workers and then copied their technique as they harvested the grapes, hoping that they wouldn't spot that he was an amateur. The work was backbreaking and as the sun got higher in the sky, he could feel sweat dripping from his brow.

Once the basket was full he carried it on his back to a barn at the end of the field and the basket was taken from him and then the grapes were emptied into a large vat ready to be crushed. Michael collected the empty basket and didn't stay in the barn for longer than he needed to, there were too many people in there and he was sure that they would notice that he was a stranger and an imposter.

Michael was glad to return to the vines where he could try and make sense of the last twenty four hours. It was a complete mystery to him how he'd got to Afghanistan and his initial eagerness to find a way to return to Britain seemed to be subsiding. He was beginning to realise that he was in fact living his dream life and was working in the fields. He'd escaped Britain, he had his freedom and his tormented history was behind him. What amazed him the most was that he had children and a partner who genuinely seemed to love him. It didn't matter that they were incredibly poor, this simple life was better than any life he could have hoped for.

Michael thought back, he could clearly remember his past up until he'd reached the Chanctonbury Ring; after that he could remember nothing and believed that his memory loss was caused by his mind closing down as it tried to repair itself. Today, mentally he felt much better and was positive about the future; he'd finally found an inner peace. He thought about Sarah and wondered if he would have been interested in her if he'd met her under normal circumstances. He hadn't really had a proper girlfriend and had lost the desire to have one as his army career had always come first. He wasn't sure how he felt about her, he couldn't say that he loved her but he did feel that they had a connection. He felt ashamed that he'd been having sex with her when she was so heavily pregnant; he hoped that she'd initiated the lovemaking. Michael wasn't sure how he would handle any further intimate encounters.

Outside of the house, in the shade of a tree, Sarah on her knees, washed their clothes in a bowl. She was hot and her brow was wet with perspiration. She wiped her brow with the back of her hand, being careful not to get any suds in her eyes and looked up at the sky, hoping that a cloud would pass over the sun and give her some relief. She longed to take off her headscarf but it would be frowned upon. The days were beginning to cool as autumn faded but today was exceptionally hot and being around nine months pregnant didn't help matters. She looked anxiously towards the fields; she could just see the men working there and hoped that Michael was coping. Jawid was at school; her neighbour wasn't home and the countryside around her breathed silently as it basked in the sunshine.

Sarah felt the baby move inside her, she was pleased to feel movement and it reassured her that the baby was alive. She was excited at the thought of having a baby of her own to love and care for but did worry about giving birth without a properly trained midwife around to assist. Her neighbour had told her that she'd delivered all her sisters children safely and had said that she was only too happy to help her when the time came. She was grateful that she would have her there but wasn't sure if her neighbour, who was old and frail, would have the strength to manage if there were complications. Sarah was also anxious to see if Michael would love and care for his child; she needed him to be a good father.

When they had first arrived in the village, she'd stopped anyone she could to ask them if they knew anything about the tsunami in England but they knew nothing about it and she came to realise that very few actually knew where England was. If she mentioned London then some would say that they had heard of it and mentioned the Queen. She'd been terrified to find herself in Afghanistan and thought that her kidnappers might find her and hold her hostage again. Fortunately for her, this wasn't the same village that she'd been held for ransom in and she gradually she became less afraid.

Desperate for news of the outside world, Sarah had gone to the school to see if she could find a computer and realised as soon as she reached a derelict building containing only a blackboard that any chances of finding one were zero. Distraught, she'd returned to Michael and Jawid with no news.

The centre of Kabul was over forty miles away, at least a two day trip. They had thought of going there with Jawid, who, when they first found him, was only a toddler but something stopped them both. Their main obstacle was the lack of food; every day was a battle to survive and making a living consumed their days; held them ransom in their village and any plans of escape faded from their thoughts.

Sarah smiled to herself; Michael had been a good man. He'd been kind and gentle and he worked hard to provide for his family. Over the past two years she'd felt a contentment she hadn't felt in years and her getting pregnant seemed to be a natural thing to happen in their lives. They had been through so much together; they'd both been caught in the tsunami and had survived. They had both had turbulent past lives and would comfort each other when they each felt low. There were times, however, when she'd seen a look in his eyes that worried her. He'd told her about his breakdown and being forced to leave the army but there was something more, something that he wasn't telling her that made his eyes look haunted and made him call out in the night.

Sarah sighed as she rinsed out one of Jawid's shirts; it was unlikely that Michael would be able to help much with Jawid and the new baby for a while. She'd prayed that he wouldn't lose his memory until after the birth or ever again. The next few months were going to be tough. She would have to support and comfort him until he learned how to relax and accept what had happened. It would be also a long while until he learned how to love her again. A tear trickled down her cheek, she didn't relish the thought of looking after two children and an invalid; his loss of memory was a blow. Sarah wished her mother could have been with her, she missed her terribly. She started to cry; she was still grieving for her loss and she felt very sorry for herself.

As Sarah hung up her wet clothes on the tree, she looked sadly down towards Michael. Things had changed since he'd lost his memory. She now felt distant from him and vulnerable, she hoped that he didn't hate her for being pregnant and hoped that he didn't blame her for holding him hostage in the middle of nowhere.

Michael stood up and arched his back to try and stretch away the ache he felt throbbing in his lower back. The sun wasn't as hot; it was starting to slide down in the sky behind the vines. The elongated shadows of the vines signified that it was late in the afternoon. He'd half-filled a basket and hoped that this would be his last one for the day. He'd eaten the food Sarah had given him but he still felt hungry and longed for some hot bread with butter and meat.

He was about to cut another bunch of grapes from the vine when he saw a child running through the vineyard to the right of him. He tried to see who it was and squinted into the sun to try and see properly. He knew instinctively that the child wasn't a local boy as he was white and had blonde hair. He seemed familiar and he thought that he might have seen him somewhere before. The boy disappeared from view. Michael shook his head and bent back down and took hold of the grapes ready to slice them from the vine and then jumped back startled, the boy stood before him and was grinning at him malevolently; it was Aaron, his nephew. Michael blinked to try and disperse this vision; he didn't trust his eyes. Helen had definitely said that Aaron had died in the house fire; he really couldn't be standing there.

"Aaron?" he asked but he didn't reply. Cautiously, Michael put out his hand to make contact as this would confirm that his eyes were not deceiving him if he could touch him and then he drew back his hand. The last time he'd seen Aaron, he'd turned himself in to a snake and his efforts to capture him had ended in tragedy. Michael didn't want another death on his hands.

"You shouldn't have let me die in the fire, Michael." Aaron whispered in a hoarse voice.

"But I didn't, I wasn't there! It was too late when I got back," Michael stammered, still not believing his eyes. He looked at Aaron's face; he was looking at him with contempt. Flames leapt from the ground engulfing his nephew, his hair caught alight and his flesh blackened. He didn't cry out at first but his expression showed Michael that he was in excruciating pain and then the spine chilling cries came slicing into the silence. Aghast, Michael watched on in horror, he'd no water or blanket to put out the flames and could do nothing but stare. Panic stricken, Michael looked around him to see if the other men could see the fire or hear the screams but they seemed not to notice and continued to work ignoring his plight.

After what seemed to Michael to be an eternity, the screams and flames subsided, Aaron had become nothing more than a pile of black ashes. Nervously Michael knelt down and stretched out his hand to touch them, still needing to feel something solid to confirm that he wasn't going mad. The ashes felt warm but not powdery as he'd expected; there was something stirring within the heart of the pile and then the ashes took on a new form. Michael moved his hand away as the ashes became black feathers and then took on the shape of a raven. At first it looked as if the bird might be dead but then it sprang to its feet and cawed at Michael, its black bead like eyes shone in the setting sun. The raven flew up into the air, pecking him on the cheek, narrowly missing his eye as it passed over his head and then flew off towards the mountains beyond.

With shaking hands, Michael wiped blood from his cheek and looked at his fingers. He'd the evidence he needed to tell Sarah of this terrible scene he'd witnessed, why he'd been on the run and why he'd been wrongly accused of murder. She needed to know the truth if they stood any chance of having a future together but he feared that she may not believe him and ask him to leave.

The other men had left the field and were putting away their empty baskets. Michael hid his basket with grapes still inside at the back of the store and hung up his knife. He couldn't face the men in the pressing shed chastising him for bringing back a basket so late; he would bring it to them in the morning.

Relieved to finish work, Michael walked silently towards his house and felt aggrieved that Aaron blamed him for his death. He thought back to the night of the fire and knew that he really couldn't have helped what had happened; it was pure coincidence that he'd decided to go for a walk whilst Aaron burnt to death; Michael was the victim, not him. Yes, he was sad that his nephew had died but he really didn't deserve to be singled out and destroyed. Tears burned in his eyes and he could feel his very soul tearing apart as his tortured past erupted within him. He prayed that he would feel the same tranquillity that he'd felt earlier but he could only feel the clawing pain of self-pity.

Sarah stood in the doorway, trying to cool herself down; she looked out into the darkness and waited for Michael to return. She dared not leave the house when it was dark and could almost feel the night drawing her out, promising her that rats and evil shadows would spring out at her if she stepped across the threshold. To break the night's spell, she looked back at the stove and at the pot bubbling away and hoped that the dinner would be cooked in time for Michael's return. She rubbed her stomach as the baby moved and she instinctively knew that he or she would arrive soon as she was sure that her skin on her stomach could stretch no more.

Sarah loved children and knew that one day she would make an excellent teacher. She was pleased that Jawid considered her to be his mother and she enjoyed looking after him. He was sat on their bed, with a small piece of blackboard and chalk and instead of working out the simple sums Sarah had written out for him, drew a picture of the sun around them. Sarah smiled; Jawid was a clever boy but had a big imagination that kept him from keeping his attention on anyone thing. She wished she could get him some paper and pencils as he seemed to like to draw very much.

Sarah fanned herself with a saucepan lid, the heat from the stove was warming the room up so that it was almost unbearable to stay inside, she was sure that she was at least ten degrees hotter than most people. Finally, much to her relief, Michael appeared in their garden out of the darkness and she was glad that he'd survived his day in the vineyard; the first day back was always the worst. There wasn't much work left to do there. Michael would have to find new work over the winter months; she decided not to mention that tonight. She smiled as he came up to her and she found herself hoping that it would be like most evenings and that Michael would hug and kiss her. Instantly she knew by the look on his face that it would be one of those challenging nights and the affection she craved so much wouldn't be forth coming. Michael looked as if he'd something on his mind that he needed to share with her.

He felt relieved to see Sarah, her smile had such warmth to it and he knew she was to be trusted and that despite what the future held, if they stayed together everything would turn out fine. He felt if he told her about the fire, the murder at the zoo and that Aaron was haunting him then she would understand and this burden would lift from his shoulders. He tried not to think negatively, he couldn't contemplate being by himself again. He decided that after he'd eaten something he would share his secrets with her, he owed her the truth at least.

Michael looked down at his work soiled hands, he needed to wash, he was covered in grape juice and dust from the dry earth in the fields. "Sarah, I'm sorry that you have me to deal with as well as running things here," he said looking at her heat flushed face. "Are you ok?"

"Yes, I'm fine, just hot and tired; I can't wait until this baby is born. I'm sure I've been pregnant for more than nine months," she replied looking at Michael's dusty face. "Jawid, show your father where the bowl of water is to wash in and then we'll eat."

Jawid put down his chalk and board on the bed and got up; he then took Michael's hand and led him outside to the water tubs. He picked up the washing bowl, placed it on an empty upturned tub and then took off the lid of another tub; it was full of water. Jawid ran back to Sarah for a jug and when he returned, he filled it and tipped the contents into the washing bowl. Jawid, picked up the soap, dipped his hands into the water and washed them. He passed Michael the tiny scrap of soap so that he would do the same. Michael washed his hands and face and realised that this was their only means of keeping clean and although he felt refreshed he longed to wash properly. He noticed that Jawid was watching him with interest and then he too, decided to wash his face.

When they went back inside, Sarah had turned the cooking ring off and had filled three bowls with the chicken and rice she'd prepared. The bowls were laid on a mat on the floor next to the bed. There was also a jug of water and an odd assortment of containers to use as cups in the centre of the mat. Sarah sat on the edge of the bed and encouraged Jawid to sit down and eat.

Michael ate with relish; it was a simple meal but tasted so fantastic that he couldn't remember a time when he'd enjoyed food so much. He watched Jawid eat and from time to time the small boy would look up at him and smile as if he knew him well. Michael felt that it was bizarre that he'd become a father overnight. He didn't feel overwhelmed but surprisingly, he felt honoured and emotional that someone so small liked and perhaps loved him. He could never hurt a small child and it distressed him that others seemed to think he could.

Michael waited patiently for her to put Jawid to bed and then waited for what seemed a very long time, for him to fall asleep. Sarah walked back to the doorway to try and cool off.

"Do you want to sit with me outside," Michael asked, concerned that she was looking hot and flustered. "You'll cool off better outside than in here," he added.

"No," she replied looking anxiously into the night. "I'll be fine; I just need to lie down for a while."

"Come and lie next to me," Michael suggested lying on the bed. "I'll fan you, until you're cool."

Sarah smiled and came over and lay next to him. It was almost like nothing had happened; he was back to his normal kind and thoughtful self.

Michael used the chalk board to fan her and gradually the redness in her cheeks began to fade.

“Sarah,” he said gently stroking the side of her face. “There’s something I need to tell you.”

17

The siren rang out bleakly, telling everyone that the raid was over and the sky and the shore were clear of the enemy. In unison, everyone exhaled with relief and allowed themselves to breathe again. Evie crawled out from the haystack, eager to get some fresh air and to avoid looking into Albert's eyes; she was frightened that he would see the truth in them. As he emerged, she tried with all her might to remember the love she'd felt for him over the years, so at least she could remember this day, the day that Edward was conceived, with some fond memories.

She patted down her clothes and pulled hay from her hair and then scanned the countryside for anyone that might be watching. Albert noticed her uneasiness. "There's nobody around," he said pulling her to him and then he kissed her tenderly on the lips. She shut her eyes and tried to move her lips so that he would feel like he was being kissed back and then she sank into his chest wrapping her arms around him. This was her very last embrace with him and then she would let him go forever. She really didn't feel the same about him now and the guilt made her body shake; her love affair with Albert was over. She couldn't bear to stay a moment longer and needed to go on her way and find Tom but knew she had to continue with the charade for a few moments longer so he could go to war and believe that there was someone back home that loved him.

"What's the matter love?" he said lifting her face from his chest, he could feel her body shaking against his. "Are you cold?"

Evie nodded but she couldn't stop the tears flowing down her cheeks. Albert watched her cry for a moment and hugged her, trying to comfort her.

"Come to me tonight," he whispered, his chin resting lightly on the top of her head. "I can't bear to be without you. I'll be back at Christmas and then we can start our lives together. Don't cry Evelyn, please don't cry."

Evie stood back from him and wiped the tears from her eyes, she needed to find an excuse to go. "I'm going to miss you so much; at least we have tonight together," she declared. "I should go home and speak to mother," she sobbed. "I'll say that I didn't feel well and needed some fresh air and ask her to ring school and tell them that I'll go in after lunch. I'll walk with you to your Granny's house and then I'll meet you at ten thirty tonight on the corner." she continued, trying to make it easy for Albert to carry on with his plans. There was a seed of doubt growing rapidly in her head; she worried that perhaps Edward hadn't yet been conceived and this would only happen if she re-enacted the past exactly as it had been. She realised that she had already, by bumping into Albert, had drastically changed her future. She didn't want to meet Albert later but knew that there was a possibility that she might have to do just that and secure her son's future. She desperately needed to find Tom, she needed his guidance and more than that, she needed him to tell her that he was in love with her.

Albert seemed pleased with these arrangements. After placing his jacket on her shoulders, he took Evie's hand, led her towards the gate and helped her over. Evie put his jacket on properly, picked up her bike and walked with him southwards as if she was going home. They walked along silently. After a while Albert insisted on wheeling her bike along for her and looked so happy to be with her. She smiled back at him, trying to show the love that he deserved but felt miserable inside. She didn't deserve his love, his complete devotion. How cruel love could be. What exactly had she done to deserve to be placed in this nightmare?

They had only been walking a short while when they reached Albert's grandmother's house. Evie looked up the drive to see if she remembered it but she didn't. In the middle of the lawn stood an apple tree with the remains of rotten apples scattered around its roots. A swing was hung from one of its boughs and swayed gently in the breeze. To the left of the lawn was a shingle path which led to a white cottage with a dark roof, which had one eyebrow window set into it. Evie hadn't met Albert's Granny before and wondered what she looked like. She imagined a small white haired lady that smelt of lavender water and who sipped Earl Grey tea form a fine bone china tea cup. Albert handed her bike back to her and then looked concerned.

"Do you want me to walk you home?" he asked. "I hate to leave you when you are so upset."

"No please don't," Evie replied, a little too abruptly. She made a conscious effort to soften her voice. "Mother's going to be furious but I'll be fine, don't worry about me. I need to work out what I'm going to say to her. She's not the easiest person to tell a tale to, I hope she doesn't see right through me. I wish she'd met you," Evie added.

"If you are sure?" Albert hadn't been that keen on meeting Evie's mother as she had a reputation for being a strict disciplinarian.

Evie nodded and walked away from Albert, he blew her a kiss and she smiled back at him weakly and then turned her back on him hoping that she wouldn't have to see him again.

She waited for a full ten minutes until she was certain that Albert had gone into the house and then with her heart thundering in her chest, she leaped onto her bike and peddled as hard as she could back past the house towards Washington, hoping that he wouldn't see her from the window as she flew by.

The journey to Washington was longer than she'd expected and as she rode, she realised just how much she'd fallen in love with Tom. She thought of the smooth pink skin on his face, his white hair and kind eyes. By the time she'd reached the village she was almost bursting with joy with the prospect of seeing him again. It did occur to her however, that it might have been only her that had gone back to 1940 but something inside of her urged her to look for him. She knew that he would help her to find a way to cope with the madness that rained down on her like shards of glass, tearing apart her past and perhaps her future.

Evie wandered around the village, wheeling her bike along and realised that she was shivering, she felt almost as cold as she did on the day she'd first met Tom. She found his cottage but wasn't sure if he'd lived in the same house all his life and then wondered if he was working as it was mid-week. He might also be in the army or navy fighting for his country. She looked up and down the road for someone that would know everyone's business in the village and might know where Tom was but there was nobody around. She then remembered the Frankland Arms and decided she would look for him there. If he wasn't in the pub, then there was bound to be someone there that could help her find him.

Evie got back on her bike and then free wheeled down the hill towards the pub and when she arrived, she dismounted and leant her bike against the low wall outside. Nervously, she walked towards the main door and hesitated, she knew she was too young to go in and it was also not considered dignified in 1940 for ladies to enter public houses. As Evie turned to leave, an old man appeared in the doorway, he swept his grey hair back, placed a flat cap on his head and steadied himself to take a step out, Evie wasn't sure if it was his age or just the fresh air hitting him that made him look unsteady. With a new found confidence the old man took a few more steps out on to the stairs and then smiled when he saw her. "Probably shouldn't have had that last whisky," he said winking at her.

"Do you know Tom Barns," Evie asked, seizing the moment to speak to what seemed to her to be a well-informed Washington resident.

"Tom Barns?" said the old man thoughtfully. "Ah yes Tom," he replied looking at his wrist watch, adjusting the distance from his eyes so he could read the dial. "Tom's getting married today. You'd better run if you want to catch the service, it started five minutes ago."

"Married!" Evie gasped. "Oh no! Thank you. Where's the church?"

"At the end of The Street. St Mary's, do you know it?"

"I... I'll find it," replied Evie running towards her bike. "I know where The Street is, thank you again."

Evie grabbed her bike, threw her leg over the crossbar and then sped off towards the church. She'd seen the street he mentioned when she'd been looking for Tom's house earlier. Evie's mind was racing; she had to see Tom, before he got married to Martha. She had to get to the church before it was too late. She was positive that Tom felt the same way about her as she did about him and if she got to him in time then perhaps he would call the wedding off and marry her. Then, the baby she hoped she was carrying would have a proper father and she could spend the rest of her life with someone she loved.

Tears of anxiety streamed down Evie's face as she raced along The Street. She could see the church ahead of her but despite her frantic peddling it took a long time to get there. Finally, she came to a stop and St Mary's Church was before her. She could hear music coming from within the walls, it wasn't the Wedding March played on an organ as she'd expected but someone singing a screeching aria in a high pitched voice. Evie jumped off her bike and, throwing it to the ground, raced up the path to the doors of the church. Hysterically, she flung them open and ran through the vestibule and into the church. The soloist, put off by her spectacular entrance stopped singing and looked at her with contempt.

Evie looked around the church and noticed that there was a small congregation who all turned and stared at her. The pews to the left of Evie were filled with the bride's family and only one lady sat on the right hand side. She was an enormous woman with a black pill box hat perched on her head - the hat looked ridiculous. She wondered if that was Tom's mother. The bride and groom were stood in front of the altar and hadn't yet exchanged rings. A wave of relief swept over Evie, it wasn't too late and there was still a chance for her.

Without hesitation or embarrassment, she yelled at the top of her voice. "Noooooo.... you can't marry her! It's me Evie. Tom I need to talk to you. Please... you really can't." she was now crying. The vicar stared at her in horror and the service came to a grinding halt. Both the bride and groom, glared at each other questioningly and then at Evie, who was now sobbing.

Evie stared at the bride's face and then at groom's and through her tears she realised that she'd made a terrible mistake, she didn't recognise the groom - it wasn't Tom. She could feel her cheeks burning with humiliation. The man in the pub had obviously not heard her correctly. The groom was dressed in an army officer's uniform, he'd dark brown eyes, a particularly larger than average nose and couldn't be by any stretch of the imagination be her Tom. Evie gasped and then wished the ground would swallow her up.

"I'm ..... I'm sorry, she stammered. "I've made a dreadful mistake. You're not who I've been looking for. Oh my goodness, I'm so sorry." Evie continued backing away from the glares of the angry guests and from the vicar who had gone a deep beetroot colour. "I'm dreadfully sorry." Evie called as she turned and ran out of the church; she needed to run away before she was dismembered by an angry mob.

Evie shut the heavy doors behind her and leaning on them, took in a deep breath of air, trying to steady herself so she didn't pass out with shock. She was mortified, she'd never been this reckless when she was a teenager and she realised that she was behaving like a fool. She needed a moment to gather her thoughts before she fled, to work out what she was going to do next. At the edge of the graveyard she saw a bench and, carefully, she walked over to it and sat down slowly; a wave of emotional nausea gnawed at her stomach. She drew Albert's jacket around her, she was shaking again; she'd never been so emotional in all her life. Evie put her head in her hands, trying to get herself to think clearly; she wasn't being sensible and things would get completely out of hand if she carried on in this way. She wondered what sort of future she was going to have and winced at the thought of having to go through a whole life time again.

"Evie, what are you doing here?"

Evie lifted her head from her hands and saw a boy standing next to her; he was wearing a school uniform and couldn't have been more than twelve years old. His tie was crooked and his hand knitted V-neck pullover had threads hanging from it and was worn at the elbows. Evie looked down at his trousers, they were a bit too short for him and his shoes were clean but looked about to fall apart. Evie looked up at his face, his hair was parted neatly to one side and his skin was pale and smooth with little freckles on his cheeks. It was his eyes that finally took Evie's breath away, she would know them anywhere.

"Tom?" she asked hesitantly. "Tom is it you?

"Yes Evie, what are you doing here? Why did you try and stop my cousin's wedding? What were you thinking?"

Incredulously, Evie stared at Tom; his voice had broken but was not as deep as she remembered it to be. "I don't know what I'm thinking at the moment, someone told me you were getting married." Evie sighed, putting her head back in her hands. "How old are you Tom?"

"I think I'm about fourteen or fifteen," he replied. "I'm not entirely sure but the boys in my class are around that age. How old are you then?

"Eighteen" she said looking back up at him. "Why did I think you would be the same age or older than me?" she asked him, laughing out loud. Tom's pale blue eyes stared back at her not understanding what she was trying to say.

Tom looked back anxiously at the church; someone was opening the doors ready to release the newly married couple.

"Look, Evie, do you want to go for a walk? They'll be coming out in a minute and my mother will be after me for slipping out during the service. She's not to be reasoned with and she'll have me by the ear if we're not careful. Come on quick; let's go before it's too late." Tom suggested, taking Evie's hand.

Evie rose to her feet. Although he looked so young, he was acting like an adult and it was comforting to find her friend again. Without delay, they left the church grounds and headed back up The Street, half running and half walking determined to escape Tom's mother and to talk.

After climbing several styles and running along the edge of two muddy fields, Tom led Evie to his camp;

it was within a clump of trees in the middle of a wooded copse. Out of breath Evie sat herself down on an upturned packing case and looked around her. A couple of planks of wood were crudely nailed to the trees, creating the walls and a rusty corrugated sheet of metal was rammed between the trunks overhead to act as a roof. The sun broke through the clouds and sunlight streamed through the cracks and onto the floor of the camp; dust particles danced in the beams of light.

Tom sat down next to her; he was so relieved to find her again. He couldn't help but stare as she was so beautiful, so slender and elegant. Her skin was the colour of milk and her wavy hair fascinated him it was such an unusual colour, it was a mixture of red, yellow and brown. He'd recognised her, as soon as she'd stepped into the church and had just stared at her in amazement. He wondered why she seemed so upset and hoped that she didn't notice him looking at her so intently.

"What's the matter?" asked Evie seeing him blush.

"Um...," replied Tom. "I'm glad you're ok and still alive. I've been so worried about you and worried for myself. Where have you been?"

"I've been in my bedroom and then I saw Albert on the way up here to see you. Do you think we're both dead?" asked Evie.

"No..., I have thought about this and no we're not dead. I'm breathing and I can feel my heart beating," he replied, holding his hand on his chest. We could be experiencing some sort of virtual reality, it could be caused by trauma after nearly losing our lives in the tsunami. You saws Albert! Was everything ok, you seem upset?"

"My life is in tatters," Evie replied, picking up a twig from the floor. She started to draw swirls in the dust with it. "I don't think I've done a very good job so far at trying to put things right. There's a very good chance that I've changed things beyond all recognition. I think back to my past life and have lost count of the number of times I've wished I could see Albert again. Do you think by some cruel hand of fate, we have been given a gift and can alter our futures? Obviously we can't stop the war but we can change our path in life and we could possibly stop someone doing something if you knew it would end badly. I don't want this to be true but I know deep down that's why we're here."

"I hadn't thought of it that way," replied Tom frowning with discomfort. "I don't want to go through my whole life again, even if I could change it. I'm hoping that I'll wake up in casualty in 2013 having had a blow to the head. Oh God no, having to go through a whole life time, even if you could change what happened, how awful would that be?"

"Isn't this your chance to change something that you wished you could have avoided or done something better if you had hindsight? Is there something in your past Tom that you would change? If there is then I would understand why we're both here in 1940."

Tom's eyes darkened and his young teenage face contorted with pain. "Yes," he replied. "I haven't thought about it for a long time but there is something I wish I could change, something I have regretted doing but not in 1940. Why would someone want to give me a second chance when I really don't believe I deserve it?"

Evie looked dismayed, Tom's eyes looked haunted and she really wished she hadn't brought up what were obviously bad memories for him. All she could do was hug him and try and make him feel better. How strange life was, that she'd suddenly become his protector and any thoughts of marrying him had dissipated. They would have to support each other now and work their way out of the surreal tangled web of deception that they found themselves caught in.

18

Amy rose up slowly and pulled out from her skirt pocket the gold watch. She hadn't noticed it before and was surprised to see it there. The casing of the watch was tarnished with age and it had an inscription on the lid. She couldn't read it without putting on her glasses but could see that the writing was in an old fashioned copperplate script. Everyone in the kitchen gasped as Amy produced the evidence and then clapped Vicki for being such a clever detective. She was confused by their reaction and she felt uneasy and wondered what they would do to her next.

Amy felt enraged; they could call who they liked and if the police came then she would put up a fight; it was ludicrous that they were accusing her of murder and having an affair with someone she didn't know. She knew that she was innocent and she wasn't going to go to prison for something she hadn't done. Her situation was laughable, ridiculous and frightening. Amy looked up to heaven for courage; she'd other things to think about. She couldn't ignore the fact that there was someone in the room that needed her help. She didn't have time to help Cornelia at the Chanctonbury Ring and she wasn't going to let another opportunity to give aid to someone else slip by. She climbed off the bench and started to walk out of the kitchen, she needed to find a quiet place to help the girl and her baby.

"Miss Warren, where are you going?" demanded Mr Firkin.

"You honestly don't expect me to reply do you? I've got better things to do than sit here with a bunch of nutcases!"

She needed to get out of the house; she needed fresh air, a moment to gather her thoughts, away from it all. She wasn't sure which way to go and hesitated at the foot of a staircase, she presumed that there was a back door but wasn't sure which way to go. Amy was just about to take the first step when she saw the young girl appear at the top of the stairs, she then disappeared. She decided to follow; she hoped the girl was showing her the way out. Amy reached the top of the stairs and then to the right, she saw her again at the end of the hall. This continued, until she found the main entrance of the house.

With relief, Amy pulled the heavy door open and stepped out into the morning sunshine, a light breeze ruffling her skirt. She breathed in what she thought to be the cool autumn air but the new leaves on the trees told a different story. The air filled her lungs and seemed real enough. Her attention was drawn again to the servant girl, she was in the garden, she stood by a small cherry tree and she pointed to the ground near the tree's roots. She was crying and she no longer held her baby in her arms. Amy knew immediately what the girl wanted. The infant had been buried there and she knew that the girl wanted her to dig the body up. Amy shivered, it wasn't something she was eager to do but the girl's need was so strong that she felt unable to walk away. She scanned the grounds for a tool she could dig with. There was a wheelbarrow in front of one of the flower beds with gardening tools laid across it. She walked across the lawn and picked up a hoe and wondered if that would break up the earth. As she picked it up, Vicki Barlow appeared on the doorstep and looked pleased to see her.

"There you are," she called, running towards her. "We've been looking all over for you."

"I bet you have," replied Amy sarcastically. Amy was uncertain about her cheery greeting; did she not just a moment ago accuse her of murdering Lord Grey? She felt irritated with her and wondered why she wasn't frightened of her. So many questions flitted through her head. She deduced that Vicki's friendliness might be a trick to keep her there and if she didn't run then she might be set upon by the others that may be hiding and waiting for their chance to seize her. Another more sinister thought crossed her mind; she'd already committed murder that morning, why should she stop at one? Amy almost laughed out loud; she shook her head to expel that thought. She was acting out of character; she would never hurt anyone.

"What are you doing?" Vicki asked, looking at the hoe in Amy's hands.

"Just digging up a body, I'm surprised you didn't work that one out too," she replied as she headed off towards the tree where she'd seen the young girl.

"You're joking right?" said Vicki, following her. "Who's body? It's... it's happened again hasn't it? I saw that look in your eyes in the kitchen; you weren't playing along were you. I could see that you were distracted you saw something didn't you?"

Amy stopped and faced Vicki. "What do you mean?"

"You've had a vision or have been visited haven't you? You're going to find another body?"

"Yes, that's right. I don't understand?" Amy was shocked; she didn't know how Vicki knew about her psychic ability and she floundered as she tried to work out where she'd seen her before and thought she might be going completely mad not to know who she was. She decided that she would pretend to know her and hoped that Vicki might be able to help her make sense of what was going on. "There was a young girl in the kitchen and she was holding a new born. I think someone killed her baby and buried it here under this tree." Amy could see in her mind Lord Grey taking the baby from the young servant girl. The girl was hysterical and fought to keep her baby. To fight her off, Lord Grey struck her with his fist causing her to fall back and she hit her head. "Yes," continued Amy, "Lord Grey took the girl's baby away and committed murder, I think he killed the servant girl too." Pitifully, Amy looked down at the ground, where the baby was buried. "The baby was a boy, he's buried here. Lord Grey was the father and he was disgusted to think that he'd fathered a bastard."

"Oh my God," replied Vicki. "That's awful, the poor girl, the poor baby."

"I know it's tragic, you wouldn't believe how many bodies are buried out here. Lord Grey, the real Lord Grey that is, was a nasty piece of work," she added. "I can sense him watching me from a window behind me; he's seething with anger and shows no remorse." Vicki looked horrified.

Amy was just about to start digging when she noticed a row of modern cars in front of the manor house and this sight took her breath away. All she could do was stand and stare for a moment; she hadn't noticed them when she walked out of the house as she'd been concentrating on finding the servant girl. The shapes of the cars were familiar but the number plates were not, she couldn't recognise the year from them. "Tell me please, I think I'm having a really bad day today. What year is it?"

"2016. Why do you ask?" Vicki looked puzzled. Amy wanted to scream out loud. "What the Hell is going on?" but thought better of it. She took another deep breath in and looked down at her clothes with confusion, she hoped that she was just wearing a costume and that fashion hadn't adopted a Victorian retro look; it really did nothing for her figure. She also couldn't believe that she'd lost three or four years of her life and was now well into her forties - she felt sick.

"Amy, before you start digging, you'd better come inside, they want to present the certificates. It was a brilliant idea of yours to organise this 'Who Done It' weekend; we've all had so much fun. Come on Amy, they're all waiting for you. Lord Grey, I mean Mr Jenkins, you know what he's like, and he doesn't like to be kept waiting. We'll call the police and get them to dig up the baby after we've packed."

In shock, Amy just nodded and followed her into the house; she was dumbfounded and lost for words. The sense of relief discovering that it was all a farce and that she hadn't been labelled a murderer was immense. Why she'd been jet propelled into the future was another matter altogether. Vicki led Amy into a reception room where chairs had been laid out in rows. In front of them was a table which had a flower display and certificates placed on it. Mr Jenkins stood by the table; he had on his head a grey wig and wore a green jacket with matching breeches and reminded Amy of a toad. Alongside him stood the widow that looked like Queen Victoria and to her left stood Mr Firkin, the bad-mannered valet.

Amy and Vicki slipped into the room and sat down on chairs in the back row.

"That was cutting it fine," whispered Vicki as she arranged her skirt. Mr Jenkins looked relieved to see them and judging by the look on his face was just on the verge of losing his temper.

"Welcome friends and colleagues to Oakwood House's 'Who Done It' certificate ceremony, to well... what will be the penultimate time I formally address you all. My last address, of course will be at my retirement party at the golf club which I hope you will all be attending. I am reassured that Treadmill Marketing will go from strength to strength in the hands of my nephew Joules Firkin." Mr Jenkins paused for a moment and looked thoughtfully at Joules. "Now to continue with the certificate presentation let me pass you over to Jane Renshaw, our kind hostess, to do the honours, I am sure we are unanimous in saying that this weekend was thoroughly enjoyed by all."

As everyone clapped, Mr Jenkins stepped back allowing Jane, wearing her widow's outfit, to call out the names of those that had won an award over the weekend. Amy had been startled when she heard the name Treadmill Marketing, she stared hard at Mr Jenkins, she recognised him; she'd seen him at Christmas parties but had never spoken to him and wouldn't have recognised him had Vicki not mentioned his name. When she joined the company as a school leaver, she only ever reported to her team manager and had left her job long before Joules Firkin had come onto the scene. She felt sorry for all employees that would have to bow down to him and didn't hold out much hope for the prospects of the company as Joules Firkin she'd decided, was a complete arse.

Amy felt elated seeing everyone's excitement at getting their certificates and then felt a small twinge of sadness; she missed Treadmill Marketing, she missed having a job and being part of a team. She also missed talking to people and having friends. Vicki seemed to be the sort of friend she would like to have.

Vicki was the last to receive her certificate and a winner's trophy and came back to show Amy. After Mr Jenkins and Joules left the room, everyone else got up to change and to pack; Amy just stood by the window and watched as they went off to their rooms.

"Are you coming?" called Vicki. "Shall we pack and then call the police?"

"Yes," replied Amy. She wasn't sure what clothes she had to wear or where they were stored, she didn't remember seeing a suitcase in her room.

"I can't wait until I get my mobile back," said Vicki as they climbed the stairs towards the servant quarters. "Without it, you feel like part of you is missing. I was going to ask to keep it as Jeff took Peppy to the vet on Saturday morning. He's got cystitis again I think. That cat's going to be the cause of my financial ruin if he keeps getting it."

"Yes I know, where would we be without them?" Amy replied nostalgically, thinking of the Chanctonbury Ring and the pile of goo that once was her phone.

When they finally reached their rooms, Vicki went into hers and asked Amy to wait for her in the downstairs lobby. Amy found the room she'd spent the night in and she hesitated before going in, she could hear Vicki a few rooms along removing clothing from hangers and she heard the clunk of the wood as they hit the back of the wardrobe, she hoped that she would find something decent to wear in her wardrobe.

Cautiously, Amy pulled down the door handle to her room, she felt like she was interrupting something as she pushed open her door. She saw a child sitting on the chair in the corner. Someone had put the chair back into her room - the girl looked cross and then vanished. She shivered, not all encounters with the spirit world were pleasant ones. She tried not to think about Lord Grey, he too was lurking nearby, oozing malice and contempt for Amy. She shivered again and she knew that she'd only a little time to leave the house before something horrible happened.

She ran to the wardrobe and flung it open, longing to find a comfy pair of jeans, a T-shirt and a sweatshirt to change into. She breathed a sigh of relief; there were clothes in the wardrobe but she didn't recognise them. On closer inspection, she realised that they all had designer labels and would cost more than she was able to afford. Amy had been reduced to buying clothes from charity shops so that Ted didn't moan at her for spending his money. She took a pair of jeans out of the wardrobe and held them up; they looked to be in her new inflated size. Without delay, she took off her costume and put on the jeans, a check shirt and then a pair of trainers that she found in the bottom of the wardrobe. There was a small holdall there too, with a few more clothes and a wash bag. With a pang of guilt, she took this out of the wardrobe, hoping that she wasn't stealing someone's luggage. Without looking back, Amy left the room and trying not run, made her way to the lobby.

She was relieved to find Vicki waiting for her, she was very worried that she might have to chat to others that worked at Treadmill Marketing and wasn't sure what she would have said to them.

"I've got your mobile for you," said Vicki passing it to her, Amy looked at the phone in her hand and she turned it over, it just looked like a rectangular mirror with one button at the side, the type of phone that a teenager might have. She couldn't remember when she'd bought her old mobile phone; it had to be more than fifteen years old.

"Are you going to ring the police," asked Vicki.

Amy stared again at her phone and then at the lobby. The atmosphere in the house was extremely oppressive and the walls felt almost as if they would bear down on her at any moment. She focused on the door at the end of the lobby, it had been Lord Grey's office and she knew he was behind the door in a highly agitated state. The door began to bow and warp as if it would explode, unleashing not only Lord Grey but any other evil ghouls caught in his malignant web. "We've got to get out of here," whispered Amy urgently. "Don't look behind you just run."

Amy tore off towards the front door and Vicki too; she hadn't questioned Amy's decision. The door behind them flew open startling those left in the lobby but Amy and Vicki had escaped in time, into the sanctuary of the garden and sunshine.

"What's the matter," asked Vicki. "Why are we running? What's going on?"

"Thank God we're out here," gasped Amy. "Even if ten priests came to exorcise this house, they wouldn't be able to do it, that house is riddled with evil. Vicki please can you ring 999 for me, my hands are shaking so much."

Without questioning she took Amy's phone and rang 999 on her mobile and passed it to her. She wasn't quite sure what she should say to the operator and she had to ask Vicki for the address of the house but finally after mentioning that she'd found a body of a child, she managed to get the operator to send someone round to investigate. Amy decided that it was best not to say that body had been buried for over a hundred years and she didn't say that she was assisting West Sussex police with their investigations as her life had been turned on its head.

"Do you mind if I go home?" Vicki asked, looking for her car keys in her handbag. "Only Jeff's parents are coming round this afternoon and I've got to get back and tidy up. The cat's ok by the way."

"No, that's fine. I don't know how long this is going to take," Amy said looking anxiously back at the house.

"Text me later and let me know how it goes," she continued, climbing into her car. "Oh yes and let me know how it goes with James tonight. I want all the details."

"James?" replied Amy. "Who's James?"

"Don't tell me you've forgotten, you're meeting your new internet date tonight.

"Oh yes," lied Amy aghast. "What about Ted?"

"Ted? Who's Ted?" asked Vicki closing the car door.

As Amy watched Vicki drive away, a strange euphoric feeling swept over her as she realised that Ted was now not part of her life - it was too good to be true. Then doubt crept in like a crack splintering across thin ice and her aspiration threatened to be shatter at any moment. Amy looked at her phone and was sure that if the phone did belong to her then Ted's name might appear on the contact list. She pressed the button at the side of the black shiny phone and watched in amazement as it sprang into life. Fortunately, it wasn't locked and there was a contacts icon on the screen but there were no other buttons to press. Amy touched the screen but nothing happened. "Where are my contacts?" Amy asked herself out loud. The contact page appeared. It took a few moments for her to realise that her phone was voice activated. "Ted," she said, trying to speak clearly. Nothing happened. As a test she called out Vicki's name and her number appeared. The sense of relief returned, Ted wasn't listed on her phone. "Photos" Amy announced and a gallery appeared on her screen. "View" she called but the screen remained on the gallery page. She touched the screen and a photo of herself and Vicki filled the screen, they appeared to be in a bar somewhere and judging by their faces were drunk and laughing hysterically. Amy couldn't remember the last time she'd got wasted. She flicked through several photos but there was no sign of Ted.

Her attention turned to a police car making its way up the drive. As quickly as she could, she switched off the phone and waited anxiously for the police car to reach her. Most of her colleagues had gone home and she was dismayed to see Mr Jenkins, Joules Firkin and the event leader Mrs Renshaw appear on the doorstep. She had hoped not to involve anyone else but she guessed that event organiser and the owner of Oakwood House would need to be informed of her findings. Mrs Renshaw's brow creased with concern, she was obviously alarmed by the arrival of the police. Amy sighed and walked over to her to try and explain.

She didn't see him at first but as she approached Mrs Renshaw, she could see a dark shadowy figure attached to her back, his legs were clasped around her waist and his bony hands hung on to her shoulders. He was doing his best to hide, so that Amy didn't see him. Mrs Renshaw and everyone else seemed unaware of the hideous ghoul she bore; she just looked jaded and rubbed her neck with stress. Amy hadn't seen a spirit do this before and she thought that Lord Grey looked like a parasite. She was thankful he hadn't attached himself to her but she knew that would have been unlikely, she could tell that he despised her.

The police officer got out of his car and looked enquiringly towards Mrs Renshaw to see if she was the one that had contacted the police.

"I rang you," Amy called to him. "I'll show you where the body is."

"What!" yelled Mrs Renshaw, marching towards her. "How dare you tell such lies. You disgusting vagabond!"

Amy was surprised by the woman's reaction, she wasn't entirely sure what a vagabond was and wondered why she was so quick to accuse Amy of telling lies, without knowing anything about it; she strongly suspected that Lord Grey was influencing what she was saying.

"Get off my land, be off with you. You have no right to be here" she continued, addressing all that stood around her.

Mr Jenkins and Joules Firkin, not wanting to be part of anything untoward, hastily got into their Jaguar and left; leaving Amy alone to try and deal with the awkward situation.

"I'm sorry, Mrs Renshaw, let me explain, today I have been informed from a reliable source that there is a body of a baby buried in your grounds. If we dig the ground by the cherry tree over there," she said pointing to the tree. "We'll find him. I know this must be upsetting for you but this needs to be sorted. Do you have a spade?" Amy asked the police officer.

"Balderdash!" exclaimed Mrs Renshaw.

The police officer shook his head, he was young, probably just out of training college and he looked perplexed. "I'd be grateful if you would calm down," he said looking at Mrs Renshaw uneasily. "I need to make a call first."

19

Michael brushed a loose strand of hair away for Sarah's cheek and continued to fan her hot flushed face with Jawid's blackboard; she stared lovingly back at him waiting for him to speak. He wasn't sure where he would start or how he would explain everything without sounding like a maniac. He decided to tell her first about Aaron's death and the haunting to see how she reacted and whether or not she believed him. He would then talk about his mental trauma he'd experienced after being dismissed from the army and if she didn't look too distressed, then he would tell her about the death of Ben George at the zoo.

"What did you want to talk about?" asked Sarah nervously, she knew that it wouldn't be good news.

"Have I ever told you about Aaron?" asked Michael, it suddenly occurred to him that he might have but couldn't remember it. He was almost beginning to think, that he had in fact forgotten the past two years.

Sarah shook her head. "Who's Aaron?"

Michael felt a mixture of relief and disappointment that he hadn't told her. "He was my nephew and he was only eight when he died in a house fire."

"Oh no! How horrible. Were you close?"

Michael nodded. He hadn't really thought about it before but he'd cared a lot about his sister's children. "Do you believe in ghosts?" he asked cautiously.

"No, not really," Sarah said turning on her side, so she was facing away from him. "I've only ever known about Jinn's - shape shifters, my mother always blamed one for hiding her reading glasses."

Michael felt that he wasn't off to a good start and the fact that she was facing away from him made him feel uncomfortable. He stopped fanning her and put the blackboard down. "I'm not sure I believed in ghosts before Aaron died," he continued "I know this might be hard to believe but I've seen him several times since his death. I saw him today in fact, in the fields, just before I came home. He appeared in front of me out of nowhere." Sarah listened silently. "And then, I watched him burn. He screamed so loudly that I thought that the others would hear and they would come running; they didn't notice. I watched Aaron disintegrate into ashes which then turned into a big black bird. As it flew up into the air, it pecked my cheek." Sarah turned back over to look at his face. "He blames me for letting him die in the fire." Michael said pointing to the wound. Sarah stared and then frowned. Her reaction made him feel his cheek with his fingertips and he discovered much to his alarm, that his face was intact and unblemished.

"I can't see anything, perhaps you're still grieving and your mind is playing tricks on you," replied Sarah sympathetically.

"Yes," said Michael losing confidence. "Maybe you're right. I haven't been myself since I left the army. I had some kind of breakdown and I know when you are traumatised you might think you see things." Michael frowned, he was convinced that he wasn't making this up. Mentally he was much stronger now and his outlook on life had changed. "I don't feel the same now. I can look back on that part of my life as a past episode and know that I'm better," he said correcting his previous statement. "I can handle the fact I might have been hallucinating, it was hot today and I might have been dehydrated but what I can't handle is that something awful usually happens after I see him. It might be just a coincidence but I'm sure that something bad will happen." Michael looked anxiously over at Jawid. "I fear for Jawid's life," he whispered.

"Why do you think that?" asked Sarah sitting up, disturbed by what he'd just said and she looked over to Jawid's bed to make sure he was there and sleeping.

"You know, I had a dream once about him and remember seeing him fall as if he'd been shot. Don't worry," he added quickly realising that he'd said too much. "It was only a dream. I'm sure that nothing will happen to him." He really regretted saying this as he'd clearly upset her.

"This is a quiet village, there's been no fighting here for years and the Taliban leave us alone. Why would you think of something like that? I couldn't bear it if anything should happen to him or any other child in this village for that matter. Is this what you wanted me to tell me?"

"No, not exactly," replied Michael uneasily, trying to pick the right words. "I think what I'm trying to say is, if something were to happen to a child in this village then it wouldn't be my fault. You have to believe me I would never hurt a child." It suddenly occurred to him that for the first time since the death of Ben George he sincerely believed that he hadn't murdered the boy.

Sarah's eyes narrowed for a moment with suspicion but then softened with what he thought to be concern.

"Michael, did Jawid tell you that one of the boys in his class has gone missing?"

"No," replied Michael feeling his chest constrict. "When did he disappear?"

"Yesterday, Jawid says that he wasn't in school today and he heard the teacher talking to his assistant about it. They don't know where he has gone; he was last seen yesterday afternoon, playing by the well. Do you remember seeing him when you went to get water?"

Michael couldn't remember anything of that day and fear surged through him as there was a possibility that their paths might have crossed. "I can only remember from yesterday evening," said Michael remorsefully.

"Tomorrow morning at first light, Jawid said that the men of the village are going to go up in the hills to look for him. You must go too, otherwise they will become suspicious."

Michael's thoughts were now racing and he got up from the bed to stand by the window for air and to try and think clearly. There was bleakness and inevitability about the day to come that made Michael shiver and his heart race. He knew what Sarah was saying was right but he didn't want to go with the other men, he feared that they would turn on him like an angry pack of wolves and tear him to shreds. He hoped Sarah didn't despise him but he couldn't read her troubled face. He needed to know what she was thinking. "Do you think I am a bad person?" He didn't know how else to put it, he couldn't ask her if she thought he was capable of murder.

Sarah, lay back on the bed exhausted and frustrated by his words. "Michael McGrath, I've known you for over two years now and am about to have your baby. I know you well enough. You are a wonderful person; you're just a bit paranoid that's all."

Michael smiled and felt comforted by her words but didn't hold out much hope that they would find the missing child and knew that the next day Aaron would cause trouble for him.

At first light the men of the village and Michael met by the well in the vineyard and formed four groups to cover certain areas of the hills where the children liked to play. Michael's group consisted of nine men, originally there had been ten in his group but one of them was very old and was persuaded to stay behind and watch out for the boy should he miraculously appear.

It was a steep climb up the hill behind the village and the going was treacherous as the ground was dry; stones fell away from the edges of the path as the men passed. Michael looked back down at the village below; the houses looked like tiny dusty bricks protruding from the earth like rotten teeth. The hills around him were barren and unforgiving and wouldn't willingly allow even a blade of grass to survive, let alone a child. Silently the men scanned the landscape for signs of life. Their mood was pessimistic and the feeling of hopeless was overwhelming.

After a good half hour walk, one of the younger men scrambled up a cliff face to a goat shelter on a ledge just above their heads and then called out to the others and showed everyone that he'd found a piece of clothing.

Michael held his breath anxiously, the garment was covered in dried blood and then a debate raged amongst the older men as they decided whether or not it belonged to the missing child. They couldn't be sure and decided to continue their search and, after drinking a little water, made their way higher up the hillside. Michael looked back at the goat shelter and watched with trepidation as a raven landed on the ledge. It cawed loudly as if it was mocking him. Michael remembered his last encounter with a bird and its presence wasn't a welcome sight. He took a deep breath and looked away, he was determined that he wouldn't be set up and drawn into a trap. The men had gone on ahead so Michael ran to join them, knowing that as long as he was with them they would be his witnesses and would prove his innocence.

He wasn't sure what it was that made him stumble and fall onto his knees; it might have been a loose rock or root sticking out from the track. As he tried to get up again, the ground gave way and Michael shot down the hillside in a shower of loose stones. The slope was very steep and every attempt to clutch onto a dry plant or rock was futile. Finally, he landed on an outcrop of rock and felt his collar bone snap as he hit the rock. Michael lay on his back as he waited for the pain to subside, the sky spun above him unsympathetically. He was grateful that he hadn't broken his back or cracked his skull. He'd broken his collar bone before and it would just take a few weeks to heal. Slowly Michael sat up and looked back up to the path from where he'd fallen. It would be impossible to get back up without someone throwing him down a rope and it would be a struggle to climb up with his broken collar bone.

He hoped that the others had seen him fall. Desperately, he called for help; he didn't want to be left behind. He looked towards the path below to see if it was possible to climb down and then inhaled sharply as he'd caught out of the corner of his eye a small naked body caught in a jagged bush just below the ledge he was stranded on. The child looked like a rag doll, his eyes were wide open and he stared lifelessly up at the sky. Michael's heart began to pound, he called again to the men that he'd found a body. He could hear them overhead shouting out in distress and then sensed by their urgent whispers that there was mistrust in the air and anger, their guarded remarks and whispers were beginning to alarm him.

Michael looked at the broken body below, the child was almost identical to Jawid and he wondered what sort of person could have done such a dreadful thing, he wondered if he was the boy in his dreams. If he'd been clothed then perhaps he may have fallen off the treacherous path above and it would have just been a tragic accident. As he was naked, battered and covered in blood then it was obviously that he been abused and then discarded. Michael felt a deep sadness inside that something so awful could happen to someone so young and that there was someone out there that could do such a despicable thing. He'd seen many atrocities in his life but this for him was by far the worst. His attention turned back to the men overhead, he wondered what they were thinking and hoped that they didn't think he'd anything to do with the child's death.

Michael sat alone on the ledge and looked down at the bush where the child's body had once been. The sun was beginning to set and his mouth was dry. He needed water and a painkiller for his shoulder. Thankfully his throbbing shoulder told him that he was alive and able to feel pain. He'd watched the men from the village carefully wrap and retrieve the body. The younger men of the group climbed up and set up a rope system so that the child could be gently lowered to the ground. He'd seen the looks on the men's faces as they worked and knew that they had decided that he was guilty. He had, using their language fluently, begged and pleaded with them from the ledge that he was stranded on and told them that he'd done nothing to harm the boy but he could see from their eyes that they didn't believe him and he sensed their hatred towards him. When they left, he hoped that they would return and rescue him and say that they were only joking but as the day wore on he knew that he'd been left on the ledge to perish as a child murderer.

In the setting sun, Michael looked over the ledge and tried to work out what would happen to him if he jumped. He stared at the bush that had caught the body of the child and thought that he might survive if the bush broke his fall. He couldn't bear the thought of spending the night alone at the mercy of Aaron who no doubt had other things planned so that he died a horrible death. He knew Sarah would be worried sick and he really didn't want her to get stressed so close to the birth of their child. He feared for his family's lives, he was useless to them trapped up on the hillside. If he could get to Sarah, then they could move to another village but he was so tired of running. After a while of sitting and thinking, Michael decided that the best idea was to find the British consulate in Kabul so that he could find a way to get them all back to England. He would get them to ring his sister; he knew her number off by heart.

As the light faded, Michael stood on the edge of the outcrop ready to jump; he really couldn't understand why he'd been branded a killer. Sarah had said that the villagers called him the quiet one and it saddened him to think that they should conclude that by having this disposition that he was capable of carrying out such a dreadful act. He wished bitterly that he hadn't lost his memory at the same time as the boy had gone missing; it made things so much more awkward as he couldn't remember where he was when the boy disappeared. Sarah had said that he'd gone to the well to collect water and he tried to imagine himself carrying the tubs but he couldn't remember any part of the journey and the more he tried to remember the less clear his imaginings became; he was becoming infuriated by his lack of memory. He needed to get back to Sarah to tell her what had happened and to make sure she and Jawid were safe. He hoped the village wouldn't turn on her for harbouring what they thought was a murderous paedophile.

Carefully, Michael lined himself up with the same bush that had caught the body of the child and it did occur to him that the drop from the ledge was a long way down and that he could die; he tried not to dwell too long on that possibility. Summoning all his courage Michael stepped off the ledge and as he fell he tried to use his arms to steer himself, the pain in his collarbone was severe. He hit the bush with force, its pointed branches dug into his legs and then because of the weight of his body, the whole bush came away from the hill and he plunged down the steep slope to the track below. He landed face downwards and then groaning, turned his battered body over so that he could see the dusky sky again. Slowly he got to his feet, his legs were bleeding from scrapes and grazes but he'd no other broken bones. He felt as if he'd once again defeated death and was back in control of his life.

By the time Michael reached the village it was dark and he was thankful to slip into the shadows of the houses as they gave him the cover he needed to reach his own house without being detected. With care, Michael circled the house to make sure that there were no unwanted visitors waiting for him. He didn't believe for one minute that the villagers would rest easy and believe that he would perish on the hillside. He hid behind the tree in the garden and surveyed the front of the house. The house was quiet and the front door was closed which surprised him as he fully expected Sarah to be standing in the doorway trying to cool herself.

He crept up to the front of the house and listened by the door to see if he could hear her or Jawid but he couldn't. He was uneasy and wasn't sure what to do. He needed to speak to her and tell her that he was going to go to Kabul to find someone to help them all. He needed to hold her and reassure her. Michael turned to slip away so that he could hide for a while and watch the house, he was sure that Sarah would open the door at some point. As he turned to leave, he saw two men standing in front of him barring his way; he hadn't heard them approach. They both had their arms folded and looked at him in a threatening manner. The larger man standing on the right, hurled himself at him but at the last moment, he stepped to the side so that the man crashed into the front door. Outraged, his attacker turned and furiously bared his teeth at him. His accomplice did nothing but just watched as they circled sizing each other up. Michael knew that the giant was going to throw a punch at any moment; this came flying towards his head. Michael blocked the punch with his left hand, grabbed the man's right wrist with his left hand and twisted it, stepped in so that his leg was in the back of his attacker's, dropped his weight and pushed the giant's chin away so that he lost his balance and watched as he fell back on the floor. Luckily for Michael the man smashed his head on the tree, knocking himself unconscious.

The other man seeing that Michael hadn't been restrained picked up a stick to strike him with. Michael swiftly moved out of the strike range and kicked him in the side of the head so that he dropped to his knees. He immediately, whilst the man was dazed went for the pressure points in his neck and pushed him to the floor until he was unconscious too. For a moment Michael thought he'd killed both of them, it was so easy to do but he could see that they were breathing.

He looked back at the door and knew that he'd very little time to escape from the village. Urgently he rapped on the door and called to Sarah. The door opened and she stood before him; a man with dark hair and a long black beard stood behind her with a gun at her neck. Tears streamed down Sarah's face, he couldn't tell if it was from fear or from disappointment. "Don't cry Sarah. Let her go, it's me you want," he called out. "I didn't do what you think I did. It's a big mistake. Do you understand? I wouldn't hurt anyone, let alone a child."

Sarah's captor's eyes narrowed as he looked at his comrades lying unconscious on the floor. "I think I have seen enough!" he snarled. "We've found an item of clothing belonging to you at the scene of the murder.

Your guilt is beyond all doubt. You will suffer for this barbaric act."

"How do you know it was mine? It could have belonged to anyone in this village. This is wrong; you can't accuse me of murder, this is ludicrous."

Michael looked at Sarah pleadingly and he could see through her fear that she believed him and her eyes told him that she trusted him and it was enough to give him hope.

Michael put up his hands to show that he was giving himself up; he had to get the bearded man to release Sarah he didn't want her to get hurt. The man pushed her back into the room and Michael could see that she was ok and he saw her comfort Jawid at the back of the room. He was hiding his face so that he didn't see anything awful happen to his father. Michael wondered if the bearded man was going to shoot him there and then. He knew he was going to die; there was no reason to keep him alive if it had already been decided that he was guilty of murder. He waited in the darkness, the breath in his body gone from his lungs, for the shot to be fired.

20

As the afternoon progressed, the autumn air became a lot colder so Tom brought Evie back to his house so that they could have a hot drink and plan their futures together. All of his family had gone from the church to his cousin's wedding reception, leaving them alone together. Evie discovered that Tom had lived in the same house all his life and the front room was almost as she remembered it to be when she had tea with him in 2013; only the wallpaper had been replaced. After much discussion, they both decided that they would find work in one of the larger southern coastal towns, rent somewhere to live and then visit the Chanctonbury Ring as often as they could in the hope that one day their pleas would be heard and they would be returned to their own time.

Evie wasn't sure how they had managed to do it but with only a few pounds between them, her grandmother's ring, an eighteenth birthday present which they hoped to pawn to raise money for a deposit on a room and with just a small bag of clothes each, they slipped away unnoticed from their villages and then ran off together.

Evie had been so nervous when she'd gone back to her house to gather her belongings; she'd prayed that she wouldn't have to face her mother. She was much relieved to find that she wasn't at home but she suspected that she might return at any moment with a policeman in tow and have her arrested for burglary.

As Evie and Tom rode on the bus to Brighton and then walked the streets looking for accommodation, she'd trembled with shock, she couldn't understand why she was so frightened of her mother; she really didn't care for her now but she remembered feeling this bad all those years ago when she'd been travelling down to Dorset to stay with her friend Milly. After sixty years, it still upset her to think that she'd disappointed her parents so badly and that their relationship would never be repaired.

Evie and Tom both had a life time of knowledge and confidence beyond their years so finding work proved to be relatively easy. Evie found work in a cafe in Brighton and Tom, with his mechanical skills worked as an apprentice in a garage. Out of school uniform and wearing some of his dad's clothes Tom just about passed as an adult.

At first Evie had been distraught that she hadn't gone back to see Albert on his last night before he went to war but Tom had persuaded her that everything would turn out all right and that somehow she would have a son and name him Edward. Tom's prophesy, turned out to be true. After four months, Evie noticed a change in her body, she knew what to look out for and when she was certain that she was pregnant with Albert's child, she decided to tell Tom. She was hesitant to do this at first and she hoped that he wouldn't be disgusted and she hoped that her news wouldn't wreck their relationship.

Although they shared a bed and cared for each other deeply, they were not lovers and were more like a brother and sister. Tom was old fashioned and she knew that he wouldn't consider being more than that until he was married. She often watched him sleeping and longed for him to hold her in his arms and make love to her; just how she imaged it should be and not how she'd experienced it.

One evening, Evie sat by the window of their small bedsit and waited for Tom to return home from work. They lived over a shop in a busy part of Brighton and as she watched for him, she massaged one of her feet with her hands. Her feet ached as her shoes were worn and she'd been on her feet all day serving customers in the cafe. Despite having to work so hard, Evie felt empowered. She enjoyed making an honest living without anyone judging her. She found herself wondering if her mother and father were still alive and if they even missed her.

Evie looked over at a saucepan of water, it was starting to boil. She was heating up the water so that Tom could wash his oil covered hands when he got in. She then wondered what she would make for their dinner that night; there wasn't much left in their larder to eat. Evie opened the door and saw a small tin of spam, a couple of carrots and a potato on the shelf and she decided that she might try and make a stew; it was so hard to make war time rations last all the week. Evie had always despised Spam but as the days passed, the lack of food made anything edible exquisite. Anxiously Evie rubbed her stomach; soon they would have another mouth to feed and she hoped that Tom wouldn't react badly to her news.

Tom smiled warmly as he came into the room and her heart fluttered, partly with anxiety but also with desire, he'd become quite muscular since working in the garage; she found this to be quite an attractive quality. Embarrassed, Evie blushed and hoped that he wouldn't notice the colour in her cheeks and read her thoughts. Tom smiled and looked at her curiously but didn't question her. From his bag he produced two eggs and placed them carefully in the empty fruit bowl in front of her.

"Where did you get those?" enquired Evie surprised by his find.

"Ahhh... now you're asking. There's a farm up the road from the garage and I managed to get one of their tractors going this afternoon and because Mr Troubridge was so pleased with my work, after he paid us, he brought over some bacon and some eggs. The boss took the bacon home and most of the eggs but he gave me these two. We're going to eat like kings tonight," laughed Tom, tipping the hot water into the sink, so he could wash his hands.

Evie stood up and taking up one of the eggs looked at it as if it were made of gold.

"Amazing," she said happily. "I'd never thought eggs could bring so much joy. When we get back to our time, I'll not be so wasteful."

"Oh yes, that's the other thing. I was talking to one of the farm hands and they exercise their horses on the Downs and are looking for people to help. We could get to the Ring a lot quicker that way. Can you ride?" Tom asked, faltering as he spoke. The look on Evie's face told him that she didn't like the idea.

"Oh dear," sighed Evie sitting heavily on a kitchen chair. "There's something I need to tell you," she said clasping her hands together on the table top. "I don't think it's a good idea for me to ride horses at the moment. Remember when we were in your camp, I told you that my life was in tatters. Well, what I didn't tell you is that I had slept with Albert, just before I met you and now I'm pretty sure that I'm pregnant. In fact I know I am. He was very persuasive and needed to seal his love in some way as we didn't have time to marry before he went to war; not that my parents would have been pleased about our marriage as Albert wasn't in our class. All I could think of at the time was about my son Edward and that I must do everything in my power to guarantee his future. I just let him do it to me, I didn't enjoy it... What I don't want you thinking is that I have no morals and that I'm a terrible person. Albert really did love me, I know that now and I'm sure if he'd survived the war, then he would have come back for me. Please don't think badly of me."

Tom sat down next to Evie and placed his warm hands over hers. It wasn't the reaction she'd been expecting. "You are not a bad person; you must never think that of yourself. This is what you wanted Evie, I said it would happen somehow, you're going to have a son and will call him Edward." Tom's face was serious yet his eyes told her that he was sincere and he didn't show any resentment.

"I'm frightened that when I'm unable to work for a while, you'll hate me because I will become a burden to you. I couldn't bear that." A tear started to trickle down her face.

"I will never hate you," replied Tom, wiping the tear away from her cheek. "You are my life now and whatever happens we will work it out. I just wish I was old enough to marry you before the baby is born."

Evie stared opened mouthed at Tom "You would marry me. What about Martha and your daughter, how do you think that will work out?" Evie didn't like to mention them but they were part of his life too and they should be considered.

Tom stared out of the window for a moment and tried not to think of them, he'd managed to blot out his future since he'd moved in with Evie. He didn't like to remember them, he was living for the moment and was taking each day as it came and had discovered that he could think of nothing better than being with Evie. He would be lost without her but he knew that he would be equally lost if he didn't have a life with Martha or see his own child in her arms. "I don't know Evie, I don't know what the future holds for me, all I know is that I'm in love with you and I will do anything for you."

He stood up and pulled Evie to her feet, held her close to him and kissed her tenderly on the lips. Evie kissed him back freely, waves of euphoria washing over her, she'd never wanted to be kissed so much - her life was complete.

That night as Tom slept, Evie lay in his arms and his warm body next to hers felt so reassuring. Earlier he'd laid her on the bed and kissed her passionately but hadn't once lost control, it wasn't his nature as he had his principles. She returned his kisses without tension or regret and knew that she loved him more than she thought possible.

The starlight caught her eyes; they hadn't drawn the curtains or eaten anything for that matter. She gazed up at the night sky, the stars shone more brightly than she'd ever seen them. Every sense she owned was heightened, was more intense, she felt truly alive; her body was wickedly throbbing with pleasure with the thought of making love to Tom. In a few years time, they could marry and their age difference wouldn't matter. She didn't care that Tom was younger than her. What was three years, it was nothing. He was everything she longed for, he was loving, handsome, he was fifteen going on forty; his young exterior was only a facade. She lay in the arms of a man not a boy. Evie drifted off into a peaceful sleep and wished that life would stay as it was; she had no desire to go back to the Chanctonbury Ring and change things. This life was all that she wanted now.

The morning stole into their room quietly, trying not to wake them. It was Sunday and both Evie and Tom didn't have to go to work. As the morning light brightened and sparkled on the clock on the wall, Tom woke with a start from his sleep and trying not to disturb Evie, sat up; he thought that he'd woken up late. As he tried to focus on the hands of the clock, he realized with a huge sense of relief, that it was Sunday and he didn't have to rush about like a mad thing to get ready and run to work. He decided to get up as apart for wanting to use the bathroom, he was starving. The eggs he'd brought home the day before were calling to him; he decided that he would cook these and anything else he could find for their breakfast.

When Tom returned to the room, he'd only been gone a minute, the communal bathroom had been empty, he smiled as he watched Evie stirring from her sleep; she looked so beautiful when she slept. He felt overjoyed that she actually cared for him and perhaps loved him too. Over the past few months he'd hoped that by living together, that she would regard him as more than a friend or a younger brother. His patience had been rewarded; he'd taken a chance when he kissed her and had known that he might ruin everything they had but he could bear it no longer, he had to declare his love for her. He hoped that her reason for stopping his cousin's wedding was that she wanted him to marry her rather than Martha.

The fact that she was pregnant with another man's child didn't bother him, it was what she wanted most of all in the world and they would somehow find the money to bring her baby up. He decided that he would ask his boss for more money; he knew he was more than an apprentice and had proved his worth. Tom dismissed this idea. It was unlikely that he would get a raise as the garage wasn't doing that well. Many of their customers were not returning as they were not using their cars as much due to the lack of petrol. Tom sighed and knew that he would have to find a better paid job.

He looked back at Evie with concern and hoped that she would wake up and be happy that they were a couple. They would have to take each day as it came and enjoy the time they had been allocated, he wasn't sure what was happening to them and why exactly they had gone back in time; this kind of thing only happened in stories.

Evie opened her eyes and smiled warmly at him and his fears evaporated like a bubble bursting and his heart pounded a little with delight.

"What do you want to do today?" asked Tom as he searched through the cupboard for the frying pan. "Are you hungry? I'm going to cook breakfast."

Evie sat up and looked down at herself, she was still wearing her waitress uniform and she hadn't taken her hair down to brush it. She decided that she must look such a dreadful sight and hoped that Tom wasn't too shocked. "I must wash and change," replied Evie. "What must you think of me?"

"I think you are the most beautiful woman, I've ever laid eyes on," replied Tom lighting the cooker ring.

Evie smiled, unpinned her hair and quickly brushed it through, until she felt that it looked half respectable. Carefully, she slipped out from the covers and placed her feet on the floor ready to stand up. The past couple of weeks she'd felt a little nauseous and light headed when she got up. She knew that she would feel fine in a moment; this was one aspect of pregnancy that she hadn't enjoyed.

"Are you ok?" asked Tom, breaking the eggs on the side of the pan, next to the spam fritters. "Do you want some water?"

Evie nodded. "Yes please, I just feel a little sick. It will pass."

Tom brought a glass of water over to her and sat down on the bed next to her.

"I do love you, you know?" he said brushing her hair back from her face.

"I love you too," Evie replied. She took a sip of water and smiled; last night hadn't just been a dream.

Tom looked back at the eggs spitting in the pan and ran back to the cooker, he wasn't that good at cooking and even the simplest of catering tasks were a challenge to him. It was a wonder he'd kept himself alive after Martha had died. Tom found a slice of bread for each of them and after laying them on the plates, triumphantly shovelled the spam and eggs on top, pleased that he hadn't broken the yolks.

Breakfast was eaten with relish, Evie wasn't sure if she was supposed to eat eggs. There were so many foods she knew that an expectant mother should avoid but she was so hungry that she was sure that no harm would come to the baby that fluttered inside her.

"Perhaps we could go for a walk along the promenade today?" she suggested looking out of the window. "It's quite bright today; I don't think it's going to rain."

"I'm not so sure if that's a good idea, there hasn't been an air raid for days. What if there was an air attack? We'd have to run to avoid getting gunned down. I'd be much happier if we went to the park and fed the ducks, would you mind terribly?"

"Oh the war, I'd forgotten. Yes the park that will be fine. I'll get washed and changed and we'll go." Evie said, leaving the table. Her life now, was all a bit surreal, the park sounded like an idyllic place to go, it could have been pouring down with rain and would still have sounded the perfect place for two lovers to spend time together. "I won't be long," she called as she left the room.

Evie walked along the dark landing towards the bathroom and joined a queue. She'd picked a bad time to change. All the lodgers in the building were waiting to get washed. Miss Roach, an elderly spinster was at the back of queue. She lived in the ground floor rooms, she smiled apologetically at Evie. She was a tall lady with grey hair and she always wore a blue woollen suit. Miss Roach had a voice in the building and spoke out for the residents if something needed saying to the landlord or to their noisy neighbours. She'd also taken it upon herself to look after cats that had lost their homes in the air raids and collected scraps from all the restaurants and cafes in Brighton to feed them. Unbeknown to the landlord, she currently had fifteen cats living with her.

"The downstairs bathroom is out of order; been like that all week!" she said angrily. "It took months to get the toilet fixed last time it stopped working. I'll have to speak to the landlord when he comes round for his money tomorrow and give him a piece of my mind."

"Oh dear, that's a shame" Evie replied. "At least you can come up here. I'll try again later," said Evie looking doubtfully at the queue waiting for the bathroom door to open. She walked back to the room and decided she would wash and change there. She would use the public convenience in the park and hoped she could hang on that long.

Evie opened the door with her key and walked in. "There's such a queue Tom, the bathroom downstairs is..." She stopped talking and looked around the room. He'd gone; it was almost as if he'd disappeared into thin air. She hadn't seen him pass her on the landing and was sure that she would have noticed if he had. She sighed apprehensively and thought perhaps that he might have slipped by when she was talking to Miss Roach. "Yes," she said to herself. "He's gone out for something and will be back in a minute." She then spotted his shoes by the bed, the only pair he owned. Surely he wouldn't go out with bare feet? In panic, Evie ran to the open window, to see if she could see him outside.

Their room was on the first floor and she wondered if Tom had climbed out of the window and dropped down. She couldn't understand why he would jump without his shoes on as there was broken glass and building debris in the front garden and he would have cut his feet.

Evie looked frantically along the street to see if she could see him. It wasn't very busy, there were a few people on their way to church or taking a dog for a walk; Tom wasn't amongst them. She couldn't tear herself away from the window; she didn't want to miss any clue, any small thing that would explain his disappearance. She flung the window up as wide as it would go and stuck her head out so she could see further down the street. She could feel tears streaming down her cheeks and she knew with a painful realisation that Tom had gone.

Defeated, Evie slumped face down on the bed and sobbed. Unhindered, every reason for his desertion circled in her head, cruelly tormenting her. She had to keep reminding herself that he'd told her that he loved her and that she must not think badly of him. Something had happened to him, something tragic, perhaps the Chanctonbury Ring had taken him off somewhere and she must believe in his love and that one day she would find him and that she should never give up hope. She tried not to listen but the thought she could hear someone whispering in her ear that it must be very hard for a man to love a girl if she is carrying another man's child.

Tom didn't come home that night and Evie tossed and turned alone in her bed, dreaming of her mother shouting at her. With a down turned mouth and deep scowl lines across her forehead; she kept calling Evie a fool, told her that she was a disgrace to her family and waved her finger at her with disapproval. Her father sat in his arm chair with his head in his hands in grief, never once looking up at his daughter and then slowly melted into the armchair. Fearfully Evie woke herself up;

she didn't want to be left in the room with just her mother. "Tom," she gasped. He didn't reply. "What am I going to do without you? Where are you? Please come back," she sobbed. The air raid siren drowned out her words. Distraught Evie ignored it, hoping that a bomb would fall on her and put an end to the dreadful pain she felt inside.

21

Not wanting to waste any more time, Amy walked over to the cherry tree and picking up the hoe, she started to scrape at the ground in an attempt to dig up the body of the baby. It had become evident that Mrs Renshaw, influenced by Lord Grey wouldn't give her or the police permission to dig without a battle. Amy wanted to get the ordeal over with and go home, she wasn't sure where home was and hoped to find in her car, a letter or bill with her address on. Before she'd met Ted, she'd rented a flat in Horsham and she hoped that this is where she still lived. The prospect of going back to that flat filled her with joy but she wasn't sure of anything since visiting the Chanctonbury Ring and wondered how long her new found freedom would last.

"Please stop digging immediately," yelled the police officer.

Amy stopped and looked down at the hole she'd created and hoped she would be able to find some evidence; a bone or a shred of material. There was a few strands of muddy material sticking out of the earth which could have been anything and with renewed confidence, Amy squatted down and pointed to the shreds. "There, look," she said. "I think this is part of the blanket the baby was wrapped in when it was buried."

Amy looked back up at the policeman to see his reaction and then was dismayed to see that Lord Grey was now attached to his back and she could see by the look on the policeman's face that he was unconvinced. Lord Grey smiled a triumphant crooked smile.

"I've a good mind to charge you with criminal damage or for wasting police time," yelled the police officer. "If you are not gone from these premises within the next two minutes then I will have no option but to take you into custody!"

Amy stood up and looked the police officer squarely in the face. "If you ring Inspector Brandon, then I think you'll find that I have been very helpful in the past and have recovered several bodies. Amy hoped that this part of history hadn't been erased too.

The police officer nodded as if agreeing with Amy's suggestion but he was only being patronizing. "Why would I want to call someone that retired two years ago?" he scoffed as Mrs Renshaw joined them. She looked concerned and her countenance had changed since losing Lord Grey from her back.

"I think you should dig some more," she suggested, urging Amy to pick up the hoe and to scrape the soft ground beneath the tree. Amy continued, determined to find some concrete evidence and stop the police officer from arresting her.

"How dare you disobey me!" spat the police officer moving towards Amy. She dodged him and he tripped over a root and fell onto the floor, almost dislodging Lord Grey from his back. She could see from the ghouls shocked face that he would be vulnerable if he should lose his host. Amy stopped digging and then without thinking about what she was doing grabbed the police officer's shoulders as he got to his feet and placed her hands through Lord Grey's hands. She knew that the ghoul was repulsed by her and he released his hand and tried to hold onto the police officer's head. Amy did the same and quickly passed her hands through his wherever he tried to hold on to his host. The police officer spun around to face Amy. "What on earth are you doing?" he yelled bemused by her actions and as he did, Lord Grey fell off him and onto the ground. Amy wasn't sure what to do next, she suspected that Lord Grey would try and latch on to the nearest person. The spirit was furious and scared; he looked around him for someone nearer enough to leap on to.

The police officer, walked across the lawn to retrieve his hat that had fallen off when he tripped and as he walked, he shook his head as if he was confused. "Where's the body then?" he asked having forgotten his past threats.

Amy looked anxiously towards him. She needed to get Mrs Renshaw and he as far away from Lord Grey as possible.

I need you both to follow me, she said running towards the pond, trying to get as much distance between them and Lord Grey.

"Why what's the matter?" asked Mrs Renshaw, following her. "I thought you found something where you were digging."

"I did," replied Amy. "Only I needed to get you to safety first, I think I might have hit... hit a gas pipe." she said desperately looking back at Lord Grey, who now clung to the cherry tree. Seeing Amy staring at him he beckoned to her and his face softened. She couldn't believe his nerve; he was actually asking her for help.

"I didn't smell gas? Did you?" she asked the police officer who had joined them.

"No," he replied. "Where is the body then?" he continued, looking puzzled.

"Didn't you see?" asked Mrs Renshaw. "Only a minute ago you asked her to stop digging? I don't think you've hit a gas main dear," she said to Amy, patting her arm. "The main will be several feet underground and you've only gone down a few inches. Perhaps you could smell gases coming up from the dead body. Oh how awful!" she exclaimed.

The police officer was still mystified and looked to Amy for guidance. Amy wasn't sure what to do next, she needed to get rid of Lord Grey for good, he needed to be exorcised but she didn't have a clue how to do it. Images of crucifixes, garlic, holy water and priests with incense flashed through her head. She'd once seen a film where a psychic had asked a bad spirit to leave a house where it had been causing unrest and it had receded back into the darkness. Amy decided it was worth a try and called out to Lord Grey in a firm voice. "In the name of all that is good," she began, she was afraid to use Jesus' name, she'd not been to church or thought about God since she was a child. "Leave this house, you are not welcome here. Go back to Hell where you belong, you, have no place here now, you reign of tyranny is over" she continued trying her best to sound as forceful as she could. Lord Grey looked at her and sneered.

"Are you ok?" asked Mrs Renshaw, kindly. "Lord Grey was one of our 'Who Done It' characters, he's not real. Would you like to come inside and have a glass of water?"

"You must know that this house was once owned by a Lord Grey," replied Amy. "He killed a maid that worked here and murdered her baby, his illegitimate son. The real Lord Grey is here in the grounds there's no gas, he's by the grave, he doesn't want us to go near it, he doesn't want the truth to be unearthed."

"Oh dear," replied Mrs Renshaw looking concerned. "Is that why you told him to go back to Hell? Didn't it work?"

"No, you'll probably need a priest to do that. I just see spirits, that's all; I don't know how to get rid of bad spirits."

"Let's get this straight," said the police officer, trying to understand what was going on. "You say there's a ghost by that grave stopping you from digging? You're having a laugh right?"

Amy was becoming exasperated; she knew if she could dig a little further, she would be able to show the police officer that she wasn't a lunatic. "Look," said Amy. "I know I sound like a mad woman but if you stay here and let me dig a bit more, I'll be able to prove to you that there's a body over by the cherry tree." The police officer shrugged his shoulders as if he'd given up hope and allowed Amy to walk over towards the grave and Lord Grey. Amy knew that Lord Grey wouldn't leap on to her; she could see that he felt repulsed by her and his face contorted with revulsion as she approached. A crazy thought struck Amy; she wondered what would happen if she drove her hand into his chest where his heart was and whether this would have any effect on him. She could see that Lord Grey had read her mind he looked horrified that she would consider such a feat. Panic stricken, he clambered further up the cherry tree until he was at the top of the trunk and just out of reach and then whistled in the direction of the house.

Amy ran to the grave and picked up the hoe and started to scrape away at the earth where she'd seen the strands of material, whilst Lord Grey shrieked obscenities at her and eventually Amy unearthed a skeletal hand. It was the servant girl's hand and she was clutching a decaying blanket. Amy stepped back and her eyes narrowed as she looked up at Lord Grey.

"You're an evil bastard," she exclaimed. "You buried that poor young girl here and put her dead baby in her arms. You make me sick. You deserve to have what's left of your heart ripped out."

"You just try it," he snarled. "Why do you think you're here? You're not all goodness and light, you've turned your back on a murder or two before, haven't you Amy Warren? You'll join me in Hell one of these fine days, that's for sure."

Amy stopped digging and stared coldly up at Lord Grey, her breath had gone from her lungs and she felt a cold chill run down her spine.

"I wasn't sure; I couldn't prove it could I? There was just the odd coincidence but there was no evidence, no real proof that Ted killed those girls. I'm no collaborator; their deaths have nothing to do with me."

"Is that so!" he replied. "Then why do you ignore their spirits when they call out to you? You don't want to hear the truth do you? You are a traitor Amy, you are no better than a murderer," he snarled.

A ghost of a Great Dane appeared by the tree and Lord Grey flung himself onto its back and the dog ran into the house with Lord Grey attached. Relieved, Amy stared down at the grave in silence, his words had cut her deep and she felt like crying. She looked up at the sky and the countryside around for reassurance but all she could hear in the distance were the cries of the girls that she suspected, no she couldn't say suspected; the reality was that Ted had killed these poor women that cried out to her for help. She had to face the brutal truth that she'd been living with a serial killer and she'd turned her back on this horrific fact as the reality was too much to bear. She shuddered; Ted did exist in 2016 and his victims were out there too.

Amy tried not to hear his victims calling out to her, she could hear them making their way to her from their resting places; staggering towards her from the shadows and was alarmed to find that there were now so many more victims crying out for help. She'd always convinced herself that Ted wasn't capable of such a terrible act. Lord Grey's words burnt into her conscience and he was right she was no better than Ted; her denial of the truth had cost lives.

"Are you all right, dear?" called Mrs Renshaw. "Is it safe to come over?"

Amy nodded and both Mrs Renshaw and the police officer came back to the grave.

"Look," said Amy pointing to the bones of the maid's hand. "I didn't realise it but the mother of the child is buried here too."

Seeing the evidence he needed, the police officer picked up his phone and called for forensic assistance. After Amy had given more details to the police officer, she looked for her car. She'd found keys in a side pocket in her bag and realised after clicking on the fob that the new Smart car parked on the drive seemed to belong to her.

She sat in the driver's seat which was in the perfect position and then looked through the glove box to see if she could find anything with her name on but there was nothing. Amy turned the key in the ignition and the engine sprang into life and she noticed that a location finder screen had lit up within the dashboard too. Seeing a home icon on the screen, Amy touched this and was pleasantly surprised to find that she lived in Horsham. She didn't however seem to live in the flat she'd once rented but instead in a street that she'd always liked. The thought of going to Findon and seeing Ted was frightening but she knew that soon she would have to go to his flat and make sure he still lived there before she contacted the police again.

Amy drove along Bartholomew Way and she looked for where she might live. The voice from the location finder told her to turn into a close and then told her that she'd arrived at her destination. Amy drove out of the close but the voice told her to do a u turn which she did, not wanting to upset the droning voice and again she was told that she'd arrived at her destination.

She decided to park on the road and then walked back into the close. She then tried to work out which of the houses might be hers; there were six to choose from. She picked one that had no other cars on the drive and as she walked up to the front door, she then tried to look through the front windows to see if anyone was at home. She really couldn't believe that she could afford to rent such a big house; she'd obviously thrived at Treadmill Marketing.

Hesitantly, she put one of the keys that looked to be a front door key, into the lock and turned it. The lock turned, she pushed the door and it swung open and cautiously she stepped inside. A large black cat appeared from a room at the end of the hall and then ran meowing towards her. Amy froze. She didn't like cats that much; especially the ones that looked like they might attack you. If this was her house then she wasn't sure why she would have a cat and she doubted whether this was where she lived. She called out to see if anyone was there but nobody replied. She felt like she was breaking in to someone else's house. The cat rubbed itself on her legs, still purring as if it was pleased to see her. Amy looked down at it and wondered why it was being so friendly.

After stroking the cat for a few moments, she decided to look around the house to see if she recognised anything that belonged to her. The first room she entered was the front room. She scanned the room for pictures she recognised or for books that she'd read but there were none. She looked admiringly at the black leather couches with modern contrasting cushions neatly placed along them. She wasn't sure if she would have left the room so organised. In the past, she'd been forced to keep Ted's flat tidy but it didn't come naturally to her. She looked at a magazine on the coffee table to see if she recognised it and smiled. It was a magazine about celebrities that she might have bought if she could have afforded it.

The next floor of the house was more rewarding; the cat followed her and waited at the top of the stairs as she entered the master bedroom which looked like it had been decorated and furnished by a designer. In one of the drawers next to a double bed was a notebook. She recognised it instantly and relaxed, she didn't have to look over her shoulder any more; she really did live in the house. She flicked through the pages to find notes about the years she'd lost. These scribbled notes formed her misery diary where she wrote down her feelings when she was sad or confused. She'd secretly written in it many times when she was with Ted, just to try and make sense of their relationship.

Amy threw herself back onto the bed, eager to read the pages. The cat jumped up onto the bed with her and rubbed its head against her arm for attention. Cautiously, she stroked its back and it purred happily as it lay down next to her. Amy looked at the cat's name tab hanging from its collar. She was named Molly and under the name was a mobile number, it was hers, she knew it well. This really was her tidy house and probably her cat too and she could hardly believe it. She lay back and turned to the front page of the notebook and started to read. Although it was her handwriting, the words were different to those she remembered. She read on and then flicked through to see if she remembered any of it.

Amy's mobile started ringing; she pulled it from her pocket and looked at the caller's name; it was James. She stared at the phone and wasn't sure whether she should answer; she remembered that Vicki had said that she was going to meet him for the first time that night. She tried to cancel the call and not knowing how to do this, found that she'd accepted it.

"Hi Amy, it's James."

The phone was on loud speaker. Amy stared at the phone with alarm. James' voice sounded upbeat and his tone was friendly. She decided to reply, it would be good to have someone to talk to, someone that might be able to make sense of what was happening to her and someone to support her when she went to the police about Ted. "Hi James, how are you?" she replied.

22

Sunlight streamed in through the shutters into the house waking Sarah with a start. She'd hardly slept at all and had tossed and turned all night worrying about Michael. She'd been too frightened to stop the men from taking him away and wished she could have done something more. Jawid believed that his father was going to be killed and had cried inconsolably; she'd allowed him to sleep with her and had held him until he went to sleep. He now slept peacefully next to her and although he was due to go to school; she thought it better that he didn't go as the other children might pick on him once they heard that his father had been found guilty of the murder of their friend.

Sarah thought back to evening before and remembered Michael's pleading eyes asking her to believe him that he'd nothing to do with the murder. She considered herself to be a good judge of character and thought that there was no conceivable way that he could hurt a child. Also, the blood stained clothing found near the murder scene couldn't have been Michael's as she could account for every item of clothing that he owned. He'd been unfairly accused of murder.

Farzad, the man that had held her at gunpoint, was regarded as the elder of the village and had the last word if there were any criminal issues. He wasn't a compassionate man and penalties for breaking the law were severe - she feared for Michael's life. Farzad was a very odd man, she didn't like the way he looked at Jawid and she suspected that he'd murdered the boy.

She became overwhelmed by grief with the thought of losing Michael. Her sorrow was paired with desperation as she wouldn't be able to feed herself or her children if there wasn't a wage coming in. She needed to speak to Farzad and convince him of Michael's innocence; she didn't hold out much hope but she would never forgive herself if she didn't try. Gently, she woke Jawid; he smiled as he opened his eyes and then frowned as he remembered what had happened to his father. "Get up Jawid, we need to go and see someone that might be able to help daddy. Get washed and dressed."

Eagerly, Jawid jumped up and ran to the door ready to wash himself and then stopped. "What about school? He asked. "I need to go today as men from the BBC are coming to make a film about us. I should go; I want to tell them about my teacher."

Sarah was surprised by his words and smiled as a fleeting glimmer of hope appeared before her. If she went to the school, she might be able to get someone from the BBC to help her. If she explained what had happened then they could contact the British consulate and let them know what was happening to Michael. Sarah got up from the bed and quickly changed her clothes. "Come on Jawid don't worry about washing, we must go to your school straight away and speak to the men at the BBC. If we tell them what happened last night, they will help," she said taking Jawid's hand.

She walked as quickly as she could to the school, her stomach was aching as she walked along and she felt hot and dizzy. As they reached the school, she noticed a pickup truck parked outside. A tall man with fair hair dressed in Western clothes stood in the back of the truck and was organising filming equipment. Sarah sighed with relief and ran over to him. "Excuse me," she called. "Are you from the BBC?"

The man frowned at Sarah as if he was having trouble understanding what she was saying. She decided to try again and thought perhaps she may have spoken too quickly and that he might not understand her.

"Do you speak English and are you from the BBC?" she asked again slowing her words down so that he could understand her."

"I'm sorry," he replied in English. "I don't understand your language. If you're asking if we are filming in the school, then yes we are. There's a translator in the classroom, she might be able to help you when we've finished filming."

Sarah was astounded; she'd spoken English to the man and yet he didn't understand her. She turned to Jawid and asked if he had understood what she had just said. He shook his head but looked confused. Jawid didn't speak English. Sarah decided that she would try again. "I'm English too, my name is Sarah Brunning and I come from West Sussex and need help," she pleaded.

"Look I'm sorry, I've nothing to give you, please take your hands off my truck and go and beg elsewhere."

Sarah took her hands off his truck and stepped back aghast; he really couldn't understand her and thought that she was asking for food or money. Despondently, she turned away from the man and walked towards the door of the school and with renewed hope went into the classroom. She would find the translator that the man had spoken about, she didn't care if they were filming, she didn't have time to wait, she needed to save Michael's life and she hoped that it wasn't too late.

***

Michael lay on the floor in a darkened room; the shutters were closed and only let in a little light. The room had no furniture and had a few sacks and packing boxes in it. There was a musty smell of old fat and mould. His hands and feet were bound and he'd a rag tied across his mouth so he couldn't call out. He could feel dry blood on his face from the blow he'd received before he'd passed out. He remembered walking through the streets to a house but couldn't imagine how he'd got in the storeroom he was now being held in. Although his head throbbed, he was undeniably alive. His shoulder was almost frozen with pain; having his hands tied up behind him wasn't helping his broken collar bone mend. He was aware of people talking in another room and suspected that they were deciding what to do with him. He hoped that they would take him to a jail in Kabul and if they did then he might have a chance of getting a court hearing.

A scuffling noise disturbed his train of thought and he blinked to make sure he wasn't seeing things. He wasn't alone, two rats were climbing over a pile of sacks on the other side of the room and then as his eyes focused on the sacks, he realised that he was looking at a body and the rats were eating the rotting flesh. The smell in the air was that of decaying flesh, he'd smelt that may times before. The body had been there a while and he was thankful that all he could see was a back and hands, bound up like his. The hands were mummified and claw like. Michael tried to drag his body as far away from the corpse as he could and feared that he too may be left there to die and would then get eaten by the rats - perhaps whilst he was still alive.

***

When Sarah had entered the school room, the film crew stopped their filming and with hands on hips looked across the room at her and Jawid. Urgent whispers spread from child to child and they pointed at Jawid and seemed shocked to see him. With wide eyes, they waited for something appalling to happen. The teacher walked over to the intruders and ushered them out of the building. Sarah resisted but his grip on her arm, showed her that he meant business and he wasn't going to listen to any excuses. Sarah could see that Jawid was mortified.

"What do you mean by, bursting into the classroom like this, especially after what has happened? How dare you show your faces here, you're not welcome; you disgust me."

Sarah was shocked by his reaction; it was almost as if he was accusing both her and Jawid of murder. "I'm sorry," she said. "Jawid's father is innocent, he's not a murderer. You must believe me."

"That's not what the villagers are saying. You know that he is not a good man. Go home and pray to Allah for forgiveness and pray for the family that has lost a child."

Sarah was furious. "How dare you speak to me like that, the villagers are all narrow minded and are being ridiculous. You can't condemn a man on hearsay. I'm not from this village or from this country. Both Michael and I are British and he has a right to be sent to trial in a proper court of law," she shouted pushing past him as she attempted to make her way back to the classroom. The teacher grabbed her arm again and dragged her to the edge of the school grounds. She could see the man in the truck shaking his head.

"Get out of here, you are a liar too," the teacher shouted as he roughly shoved Sarah away, "Don't you dare come back here again or I will send Farzad after you too."

Sarah cried out with despair and then tried to suppress her sobs, she didn't want Jawid to be alarmed but she couldn't hold back the tears as she walked away. She couldn't believe what had just happened; she was being treated as if she was unclean. She felt like she was going mad and was convinced that she'd spoken English to the man in the truck and couldn't understand what was happening to her.

Holding Jawid's hand tightly, Sarah walked away from the school with her mind racing. Jawid was crying and she was worried that he might run off. When she was out of sight of his teacher, she stopped and stood mesmerised for a moment; the people of the village were all like strangers to her and they scowled at her and Jawid with disapproval. She needed to talk to the translator, it was her last hope. She was an old Afghan woman from another village; she'd seen her in the classroom sitting at the top of the classroom by the blackboard. The woman had a kind face and Sarah had noticed that she'd looked on sympathetically when the teacher had marched her out of the classroom. There was a chance that she would listen to her and be able to persuade the camera crew to help.

Sarah sat down on a wall on the main street and rubbed her stomach, it ached and she hoped that the pain would stop if she ate something; she hadn't eaten properly for several hours. Jawid sat next to her and swung his legs anxiously, she knew that a flurry of questions would follow and they did. He was upset that his teacher didn't want him to go to school any more and thought that it was because he talked too much. Sarah tried to reassure him that this wasn't the case and with the last of her coins in her pocket bought him some fruit and bread to eat to take his mind off things. As Sarah waited she watched clouds gathering overhead, there was a distinct chill in the air and it looked like it would rain soon. Crows began to gather on the roof tops and strutted along the tiles in an agitated manner as if they were waiting for someone to die.

***

Michael squinted when daylight hit his eyes but couldn't shield his eyes as his hands were still bound. He'd been dragged out of the room by two of Farzad's men and his legs had been untied. He'd been shoved out into the street and was relieved to be outside away from the storeroom and the decaying body. He wished he could run but he could feel a gun pointed into his back. He wasn't sure where he was being taken and hoped that he was going to a court house or back to Sarah but that was unlikely.

As Michael was pushed along the streets, the people of the village shouted or spat at him as he passed them by. He felt humiliated and frightened and he knew that his future was bleak, there was nowhere to run to and he knew that the end of his life was imminent. All hope was draining from every pore of his body as he walked along. Every ray of sun that caught him dropped a tear on his brow and was unable or unwilling to tell him what his fate would be and then without warning the sun hid behind storm clouds, leaving him to the mercy of his captors.

***

Large drops of rain hit the dry ground and greedily the dust gulped at the water. Sarah stood up and looked for shelter and then gasped as she saw Michael step out onto the high street from an alley opposite to her. She was about to call out to him but realised that some of Farzad's men were escorting him. She was relieved to see that he was still alive but she knew what was about to happen, she'd seen it happen to others that broke the law. Michael was being taken to the village square to be executed; several of the villagers followed eager to see the spectacle. Michael hadn't seen her or Jawid.

Jawid seeing his father, jumped off the wall and chased after him. Sarah called him and told him not to go but he didn't hear and he then disappeared into the crowd as he tried to find his father. A stabbing pain in Sarah's stomach stopped her from chasing after him. When the pain subsided, Sarah fled towards the school to get help, she had to make herself heard; it was a matter of life or death.

As she reached the school she could see the BBC men loading up the camera equipment into the pickup truck and she could see the translator standing outside the school; she seemed to be waiting for someone. Sarah wasted no time, and, trying not to appear hysterical, calmly walked up to the old woman and then couldn't speak to her as she felt a sharp stabbing pain rip around her stomach again. She gasped out loud with pain. The woman seeing her plight, immediately came to her aid. "Are you in labour?" she asked gently.

Sarah nodded with a startled realisation, she'd just passed the cramping feeling she felt as being hunger pains but now she knew that her baby was on its way and had chosen probably the worst time possible. "I must be," she replied holding her swollen stomach. "But it can't come now; Farzad's men are taking my husband to the village square. They're going to kill him for something he didn't do. I came earlier; I thought these men from Britain might be able to stop this murder from taking place. Please can you talk to them, if they go to the square, they might be able to stop this atrocity. I can speak English but they couldn't understand me and thought I was a beggar. Please, you've got to help me." Sarah realised that she'd been speaking English and hoped that the woman would understand her.

The translator frowned as she heard Sarah's problem and then looked towards the camera crew and she was thankful that she understood and would try and help her. "You wait here, I'll see what I can do. They are an arrogant lot but if they take their cameras to the village square, after a good story, some good might come of it. If their presence is noted, it might stop this tragedy from happening."

"Thank you," Sarah wheezed as another contraction took hold; she held the wall to try and steady herself.

Sarah couldn't quite hear what she was saying but she was causing quite a debate and then with an immense sense of relief a camera man and two of the crew charged off towards the village square.

The translator came back to Sarah with a look of triumph on her face. "There, I have a quick tongue and I stirred them up by telling them they would make a fortune. They have taken a camera with them. Now, we need to get you home before you have your baby on the street."

Sarah cried out as she had another contraction and when the pain subsided she took the hand of her new friend and slowly they made their way back to her house. As they walked along, Sarah looked back towards the village square and in the distance she could see the crowds and again she saw the crows; impatiently they circled above the village square.

***

Isolated and accepting what was about to come, Michael stood in the middle of the square and looked at the faces of the villagers. They showed no compassion or forgiveness, their stares were contemptuous and condemning; they jeered and made rude gestures. Michael realised that there was no hope for him and that he was to meet his end playing his part in a mad charade. Aaron had won, he'd reaped his revenge and he hoped he would be satisfied that his uncle had been executed. He could see the blood thirsty crows flying above him and wondered if one of those was Aaron mocking him for feeling afraid.

Michael could sense the crowds tensing as a gun was lifted ready to take aim and then he turned to face them. He didn't want to be shot in the back; he didn't want to die a coward. The crowd became quiet as Farzad's men took aim. Michael didn't feel afraid, he just felt a deep sadness that they thought him to be an evil murderer and that their judgment had been impaired by the people that led them. The rain began to pour down.

A shot fired. He felt it enter his chest and he heard the crowd scream. Michael was surprised by their reaction; he thought that they might cheer. Perhaps, he thought, that there was some humility left in their hearts, perhaps there were some that cared about this travesty of justice. He wished they could have left him alone to continue with his simple existence and allow him be with someone he truly loved. He knew it now, as clear as it was day; he loved Sarah and wanted nothing more than to spend the rest of his life with her. He was grateful that he couldn't see her in the crowd; he didn't want her to see him die in such a brutal way.

Exhaustion swept through his body and he felt himself fall to his knees and he twisted around so that he was facing away from his executioners and it was then that he understood what it was that had distressed the crowd. He saw a small boy, lying dead on the ground in front of him with a gunshot wound to his head. The boy's eyes were wide open and looked towards him, accusing him of shooting him. Michael looked down at his chest; the bullet had gone right through him and into the boy's head. As Michael collapsed onto the floor, he felt the darkness rushing in on him from all sides and felt his breath being squashed from his body. His last thought was that they had shot Jawid too, just like in his dream and this was too heart breaking to bear. Michael stretched out his hand and held on to Jawid's foot to apologise, there was nothing more he could he do.

***

Sarah screamed, she'd never felt such pain in all her life but the lady that had helped her home assured her that the baby's head was crowning and on the next contraction, she was sure that the baby would be born. Sarah wanted to push but knew she must wait and when the contraction came with the little strength she had left she pushed hard and then felt her baby slide out of her.

"We were lucky to get home in time that was a very quick birth. It's a boy, she said cheerily," as she wiped the baby down. The baby began to cry so she wrapped him up and passed him to Sarah. "He probably wants feeding, he's strong and healthy and I think he'll be a hungry one."

Sarah took the baby and looked at his puckered face; he'd lots of dark hair and reminded her of Michael. "Oh he's wonderful, thank you so much for helping me, I don't know what I would have done without you."

"I have delivered many babies. I'm glad I was here for you. I'm sorry about your husband, I hope he comes back. He will be a very proud father."

Sarah looked at the door and prayed that he would walk in and hold his son but a wave of doubt prevented the door from opening. "We'll see," replied Sarah, "I have faith in Allah."

After the translator left, Sarah thought about Jawid, she wished she'd asked the woman to find him but she really didn't want to impose on her any more. She didn't feel strong enough to leave the house and hoped that he would return and thought it was a good sign that he hadn't come running back to her to tell her that his father had been killed. Sarah looked at her new baby with pride; he'd fed from her and was now asleep. She felt very tired and decided to go to sleep for a while, and then, if Michael and Jawid hadn't returned in half an hour, she would take the baby and go and look for them. She fell into a deep sleep exhausted from giving birth.

The next day pictures of a man and child that had just been executed in a village outside Kabul appeared on the news in the western world. Insurgents were accused of carrying out this barbaric act. So shocking was the film that it caused a public outcry and some asked if it would ever be possible for law and order to be maintained in Afghanistan. A man from Kabul told reporters that he would leave his country when the troops were withdrawn as he feared that the Taliban and other insurgents would return and wreak havoc.

23

Evie wasn't sure what had woken her, perhaps it was a bird singing or someone coughing. She breathed in, she was still alive and had managed to survive the bombing raid. She still felt dazed and confused and wondered why Tom had declared that he loved her and had then run off leaving her alone and pregnant. In retrospect, she didn't blame him for leaving her as bringing up another man's child was a lot to deal with. Things would be so much easier if she hadn't fallen in love with him and now she was grieving for his loss; she felt badly let down.

Evie opened her eyes and looked around her room trying to get her bearings. From her bed she could see a window opposite to her, instead of it being to the left of her, where she remembered it to be. In place of war torn buildings, through the window, she could see green hills with dark angry clouds above threatening to rain. She shut her eyes tightly as she was obviously still dreaming. She was dreaming of another time, another life, she was in a familiar place but not her room in Brighton. A wave of sadness flowed over her like a heavy blanket, suffocating her, throwing at her memories of the night to haunt her. She wondered if her grief was making her hallucinate.

Evie opened her eyes again and frowned; perhaps she'd been caught up in the bombing raid and was now in a hospital room or was dead. She rubbed her eyes to confirm that she wasn't seeing things. She looked at the bed she was lying in, it wasn't a double bed, just a single one and across the room, piled neatly on a chair, were clothes that she used to wear when she worked on the farm. There was a small chest of drawers next to her bed and a white door with a black latch, leading to a dressing room. Her heart was now racing; she'd somehow woken up in her room she'd stayed in when Milly had taken her in. Evie's eyes cleared and she looked nostalgically around her room.

Her hand shot up to her hair and she gasped as she realised that it had been cut short. She'd always regretted cutting her hair but there had been a practical reason for this needing to be done. Her long hair had become a nuisance when she'd changed Edward or hugged him, he often got his fingers caught in it and then pulled it. One afternoon, Milly had cut it for her and she'd cried when she saw her beautiful tresses lying at her feet. Short hair, however had turned out to be easier to wash and manage and she soon got used to having a bob.

Evie sat up in bed and slipped her feet on the whitewashed floorboards to make sure that the room was real. Her life had become a bizarre scrapbook of her past experiences. She'd just got used to her life in Brighton and being with Tom and then the rug had been pulled from beneath her. She thought that she'd been allowed to rerun her life but she wasn't so sure now. If she hadn't slept with Albert then perhaps her life would have taken a completely different course. She'd got pregnant and by doing so, hadn't really changed things very much. She wondered why she'd been deposited in Milly's farmhouse; she couldn't understand what her purpose was, she felt so alone and helpless.

Evie felt her stomach to see if she could feel Edward moving inside her but it felt flat and strangely empty - she didn't feel pregnant; she was beginning to panic. It was then that she noticed the cot at the foot of her bed that Milly had lent to her when she'd given birth to Edward. Within the headboard, there was a goose and a chicken with six chicks each delicately carved in to it; she'd always admired the workmanship.

Edward had loved feeding Milly's chickens and they didn't mind if he picked them up. She smiled as she remembered him growing up on the farm and then like a mirage he appeared before her, he was just tall enough to peer over the headboard of the cot. He smiled widely, elated that he could see his mother and held up his arms to be lifted out of the cot. Evie's mouth fell open, he had to be no more than eighteen months old and his blue eyes shone. His cheeks were rosy as he still had teeth growing, his blond hair looked ruffled and in need of brushing. Without hesitating, Evie got up and went to him. She gently lifted him out of his cot and hugged him. He clung to her, pleased to see her and laid his head on her shoulder. If she could be given anything, holding Edward as a baby was more than she could ever have wished for.

Edward had been such a good child, always happy and always hungry. She felt his nappy; it was soaking wet and knew she would have to get dressed and change and feed him. Evie tried hard to think how she used to look after him, her mind become crowded by the adverts she'd seen on the telly showing disposable nappies and milk and then she remembered that Edward only ever had towelling nappies and that it had been hard work keeping them washed and dried. If her memory served her right, she hoped that she would find some nappies on a rack, next to the range and some cereal in the kitchen. Evie set Edward down on the floor and then got dressed. She smiled as he toddled around the room and she watched him stop to play with the metal handles on the drawers. He'd always liked them; he liked the sound they made when he let them swing back against the drawer.

When Evie was dressed, she scooped him up and made her way downstairs into the kitchen. The kitchen was empty, she hadn't thought about what she would say when she saw Milly and her boys. She bit her lip anxiously; she wasn't sure how she would explain how she'd materialised out of nothing. She hoped that she might have been with Milly for a while and her best friend would just act normally as if it was just another day from their war days together.

The kitchen was just as she remembered it, with the large pine table and chairs in the middle. Her gaze lingered momentarily on the fire blazing in the fireplace and she remembered scooping the ashes into the biscuit tin. To the left of the door was the range and there next to it was a rack full of towelling nappies. She felt one to see if it was dry and then pulled it off the wooden rung. She found Edward some clothes in a basket at the foot of the stairs that had been left there for her to take up to her room and then carried Edward and his clothes through to the scullery. She laid him on a towel on the wooden drainer next to the sink. It was almost as if she was on autopilot, it was second nature to her. She washed, changed and dressed Edward with ease and then, after leaving the wet nappy to soak in a bucket in the corner carried Edward back into the kitchen to find something for him to eat. Seeing his highchair, Edward struggled to get into it, eager to have his breakfast.

Evie looked at the clock. It was just after seven. She wondered what day it was and tried to remember the weekly routine. She could feel her hands shaking; she knew she was in shock but there was something really quite wonderful about finding herself back in the farmhouse with Edward. She'd often thought back fondly about those days and although there had been bad days, there had also been many good days, when it had been warm and sunny and they had gone for walks through the countryside together, had picnics or swam in the streams.

Evie looked out of the window; the rain was pelting down and beat on the window angrily. Through the rain, Evie could see Milly running across the yard towards the farmhouse trying to out run the rain. Milly went to help with the milking first thing and would then have breakfast, which Evie usually had ready and she would then get the boys up for school. Evie looked guiltily towards the pot of porridge oats; normally she would have a large pot of porridge simmering on the stove. Milly burst into the kitchen laughing.

"Look at me Evie," she said taking off her mac and wellingtons, "I look like a drowned rat." She smoothed back her shoulder length brown hair that was wet through and then went to the range to warm her hands over one of the hot plates.

Evie breathed a sigh of relief; Milly hadn't questioned her being there and seemed as bubbly and happy as ever. Evie sprang into action and got the porridge oats out ready to make breakfast. Edward looked enthusiastically towards her hoping that his breakfast was coming.

"Oh don't worry about porridge, Evie, as the boys are staying with Mum, we'll just have toast today. It's a shame about the rain; the village fair is going to be a bit of a washout."

Evie sighed as an old memory took hold. She remembered this particular village fair, it was on a Saturday and that rainy day all came back to her in a flash. It was the day they'd gone to the fair and got soaked to the bone and more memorably it was also the day that Milly got a telegram letting her know that her husband had been killed in action. An overwhelming feeling of loss and how hopeless they'd all felt washed over her and she felt so sad for her friend.

"It might just be a shower; maybe the sun will come out later," replied Evie, taking a loaf out of the bread bin and trying to sound relaxed. The truth was that she felt almost sick with anxiety. She thought that she might be going mad and having delusional episodes - after all she really was over eighty. As she sliced into the bread it occurred to her that if she changed the day's events then she might be able to change not only her own destiny but more importantly, she could change Milly's too. She now understood why she was there.

"I don't want to go to the fair," she said. "The rain looks like it is set for the day and the village green gets so muddy. Why don't we see if we can get Edward some shoes in town? We could also get the boys some sweets. The market is there today, we might find ourselves some bargains."

Milly nodded in agreement and came over to help toast the bread. She put two slices of bread on toasting forks and took them over to the open fire and as she past Edward she tried to smooth down his hair. "Do you want to go to town Eddy?" she asked but he was more interested in the bread and jam that Evie was going to give him. "Yes, why don't we?" agreed Milly. "I need to pick up some candles and some string in Millers."

Evie smiled to herself, the day was set to change and she hoped that her plan would work.

***

Quite near to the farm on a steep hill, a large rust coloured fox sheltered beneath an oak tree to keep out of the rain and stared wistfully at the farmhouse in the distance. The lights in the kitchen had been turned on as the day had been made dark by the storm that raged above. There was something special about the building, he wasn't quite sure what it was but he'd spent many afternoons watching and waiting, quite sure that at any moment his patience would be rewarded.

Since he'd arrived in the area, he'd spent several weeks learning how to catch rabbits and other creatures in order to stay alive. He'd seen the chickens in the farmyard and, although he was often near starving, he'd never once been tempted to steal one as he knew that to be wrong. He didn't know why but he felt very protective towards the farm and felt obliged, each night to skirt around the edges to make sure that it was safe from intruders or vermin and he did this diligently.

He lay down on the grass waiting for the storm to pass and thought back to the day he'd woken up by a stream not far from the farm. It had taken days, perhaps weeks, to understand what had happened to him. His first memories of his past had come in dreams and he'd woken up each morning piecing together the jigsaw. One night he dreamt that he'd been human and when he opened his eyes he knew that it wasn't his imagination, he really did remember being a man once. It was difficult to comprehend and he felt uneasy knowing this, thinking that it would have been much kinder if he'd only known himself as a fox. There were still gaping holes in his memory, one of which involved another human and he felt a sense of loss, he wasn't sure why. Perhaps he was pining to be human again but he could remember very little about it, only that he walked upright and might have been called Tom. How strange, he thought, that humans named themselves. He could also just remember the voice of another female human talking to him and he longed to hear her voice again. His last memory of her was in a room somewhere, just before he'd leapt out of the window onto the roof of the porch, frightened and confused.

Shaking and trying to understand what had happened to him, that night he'd hidden behind some dustbins near to the house he'd jumped from. When he heard the terrible noises made by the sirens, aircraft and the explosions; he'd fled for his life. These sounds terrified him and filled his ears and were so unbearable that he thought his head and heart might explode.

The following morning he'd woken up in a green oasis, filled with poppies and cornflowers; he didn't know how he'd got there. He could hear the birds singing and the crickets rubbing their legs on their bodies, he could hear a wood mouse making a nest and water running along the edge of the field; his hearing was better than it had ever been. This new habitat was a welcome change but he couldn't understand what had happened to him. After he'd drank from the stream he'd seen his reflection in a pool by the stream. He wasn't alarmed by what he saw, it was reassuring to see that he existed but there was something odd about his reflection, he didn't recognise it.

Tom had slept for a few hours and now felt restless. The storm hadn't passed over and the rain poured down relentlessly. His stomach felt empty, he hadn't caught anything decent to eat for days and needed to hunt but there would be nothing around until the rain stopped. He stood up again and sniffed around the roots of the tree to see if there were any insects hiding there. He found a beetle and snapped it up into his mouth; it was crunchy and tasted bitter.

His attention then turned to the farmhouse. Two females were leaving the building, one of them was carrying a baby; he'd not noticed them before. He narrowed his eyes trying to see more clearly, there was something familiar about the woman with the baby; he needed to get closer to see her. Tom watched them get into a car and decided to run down the other side of the hill he was on and watch the car as it went by.

The farm's drive skirted the foot of the hill. He ran swiftly through the rain, stationed himself on a mile stone at the entrance of the farm and waited for the car to arrive. He didn't have to wait long, he could see the car bouncing its way along the farm track, swerving this way and that as Milly tried to miss all the potholes. There was a particularly large pothole near to him and he knew that the car would have to slow right down to go past him giving him a chance to see the passenger.

As the car past him by, Tom stared intently at Evie, trying to place her in his memories. He knew he'd seen her before; her face was familiar but not her hair. Perhaps he remembered it being longer or a different colour but it didn't matter, there was something warming about her smile and he understood why he'd been protecting the farm. He'd been protecting her; instinctively he knew he would lay down his life for her.

"Did you see it Evie," exclaimed Milly as she drove off the farm track onto the main road. "Did you see that fox sitting on the stone by the gate as bold as brass. I didn't think they came out in the day. If it goes anywhere near my chickens, I'll have to get the shot gun out."

"Oh don't do that Milly," Evie cried, trying to stop Edward from getting off her lap. "Perhaps it's sick, it looked a bit bedraggled. I don't think it will harm your chickens."

"One year, I lost the lot to a fox" replied Milly. "Just slaughtered them all and left them there dead. It did it just for fun. Can you believe that?"

"No, that's awful," replied Evie. "But please don't shoot it."

"You're not really a country girl are you Evie? Don't worry as long as it keeps away from my chickens then I won't shoot your fox. Do you think it's worth going into town, the rain is getting heavier?" asked Milly trying to clear the steamed up windscreen with her hand.

"It'll be fine, I think the rain will stop soon and the sun will come out for a bit." Evie could remember that all those years ago there had been a sun break, just before the village fair had started. The dry spell had just been long enough to entice all the villagers to brave the weather and pay to go into the fair. As the sheep herding commenced, the heavens had opened sending people scattering to find cover. Eventually, because of the rain, the fair had been cancelled as it was too wet to proceed.

"Ok, Evie, let's take a chance."

She hoped that her plan to change history would work, she knew how much Milly loved her husband, they'd been childhood sweethearts and it had been such a tragedy when he'd died. Her thoughts turned to Tom; she wondered what had happened to him. There was a faint hope that he too might have been taken off to another time and he was out there somewhere feeling the same pain of loss that she was experiencing. She knew that she would have to be strong and be positive. There was always the chance that they would meet up again. With her spirits raised, Evie looked towards the sky searching for a break in the clouds that would let the sunshine through.

24

"How did your team building event go?" asked James. "Did you have fun?" Amy took a deep breath and tried not to laugh; considering what had happened to her, she found James' question amusing. She decided that talking about her day would be easier than asking him things that she may have asked him before.

"I wouldn't say fun exactly, it didn't go as expected. It turned out that I killed Lord Grey, that was quite a shock and then I met the real Lord Grey and unearthed two murder victims in the grounds of the house. I told you that I have some psychic ability didn't I?" Amy regretted saying that, there was a moment's silence and she fully expected the phone to be put down on the receiver.

"Really? No, you never said. Murder! I look forward to hearing more. I was just going into a meeting and thought I'd ring you up to see if you're still ok for tonight. Shall I pick you up from your house at seven?"

"Oh, yes that'll be fine, I'll be waiting for you on Bartholomew Way, do you know it?" Amy didn't want James to know exactly where she lived; it would be just her luck to be dating another serial murderer.

"Yes, I've got a friend who lives just off there. I've booked a table at an Italian restaurant, is that ok? Do you like Italian?"

"That sounds wonderful," replied Amy and she realised that she was really hungry and the thought of eating out seemed more appealing than going to the supermarket and then trying to work out how to use the cooker. "What car do you have? I'll look out for you."

"It's a yellow open top kit car; you'll see me coming a mile off. I just finished building it last weekend and this is her first proper outing."

"Great, see you at seven," Amy said as cheerily as she could. James said goodbye and his call ended. She sank back onto her pillow and could feel butterflies in her stomach as well as hunger pains. It had been a long time since she'd dated and her new larger size didn't make her feel that confident. A sudden scary thought popped into her head as she thought about James' kit car. What if she didn't fit into the seat? She would feel so embarrassed and humiliated if this happened. Another irrational thought followed; what if James saw her standing on Bartholomew Way and then kept driving as he was too shocked at the sight of her to stop, how awful would that be?

Anxiously, Amy looked at the clock. It was lunch time; she only had seven hours before James came and there wasn't enough time to perform a miracle and lose half her body weight. She felt that she was on the verge of insanity to consider going on a date. If she did go out with James, she might be helping whoever it was playing games with her life to set her up for another fall. So much had happened to her in the last twenty four hours it was almost beyond belief. If this was punishment for harbouring a murderer then maybe she deserved it. In despair, Amy picked up her notebook and started to read hoping that she could make sense of everything. If Ted didn't appear in the pages, even if the slate had been wiped clean and she'd been given a second chance to re-live her life, then he would always be out there killing girls; she couldn't carry on with her new life knowing that. Her only hope of redemption would be to find Ted and get him to turn himself in. Amy started to read the first page, January 2007 - the year she'd met him.

The cat nudged Amy's hand and rubbed its head along her arm trying to get her to wake up. When Amy opened her eyes, Molly began to meow continually. She pushed her away gently and looked around her room; the curtains were open and it was dark outside and she wasn't sure how long she'd slept for. Amy looked at the half read notebook discarded on the floor; there had been no mention of Ted, just pages about nights out with Vicki and other friends and quite a lot about her male conquests. It was almost as if she'd been reading about someone else. The woman in the notebook was outgoing and self-assured, especially with men and she knew that she was just a shell of that person in reality. Amy wondered if this is how she would have turned out if she hadn't met Ted. She wasn't sure that she liked that person; perhaps Ted had been right all along and that she really was easy.

She looked at the clock again; it was nearly six o'clock. She then remembered her date with James and began to panic, she needed a shower and to get ready and had very little time to achieve this. Just before she'd fallen asleep, she'd decided to cancel her date but now she felt it was too short notice. She jumped off the bed and ran to the wardrobe to see if there was anything decent to wear. Frantically, she flicked through the rows of clothes for something that wasn't too smart but not too casual. The dresses hanging there were fitted and far too short for somebody of her age and size to wear. Nearly all the shoes, lined up in the base of the wardrobe had six inch heels and looked impossible to walk in. After ten minutes with the cat winding itself between her feet, Amy chose a smart pair of black trousers and a top that looked to her like a maternity dress but it was the best she could find and at least covered her stomach. She hoped that the swirling pattern on the fabric would distract James and he might not notice how large she was. She also found tucked away at the back of the wardrobe a pair of flat shoes that looked comfortable rather than glamorous. Her underwear drawer contained an assortment of fancy garments that she couldn't ever imagine wearing. In one corner of the drawer she found a black bra and matching pants and with these she ran through to the bathroom almost tripping over the cat. Molly followed her into the bathroom and meowed loudly complaining about something. Amy looked at Molly and was puzzled by her behaviour, she didn't realise how vocal a cat could be. She suspected that it might be hungry and decided to feed her before she left the house.

She turned on the shower and the cat ran away disturbed by the noise made by the jet of water. Amy locked the door of the bathroom, she felt much safer with the door bolted; her nerves were on edge and she didn't want anyone creeping up on her. It was such a relief to have a hot shower and wash her hair; if only she could wash away the past too.

Amy was glad that James had decided to bring a normal hatchback and not his open top kit car and she'd gracefully slid into the passenger seat just before the rain started. Nervously, she relayed her whole weekend at Oakhill House and decided to tell him all about the ghosts she'd seen and how Lord Grey had tried to stop her from digging up the bodies. James listened patiently and didn't stop the car once to let her out; he smiled at her and she wondered why. "You think I'm mad don't you?"

"No," said James laughing. "I was just thinking what an interesting and wonderful person you are. My life must have sounded very dull compared to yours"

Amy was beginning to feel uncomfortable; she knew nothing of James' life only that he'd built a car and attended a meeting that afternoon. She didn't know where he lived, what job he did or if he had children. "You're so clever though James, building a kit car; I wouldn't know where to start."

The rain hit the restaurant window with force and people ran inside to escape the deluge. As James looked at the menu, Amy studied him hard, he had a round face with laughter lines at the corner of each eye and she couldn't help staring at him. Although his hair was grey, he still had a full head of hair. From listening to his voice on the phone, she'd expected him to be about thirty but she guessed he must be over fifty. He wore light coloured chinos and a pink shirt and he looked very smart. Ted never bothered to dress up and take her out anywhere.

Amy picked up the menu and tried to read it but she found it hard to see the writing, she really did need to get herself a pair of glasses. She hoped that they did Bolognese or meat balls and pasta, she was so hungry and she wondered if James would mind if she ordered a starter and pudding as well. When he'd chosen what he was having, she would have to ask him to read the menu to her.

Amy looked around the busy restaurant and then at the rain streaming down the windows; she felt on edge and fully expected something horrible to happen at any moment. Her attention was drawn to the restaurant door, her flight instincts were screaming out to her, warning her to run and escape from what lay on the other side of the door; she could feel the hairs on her neck rising with fear. She could see a silhouette of a man outside the restaurant; his profile was familiar and horrifying. The door opened and Amy's mouth fell open as Ted entered the room. He turned and scowled at a woman that had followed him in, she was small and mouse like. They were both very wet and she could tell by Ted's expression that he was cross with her. He threw scathing glances towards the woman as if he was blaming her for being so wet. They waited impatiently for a table; there was one near to Amy's that was free and her heart thudded painfully in her chest as she waited to see where they would be seated. They were shown to a table on the far side of the restaurant but it didn't seem to be far enough away. Amy didn't know what to do, she wished the walls would draw her in and hide her; she buried her head in the menu so Ted wouldn't notice her.

When she composed herself, she peeped over the menu hoping that Ted wouldn't see her. He was rearranging the cutlery as if it was not placed correctly and was talking to his companion in an aggressive way. Amy was beginning to feel hot and her head spun; she stared at the wall behind Ted and thought she saw it move, she was sure that she was seeing things. She held her gaze and saw it contort and stretch; the wall had become like dough and she watched in terror as the spirits of the girls that Ted had killed seeped out into the restaurant and gathered behind him. They flowed out of the floor too and floated around him. The girls were holding each other's hands, bound together in misery. The desolation in their faces was all too evident and what was worse they were all looking towards her with reproachful eyes. Amy could feel the heat rising in her cheeks and she thought she might pass out. She couldn't help but gaze across the busy restaurant at the spectacle and then looked at the reaction of those around her and knew that she was the only one to witness this haunting.

Amy froze and then shivered as Ted looked her way. She fully expected him to charge across towards her and accuse her of being unfaithful but he didn't seem to recognise her. He was more interested in the woman he was with than in her. She might be his next victim Amy thought. She wondered if this is what he did, wined and dined his victim and then took them somewhere to rape and then murder them but then thought otherwise. The woman he was with was too old and was more likely to be his partner or his wife. Looking at the woman's clothes and body language, Amy thought that she appeared to be downtrodden and submissive. With horror, she realised that this woman was a carbon copy of her former self. Amy felt disgusted and sickened by Ted's callousness, how could he show his face in public when he'd committed so many murders and she knew that she couldn't stay for another moment longer in the restaurant.

"Are you feeling ok, you look a bit flushed?" asked James, he looked concerned.

"No, I'm not feeling that good, I don't know why. Would it be ok if we went back to mine and ordered a takeaway?"

James agreed but Amy could see that he was confused, he apologised to the concierge and they walked up East Street to the car park in silence.

"You don't want to go out with me do you?" James blurted out as they got into the car. "I'll understand - I'm getting used to being dumped."

"Oh goodness me, no," replied Amy, mortified that he would think that she'd cancelled their meal because she disliked him. "I felt faint but I'm feeling much better. You are lovely person, don't be daft. There was someone in the restaurant that gave me a fright, I really couldn't sit and eat knowing what he's done."

"Who was it?"

"Just someone I used to know; not a very nice person at all. In fact, I would go as far as to say he's positively vile. Let's get a Chinese takeaway and get a bottle of wine and I'll tell you all about it."

As they drove to the takeaway, Amy told James all about Ted and her sighting of the woman he'd murdered; she didn't say that he'd been her partner as she felt that might be too much for James to absorb and as there was no record of her ever living with him, it didn't seem relevant to mention it. Amy was convinced that James would think she was a crackpot but it turned out that he did believe in ghosts and he sympathised over her dilemma. At first he suggested that she should go to the police and say that she suspected Ted of being a serial murderer but then doubted whether they would believe her as there was no hard evidence. He begged her not to approach Ted and ask him to turn himself in as this would be a dangerous thing to do. After some thought James thought that the police might investigate if she mentioned her success rate finding the bodies of murder victims and if she could find where he'd buried one of his victims, this would back up her statement. She was pleasantly surprised when James said he would go with her to the police for moral support. Someone, she wasn't sure who or why, was giving her the opportunity to put things right.

Amy had eaten too much and she fell back on the sofa and tried not to spill her fourth glass of wine. "So you don't think I'm a mad woman? Most men would have run a mile by now."

"No, I don't, you seem to have had a colourful life and I find you interesting. You're not like other women I've met," he said as he sat next to her. "I could tell you a few dull stories about my ex-wife but I wouldn't want to depress you. The last date I had was a disaster as she had a handbag dog and that was all she could talk about, she was so shallow. We fell out when I said I didn't like dogs."

"Have you been on many dates then James? Are you looking for a relationship?" Amy looked at her wine and thought that it had gone to her head as she was asking very leading questions and she'd only just met him. She wasn't sure how she felt about him, it was only days ago she was in a relationship and although she knew it was over, she felt it was far too soon to test the water again; she wasn't sure whether she would ever be ready for relationship. At the moment all she needed was someone to hold her tight and tell her everything would work out. She decided that she really must be drunk as a more startling feeling of actually desiring James was taking her over. She knew she shouldn't but she couldn't help herself. She took a sip of wine and put her glass on the side table, she brushed her hand along the top of James' thigh hoping that he wouldn't reject her. He smiled and moved closer. "Do you want to go upstairs?"

Amy nodded and smiled, suddenly she felt beautiful and an object of desire: she happily allowed James to lead her to the bedroom. She thought she would feel nervous as she undressed, embarrassed by her size and being naked but as the kisses became more urgent all her inhibitions drifted away and she'd no regrets. Her desire to be loved was too overwhelming to resist and James seemed to be a very caring and gentle lover. His hands and lips caressed her body allowing electricity to run through her veins. She'd not felt this level of desire for a long time and thoughts of Ted's mechanical efforts in the bedroom were soon forgotten.

25

"Did you see it Mr McGrath? It's shot out from under the shelves, ran around the edge of the room and I think it's gone behind the boiler."

Michael's eyes snapped opened, he was lying on the floor, he held in his hand a torch and he was directing the light at the back wall below what he thought might be a storage rack. He drew in the air, he could feel it filling his lungs, he was no longer gasping for breath and he felt no pain in his chest; he was relieved to find that he was still alive and could breathe like anyone else. The person who had just spoken to him sounded young but it wasn't Jawid and not anyone that he knew. He remembered seeing Jawid die before him, only what seemed to him to be seconds ago and he couldn't understand why he'd been spared and not Jawid. He could feel tears welling up as he realised that he'd lost him and he cried out in distress.

"Are you all right Mr McGrath? Are you hurt? Do you need a hand up off the floor?"

Embarrassed, Michael suppressed any further sobs and tried to pay attention to the boy standing next to him. He composed himself, shook his head, slid out from under the shelf and hauled himself up using the shelves for support; he found that he could stand quite easily and there were no signs of a gunshot wound in his chest; he wasn't injured.

The boy smiled back at him uneasily and looked relieved that he didn't have to assist him. Michael didn't recognise the boy, he wasn't from the village and he found it strange that he was wearing a school uniform. He looked past the boy and noticed that he was in another dimly lit storage room; it was hot and unfamiliar. The boy had mentioned a boiler and he saw that there was a large modern one in the corner of the room which was now harbouring a creature.

Michael felt his chin, he was clean shaven and then he looked down at himself again in disbelief; he was wearing a brown overall coat, trousers, safety shoes and held in his hand a torch. The torch had writing on the side so he held it up in the dim light and read that it was the property of St Catherine's Secondary School. Michael was shocked; he'd been ripped from death and from those he loved and had ended up in an English school. He wondered why and what he might have done to deserve to be tormented in this way. He needed to understand why he was being hauled through such an emotional obstacle course. He felt like he was dreaming and knew that the boy was becoming alarmed and would soon question his state of mind if he didn't act rationally. "Remind me what we're looking for?" Michael asked.

"A cat, I told you, I saw it run down here; someone must have left the boiler room door open. It would be horrible if it got shut down here and died."

Michael was beginning to panic, he felt uncomfortable being alone with a minor; if the last few days had been anything to go by then the boy was in mortal danger. He needed to get out of the boiler room and outside where there were plenty of witnesses should anything disastrous happen. Most of all he needed to find Sarah and make sure she was safe and be there for her when she gave birth. He couldn't contemplate having a life without her. His chest was in pain and he felt that he was on the very edge of a breakdown as he'd been when he'd been discharged from the army. He refused to go down without a fight, he was determined to wrestle with his demons and not let them drag him into darkness.

Frantically Michael looked towards the boiler room door, it was wide open and he knew if he didn't hurry then at any moment it would swing shut and terrible things, would happen to the boy that were beyond his control.

"Will you take me back to my office, please," he asked the boy, he hoped that he would have an office or a flat to go to. "I've got a visual migraine and I'm not seeing clearly. We'll leave the boiler room door open and hopefully the cat will come out by itself. I'll check for it later."

"Ok, that sounds like a plan, it's probably too frightened to come out now. Follow me. Do you want me to get the nurse?"

"No, I'll take some tablets and I'll be fine in a while," replied Michael rubbing his forehead to make his imaginary migraine seem more real. The truth was that all his senses were screaming out in disbelief and he needed a quiet corner to find out what was happening to him and to form a plan.

The door didn't swing shut and allowed himself and the boy to leave the boiler room; Michael thought this was odd and then he almost laughed out loud at his own paranoia. They arrived at a small office in a courtyard and the plaque above the doorway read 'Michael McGrath – Caretaker'.

Michael thanked the boy and then he quickly shut the door of his office and looked around. At the back of the room were shelves full of cleaning fluid, cloths and various tubs of cleaning products to deal with any emergency, he also had a polished mahogany desk with a computer and a telephone on top. Michael switched on the computer and sat down on the leather covered swivel chair. He hoped that the computer wasn't password protected; after a few moments a login screen appeared. With impatience, he looked at the space to add his password, it could be anything. Sceptically, he typed in his favourite password 'brown_fox5' and waited and was amazed when his desktop appeared. There was so much he could do now that he'd the use of a computer. He could go on the internet, get news, see if he was still being hunted and most of all he hoped he would be able to find Sarah. It was quite plausible that if he'd been sent to England then she too could be in another country, he hoped it was the same one

Michael moved the mouse and held the pointer over the time. It was 15:05, 31st October 2015. He stared at the date, he'd lost three years of his life; it was quite shocking to see his life speeding by in years when to him only days were passing. Michael sighed despondently, he wondered if Sarah would remember him and forgive him for leaving her alone with a child to bring up. He was distraught that he'd missed the first few years of his child's life.

He stood up and took off his overall and flung it in the far corner of the room, the garment was irritating him; it was too constricting and he wasn't going to be a school's caretaker and slot in to that roll as if nothing had happened. Trying to calm himself, he sat back down and stared at the screen and waited to be connected to the internet. He didn't recognise the home page or the internet provider or even the keyboard which was a touch screen. He didn't know what to type in at first as he didn't know Sarah's surname, he'd never asked her, so he decided to type in 'Sarah, hostage, Afghanistan'. Details of her kidnapping appeared in the listing and he discovered that her surname was Brunning but little else. There was no mention of her after 2013 and he didn't recognise anyone with that name on Facebook. Next he typed in tsunami in England and found records of historic floods but nothing about a tsunami at the South Downs. Michael frowned, he wasn't having much success. He typed in Michael McGrath and found an actor with his name, a politician and several people on Facebook. Finally and reluctantly, he typed in 'murder' by his name and waited anxiously for the listing page to reload. There was nothing about him being wanted for murder, just someone with his name reported to have been beaten to death; he wasn't sure if this was a comfort to him or if this fact annoyed him; he could find nothing about a child's murder at the zoo.

With frustration, he pushed the computer away from him and threw the mouse across the room. As he did this a bell on the wall above his desk, rang out loud making him jump and he wondered if he'd set it off. The bell stopped and then after a short pause he heard outside, the excited voices of children as they burst out of their classrooms and poured into the courtyard outside his office. Lessons for the day were over. Michael sighed with relief, soon all the pupils would go home and leave him in peace. He leaned over the desk and lay his head on his arms as he waited for the children to go; he wasn't sure what he should do, Aaron was obviously not content with him being executed and must have something far worse in store for him but he couldn't think what it could be, he was still reeling from being shot. He couldn't take any further punishment, if that what it was; he needed to find a way to stop the nightmare he was in. A school was a very bad place to find himself in; he could feel the evil beginning to build within its walls.

Michael sat up and picked up a bottle of whisky that he'd found on the desk, he poured some into a glass and then swallowed a mouthful; it burnt his throat as it went down and he hoped it would help to calm him. He took another sip and felt a bit better; he hadn't had alcohol for a while and he could feel his muscles relaxing. Michael found himself thinking about Sarah again; he had to find her and make sure she was safe and he hoped that she wasn't suffering in any way. Michael shut his eyes and tried to remember her face but felt too sleepy to concentrate and he realised that he was exhausted, both physically and mentally; he needed to sleep and recharge his energy levels. If he shut his eyes for a while and slept, he might wake and be able to think sensibly.

Michael woke with a start, someone was knocking on his door in an urgent manner, he wanted whoever it was to go so he could sleep some more but the knocking persisted. Michael could stand it no longer; he leapt up from his chair and flung the door open. A small boy, dressed in school uniform stood before him. The pocket on his blazer was torn and hung down and he looked dishevelled as if he'd been in a fight.

"You took your time opening the door," he said looking at the glass in Michael's hand suspiciously. "You were wrong, I ignored him and he still took my money and pushed me about. What sort of advice was it to tell me to just ignore him? He still beat the crap out of me. I think you should call the police, Troy Tomlinson needs locking up. You need to do something about him. I'm not willing to live in fear of my life any more."

Michael stared incredulously at the boy as he ranted on, in many ways he reminded him of himself. He too had been bullied at school and it was one of the reasons why he'd joined the army. He wanted to just shut the door but felt that he couldn't as the boy was clearly distressed and needed his help. The boy had it seemed, come to him in the past and had listened to his advice. He wasn't sure if he would have recommended ignoring a bully. Calling the police wasn't going to be an option, he wanted nothing to do with them, he was sure that he was still on their wanted list.

"Look, I'm sorry," said Michael impatiently. "I'm sorry things didn't work out, you need to tell your parents and get them to speak to the Head."

The boy looked at Michael with disgust. "Well what do you think I'm doing, you're my father aren't you? You need to speak to mum and sort this out for me, before I get beaten to a pulp."

Michael silently yelled out "What the Hell?" when he heard what he was saying. He was inferring that he had a son and a wife. Michael frowned; things were starting to get out of hand and were way too freaky. Michael stared at the boy without speaking; he was a replica of himself at that age and could have easily been mistaken for being his child.

"Well what are you going to do about it?" the boy demanded.

Michael had barely enough energy to stand upright and felt that he was being browbeaten in to taking action.

"Nothing, were going to do nothing. You need to learn to stand up for yourself." Michael was determined not to play along any longer. The boy in front of him couldn't be his son and the only person he wanted in his life was Sarah. A fleeting thought filled him with hope for a moment. "What's your mother's name?"

The boy look puzzled and replied hesitantly "Sarah McGrath? Why do you ask?"

His reply made all the difference, Sarah was around and not too far away. "Look, I'm just testing that you don't have concussion. I've got one more question, where do we live?"

"Here," said the boy, rolling his eyes and pointing across the courtyard. "In the gatehouse, at the beginning of the drive." Michael smiled, Sarah was in walking distance and he needed to get to her as soon as he could. "Come on, let's go home and discuss this with your mum. I'm done for the day."

"Ok," replied the boy as he walked across the yard. "She's going to be mad, this is the second blazer this month that's been ruined."

The school drive was longer than he expected and it took them a long time to reach the gatehouse. It was a stone building with a slate roof and the gardens around it had been well maintained. He was surprised that Sarah had time or the energy to keep it so well with a three year old, his real son and an annoying teenage to look after. Someone came out of the house and picked up a broom and started sweeping leaves off the path.

"Mum" the boy called out as he ran to her, the woman turned around, responding to the boy's call.

Michael stared at the women's face with disappointment; it wasn't the Sarah he knew. She however, did seem to know him and didn't look as if she was pleased to see him. Michael instantly felt like he'd done something wrong. Perhaps she was blaming him for their son's dishevelled appearance or perhaps there were some underlying issues. Either way, he wasn't prepared to find out; he wasn't prepared to carry on with this farce any longer. Michael stopped and turned around, he would find another way out of the school and then try and track his Sarah down. It then occurred to him that he owned nothing, only the set of clothes he wore. If he was going to go travelling, then he would need supplies and if he was the husband of this woman then he would have a bag and clothes he could take with him within the house.

He felt a surge of pain run through him as he started to turn back towards the house, it wasn't only the dread of having to face the woman who clearly loathed him but he could sense something more sinister nearby. He'd the distinct feeling that he was being watched; there was something or someone hiding in the bushes next to the drive, lurking there, judging him and laughing at his vulnerability. Out of the corner of his eye, he was sure that he saw a bush move. A dry leaf tumbled to the ground confirming his suspicions. It had to be Aaron, the source of all his problems. He would have no peace until he dealt with him. He'd no idea how he would do it but there had to be a way to stop him, send him back to Hell or even destroy him but he'd no idea how.

The bushes began to quiver and part as a creature tore back up the drive towards the school as if his last thought had frightened him. Instinctively, Michael ran up the drive following the movement in the bushes. Aaron was too fast for him to catch up with him and he wondered what form Aaron had taken. It had to be a weasel or a hare to travel so fast. Michael ran with conviction, he couldn't let Aaron out of his sight and wondered what he would see when the shrubbery ended at the top of the drive. His curiosity was rewarded, Aaron stepped out of the bushes in human form. He appeared as a boy dressed in the St Catherine's uniform and he smiled cruelly at Michael and then ran off towards the school buildings. Undeterred, Michael ran as hard as he could, the adrenaline coursing through his veins and as he burst into the deserted courtyard, he just caught sight of his nephew as he disappeared inside the chapel. This confused Michael for a moment and he wondered how something so evil could have the audacity to enter into a place of worship.

Michael stopped outside the heavy oak doors of the chapel and then after getting his breath back entered the building. The smell of incense and mildew in the air filled his lungs bringing back painful memories of being forced to go to church when he was a child. He'd been the youngest of thirteen children and his mother a devote Catholic had taken them to church every evening. He'd loathed it, the prayers and lessons he endured had always been meaningless to him. He couldn't understand what benefit his mother had received from going to church as she was the most miserable person he'd ever known and even on her deathbed, she'd tried to make those around her, her so called loved ones, accountable for her illness.

Michael scanned the church for any signs of Aaron but couldn't see him; he paid particular attention to the back of the church as he imagined that it was unlikely that he would to go near the altar. Michael walked up the central isle over the graves of various dignitaries who had contributed to the foundations of the chapel and wondered if they ever considered that their very bones might support the church itself one day. There was one large stained glass window above the altar and it let in a limited amount of light. Michael could just make out scenes of Jesus' resurrection but the glass was in need of cleaning and restoration.

He decided to sit down on the pew at the front of the church to rest and to try and think. He needed advice, he'd no idea how to deal with Aaron, and he hoped that the church might bring him inspiration. On the corner of the pew, hung some black rosary beads left by a student, Michael picked them up and ran his fingers along the beads and then worked his way down to the small cross at the bottom. He looked at the cross with contempt, it meant nothing to him. He imagined himself strangling Aaron with the beads and them burning into his neck as he choked to death.

"You'll have to do better than that!" smirked Aaron.

Michael's head snapped around in shock, Aaron was sat on the same pew as him an arm's length away. Automatically, Michael whipped the beads around Aaron's neck determined to strangle him with them. He could feel the beads tighten around his windpipe and as he applied pressure Aaron just smiled and the necklace broke sending beads scattering across the floor.

"I told you Uncle Michael. You like to hurt innocent children don't you? Now things are going to get really nasty!"

26

The rain had stopped and the market bustled with life even though there wasn't a lot to buy. Turnips however, seemed to be plentiful. Evie carried Edward on her hip and she smiled politely at the traders as they called out to the passers-by to come and look at their wares.

On the second hand clothes stall she managed to find a pair of T-bar sandals that were in good condition. She didn't have much money left in her post office account and could only afford to buy a cheap pair of shoes for Edward. She slipped them onto his small feet and set him down on the pavement. The sandals were too big for him and as he walked along, he looked comical; almost penguin like. He was fascinated by the buckles and stopped every few steps to inspect them. She paid for the shoes and looked up at the sky at the dark clouds above and hoped that the break in the weather would continue for a bit longer. She hoped that if they stayed out until mid-afternoon and not be in at lunch time when she remembered the telegram arriving then there might be a chance that she'd changed history enough, that it wouldn't come at all and Peter would survive the war.

Milly appeared and smiled broadly as she held up a brown paper bag. "I'm so excited; I've bought Peter some of his favourite cigars. I've been putting money by for ages to get them. It's his birthday next month and I'm going to make up a food parcel and put the cigars in it. He'll be over the moon when he sees them."

"Does Peter smoke? I don't remember him having a cigarette," asked Evie as she looked at the two large cigars at the bottom of the bag; she could smell the tobacco. The smell reminded her of her father's pipe tobacco and she could picture him trying to light it on a Sunday afternoon.

"Only on his birthday and Christmas," replied Milly tucking the bag away into her shopping basket. "I'll just get the boys some sweets and then will go over to Mum's and pick them up. They're probably bored to tears by now. Mum does tend to tell them the same stories about her childhood and they're not that good at sitting still and listening. Evie found it hard to pay attention, her mind was wandering. They needed to stay away from the farm as long as possible but she knew she would have to go back soon as Edward would need lunch and his afternoon nap; she hoped she'd changed things enough to make a difference. She didn't remember Milly's children being around when the telegram came. It was a good idea to change things further and pick them up. "Ok, I'll see you back at the car. I'm just going to get some stamps so I can write a letter to Albert later."

"You've still not heard from him have you?" asked Milly looking concerned. "Are you sure you've got the right address, he might have been moved to another part of Africa?"

"I really don't know," Evie tried to remember her efforts to trace Albert. "His sister sent me his address but I've not heard from her recently, I don't think she liked me much, I don't think she thought I was good enough for Albert."

"Why don't you contact his mum and dad, they're bound to know where he is?" Milly suggested.

"Yes, that's an excellent idea," she was surprised that she hadn't thought of doing that all those years ago. She knew the village store's address but not the postcode. She couldn't remember if buildings had postcodes during the war, she didn't think that they did. Then she thought of Tom and a wave of guilt ran through her, she knew that any ideas to write to Albert were just a charade - she'd no intention of writing to him.

As they returned home, Evie watched the countryside fly past and was glad that the rain hadn't returned. There wasn't enough room in the cab and Milly's boys had sat in the back on sacks. Evie looked at them and smiled, they didn't seem at all phased that they were not strapped in and were not sitting on booster seats - how things had changed.

As Evie's head turned away, she had to shield her eyes from the bright sunshine streaming in through the window and it promised her that the evening would be different to the one she remembered. She could almost feel the day physically shifting before her, like an untamed beast she'd modified its behaviour and had tamed its spirit.

***

When the rain stopped Tom had gone off to hunt and had managed to catch himself a rabbit. This he'd taken back to a hollow tree on the edge of a wooded copse and he'd eaten it hungrily. As he settled himself down to sleep, he thought of Evie, he could recall her voice and see her face in his mind and it was a comfort to him to have found her. He licked his paw to clear the last of the rabbit blood from it and then curled up ready to sleep.

He closed his eyes for a moment and then opened them again as something was bothering him; he couldn't stop thinking about her and he realised that seeing her wasn't quite enough for him, he needed to let her know that he was there for her and that he would protect her. He had to communicate with her but wasn't sure how; he couldn't speak and he couldn't write, he would have to find another way. If he could bring her something that would immediately make her think of Tom, then that would be a start. His brow creased as he tried to think of something that Evie would recognise before drifting off into a restless sleep.

***

After lunch, Evie laid Edward down in his carriage pram by the kitchen door. As she hooked him into his harness and covered him up, she noticed Milly approaching carrying a handful of letters. Her heart began to thump and she hoped that the pile didn't include a telegram. She thought that it was unlikely to be delivered with the other mail; she was sure that telegrams were delivered by hand. Milly though, did look unhappy and held up a brown envelope with the address typed out in bold black letters and Evie held her breath nervously. "Look Evie, I've got another letter from the Inland Revenue, I'm just going to burn it. I bet it's about outstanding taxes that we can't possibly owe. I wish Peter was here, he'd sort it out. I'm not that good with the paperwork side of things. Running the farm is no problem but bills and horrible letters I really can't tolerate them."

Evie, sighed with relief as she rocked Edward to sleep, the pile of letters didn't include a telegram but as she recalled Milly's phobia over opening official letters had resulted in her eventually losing the farm. "I'll have a look at the books if you like, it's the least I could do for taking me in."

Without hesitation, Milly handed Evie the letter and then smiled broadly. "Oh yes, how could I forget? There's a letter for you too." she said handing Evie a crumpled envelope. "It's from abroad. Is it from Albert?"

Evie examined the faded handwriting and nodded in amazement. "Yes, oh my, it's Albert's handwriting all right," she said trying to sound enthusiastic to please Milly but she honestly wasn't sure how she felt.

As Edward was asleep, Evie decided to hide away in the barn and read the letter in private. Milly realising that she needed some time alone, had gone into the farmhouse to start some washing but insisted that she tell her all about the letter when she'd read it.

Evie stared at the envelope wearily and wondered what Albert had to say for himself. She half hoped that he would tell her that it was all over and he'd found someone else. Slowly Milly opened it and pulled out two pages of paper. It was written in ink and although Albert's writing was easy to read it was a little smudged here and there. Evie took a deep breath and began to read.

My Dearest Evelyn,

How are you my darling? I miss you dreadfully. I sent a letter every week to your address in Goring until my infuriating sister finally gave me your new address. She also told me about Edward, she says that you have had to go and stay with your friend and that your parents have disowned you. I feel dreadfully about this and ask you to forgive me. I am so proud to have a son but feel distraught that I have put you through so much.

I can't help wondering why you didn't meet me like we arranged the night before I went to war. Did your mother catch you sneaking out to see me and stopped you? Is that why? I hope that is all it was. Please my darling write, nearly two years have passed and I have heard nothing from you. Write and tell me more about Edward; he must be walking by now? I long to see a picture of him I cannot believe that we have a son. As soon as I am able, I will be back to make an honest woman of you and we will become a proper family.

Surely this war must end soon? I won't be able to bear it for much longer, conditions in the trenches are atrocious and we can barely sleep for the fear of being shelled or eaten alive by mosquitoes - our nightmares haunt us. I will not tell you any more, the things I have seen would make grown men cry and I do not want to upset you. All that keeps me going is the thought of seeing you and Edward when I come home.

Please write to me soon, I have written my address on the back of this letter. I pray that you still love me and that you forgive me.

Yours for Ever
Albert

Evie quickly put the letter down next to her and stared at it as if it might bite her; she felt guilty and cross at the same time as his words replayed in her mind. Albert declaring his love for her and praying that she felt the same way about him was a blow. She also felt cross that she'd spent her whole life grieving over the loss of Albert and now here he was writing to her, telling her he was still alive and wanting to be part of her life. She knew she should be happy that the whole course of her life had changed for the better and that Edward would have a father but she couldn't imagine being with Albert and ever loving him again. Tears of frustration and confusion ran down her face. She wished Tom was there to put his arm around her and tell her that he was there for her.

***

As dusk turned to night, Tom stretched and then left his den. There was a full moon and he could see clearly as he ran through the fields towards the farm. When he reached the farmyard, he could sense that he was being watched. There was another fox by the chicken runs and it was trying to hide in the shadows so that it wouldn't be detected.

Angrily, Tom shot forward to challenge the rogue fox as it had no right to be on the farm and judging by its behaviour, it was obviously up to no good. As he got closer, he could see its eyes narrow as it prepared itself for defence. To Tom's surprise the trespasser boldly leapt out of the shadows to face him. It curled its lips and growled, showing its sharp teeth. Tom came to a stop and re-evaluated the situation. He hadn't bargained on the intruder putting up a fight. He wasn't sure what he expected, he half hoped that the fox would take fright and disappear into the night. The trespasser was slightly bigger than he but didn't look to be in good condition. Tom could see his ribs and there were gaps in his coat where mange had eaten into the skin. Instinctively, he launched himself at the fox, knowing that he'd a good chance to win back the farmyard and Evie.

***

"What's that noise?" Evie asked Milly as she helped her to clean the silver by the fire in the sitting room.

Milly stopped buffing a candlestick "What noise is that?" asked Milly. "Oh yes, I can hear it now. I don't think it's Edward or the boys. It's coming from outside. It's probably cats fighting."

"Maybe," said Evie holding up a spoon and looking into it. She could see her reflection which in her mind passed as being properly polished. She placed the spoon back into the felt lined box and then picked up a knife to clean.

"You're very quiet tonight Evie. I thought you'd be over the moon about getting a letter from Albert. You've been waiting long enough for it."

Evie sighed. "You're right, I should be happy but it's been so long Milly; two years is such a long time. I'm not sure how I feel about him any more. Do you ever feel like that about Peter?"

She could see by the surprised look on Milly's face that this wasn't the case. "Goodness me, no, Evie! I miss him desperately and although I am still cross that he went off to be a fighter pilot when he could have stayed on the farm; the truth is that I love Peter with all my heart. You didn't go out with Albert for that long before he went to war so I can understand why you say that. I'm sure that when you see him again, you will have feelings for him. You have to; you've had a child with him. It's your duty to stand by him."

Evie shook her head; she was in danger of making Milly cross but she found her old fashioned values difficult to take. If only she knew how long she'd stood by Albert, nursing his ashes, nursing her memories of him and all for nothing. "Milly, I'm not in love with Albert any more, there's someone else."

Milly's mouth dropped open. "Who Evie? When did you meet him?" she sounded shocked.

Evie was taken aback by her reaction and wasn't quite sure what to say. She wanted to tell her the whole story, about the future, about the Chanctonbury Ring and about Brighton and Tom's disappearance. "He's called Tom Barns; he's from a village near to Goring. I met him the day before Albert went to war. We ran away together and we lived in Brighton for a while until he disappeared. I need to find him again Milly, I miss him so much."

"You never told me about him before. Why now after all this time? You poor love, you're confused, it's no good though Evie, you need to marry Albert for Edward's sake."

Evie looked at her incredulously. She realised that Milly must really be bewildered as she'd never mentioned Tom and had probably, for almost two years, gone on incessantly about Albert. For Evie it had only been a day and the pain of being separated from Tom was still raw. It then occurred to her that not only had she changed Milly's future, sparing her that awful telegram, but she'd also changed her own destiny too.

Wiping away a tear, Evie stood up; she needed to go back to Washington to find Tom as that was the only place she could think he might have gone to. She just needed to speak to him and find out what had happened. She hoped that she could persuade him to take her back. "I need to go home and find him Milly. I know you think that's bad of me and you will probably hate me but I really can't help it, I think my heart will surely break if I don't find him soon."

"I will never hate you Evie, you daft thing but I think you will be disappointed, he must have left you for a reason. Oh my, Edward isn't Tom's is he?"

Evie shook her head. "No he's Albert's, I didn't sleep with Tom."

"Thank goodness for that. You shouldn't go looking for him, he's been a beast and you deserve better."

"I don't know what to think, it's late, I'm tired and maybe I've become irrational. I'll try and sleep and see how I feel in the morning. I'll finish off cleaning the silver for you tomorrow. Good night Milly."

When Evie got to her room, she burst in to tears and sat on the bed trying to stifle her sobs as she didn't want to wake Edward. After a while, she managed to stop crying and tip toed over to his cot to make sure he was asleep. He'd kicked off the covers so Evie carefully covered him up without disturbing his sleep and then took her night clothes and wash bag to the bathroom. She was determined not to think about Albert or Tom but their faces kept flooding her mind. She imagined Albert lying awake listening to bombs falling, counting the days until he returned home and then she thought of Tom, alone in a bedsit somewhere regretting leaving her and resolving to finding her again. A howl and a yelp of an injured animal crying out in the night broke her thoughts and she felt sad that animals could be so cruel to each other.

***

Tom staggered back towards his den, his ripped neck dripped blood as he walked. Although in agony, he did feel a sense of triumph that he'd seen off the fox that had intruded and suspected the injuries it had received may be enough to finish it off. As Tom disappeared into his den below a decaying tree, he thought of Evie and was glad that she was safe inside of the farmhouse. He half hoped that she might have realised that it was him out there defending her, standing by her but knew that was too much to hope for. When his wound healed, he would take her a flower every day and lay it at her feet until she finally realised that it was him and not just a fox. He smiled to himself as he drifted off into a deep sleep, exhausted from the battle.

27

In the confined space she found herself in and in the darkness she feared so much, with her hands bound behind her, Sarah carefully flipped herself over as she frantically searched around herself for her baby, using her head, her feet and her hands. Her hunt was futile, she couldn't find him and so she called out for help but her cries went unheard. Exhausted, she stopped her fruitless search and tried to calm herself down so she could think rationally and work out where she could be. She listened to her surrounding for any clues; she hoped she could hear her baby, hear him move or cry or at least breathe but all she could hear was the drone of an engine and she realised with dismay that she was locked in the boot of a car.

She wondered how long she'd slept and how she'd ended up bound and trapped in a boot. She'd no recollection of being abducted and for a moment thought it might be her kidnappers, taking her off somewhere, still greedy for ransom money. After considering this for a moment, she decided this was unlikely as she'd been released as their attempt to raise money for her had failed.

It slowly dawned on her that car was moving as she could feel the bumps in the road; she wondered where she might be going to. She didn't like being so cramped up and a wave of claustrophobia took hold and she kicked out on the lid of the boot again and again to try and break open the lock and release herself from her dark prison. Sweating and crying with frustration, she drew her feet up, so her knees were under her chin to try and make herself as small as possible. Instinctively, she knew that she was in danger but what upset her most was the thought that someone had taken her baby from her. Tears rolled down her face as she thought of him being harmed or left alone in her house with nobody there to look after him. She prayed that Michael or Jawid would find him and comfort him.

By taking deep breaths in and holding her breath and then exhaling slowly, she managed to keep herself calm enough to think of how she would defend herself when the boot opened. There wasn't a lot she could do with her hands bound; she would just have to kick her kidnappers. She sensed that they had turned off the road and were on a track as she could feel every pothole or ridge vibrate through her body as the car bounced along and she suspected that they were about to reach their destination; she could feel herself shaking.

As soon as she heard the car stop, she placed her feet on the roof of the boot and planned to try and force it open violently and take whoever opened it by surprise. She would then kick the attacker in the chest or face if she could and throw herself out of the boot and run for her life. With adrenaline flowing through her veins, she listened for footsteps. A car door opened and closed; she could hear only one person walking around the car towards her and although she feared him, she didn't want to stay another minute in the boot that smelled of oil and damp magazines. The boot clicked as it unlocked, Sarah's leg muscles tensed ready to push the boot lid upwards. A glimmer of daylight seeped in and immediately, she forced the boot lid upwards.

The daylight was intense and made her eyes stream but she squinted and tried to focus on her kidnapper. She fully expected to see one of Farzad's men but instead she saw a white man in his late forty's staring at her with an amused expression on his face. He'd black curly hair, a sweaty face and a beer belly; his stomach hung over his belt. He wore over a brown checked shirt a green sleeveless jacket which had several zip pockets and he looked like he was on a fishing or hunting expedition. She brought her legs back, ready to strike him in the chest but by pausing too long to look at him, she'd spoiled the element of surprise and the man lunged forward, knocking her legs out the way and grabbing one of her arms, started to drag her out of the boot. She screamed for help and then with pain as her back grated on the boot lock.

"Feisty little thing you are. You need teaching a lesson. If you know what's good for you - keep quiet. All the same you young girls, all fucking bitches!"

She was shocked by his vile language and surprised that he spoke English. She looked at the countryside around her; she was clearly not in Kabul and the ring of trees at the top of a hill in the distance confirmed this; she was in West Sussex again not far from the Chanctonbury Ring and she was dumbfounded. The man started to walk away from the car towards some woods and pulled her along; she looked back at the white car determined to remember every detail so if she ever spoke to the police she could give them its make and number plate. To her surprise she noticed that it was a white taxi cab which had the company's logo on the sides and roof; she knew this taxi cab company well and had used them before. It was obvious he was going to kill her as he wasn't keeping his identity a secret.

Panic stricken, Sarah tried to pull away from her captor. She wasn't going to comply with anything this mad man wanted but he was too strong for her and he relentlessly yanked her along, through the woodlands. The trees were becoming denser and the ground more uneven and she tripped on a root. She fell heavily to the ground as she was unable to put out her hands to save herself; the man pulled her to her feet and then brought his face close to hers, his breath stank of stale cigarettes. "You be a good girl for me and I might let you live."

Desperately Sarah looked around for a house or for another person that she could run to and try and get help but the woods they were in were deserted. Miserable and in shock, Sarah allowed herself to be dragged further into the heart of the woods. She looked up at the sky through the branches to try and work out what time of day it was. The sky was grey and gave nothing away, she thought that the light was beginning to fade and that evening was approaching but she couldn't be sure. She wasn't sure of anything any more.

She felt cold and looked down at herself she was wearing jeans and a t-shirt, they were familiar but were clothes she'd worn as a teenager and this confused her; she wondered what had happened to her. She couldn't believe that her two years with Jawid and Michael and the birth of their son had been a dream or a hallucination. She couldn't help thinking that it was all just make believe and that she was in a terrible dream and her captor wasn't real. She'd been thrown into a barbaric game and this potential murder simulation was to test of her strength of mind and ingenuity. The dirty nails digging into her arm was too real and any ideas of this being virtual reality sunk into the fallen leaves around her feet. Sarah looked at the man dragging her along with disgust, she'd a feeling he'd brought others to the wood and expected to see nobody else as he was quite happy to keep her hands bound.

To her, he looked like a normal man, like a father or an uncle and she would have got into his cab quite happily not suspecting him of anything. She tried not to think of what he was planning to do with her but instead looked around for places where she might run to and escape.

They had been walking for nearly an hour and the light was beginning to fail. Ahead of her, to her dismay, she could see a crudely made shack and realised that this was where he was taking her. She was determined that he wouldn't take her inside it; if she allowed this to happen then she knew it would be the end for her. Desperately she tried to think of something she could say to save her life. She remembered the last thing he'd said to her, that he might let her live if she was nice to him. She didn't believe this but her only hope of surviving was to try and befriend him and persuade him to let her go. She had to believe that whoever was playing games with her life had let her live this long and surely had no reason to want her dead. She needed to say something that might make him question his motives. Calmly she spoke, trying to keep her voice gentle and she tried not to show that she feared him.

"I've not seen my mum for a while and I know she is missing me. Is your mother still alive?" She was gambling with her tactic as if he had issues with his mother then she would only enrage him. She looked hopefully at him for a response; she could see that he was thinking about what she'd said.

"She's not alive now," he replied looking puzzled and then his expression darkened. "She was a good woman, too good for him though. He treated us like dirt - the bastard."

Sarah had clearly opened a raw nerve but if she steered the conversation back to his mother only then he might soften. They had reached the shack and as he took away two packing case bottoms used to make a door, she tried again. "Do you think your mother is with us now, do you think she would want you to hurt another person?"

"Look you, just shut the fuck up!"

"But you cared for her, you don't have to do this it's not too late" she was beginning to sound like she was afraid.

"Don't you see, you slut? I'm doing this for her! She told me that no woman would ever want me; I was too much like my bastard of a father. She was wrong, I've got a steady job and I've got a girlfriend."

"Then you've proved to her, to yourself that you are better than your dad. If you do this you'll just sink to his level, you'll be as bad as him or worse." She could see that she wasn't getting through.

"I can have any young woman I like and when I like," he said proudly, ignoring her last comment but then he looked cross. "You're all the same, can't keep your eyes off other men," he hissed as he yanked Sarah by the arm trying to drag her into the shack.

Sarah struggled and pulled away from him, fighting with all her strength from being pulled into his lair. She felt foolish, she was no psychiatrist, she couldn't play mind games like they did in the movies. She could feel herself shaking and didn't want to go into another disgusting cell and then be violated. With all her might she turned and kicked him straight into the groin causing him to double up in pain. As he dropped to his knees, she kicked him in the face and he yelled out again. Without hesitating, she ran as fast as she could away from him, hoping she would find a house or someone that could raise the alarm, she darted this way and that, looking for a track or path that might lead her out of the wood and to safety. For once in her life, she was glad that night was coming, where she once feared the darkness it was now becoming her comrade. She looked over her shoulder, she wasn't being pursued.

Sweat poured down her face as she ran, she'd been running for ages and being bound made running awkward; she needed to remove the metal cuffs from her wrists, they were digging into her skin and bruising her wrists. She knew it would be impossible to break the chain without someone helping her. With her chest heaving she stopped to look around, it was getting difficult to see where to go next. She'd left the woods and had entered a field but the edges of the field were fast disappearing into the darkness and soon she would be walking along blindly.

She sank down to her knees to rest; there was no way that anyone would be walking through the fields now - it was too dark. For a moment she felt comforted as the night shielded her from harm. She was shivering for shock and her t-shirt had become wet from cold evening air; she wanted to rub her arms to stop herself shaking and warm herself but she couldn't. All she could think about was being in Michael's warm arms and cradling her baby. She had to keep moving to keep her body heat from dropping or the night might claim her for himself.

Sarah looked up to the sky for inspiration, she knew that before she could find her family, she needed to get to a phone and call the police and tell them that there was a maniac on the loose and he had to be stopped. She couldn't believe how desolate the countryside could be. All she could hope for was to stumble across a farmhouse or road and hoped that it wouldn't be long before she found civilization. She walked up hill and when she reached a ridge at the centre of the field she smiled with relief as she could see headlights of a car as it drove along a road in the distance.

With renewed hope, she walked as quickly as she could towards the edge of the field, in the direction she'd seen the lights and then fell into a ditch that ran along the hedgerow. With difficulty, she climbed out of the ditch and looked for an opening in the fence to squeeze through. After crossing several fields, eventually, she found a style and clambered over it and then dropped to the floor as she missed the last step.

She had reached the road and saw another car speed past her and she got to her feet hoping to flag it down but it was too far away to see her. Exhausted now, Sarah crossed the road, she would have to stand in the way of oncoming traffic and she hoped they would see her and stop before they hit her. She'd no other way of attracting attention as her hands were bound and she couldn't flag them down.

Anxiously, Sarah waited for over ten minutes until she heard the sound of another car approaching. All she could do was jump up and down in the road and hope that she would be seen before it was too late. She could see the headlights of the car speeding along but the road was long and straight so they should see her from quite far off. Her heart pounded as the car didn't seem to be slowing down and she jumped much faster but was also ready to dive into the verge if need be. The car didn't stop and she just managed to throw herself out of the way onto the grass. The car sounded its horn at her, believing that she was drunk or was some kind of nuisance; she couldn't believe how unkind people could be.

She struggled to her feet, she could see another car approaching, this one wasn't going so fast and she thought she might have a chance to stop it. She ran back into the road and started to jump about to attract attention. The car was almost on top of her and the headlights were blinding. With relief she saw the car slow down and then finally it stopped just a short way from her. She squinted; the car headlights were so bright. The driver's door opened and a man leapt from the car. She was relieved that someone could see that she needed help and cared enough to stop and assist her.

Elation suddenly turned to fear as she saw the mini cab logo on the roof of the car and her worst fear was confirmed as she saw the driver run towards her, it was her foe. Sarah turned and ran as fast as she could along the road but she felt like she was running in slow motion, she was tired and it wasn't long before he caught her. She screamed and looking at his crazed eyes, she thought that he might kill her there and then. With a look of disgust, the man grabbed hold of her: gently he caressed her hair and then took a great handful and almost yanking it out of her head. "You bitch, kicking me like that. You'll be sorry," he snarled as he slapped her across the face. Sarah squealed in pain and then by the hair he dragged her back to the car. Sarah prayed to see another car go past and knew if they saw how she was being treated they couldn't fail to see that she was in the hands of a nutter and raise the alarm. The lane remained eerily quiet.

Sarah looked at the boot with trepidation, she couldn't bear to be trapped in there again and she tried to resist but he held her firmly; she was exhausted and had no fight left in her. "You're a disgusting creep and I bet your mother is turning in her grave. You're just a pathetic coward."

Without replying he punched her hard in the face and smirked as he did it. Sarah felt her head fly back and her jaw crack. A searing pain ripped through the broken bones and she could feel herself slipping in and out of consciousness. The last thing she remembered seeing was the tree in her garden in Kabul crying tears of blood on her baby that lay naked at its roots; she wanted to go to him but she wasn't allowed.

She didn't see the lid of the boot closing or Ted banging the steering wheel, seething with anger because the slut in the back and given him so much trouble and he was now too sore in the groin to finish her off properly. She didn't notice as he put his foot down on the accelerator and sped off down the country lane back to Findon - to his excuse of a girlfriend Amy.

28

Aaron disappeared from the seat next to him and Michael exhaled sharply as he felt someone place their hand on his shoulder. He automatically jumped to his feet bringing his fists up ready to defend himself. He fully expected it to be an assailant sent by Aaron to finish him off again. He relaxed; he wasn't in danger, a priest stood next to him, he looked frightened and he held up his hands shaking them as if he feared being struck. Michael sighed with relief, the priest posed no threat and he dropped his guard and turned his head back to where Aaron had been sitting hoping that he'd materialised as he wanted the priest to confirm that he wasn't seeing things and that his nephew did exist.

"What's wrong Michael," asked the priest. "I've been watching you for a while. You seem distressed. Are you seeing things again? What's the matter? Why did you break the rosary beads?"

Michael looked at the priest suspiciously, he sounded if he cared about him and as if he knew him well. He'd asked him if he was seeing things and he detected that he'd a history of hallucinating and it was obvious that he hadn't seen Aaron. Michael stared long and hard at the man, trying to reassure himself that he was real and not a mirage and that he really was trying to help him. He was an elderly man, had a kind face and he wore a black shirt with a white collar. There was a smear of something on his shirt, perhaps jam and his trousers needed pressing. Michael could still hear Aaron's last words ringing in his head saying that things were going to get nasty. He wasn't sure if he could trust anyone any more but he needed questions answered so he could formulate a plan of action. If he was indeed a man of God then surely the evil Aaron wouldn't be able to harm him or influence his thoughts or actions. Out of desperation, he decided to speak to him but he couldn't talk to him in the church in front of Aaron, who wasn't visible but would no doubt be close by.

"Is there somewhere private we could talk, Father? Somewhere safe? A place where no evil spirits can reach us? Something is following me and listens to my every word; even this church is not a sanctuary. I need you to take me to a safe place but not tell me where we are going or I am sure something terrible will happen."

The priest looked scared for a moment and then smiled and he hoped that he wasn't making light of his request. Michael sensed that the priest was pleased that he wished to confide in him. He nodded and beckoned to Michael to follow him; he was grateful, the priest could have quite easily turned him away. As they walked out of the back of the church, although he couldn't see Aaron, he knew that he was following them and thought that he might strike at any moment. He didn't want to see any more bloodshed and another innocent life taken.

"Hurry Father, we don't have much time," he whispered.

The priest looked at him thoughtfully as he took him through his garden to the vicarage. The garden had a row of gnomes along the path - their expressions annoyed Michael; they all had stupid grins on their faces as if they were mocking him. As they entered the house, Michael could feel a change in temperature and it felt eerily cold in the kitchen as if the very air would turn them to ice. He noticed that the priest looked uneasy and his pace increased as they climbed the stairs to the landing and then as they entered one of the bedrooms he realised that the priest could sense Aaron was following too. Looking over his shoulder he ran towards a cupboard and then beckoning to Michael, darted inside. Michael followed, hoping that the priest didn't think they would be safe to talk in a cupboard but as he entered, he saw him release a hidden switch and a heavy door swung open.

They entered a bolt hole, a small room hidden away. Triumphantly, the priest shut the door behind them; he seemed pleased that he'd shut out their pursuer. Michael heard the priest strike a match, the flame lit up the small room and Michael watched him light a candle on a shelf in the corner. He looked around the room, there were no windows and appeared to be no ventilation holes. This room had the sole purpose of stowing something away or hiding someone for a limited amount of time. In the room was just one wooden chair. The priest sat on this and Michael slid down to the floor and leant against the brick wall; he felt mentally exhausted. "It's a priest hole, isn't it?" he asked. "I've seen one before." His attention turned towards the door as if it would burst open at any moment.

"Yes, you're right, this is the most sacred place I know; it must have been blessed hundreds of times over the years and has kept priests safe from those that wanted to cause them harm. It dates back to the sixteen century when the Catholics were persecuted; nothing can get in here, not even whatever is after you."

Michael sighed with relief and knew that the priest had felt Aaron's presence too. He wasn't imaging it. "You sensed him, didn't you? You felt him chasing us? Tell me I'm not going mad."

"No you're not going mad Michael, we all have our crosses to bear and sometimes what haunts us can take on a physical form. I do not doubt that what you fear is real and yes I did feel it following us. Did you notice how cold it was in the kitchen? You mustn't fear it, it will not harm you."

Michael laughed sarcastically; the priest had no idea what Aaron was capable of.

"I know you're unhappy," the priest continued, ignoring Michael's outburst. "Sometimes the demons that torture us become tangible. The only way to rid yourself of these spirits is to face up to your problems. You are probably not going to like what I have to say but it must be said. We all know you have a drinking problem, your work is suffering and a rift has formed between yourself and Sarah. You must stop drinking and talk to her and in time she will forgive you and the love will return. Please Michael you can't carry on as you are, you need to repair the damage that has been done before it is too late. You need to do this for your son, your wife and most of all yourself."

Michael stared incredulously at the priest. He was talking to him as if he was an alcoholic! He was about to protest at being labelled a drunk but thought better of it as he would only fuel another lecture. He laughed inwardly this time; he hated alcohol since being forced, as a child, to drink the blood of Christ at church. The red wine had always tasted sour, like vinegar and it had put him off both vinegar and alcohol as an adult. He then remembered drinking the whisky earlier and it hadn't bothered him; he'd drunk it as if it was water; this he found disconcerting and he understood that in this life, he had an alcohol problem.

Michael knew the priest was only being kind and had actually found them a place where they could talk freely without Aaron interfering. However, he knew his nephew would be outside the vault and hoped he couldn't hear what was being said. It was such a relief to be free of him - just for a few moments.

Michael decided to play along with the alcoholic theme, just long enough to give himself time to think. "I have been a fool father," he lied. "I will stop drinking and sort things out with Sarah but I need someone to help me get rid of the spirit that haunts me. The boy that follows me blames me for his death. I need someone to talk to him and ask him to leave me alone. I didn't start the fire that killed him and I'm sorry that I wasn't around to rescue him from the flames but I wasn't well at the time and, although I will live with the guilt, I really shouldn't be punished. I shouldn't have to endure seeing others suffer because of this tragedy. Please Father, can you help me?"

As Michael waited for a response he noticed that the candle light had begun to flicker as if it was being disturbed by a draft and out of the corner of his eye, he could see the wall shift a little as Aaron pushed against it trying to force his way in. He could see the shape of his small hands outlined in the wall. "We don't have much time," whispered Michael "I need you to carry out an exorcism."

The priest shook his head, "I don't have that training and as I have said this demon is of your own making. If you want to get rid of it, then you need to work out when you first saw him and address the problem. Michael, I believe that if you spoke to a counsellor then you will find peace and your evil spirit will leave you. I have a friend that can help you."

Michael looked wearily at the priest; he really didn't understand how much danger they were both in. If only Aaron was what the priest had said, an inner demon, an illusion that would dissipate when he got therapy, then he would have nothing to fear but his own conscience - that he could live with; he knew this wasn't the case.

He tried to remember when he'd first been troubled by Aaron; he'd spent weeks looking after his nephew and niece to help his sister, whilst she'd been in hospital and although it was a disturbing thought that Aaron had only been a ghost and he'd blotted out the fact that he'd died in a house fire, to him he'd been a normal child and not a demon. His problems had started on the last night of their stay in the caravan when Aaron had turned on him, long before he went up to the Chanctonbury Ring. On the following day at the zoo, his life had changed beyond all recognition but it was the Chanctonbury Ring that disturbed him the most and he was sure that there was some evil being lurking within the hill that wanted to persecute him. He remembered seeing a dark figure trying to hide from him when he'd swum out for his backpack. He realised that he hadn't been alone as others must be suffering at the hands of this villain too, including his poor Sarah; it was inexcusable and he had to do something about. He knew that it was a crazy idea but he'd the gut feeling that, if he went back to the Chanctonbury Ring, there was a chance he could face the instigator of the madness, even if it was the Devil himself and call a truce. With urgency, Michael turned to the priest. "How far away is the Chanctonbury Ring, do you know it?"

"Not far, I think you can get to it from Washington, that's just up the road. Why do you ask?"

Michael was surprised, he could have been anywhere in England and was relieved to find himself to be back in Sussex. "I know you're trying to help me but I'm certain if I go up to the Chanctonbury Ring, I'll be able to start the healing process, not only for myself but for everyone that is involved. Could you take me?" Michael asked. He'd no idea if the priest owned a car and he hoped that he did. Another reason for asking that the priest come with him was for protection from Aaron. The priest hole had offered them sanctuary and the priest seemed not to be fazed by his demon. There was a chance that they could get to the Chanctonbury Ring in one piece. The priest didn't respond immediately, he looked like he'd been weighing up the situation. Michael pressed him harder. "You can leave me up there; I'll make my own way back. Please, I don't expect you to do anything, just drop me off."

"Ok, Michael, if you think it will help. There's nothing like fresh air to focus the mind but we'll have to be quick, I have a meeting to go to in an hour. I'll get you the number of the counsellor."

"Thank you, I really appreciate your help," replied Michael eager to get going. "I'll get the number from you later if that's ok, the sooner I get up that hill the better, it will be the best for all of us."

They'd practically run through the house to get to the car. It wasn't Michael who had encouraged this but the priest, who seemed to sense again that they were being followed as he'd looked over his shoulder several times, checking to see what it was that was following them. The priest was becoming more anxious as the minutes ticked by and for a moment Michael was cross with him for dismissing Aaron as just a problem that could be expelled through counselling. The priest was becoming a burden and the thought of keeping him alive seemed to be a daunting task.

As they sped along the A24 towards Washington, he could still picture, his 'so called' wife's puzzled expression as they'd passed the gatehouse without stopping. The priest had asked if he wanted to tell her where he was going but hadn't questioned him when he'd said no. Michael had looked at this woman's expression and he could see resentment in her eyes and felt guilty knowing that he'd caused her so much pain. She looked to be a hard cold woman and he couldn't imagine ever living with her. He missed his Sarah desperately and wished that he could find her soon.

Michael stared out of the window, willing Washington to appear before them. He hadn't heard of it before and searched the horizon for a road sign, eager to reach his destination. He rubbed the window next to him, his breath was steaming it up and he shivered, the temperature had dropped. He'd the uncontrollable urge to look over his shoulder. His worst fears were confirmed, Aaron was sitting on the back seat staring at him malevolently.

"Father pull over, you must stop" Michael yelled. "I'll go on alone, how far are away are we? Aaron is with us, you know this don't you?"

"Don't worry about me, we're nearly there, it's just up ahead. We'll be there in a minute."

Michael looked back at Aaron and knew he was about to do something despicable. Unable to stop him, he watched as his nephew, sprung from his seat and placed his hands over the priest's eyes. Immediately he screamed out from the shock of being blinded and then rubbed them furiously to try and make his eyes see again. Michael too tried to peel off Aaron's hands but they were too hot to touch. He could smell the priest's skin burning and then grabbed the steering wheel as the priest was drifting into the outside lane and into the path of a lorry; a horn blasted. The priest screamed out in pain.

"Stop, for goodness sake stop, before we kill someone!" yelled Michael.

The priest put his foot down heavily on the brake and then sharply turned the steering wheel to the left as if he'd made a snap decision to leave the dual carriage way. They missed the lorry but hit a motorcyclist side on and knocked him off his bike. The car tore into the verge and into the bushes and then finally came to a stop. Michael flew forward but the seat belt stopped him from going through the windscreen and he fell back into the seat unhurt but was shocked. The priest however wasn't so lucky, his head hit the glass smashing it and he slumped over the dashboard with his head twisted at a peculiar angle. Michael was sure that the priest's neck was broken and he didn't appear to be breathing. Aaron had disappeared but he could see where his hands had been as there were hand shaped burn marks over the priest's eyes. He was motionless and where his eyes had been at the centre of the hand print, Michael could see black holes. He looked away, revolted, undid his seat belt and then pulled at the door catch to open it. He managed to open the door a fraction as he heard all the other door locks click shut and then felt the door he was holding push against him as if something was trying to shut him back in the car. With all the strength he had, Michael pushed the door open wide enough for him to slip out and the door sprung shut behind him; Aaron had wanted to lock him in the car for some reason. He looked back at the priest and wished that he'd listened to him and pulled over when he'd the chance to do so - now he was dead.

Michael was about to continue his journey on foot when something chilling happened; he saw the priest move and then sit up. His movement wasn't smooth and his whole body jerked as his neck clicked back into place. He turned and looked his way as if he had eyes and not just empty sockets; he looked furious. The priest then started the car, he watched him put the gear stick in reverse as if nothing had happened to him. The wheels of the car spun around; the ground was muddy and the car didn't move. Panic stricken, Michael looked around him for help; he had to get to the Chanctonbury Ring. Two motorists had stopped and were running towards them to assist. One of them went to the motorcyclist; who seemed to be just shocked and sat on the grass verge to recover. Michael looked anxiously back at the priest as the car's engine roared; this wasn't right, it wasn't possible, Aaron had to be moving the car but he couldn't understand why. He had to get away; he couldn't put anyone else in danger.

"Are you both all right," a man called out to him. We've called an ambulance and the police. Is your friend trying to leave? You need to wait until the emergency services get here."

Michael didn't know what to say. "I wouldn't go near the driver," he replied, trying to think of a reason why. "He's not hurt but he's lost the plot and could be dangerous. I won't be asking him for a lift again. Let the police sort him out."

"Oh, right," replied the man, looking anxiously at the car behind Michael that was now beginning to move back through the mud.

Michael shook his head, "He's a head case. Is the motorcyclist ok? Is there much damage to the bike?" he asked as he walked towards him away from the car. He thought that Aaron might make the car charge at him and he looked for a place to run to if this should happen. He needed to make a fast getaway and if the motorbike was still working then that would be ideal. He'd ridden a motorbike as a teenager and he was sure he could remember how to change the gears. The bike had been put on its stand on the side of the road and seemed to be undamaged; the key was in the ignition.

Michael looked back at the priest's car; it had reached the tarmac and was turning towards him. He doubted if running him down would be enough for Aaron, he'd been shot in Kabul and that hadn't satisfied his thirst for revenge. He wondered what he was trying to do and thought that he might be trying to kill him in as many different ways as possible and he would find himself in various life threatening scenarios for eternity. Being killed in a traffic accident, he decided wasn't one of Aaron's best schemes and he suspected that he might be trying to stop him from going up to the Chanctonbury Ring.

Michael ran to the bike and jumped on it and turned the key. It didn't start so he tried again and on the second attempt the engine roared into life. As he kicked the stand away, he noticed both the priest's car roaring towards him and the man that had come to help him was approaching - he looked worried.

"I'm only borrowing it," he yelled at the man and the owner of the bike. "Watch out for that nutter coming straight for us," he called pointing to the car.

Michael sped off towards the Chanctonbury Ring just as the car charged into the space where he'd been; the man managed to throw himself out the way and Michael was glad that his life, at least, had been spared.

29

Evie had slept badly; she'd spent the whole night thinking about Albert and the words in his letter had replayed themselves in her mind over and over. Her body felt achy as if she was coming down with the flu and she was sure that she had a temperature. She opened the bedroom window to cool off and then stared out at the hills around the farm hoping they might provide her with answers to her problems.

She tried to remember everything she could about Tom and felt guilty that her fevered mind, had that night, only featured Albert. She tried to remember the first time she'd met Tom but her cheeks, already flushed, reddened further from embarrassment as she remembered the awful day she'd burst into the church and stopped the wedding and then she smiled as she remembered him kissing her and telling her that he loved her. She really couldn't believe that he'd deserted her; there had to be something more, something she'd missed. She had to trust him and believe that he did still love her and that he'd been mysteriously taken off somewhere as she'd been - otherwise she would lose her mind. She hoped that he hadn't gone to war.

Evie wanted to try and find him and she thought about going back to Washington but the prospect of going on this journey with Edward seemed daunting; she looked down at him sleeping peacefully in his cot. She couldn't expect Milly to look after him as she had the boys and the farm to cope with. If he was to come with her and they went on a train, then she'd have to bring his pram and a suitcase; she couldn't see herself hauling them all aboard and she realised that going on this journey would be impossible. She sighed despondently and put her hands up to her cheeks feeling sorry for herself, her face was burning and she felt very thirsty.

As Evie went down to the kitchen, she felt relieved that it was Sunday and the day would be a bit more leisurely. If she could get the money together she thought, then maybe Milly's mother would babysit Edward; she knew he would be well looked after but she suspected that she would probably tell her off for being so headstrong. She really couldn't face being reprimanded by her.

Evie let the tap run for a moment, filled a glass and then held it up to make sure it was clear, sometimes the water had a brown tinge to it but today it was clear.

"Evelyn don't be afraid, I've let myself in. I hope you don't mind?"

Evie spun around to see who was in the kitchen and her worst fears were confirmed, Albert was sat at the kitchen table, she'd not noticed him; the glass fell from her fingers and shattered on the floor. She held her gaze and hoped that he was just her imagination; she hoped that he might disappear but he didn't and continued to look at her. His eyes had a haunted and troubled look about them; he looked tired, his uniform was dusty with fine sand and his skin was dirty. Evie was speechless as she'd only just got his letter and she'd not got over that blow; she couldn't believe that he was with her in the kitchen smiling at her, presuming that she would fall into his arms. She could feel the heat in her cheeks intensifying as a wave of sickness washed over her and then the room began to spin. Hopelessly, she grabbed the edge of the sink to try and steady herself. She wasn't sure if she was ill or was keeling over from shock but she couldn't stop herself from falling. As she sank to the floor, she could see his face; he'd stopped smiling and looked concerned. She couldn't speak and waited to hit the floor but instead darkness washed over her and then swallowed her whole, taking her away from him.

***

Tom, despite his battle wounds, had slept soundly and after stretching and licking away the dried blood from his fur, was pretty sure that the rip in his neck would heal. He felt pleased with himself as he had a plan; he would take a flower to Evie every day after lunch when she put her baby in his pram to sleep. He'd seen some oriental poppies growing in a garden nearby and would pick a different colour each day and drop it at her feet until she recognised him or at the very least considered him to be her friend. Confident that his scheme would work, he ran across the meadow towards the farm next to Evie's. He would have to pick the flowers before it got light, before the occupant let her dogs into the garden. He'd been into her garden many times and gained access by climbing up onto a shed roof and by dropping down onto a water butt and then a bench.

He particularly liked visiting this garden as it reminded him of another he'd known when he was a boy. He thought it strange that his memories of being human constantly bombarded him; this he found most disturbing but on the whole, he was glad to know more about his past.

He remembered having a mother and holding her hand when he was a toddler. He remembered being in a garden full of flowers and chasing dandelion seeds that floated in the wind. He found great pleasure in being in a beautiful garden and he appreciated the effort that humans went to keep them.

He trotted over to the flower bed and selected a big red poppy. He was certain that this was Evie's favourite colour, he wasn't sure how he knew this but he did. Carefully he bit the stalk to try and cut it in two but ended up mashing it. Eventually he found that if he bent the stalk more than ninety degrees it snapped and he was able to severe the final strands joining it together with his sharp teeth. Pleased with his efforts and holding the flower in his teeth, he hopped back on the bench and finally jumped from the shed on the other side onto a pile of logs. He then carried the poppy through the meadow.

As he trotted through the long grass, out of the corner of his eye he noticed a rat creeping along the edge of the field and thought that it would make a tasty snack. He really wanted to take the flower back to his den but his stomach was rumbling and he knew that he should eat; he'd spent too long sleeping after the fight. Carefully, he laid the flower down and then keeping low, crept through the grass ready to leap on to his prey. The rat wasn't aware of him approaching; rats were sometimes too confident for their own good. Giving it no chance of escape, Tom shot out from his hiding place and caught the rat skilfully in his jaws. Automatically, he broke its neck and then after a moment of deliberation, decided to eat it there and then as he didn't think he could carry both the flower and the rat together.

***

"Evie, do you want me to call the doctor? Evie wake up. No, it's no good, I'm going to fetch him, you're burning up."

It was Milly's voice; Evie could just hear her and she wanted so badly to tell her she was fine but she couldn't open her mouth and speak. It was almost as if she was shut away somewhere, unable to move and she'd no energy to do anything about it. Evie sank back in to her half-life away from Milly's voice where she had no responsibility, nothing to worry about and no-one needing answers. She felt safe and cocooned from all that worried her.

She became aware of something happening in the distance, her eyes wouldn't focus at first but after a while she saw a silhouette of a hill with a ring of trees on its summit. She stared at the hill in trepidation and remembered those trees in her memories but couldn't make sense of what she was seeing. As she continued to stare, the trees parted and the hill split in two and a fire roared up into the sky. She could hear laughter from a faceless crowd that had formed around her; they seemed familiar but she couldn't quite remember where she'd seen them before. She sensed that the crowd were becoming concerned that one of their members was missing. She knew that it was Tom and she asked them to look for him but they ignored her and stared at the flames as if it was a bonfire.

Frightened by what she saw Evie opened her eyes wide and hoped that she was awake; more importantly she hoped she would be herself again, old and grey with a liking for tennis and good books. Gradually, Milly's front room came in to focus and she found that she was still a young woman and she found that she was lying on a sofa. Again she saw Albert; he was sitting on a wooden chair close to her and was holding her hand. He'd changed and was wearing trousers with braces, a brilliant white shirt and his skin was clean as if he'd bathed. Evie couldn't help smiling at him; he looked so different from when she'd seen him in the kitchen.

"Thank goodness, you're awake Evelyn. I must have scared the living daylights out of you. I'm so sorry," he said squeezing her hand. "You're not well though; Milly's gone for the doctor. You've got a fever."

"No, I'm fine, I just need a couple of paracetamols and the fever will soon go."

"A few what?" asked Albert, he looked puzzled.

Evie realised that he wouldn't have heard of the tablets, they were before his time. "Just some medicine to take away my temperature, I might not need them, I don't feel that bad."

"Let's see what the doctor says," continued Albert. "I know you're not feeling very well but I just need to know one thing."

Evie had been dreading this moment but it wasn't what she'd predicted.

"Is it all right if I go and get Edward, he's calling for you?"

"Oh yes, Edward!" she'd forgotten all about him and now she could hear him calling out. She tried to sit up but immediately felt sick and dizzy and sunk back on the pillow. She'd no option but to let Albert go to him. "Yes please, he'll need changing, he'll be soaked I'm afraid; there's a pile of nappies on the side in our room. If you bring him to me, I'll try and change him here."

Albert got to his feet and patting her hand, he gave it back to her. "I'll change him; you're not strong enough to do it. I've put a nappy on my sister's baby before. Don't worry, I'll be fine and then I'll bring him down to see you."

She watched him leave the room and then tried not to move her head too much as it made the room move too. She realised that she was quite ill; she'd had the flu once but this was different, she really didn't feel well at all.

Her thoughts turned to Albert, he'd been so gentle and kind, not how she remembered him to be when they'd taken shelter in the haystack. There was something different about him but she wasn't sure what. Perhaps she thought, he'd grown up and had become a man. She felt so emotionally confused and knew that what she was experiencing might not be real. She'd imagined him to be fighting somewhere in Egypt and it was very unlikely that he would suddenly appear in Dorset; yet she'd felt his warm hand on hers.

She thought back to what Milly had said and wondered if she felt any differently towards him now that she'd seen him. She tried to think how she felt about him and decided that she couldn't make a rational decision whilst she was so ill and would have to give it time. He looked like he'd been through a lot and was psychologically frail; she didn't want to hurt him any more than she needed to. She was grateful that Albert could see and hold his son, it was something she'd only dreamed about and she was sure that the pleasure of seeing Edward smiling up at him when he lifted him out of his cot would be something he would never forget and would perhaps leave a positive imprint somewhere in history.

Evie could feel herself burning up and was beginning to doubt her earlier declaration that a couple of tablets would cure her; she closed her eyes for a moment to rest and found herself drifting off in to a troubled sleep.

Just after the clock struck eight Albert reappeared, holding Edward in his arms. He'd washed and dressed him and brushed his hair; it was almost as if she'd done it herself. Albert sat down in the arm chair with Edward on his lap. "He's a fine lad," remarked Albert. "He looks like you Evelyn, he has your eyes."

Evie looked at Edward and Albert together, it was almost as if he hadn't gone to war and had been with Edward and her from the beginning. "I'm so glad you've met him, he knows you're his father, you can tell," Evie said as she tried to keep them both in focus. She knew that Edward was in safe hands. "I'm glad you're here too. How did you get back to England? She could feel herself beginning to drift off to sleep again. She really wanted to hear what Albert had to say. He began to speak but she couldn't make out what he was saying. She was determined not to lose consciousness again but she couldn't fight sleep any longer and she was unable to stop her eyes from closing and didn't want to return to the burning hill; she feared and loathed it.

***

In the shadows cast by the haystack in the barn, Tom waited silently for Evie to bring the baby out from the farmhouse and put him in his pram. He felt nervous and excited at the same time; he hoped she wouldn't scream when he saw him approach. The shadows grew longer and Tom realised that she was late, she always laid the baby down to sleep at the same time every day and instinctively he knew that something was wrong. He had to get closer to the house and perhaps go inside and find out what was going on.

The thought of entering the farmhouse terrified him. He didn't understand why but he guessed it was something to do with entering the den of a human and going against the laws of nature. His ears pricked up, he could hear the baby crying - it was an unusual noise. After a few moments the crying stopped and Tom felt relieved as it was most unsettling to hear a human in distress. He then remembered himself crying over a broken toy when he was a child. The toy was in two pieces and was made of wood but he couldn't think what it was. He hoped that later he would recall what it was called.

The kitchen door swung open and Evie's friend came out with the baby, who appeared to be asleep and she put him in his pram. This turn of events wasn't good; he had the feeling that he wouldn't see his Evie today. There was something wrong with her - he could feel it in his bones. He sank down onto the floor and placed his chin on his paws to rest; he felt tired but couldn't risk falling asleep in case he missed seeing her. He couldn't understand why he always felt so tired in the day and so wide awake at night.

His eyes were beginning to close when he noticed Evie's friend getting into the car. She looked anxious and in her haste to leave, she'd left the back door ajar. As soon as the car was far enough away, he got up, picking up the flower he'd laid in front of him and then trotted swiftly across the farmyard towards the door. He could feel himself shaking and wasn't sure what he would encounter once he was inside but he knew that he had to see her and make sure she was well. He pushed the door open a little more and walked into the kitchen. He stopped to sniff the air and his nose was bombarded with strange smells. Some he knew, he could smell onions, cinnamon and soap but there were others that mystified him.

Cautiously, he worked his way around the house until finally he sensed he was outside of a room that housed his beloved Evie. The door was open and he could see her hand sticking out from the covers and he found it very strange that she should be in bed when it was day time. He walked into the room and sat by her bedside with the wilting poppy still in his mouth. He was beginning to relax, it wasn't too bad being inside a house and his surroundings were not too alarming.

He watched Evie as she slept, she seemed to be agitated; she mumbled the odd word, an incoherent sentence and most startling of all she said the word 'Chanctonbury' over and over again. He knew that word but wasn't sure why it bothered him so much to hear it. Suddenly without warning she called out his name and for a moment he thought that her eyes had opened and she recognised him but he was wrong; she was still asleep and seemed to be in pain. He wished he could help her but didn't want to cause any further anguish and knew if she saw him sitting by her as a fox she may get frightened. He was sure that she wouldn't believe her eyes so he thought it best to leave. He left the poppy on the floor next to her bed where she would see it and crept out of her room.

As he reached his favourite oak tree at the top of the hill near to the farm he could see the car racing up the drive and watched as Evie's friend jumped out; she quickly looked at the baby in the pram and then ran into the house. She was holding a bottle of dark coloured liquid and he prayed that it was for Evie and that it would make her better.

30

Amy stirred from her sleep, her night of passion was still vivid in her mind; she stretched out a little trying to wake herself. She could sense it was morning and knew that she should start to think about getting ready for work but the prospect of arriving at Treadmill Marketing, not knowing who everyone was seemed daunting. She decided that she would phone in sick and say she'd a migraine but in reality her head didn't feel too bad which surprised her as she'd drunk a lot of wine. She smiled and turned over to see James and then opened her eyes; he wasn't there. She was puzzled and wondered if he'd gone home without saying goodbye. Her anxiety dissipated as she heard the toilet flush; he'd gone to use the bathroom.

As she waited for him to return her attention turned to the layout of the bedroom; it wasn't the same. With her heart rate quickening, she waited for the walls and furniture around her to transform to her bedroom at Bartholomew Way but they remained static. She knew what bedroom she was in but this truth was too horrific to comprehend. She drew the covers up to her chin as if they would shield her from danger and protect her from the person that was in the bathroom. She looked around the room for a weapon and then in her head tried to plan a route of escape and what she would take with her. Her old mobile was on the bedside cabinet, not her new age one and she grabbed it ready to dial 999 if necessary.

Ted walked into the bedroom and just by looking at his face; she knew that he was in a foul mood. She was sure that he would know that she'd been unfaithful but worst of all she feared that he would detect that she was aware that he was a serial rapist and a murderer. She fully expected him to attack her but he didn't and she was confused. He was carrying out his usual morning routine as if nothing had happened. Amy stared at Ted in disbelief, she was shocked to see him again; he disgusted her. He didn't look at her and went over to the wardrobe and opened it; he was only half dressed and started to hunt for a shirt.

"Where's my green shirt," he asked stopping his search and turning towards her. She was so frightened she could barely reply. "I don't know. In the wash?" she stammered.

"What's the fuck's wrong with you? If it's in the wash then it's about time you washed it, it's been in there for at least a week - lazy cow," he grumbled taking a check shirt out of the wardrobe.

Amy didn't reply, she knew better than to retaliate. She stared at his face; he looked a little younger than she remembered. He'd a black eye and a scratch on his arm. "What happened to you? You've got a black eye," she asked trying to make conversation so that he didn't suspect anything.

"I got it caught on the car door," he replied after a short pause. Amy knew that he was lying and that he'd been up to no good. As he buttoned up his shirt, she concentrated on the spirits she remembered seeing in the restaurant and in her mind asked them to come forward.

She didn't have to wait long for a spirit to appear. She could see the shadowy image of a teenage girl - she remembered her. She was very thin, had long fair hair and her school uniform were ripped. She looked sadly at Amy, her eyes pleading to find her body and release her from Ted's dark soul.

Amy concentrated harder and asked for any other spirits to come forward but there were no others. She tried to make sense of what she was seeing. She couldn't understand why there was only one spirit attached to him when she'd seen so many before. The only reason she could think of was that she'd gone back in time, Ted had only killed one girl and she'd been given the chance to stop him from carrying out further murders. It was what she'd wanted but this mission was overwhelming, she wasn't sure how to go about it. She needed to find the strength to face up to her duty and not let Ted wear her down; setting him up would be dangerous and more than likely be fatal.

Ted had finished dressing and then as he started to walk out of the bedroom, he stopped. Amy's heart almost stopped too. "What's your plan today?" he asked his tone now less stern.

"I'll put a wash on and probably tidy and clean the flat, it could do with a good going over," replied Amy, knowing that this response would please him. If she'd said she was going out for a walk, she would rile him and he would question her until he was satisfied that she wasn't going to go to a place where there might be men.

Amy's attention turned to the spirit who now stood by the window, she seemed to be pointing outside and making out she was driving. She stayed for a few moments continuing with the same charade until Ted left the bedroom and then wearily followed him out of the room.

Amy listened for the sound of the kettle and the toaster to go on and as soon as she was sure that Ted was in the kitchen and getting his breakfast she swung her legs out of the bed and sat on the side. She was still naked and she was glad Ted hadn't noticed as that would have drawn unwanted attention to her. With great relief she realised that her body had dropped down several sizes and she felt much healthier; she planned to stay at that weight. She was surprised how calm she felt considering how frightened she'd been earlier.

Amy put on a dressing gown and then walked to the window and drew back the curtains to try and see what the spirit had been trying to show her. She looked out of the window and could see nothing unusual. The wind blew rubbish across the car park and in the flowerbed that ran along the edge; a cat was digging in the earth. She could see Ted's taxi on its own in the car park; her car was out on the road as they only had one allocated space. As far as she could tell the spirit had been pointing to Ted's car. She thought that she was trying to tell her that she'd been in his car; perhaps she was trying to say she was still in there. Amy thought that was unlikely as she sensed that the girl had been dead for a while. She couldn't get her pleading eyes from her mind and knew that she wouldn't find peace unless she looked in the boot of the cab as this part of the car concerned her most.

Quickly she got dressed in to a comfortable pair of jeans, a t-shirt and a favourite sweatshirt that Ted hated. She looked at herself in the mirror as she brushed her hair and liked what she saw; she looked so much younger.

Amy's attention turned back to the car and for a moment she thought she saw the spirit of the girl standing by the boot, confirming that she must try and get out there and investigate. She walked through to the kitchen to make herself a cup of tea; she'd have to wait for the right moment to slip out of the flat. She knew that he was up to something as normally he would have left before she'd got up; it wasn't like him to miss the morning rush hour fares; she looked at the kitchen clock, it was nine thirty. He sat at the table, reading the paper whilst eating his toast and drinking a cup of tea. His usual routine was, to go to the bathroom after breakfast with his paper; he'd be in there for at least ten minutes. If this happened then she would get his keys and go and look in the boot.

Amy made her tea and walked through to the lounge to check if Ted's keys were on the hook by the door and much to her relief they were. Hanging from his key ring was a wooden cross; she couldn't believe that he displayed a religious symbol so blatantly and then so violently murdered innocent women - it was ironic. Amy turned on the television to create some background noise so he wouldn't hear her open the front door. The channel was a breakfast programme and the presenters' clothes and hairstyles were so dated that it made her smile. She sipped her tea but couldn't concentrate on what they were saying as nerves were beginning to kick in.

Finally, as Amy finished her tea, she heard Ted take his plate and cup through to the kitchen and she patiently waited for him to appear. After what seemed like ages, he walked across the lounge, with the paper tucked under his arm and headed towards the bathroom.

He didn't even acknowledge that she was there and she realised then that he'd never really loved her. As soon as she heard the bathroom door shut, she leapt up and collected his keys from the hook, making sure they didn't jingle. She put on some shoes and leaving the door ajar ran down the stairs to the ground floor and into the car park. She sprinted towards the taxi and released the alarm. It beeped loudly and she hoped that he didn't hear it. She turned the key in the lock of the boot, pulled the lid up and then drew in a sharp breath; there was a girl lying in it and her eyes were open wide with fear. Amy was shocked; she was really not expecting to find somebody in there. The girl looked familiar; half of her face was bruised and swollen. She looked back at the flat to see if Ted was at the window, she knew she had to hide her somewhere; there wasn't time to call the police.

"Don't be afraid, I'm going to take you to a place of safety. Are you able to walk?" she wasn't sure how badly injured the girl was but she nodded and sat herself up. Amy looked desperately around the car park for a place to hide her but there was nowhere suitable. Then she saw her own car and looking on the key ring, she saw that her spare key was attached.

"Quickly," Amy said urgently as she helped the girl out of the boot and then she realised who it was. "Sarah, Oh my God it's you! Come with me I'm going to hide you in my car until Ted's gone and then we'll call the police and get the bastard arrested."

Amy had to practically hold Sarah up as they made their way to her car; she was weak and seemed to be in a lot of pain. Fortunately, the key to the handcuffs was on the key ring and after removing them from Sarah's wrists, stowed them in her glove box to use as evidence. It took longer than she expected to get her onto the back seat of her car and to make her understand that she needed to lie down. The whole time Amy's heart was pounding as she knew at any moment Ted would come out of the bathroom. As she covered Sarah up with a coat she'd found in her boot, she hoped that she could make it back to the flat in time.

"Thank you," Sarah whispered. "Be careful."

Amy ran across the car park, watching the front room window as she ran. She tripped up the stairs and when she reached the front door she stopped for a moment frightened that she was too late and Ted would work out what she'd done; he wasn't stupid. She closed the door and stepped into the lounge and much to her relief found that Ted wasn't there so she headed towards the bedroom as she really didn't want to see him again and she was sure that her face would give the game away. She heard Ted come out of the bathroom and then heard him go into the kitchen. Amy waited in the bedroom and then realised that she still had the keys in her pocket; she had to get them back on the hook before he left. She could feel herself shaking as she walked back to the lounge. Holding her breath she put the keys on the hook and turned around; her heart stopped dead for a moment, Ted was stood in the lounge doorway. She exhaled, he wasn't looking at her; he'd a letter in his hand and was reading it. Amy tried her best to look relaxed and was relieved that she'd got away with it.

"We need to provide a meter reading, this electric bill is far too much. They keep estimating it. Can you take a reading and give them a ring? It should be at least half. They want two hundred and fifty three pounds.

They're having a laugh. Can you sort this out? I'm not going to have time today."

"Ok," lied Amy, she desperately wanted him to leave, she couldn't stand being near him, he was an animal, worse than an animal, he was the Devil himself.

Amy sat back down on the sofa and he passed the bill to her; she noticed the scratch on his arm again and hoped that Sarah would have his skin under her nails as that would be crucial evidence. Ted put on his coat and collected the keys from the hook and then without saying goodbye left the flat. Amy took a deep breath; she was so pleased to see him go. She couldn't believe how casual he was, knowing that he'd a girl trapped in his boot. If she hadn't developed her psychic ability there would be no way she would have suspected him of being a murderer. Amy turned off the television and walked to the window; the taxi had gone. She knew it wouldn't be long before Ted opened the boot and discovered that Sarah had disappeared and then returned. Without hesitating, she got her bag, phone, coat and keys and headed off towards the car. As she approached it, she could see that Sarah was sitting up and hoped that Ted hadn't seen her.

Amy got into the car and turned the key in the ignition. "I need to take you to the police station and they'll get someone to see to your face. You poor thing, you mustn't worry you're safe now."

"I don't feel very good; I need to go to the toilet. I don't think I'll make it to the police station," Sarah replied, her stomach was in pain.

"Ok, we'll go back to the flat first, sorry I didn't think." Amy turned off the engine but her instincts were screaming at her to carry on and that it was too dangerous to go to the flat as Ted could return at any moment.

When they finally got back to the car, Sarah felt a lot better and she'd managed to stop shaking, it had been a very cold night trapped in the boot and the pain in her jaw was excruciating. She couldn't believe that the vile man that wanted to rape and murder her was Amy's boyfriend. She felt sorry for her, she was a victim too and she was very grateful that she'd rescued her and wondered how she knew that she was in the boot. She thought back to the day they'd met at the Chanctonbury Ring and how protective she'd been when Nabeel had been after her. "You know that this is just a mad game someone is playing; just the fact that we know each other is real. I'm not sure what's going on, it's like being in a game show and someone out there is laughing at us. What I want to know," continued Sarah, "is what we have done to deserve this. This isn't my first bizarre situation I've been in since the tidal wave hit the South Downs and I bet it's been the same for you. We need this to end, to return to normality and carry on with our lives. Please tell me I'm not going mad."

Amy turned out of the close and began driving towards the nearest police station. Even if it all was just a game then she still needed to get Sarah to a place of safety. "I know what you're saying is true but for me, I feel like I've been given the chance to address a situation I tried to ignore for many years. If I'd been more observant and not turned a blind eye then I could have stopped many horrific deaths. I'm not sure if I can stop him but I need to try my best. He's killed one girl already. I saw her ghost and she let me know that you were in the boot and I got to save you. He nearly killed you and I know that he will kill again. Please, Sarah, come with me to the police station, you know what he's capable of, I have to try at least or I won't be able to live with myself."

"Of course I'll speak to the police but you mustn't be so hard on yourself; he doesn't look like a maniac, does he?" Sarah replied. She was starting to feel faint and she wished Michael was there for her. "The police might be able to find Michael too. I was with him just days ago and I think wherever he is; he'll be worrying about me if he's not been executed! We were together for over two years in Afghanistan, can you believe that? He was taken away for killing a child - it was like a nightmare. I don't think for one minute he's capable of such a thing; he was the kindest and most loving man, he wasn't a killer. We... we had a baby and we had Jawid to look after. I miss them all desperately, especially my baby, I only gave birth to him hours ago...it's too awful," Sarah sobbed.

"It's ok Sarah, we'll find them again. If we've met up again, then I'm sure you'll find them again. You mustn't give up hope. There must be a way to end this all."

As Amy pulled up at the roundabout, she looked in her rear view mirror and she gasped, Ted was in his taxi behind her. She could see his face in the mirror and he looked furious. She could feel a cold chill run down her spine as his expression changed and she saw his face twist into a sinister smile.

31

By luck Michael found his way to the foot of the Chanctonbury Ring and as he tore through the car park, he could sense the disapproval of the hikers and tourists as he roared past them. He paused for a moment at the edge of the car park to get his bearings and then on deciding on the best route to go, raced off up the winding chalk path towards the hill top. He knew he had to go as fast as he could to prevent Aaron from catching him up and he dreaded what might happen to him; he didn't want to have his eyes burnt away too.

The path was steep but the bike had a big engine and it handled the incline well. He found it easy to handle and wove his way through the crowds making their way up the path. The trail levelled as he reached the top of the hill and he could see the ring of trees ahead of him on the next peak. Between him and the Chanctonbury Ring were a large group of students, dressed in costumes. This puzzled Michael for a moment and then he remembered that the date was 31st October - it was Halloween. Michael's heart began to sink when he realised how many people were making their way to the Ring. This development was annoying; he was hoping to summon the Devil or whatever it was in private.

He felt a cold chill run down his spine; he could sense that Aaron was nearby. Desperately, he looked for a place to escape and then thought that if he joined the students then he might be able to hide from him and hoped that he wouldn't try anything when there were witnesses. Michael stopped the bike and leaving it on the side of the path ran to join the students; he caught them up and then looked nervously over his shoulder for Aaron.

"You going for soup too?" asked a young man dressed up as Frankenstein's monster.

"Something like that," mumbled Michael, puzzled by his question. "What are you going to do to get the soup?"

"Walk around the trees anticlockwise seven times and the Devil will either give us a bowl of soup or grant us our dearest wish. Of course, I'm going to wish to win the lottery. It all sounds like a bit of a laugh to me. I wanted to come up here at midnight but Jessica was too scared," he said pointing to a girl dressed as a witch. She'd a mass of back combed purple hair and her skin was green; she frowned at them when she heard her name being mentioned.

"Seriously," Michael warned. "I really wouldn't do that. You might get more than you bargained for." He looked over his shoulder and for a moment saw Aaron and then watched him hide behind one of the students at the back of the group.

As they climbed the last grassy slope to the path that ran around the trees, Michael started to feel nervous as there were far too many people around and he was concerned about their safety; anything could happen, especially as it was Halloween; the day when the dead might rise from their graves. Whatever it was that lurked in the hill, it could at any moment unleash a terrible catastrophe and everyone there could perish. He couldn't bear that to happen and he felt helpless.

When he'd been at the Chanctonbury Ring the last time, no one had walked around the Ring and summoned the Devil; he'd just made his presence known in the most startling way. There had been six of them that day on the hill - the Devil's number and he thought that might have been the trigger that began the crazy chain of events that had made everyone's life a misery. He was beginning to lose control and knew that he was running out of time. He didn't have time to walk around the Ring seven times; there had to be a better way to get the Devil's attention.

Michael left the parade and walked towards the centre of the Ring through the copse, he had to draw Aaron away from the students and face up to whatever he threw at him. He passed a group of women dressed in black; they were sat around a fire and were chanting. As he passed the women, they glared at him as if he was disturbing their incantation and was trespassing. Michael shook his head in disbelief at their stupidity.

He stopped and looked around, there were still quite a few people nearby, groups of people chatting and laughing as if they were waiting for something to happen. The light was beginning to fade and lanterns hung in the trees glowed brightly. Children in costumes ran around chasing each other, pretending to be monsters – if only they knew the truth.

Michael was beginning to sweat. He needed answers. He remembered the night he'd fought off Nabeel, saw him fly through the air and then fall on a tree stump and die. He'd been accused of murder that night and he wondered if he was capable of such a terrible act. Could he be a murderer? Did he kill children? He could feel himself shaking and his head was in pain. He took a deep breath; he had to be in command of all his faculties if he was going to face up to the truth. He looked down at his hands and then at the children nearby and felt no desire to kill them. He prayed that he didn't have blood on his hands. His only crime was wishing that his nephew would leave him alone and then burn in Hell.

He concentrated as hard as he could on Aaron, calling him in his mind to come to him, almost begging him; he had to face his demon. Out of nowhere, Aaron leapt onto his back and Michael yelled out in triumph; his soul screamed too. He knew that he was unable to hold back any longer; his desire to cause Michael pain and misery was too great. Instantly, he felt the heat from Aaron's body; it was like having hot irons put on his back. He tried to pull Aaron's arms from around his neck and tear him from his back but he was too hot to touch; he could feel his clothes burning on his back. He felt Aaron bite into his neck and the pain was excruciating.

Desperately, Michael grabbed a handful of his nephew's hair to pull him away but he couldn't move him. All he could think of was to roll onto the floor as his clothes burst in to flames and to shake Aaron off. Catching him off guard, he managed to dislodge him and then stood up quickly ready to fight him, should he attack again. Aaron circled around him, ready to pounce, there was something cat like about him, his eyes were more feline than human. Michael knew he would have to think of something quickly to save himself. He needed to end this madness and speak to the organ grinder and in desperation he shouted out loud "What do you want from me? Haven't I been through enough? Are you not satisfied? You send a child out to hunt me down and destroy me. I think that makes you worse than a coward. Come and show yourself and face me. Face me and do a deal with me. Everyone that came up here when you tore the hill in two must be released and their lives restored. Come out here and do this deal, you bastard!"

Michael waited. He was beginning to draw a crowd and they looked shocked as if they were watching an escapee from an asylum. It reminded him of the cold hearted crowd, from the village near Kabul as they waited for his execution. If this was going to be a rerun of that day then so be it, he didn't care about himself any more, he just wanted Sarah and the others to be given their lives back. He looked at Aaron; his arms were down at his sides with fists clenched, he looked furious as if what he'd said had stopped him from finishing him off.

Michael watched and waited, knowing that at any moment he would face something unspeakable. He could feel the ground shaking, though not as violently as before when the hill had split in two. The earth and leaves in front of him rolled back and the ground opened to reveal a small stone staircase which led downwards into the earth and into darkness. Aaron turned himself in to a rattlesnake and without hesitation, wound his way to the steps and then shot down the stairs. The crowd around Michael applauded and he looked at them incredulously as if they were mad. They didn't realise what was happening and thought they were watching a show.

Michael looked at the steps warily, he didn't want to follow after Aaron and wasn't sure where the steps would lead to but he knew that this was his only chance to put things right. He stepped onto the first step and then realised that the crowd intended to follow. He spun around angrily. "Do you not realise, that you are all crazy, this is not a game or a play. You're not allowed down here. Do you understand?" The crowd took no notice and surged forward eager to take part in the festivities. Michael was going to shout again to warn them but the stairs transformed in to a slide and he shot downwards and was plunged into darkness the entrance sealing up behind him; shutting out the real world. As he slipped down the slide, he could feel the temperature increasing and wondered if he was going to be plunged into a pit of fire. He could feel his hair singeing. Finally he was cast into a windowless room, lit by lava pools.

Michael slid on to the floor, the room smelt of charred flesh, he looked at his body to see if it was himself that was on fire; he was sore and burnt but the smell oozed out of the walls and was overpowering and he coughed as he tried to breathe properly.

"You took your time getting here! So, you want to do a deal? What sort of deal do you have in mind?"

Michael got to his feet and looked around but could see no one. He could hear him so clearly as if he was next to him.

"Why don't you show yourself? I prefer to face people when I speak to them," Michael shouted.

"Well I'm not people am I? I make my presence felt where there is death and destruction and take pleasure in creating mayhem. There is no need for me to take on a worthless human form. If I did, what would you have me wear? Would I have horns on my head, wear a red leotard, have a long tail with a fork at the end of it? I don't think so."

"So here you are Michael, an ex-soldier, deluded, deranged and outraged that you are still being tortured after all you have been through. You wonder why I chose you and your friends to toy with. It was nothing more than a whim, it can get so tiresome down here and one needs a little entertainment to make life more interesting. To dwell here, or should I say be incarcerated here, I am bound by an ancient and unwritten rule to give the odd bowl of soup or grant the occasional wish. That is exactly what I did for you all; granted you all your pathetic little wishes but I might have made things a bit more interesting. You all got what you deserved and now you have the impertinence to want to do a deal. Hear me Michael McGrath, I don't believe in happy endings - there will have to be a trade-off."

Michael listened to what he believed to be the Devil. He could hardly believe what he was hearing and realised that there was very little chance of doing a straightforward deal. "We didn't walk around the Ring or summon you. None of us made wishes; you had no need to pick on us especially. Sarah has been through enough, she didn't deserve to be sent back to Afghanistan again."

The Devil laughed. "She was just in the wrong place at the wrong time. It happens! I could just pulverise those irritating people on my hill if I wanted but that would be too dull, I much prefer tormenting the Ring barnacles one by one. You may say that you didn't deserve to have your dearest wishes granted but I was doing you a favour. You all had your problems, fears and dark secrets. Take you for example; you're a casualty of war; your mind is spent and you're not quite sure if you murder children when you lose your mind. You wished to start a new life abroad and that is what you got."

"Why didn't you leave me alone, why did you send Aaron after me? I could have been happy there with Sarah," replied Michael angrily.

"Where's the fun in that. If I grant a wish then there is a price to pay. Aaron has his own axe to grind but shouldn't bother you again should we come to an arrangement. I told you, I don't believe in giving something for nothing."

"You've had your fun with us and it's time to let us go, God knows what they've been through. It's time to do a deal and do as I ask, release us and restore our lives."

"Don't mention that name here! This is all a bit one sided - what do I get out of it? You realise that I could just strike you down dead if I chose."

"I think there is a reason why you can't. I think this hill will only let you go so far. You said that you were trapped, there must be a power greater than yours to contend with otherwise you would rise up from here and end all of mankind. You know what I say is true." Michael gritted his teeth and waited to die, he was shaking with fear but no lethal blow was dealt and he was met with silence.

Michael scanned the room and waited to be attacked and then noticed Barney, Tom's dog, sat in the corner; he was whimpering. Michael thought that he'd died in the explosion. Although he didn't particularly care for the dog, distressed by the sound of his cries, he walked over to him to see if he could help and he called out his name to let him know he wasn't going to hurt him. The corner he was in was dark as if he was trying to hide away. Michael bent down to look at the old greyhound to see why it was crying and then saw to his dismay a barbed wire collar wrapped around his neck. The rusty wire had been wound around several times; the barbs stuck into his flesh causing puncture marks and blood dripped down on to the floor. Michael was cross and couldn't understand why such needless cruelty had been inflicted on him. He sat down on the hot stone floor to see more clearly and to look for the join in the collar. He found the end of the wire and gently unravelled it, trying not to cause the dog any more pain. His fingers were burnt and sore from trying to tear Aaron's arm away from his body earlier. It was a difficult job to remove the last length as the barbs were embedded in the dog's skin.

Finally, Michael threw the wire to the side and stared at the dog hoping that it would stop making such an unbearable noise. The dog gradually stopped whimpering and then his eyes narrowed as if he blamed Michael for the cruelty and he began to snarl. Michael backed away from the dog and hoped that it wouldn't bite him. He was disappointed that the greyhound didn't understand that he was trying to help him.

"See what happens when you carry out an act of kindness," the Devil shouted. "There is no reward. There is nothing to be gained by granting wishes. With my help, mankind will eventually wipe themselves out; it is only a matter of time and then I can walk the earth again as I did when the earth came in to being."

"I didn't need a lesson from you! Don't you think we've had enough of those? I am a good man, I don't care that the dog hates me, I can take that and yes some people can be heartless and cruel but most wish to lead peaceful lives. You shouldn't mess with the innocent."

"The innocent are fools, irritants, barnacles, filthy parasites and they breed like rats. I don't care for the guiltless; I get my pleasure from filling my dungeons with the bad, the corrupt, the evil and then watch them squirm as their souls burn for eternity. That is, my music and their hearts a light hors d'oeuvre. So Michael what will you give me in return for your freedom? Your new born? I guess your soul is out of the question, your right arm perhaps?"

"What do you mean, new born? Did Sarah give birth? Where are they?" Michael could feel angry tears burning in his eyes. "You know I haven't seen my child; you had me shot! I would give anything to be with them again. What have you done to them?"

32

Evie had been engulfed in a white mist for hours and hours, she felt as light as a feather and thought that she might be floating in a warm sea; aimlessly drifting in no particular direction. She believed she was in a tropical sea somewhere. Sometimes she could hear sea birds cry and surf washing onto a beach and at other times she thought she was in a train carriage and could hear the wheels as they rattled along the tracks. She was alone in her peaceful ocean and wondered if she was the only person left alive in the world. She wished that she could stay there forever but for the terrible thirst that consumed her.

The air around her was hot and she could see steam rising off of the water. The warm water sifted through her fingers and taunted her as she suspected it was undrinkable as she could smell the salt in the warm breeze. The steam reminded her of a sea mist at Goring; she didn't like to think of that place and tried to close her mind to seeing a picture of her mother wagging a finger of disapproval at her. She could see her mother's lips moving but, all she could hear was a siren and Evie's pleas for cool water went unheard.

"Evie, please wake up, we've got to take shelter," begged Milly. "I haven't got time to get someone to carry you. I was dreading this day."

Evie opened her eyes with a sense of relief; she couldn't bear to look at her mother for a moment longer. Milly was by her bedside and she was carrying Edward, he had his head on her shoulder and was asleep. Her two boys stood by her and looked anxiously at their mother, willing her to hurry and take shelter. Evie looked at Milly curiously and then realised the gravity of the situation. "Where's my dressing gown," she asked with difficulty as her mouth was so dry. Milly unhooked it from the back of the door and passed it to her.

"Thank goodness you're awake. How are you feeling? Your fever's all gone now, you've made it Evie but if we don't take shelter soon, we could all be in trouble."

"You go on, I'll slow you down, please take Edward and your two to safety, I won't be far behind you, I've got to get my land legs back again."

"I don't like to leave you."

"No, go," insisted Evie. "I promise I'll be fine."

Evie watched Milly leave her bedroom and then run off with the children to their Anderson shelter that was buried in the orchard behind the farmhouse. Evie sat up pulled back the covers and swung her feet on to the floor. The whitewashed boards felt cool against the skin on her feet. She put on her dressing gown and using the corner of her bedside table stood up. She felt very light headed but felt strong enough to walk. There was a glass of water on her bedside table and she knew she would have to drink before she attempted going down the stairs. She gulped down the water, thankful that it wasn't salty and then set the glass down next to a jug of poppies.

She knew she didn't have much time left to get to the shelter. Carefully, she made her way down to the kitchen and then putting on her wellington boots, she walked outside into the darkness; she'd no idea that it was night time and this surprised her and she wondered how long she'd been asleep. The night was warm and a light breeze ran through her hair. She ran her fingers through it and wished she'd brushed it before leaving as it was matted with dried sweat.

It was very dark outside and she had to feel her way along the side of the house so she didn't stray off the path. Her attention turned to the sky, she could hear a familiar humming noise in the distance; there were enemy planes approaching and she knew that she wouldn't reach the shelter in time. She looked around for a safe place to hide and it was then that she heard bombs falling and exploding. Terrified she pinned herself against the wall of the house and shut her eyes praying that the Germans wouldn't target the farmhouse. She turned her face away from the planes as they flew overhead. She felt frightened and she closed her eyes until the planes had passed over and then, using every ounce of strength she'd left in her, ran towards the shelter, stumbling as she went She still remembered the way and realised that it had been over sixty years since she'd been to the shelter.

"Oh, Evie!" cried out Milly "I thought you weren't going to make it. Where have you been? Sit down, you poor lamb; you look worn out. I knew I shouldn't have left you."

Evie sat down on her cushion on the bench next to Milly and couldn't speak for a while as her breath had been taken by fright. As she recovered, she looked at Edward who was fast asleep in Milly's arms. Evie held on to his warm foot, just to make sure she wasn't dreaming. Milly's boys were in their bed, one at each end. They looked sleepy but looked frightened and were unusually quiet.

"Did you hear those bombs come down?" whispered Milly as if the very word would explode in their faces. "I wonder where they fell? They sounded so close to us. Do you think it was the village center?"

"I don't think so, it was further away, maybe nearer to Weymouth," Evie looked around the shelter. "Where's Albert?"

"What do you mean Evie," he's not here. He's fighting for us in Africa.

Evie stared at Milly in amazement. "No, Milly, he's here, don't you remember, he came on the day I got sick and when you went for the doctor, he stayed with me."

"Oh Evie, you must have been seeing things. There was no one there; it must have been your fever. You were so ill, I thought we were going to lose you; you've been unconscious for three days. You must have seen Albert in your dreams. I know you are missing him, he'll be home soon, you'll see."

"Oh dear, it's as I thought," sighed Evie. "I won't, see him again - he's dead."

"That's an awful thing to say Evie, you don't know that."

"He came to say goodbye and to see Edward. I understand what happened now. One of my greatest wishes was that Edward could have met his father and someone out there granted that for me. If you don't believe me, how did Edward get dressed and fed that morning?"

Milly shook her head, not wanting to cause any further distress. "I did wonder," she replied, remembering getting him from his cot that morning. She'd dressed him and took him down to the kitchen and given him his breakfast.

Evie looked at Milly and knew that she didn't believe her. "Do we have anything to eat with us? I'm starving."

Milly pointed to a tin of biscuits. "There are a few biscuits in there and a bit of cake that mother made but it might be past its best."

Evie helped herself to a biscuit and ate it slowly; her throat was still tender from being so dry. She thought of Albert and how angelic he'd looked holding Edward and then remembered Albert's face when she'd first seen him in the kitchen; he looked as if he'd just stepped off the battlefield. She now understood that what she'd seen was his ghost and she knew that was the last she would ever see of him. She still believed that Albert had come to see Edward and would remember their time together as being magical. Now she knew that Albert had died, she could get on with the rest of her life as a single mother. She sighed as she thought of Tom and knew that she must try her best to forget him as the reality was - he'd deserted her.

"I'm so glad you're feeling better but you're looking so thin. I'm going to have to fatten you up somehow," Milly said putting Edward in his make shift cot, made from an old drawer. "Oh yes," she exclaimed. "I forgot to tell you. The strangest thing happened when you were ill. Did you notice three huge poppies in a jug, in your room, next to your bed?"

"No, where did they come from," replied Evie intrigued.

"I don't know, I thought you might," continued Milly. "I found them on the floor by your bed. The first red one appeared on the day you got ill, the second pink one on the next day and today I found the orange one, roots and all. Who do you think left them? And why would someone leave you a flower with a root?"

Evie tried hard to remember the jug of poppies but hadn't noticed them. She couldn't think of anyone that might leave a flower for her and then she looked at Milly's boys who were now asleep. "You don't think it was Christopher or Charlie who left the flowers there?"

"No, it wasn't them, I did ask and when I thought about it, on two of the days, the boys were at school when they appeared. You haven't got another secret lover hiding in the wings have you?"

"No Milly," Evie replied a little surprised by her comment. "I really can't think where they've come from. How strange, I wonder if I will get one tomorrow? It's all a bit creepy don't you think?"

"Yes, I do," replied Milly now looking alarmed. "We should make sure all the doors are locked, night and day. I've been really lazy and often forget to lock up at night. I can't believe I've allowed a stranger to walk into our house; for all we know he could be a criminal!"

"I'm sure that's not the case. There must be a rational explanation for this but I can't think of one at the moment. Don't worry Milly; I'm sure there must be a sensible reason; there's nothing to worry about."

***

Wearily, Tom made his way to the farm with a duck egg in his jaws. The sun was high in the sky and he felt hot. He'd remembered bringing eggs back to the flat in Brighton and had seen the look of joy on Evie's face and hoped that the egg would make her realise it was him. His heart was heavy, three days had been such a long time to be unconscious and he wondered why she'd not been taken to hospital - if he'd been human, he would have taken her.

He stopped and put down the egg by the edge of the field, in the shade of the post and rail fence, to get his breath back and looked sadly up at Evie's bedroom window - he hoped she would be better today. He looked over to the kitchen door and was dismayed to find that it was shut. For the past few days, it had been very hot and to let fresh air into the kitchen, the door had been left open. He'd crept into the house each day whilst Evie's friend put the baby in the pram. He then checked on Evie and left her a poppy. He was pleased to see that the other flowers had been put in a jug by her bed. Getting out of the house had been a bit trickier and one of the days he'd hidden for an hour in the room next to the kitchen, with his heart thumping, waiting for the right moment to escape.

Tom picked up the egg, crept behind the barn and then hid behind the chicken coop to wait; this was the closest he could get to the kitchen door without being seen. The chickens didn't appreciate him being there but soon settled down when they realised that he wasn't interested in them. Whilst he waited, he watched them pecking at the ground randomly for bits of grain and found them to be the most irritating bird that ever existed, followed closely by ducks and could fully understand why foxes liked to wring their necks and not even bother eating them.

He didn't have to wait long and then to his great delight, Evie appeared carrying her baby in her arms - Edward, he'd remembered his name. She looked pale and much thinner than he remembered but her eyes were bright and her hair shone in the afternoon sunshine. His heart began to pound with a mixture of anxiety and excitement. He picked up the egg and walked over to her and stopped a short distance away so that she wouldn't be alarmed when she saw him; he hoped that she wasn't afraid of foxes. She put Edward in the pram and then holding the handle rocked it gently to get him off to sleep.

When she was satisfied that he'd settled, she turned to go back in the house and it was then that she saw Tom with the egg in his mouth. He didn't know what to expect but her look of amazement and shock was evident on her face. She stared at him and remained frozen to the spot. He carefully walked a few steps towards her and placed the large duck egg at her feet and retreated. Evie smiled at him and she didn't move a muscle as she called out to Milly to come and see. Tom wasn't at all sure that Milly would approve. She called her again and she appeared in the doorway but scowled when she saw him.

Tom was about to run off when he noticed something move in the barn. He thought it was a rat at first but he could hear and sense that it was a much larger animal - it was the rogue fox after Milly's chickens again. Without warning, it shot out of the barn, tore across the farmyard, upsetting the chickens and leapt up onto the pram. Tom stared at the fox and couldn't believe what he was seeing. It was emaciated and desperate to for food but he couldn't believe that it would attack a child. He heard Evie scream out and Milly yell at the demon fox. He knew that it had to be stopped and quickly, before any damage was done. He raced over to the pram and jumped up onto the back of the fox and managed to pull him off Edward and drag him onto the cobbles below. There they wrestled and battled until there was no fight left in the beast. Tom, with his sides heaving for breath, watched the rogue fox run off into the field beyond the post and rail fence and knew that it was badly wounded and would die - he felt no remorse.

Tom looked back at Evie and Milly to try and reassure them and was alarmed to see that the friend was loading a shot gun. Confused, he looked at the other fox running across the field and thought she might try and finish it off. Slowly, it dawned on him that he was in danger too and he knew he must flee. In panic, he ran as fast as he could, choosing to go the same way as the rogue fox. This was a fatal mistake; he should have found a better escape route.

He felt the bullet enter his head and a sharp pain took his breath away, he heard the shot echo around him in the hills, saw the sun for a fleeting moment and then - nothing.

"Oh Milly, you've hit the wrong fox. Didn't you see it fight off that bad fox and save Edward? Why did you kill it? It did nothing wrong," yelled Evie in tears as she attended to Edward who was crying too.

"Oh, don't be ridiculous!" snapped Milly lowering the smoking shot gun. "They were both filthy vermin; either of them could have ripped Edward's face off. I've never seen anything like it and in broad daylight too. Grow up Evie!"

Evie watched Milly storm into the house. She'd stepped on the duck egg and its contents spilled out. Evie picked up Edward to comfort him; he'd just a puncture wound in his cheek which was bleeding a little. She wiped away the blood with a tissue and then cuddling him, rubbed his back to soothe him. She looked over to the fox lying on its side under the fence. She wished it had run a little faster, taken cover in the shrubbery and missed the shot. She couldn't bear to look at him again, it was too awful.

Edward had stopped crying and was looking sleepy; the wound on his cheek had stopped bleeding. She continued to rock him but she couldn't help weeping as she thought about the dead fox. She couldn't understand why she was crying so much. There had to be a reason why the fox had brought her the egg and possibly the flowers too. It was all so surreal; nothing surprised her any more. She'd a strange feeling inside - it was almost as if she'd lost a good friend. Evie leant back against the wall, holding Edward close to her for comfort and tried to compose herself before she went into the house to face Milly. She knew it was daft and she'd told herself that she must continue her life without Tom but there was something desperately sad about losing the fox. She couldn't help but feel that she'd lost him too.

33

"Sarah, I don't want you to panic," Amy said as calmly as she could. "Don't look will you? Ted is in the car behind us. It's just typical, I can't believe it! We've just got to pretend he's not there and get to a police station as quickly as we can. There's two of us and only one of him, so we mustn't be afraid."

As they waited to take their turn to move on to the dual carriage way, Sarah felt frightened and she stopped herself from looking in the mirrors to see him; she could feel his eyes boring into the back of her head. She stared at the cars flying past, the roads were still busy with the morning rush hour traffic; she didn't feel confident that they would make it to a police station in one piece. She was grateful Amy was with her and was surprised how calm she was considering the circumstances; she didn't seem to be afraid of Ted at all. As they pulled away and built up speed, Sarah allowed herself a quick look over her shoulder to see if the white taxi was following; she gasped as it was tailgating them and was almost touching their rear bumper. She looked anxiously at Amy and could see that she was worried too; her teeth were clenched together and her foot was pressing hard on the accelerator but the car wasn't powerful enough to speed away from their pursuer. "You don't think he's going to ram into us do you?" whispered Sarah. She could barely speak now as her jaw was so swollen.

"I don't think so; he loves his car far too much to damage it. He's just trying to scare us," she replied trying to remain calm but deep down she was feeling vexed and her heart was beating hard. She also felt guilty and couldn't understand why. This was the first time, she'd stood up to him and retaliated; she knew it was crazy but she felt like she was betraying him and ruining their relationship. She knew she didn't love him any more and she couldn't understand why she was feeling so miserable. She guessed that it would take a long time for her to recover from the emotional damage that he'd caused and that she must try her best to ignore her guilty feelings and give herself time to mend.

When they came to a large roundabout, Amy managed to get away from Ted and sped out in front of a car approaching them from the right; Ted was unable to follow. She wondered if he knew where they were going. She suspected that he might and thought about pulling up in a garage or supermarket and calling the police from there but she was too frightened to stop.

After a torturous twenty minute drive, Amy drove into the police station car park and looked for a place to park. There were no spaces left and she knew that Ted wouldn't be far behind them; she half hoped that they had lost him but that idea evaporated as a white taxi appeared in the car park entrance. Amy slammed on the brakes and stopped the car in front of the main entrance of the police station. She jumped out of the car and then helped Sarah out; she was looking very pale and had beads of sweat on her forehead. "There's nowhere to park and for our own safety, I think it's best if we just leave the car here and get inside the building as soon as possible. You poor thing, you're looking terrible."

Amy hadn't been inside a police station before and thought it would be bustling with life and be more welcoming than what she saw before her. The reception area was dimly lit and in a poor condition. The front desk had scuff marks up the front of it and the top was chipped and worn. There were padded bench seats around the waiting area which had rips in and the floor didn't look clean. Behind the front desk stood a female police officer, her uniform stretched around her ample body and looked as if it would split at the seams at any moment. She was assisting an elderly man who was trying to explain to her that he'd lost his driving licence when he moved to his nursing home and he suspected Gillian Scrimp of stealing it from him as she was the nursing home's magpie.

Amy sat Sarah down on one of the cleaner looking benches and looked anxiously at the doors, hoping that Ted wouldn't follow them in. If he knew what was good for him then he would keep away, flee perhaps, realising that it was all over. He might have guessed that she'd helped Sarah out of the boot but what he didn't know, was that she knew he was a murderer.

"You're going to have to wait, you know. I'm going to be a while!"

Amy's attention turned to the police officer's unwelcoming greeting and she wondered why she sounded so hostile. If she understood how urgent the matter was then she might be a bit more willing to help."

"My friend's been assaulted and the man that did it is in the car park. She needs medical attention."

"Not another domestic. The young people in this town cause nothing but trouble!" the police officer exclaimed. "No discipline, that's the problem. Now if you don't mind, I need to establish exactly where this man had his car accident and it may take some time. You can wait if you want."

Amy scowled at the police officer she was making some wild assumptions. Sarah looked very pale and dazed. She could see that she was now too ill to give a statement and was in need urgent medical attention. She took her phone out of her bag and called 999 for an ambulance.

As she finished the call, to her amazement Ted walked into the police station, smiling as if nothing had happened.

Amy didn't know what to say to him and promptly sat down next to Sarah to comfort her and wait for an ambulance to arrive. She seemed to be deteriorating rapidly and didn't seem to register that Ted was standing near to her staring directly at them.

"So what are you doing here then Amy? I saw you leaving Findon and was worried about you. Why didn't you ring me?"

Amy glared at Ted, she couldn't believe her ears; he was acting as if he was innocent. "You know why I'm here," snapped Amy.

She could tell by his reaction that he wasn't used to her being so aggressive and fully expected her to be her usual submissive self. Amy looked over towards the police officer to see if she was likely to finish soon; she didn't like being so close to him, his attitude was making her skin crawl. She held Sarah's hand to try and comfort her.

"She doesn't look very well. She needs to see a doctor. I can take her to one."

"I don't think so! An ambulance will be here in a moment," Amy replied proudly. She could see that this revelation had annoyed him. She could hear a siren in the distance and hoped that it was the ambulance approaching. Ted sat down opposite them and she suspected that his friendly facade was about to crack. Amy said nothing more to him. She was worried and wasn't sure if she should go with Sarah to the hospital or stay and give a statement. She decided on the latter as going to the hospital would delay Ted's arrest and put them both in danger.

Amy looked over to the police officer with impatience; she seemed to be taking her time. She was showing a stretch of road on a screen to the man who seemed to be getting more and more confused. There was an air of sarcasm in her voice as her patience waned. "Are you sure you were a victim of a hit and run? It seems very unlikely," she asked him.

"I have a large bruise on my right thigh, do you want me to show it to you?" replied the man not realising that the police officer was being rude.

Amy looked at her watch and was praying that Sarah wouldn't collapse before the ambulance got there. She stood up to see if they were coming and felt very relieved when she saw two men in green uniforms making their way into the building. Ted said nothing but had a very sour look on his face. "I rang you," she called out to the ambulance men. "This is Sarah, I don't know her last name, she's not able to talk, I think her jaw is broken and she might be in shock. I would have taken her to casualty myself only we were going to report the assault but she's suddenly gone downhill."

The ambulance men swiftly worked on Sarah, much to the disapproval of the police officer who was annoyed that an ambulance had been called without her permission. As Sarah, who was now unconscious was put on a stretcher, Ted stood up. "I'll go with her," he announced.

Amy was shocked by his audacity. "You're the one who did this to her, you can't be serious?"

"I am serious, you know I wouldn't hurt a fly, look what you did to me!" he said showing Amy his eye and the scratch on his arm.

"I don't think that would be a good idea if either of you came," said a distressed ambulance man. "If she comes round, she might want to make a complaint and if she sees you both, it might upset her."

Amy felt comforted as she watched the ambulance drive off and knew that Sarah was in safe hands for the moment. Her plan was to make her statement, accusing Ted of assault and murder and then go straight to the hospital after he'd been arrested. She glanced briefly over at him and could see the fury in his eyes; he was becoming desperate and she wondered what he might do next. She could wait no longer and approached the police officer again. "Look I'm sorry but I need to speak to someone, it can't wait. Surely there must be someone else here that could help me? I need to make a statement and get this man arrested."

The police officer looked as if she was about to explode. "How dare you..." she didn't finish as Ted interrupted

"You don't have to do this," he said looking slyly at her. "You know it wasn't me that hurt Sarah, it was you. It's not your fault though, you are depressed and you have a terrible temper. I don't know why you hurt her or why you're here. I think I should take you home, we need to work this problem out and get your medication reviewed."

"What on earth are you talking about?" screamed Amy. "I'm as sane as the next person. Why are you saying all this? You're the one that punched Sarah in the face and you're the one that committed murder! Don't you dare turn this on me you bastard!"

"If you don't mind!" boomed the police officer. "If you could take your domestic spat out of this office into the car park I would be most grateful or I'll have you both arrested for disturbing the peace."

"I'm not going anywhere, this man needs arresting, he has blood on his hands and is a danger to women. I am not taking his shit any more, if you don't do anything then I'm going to ring the police here and now and have you reported!"

"See what I mean," Ted exclaimed calmly. "She's completely nuts; I don't know why I'm still with her. I must be mad," he said snatching her mobile out of her hand. "Her whole family are just the same."

Amy stared at the police officer, pleading with her to see sense but her outburst had done more harm than good. She could tell that she was sympathising with Ted - he'd charmed her.

"I agree, she obviously needs help," she said trying to avoid eye contact with her. "If you could both leave this police station, I would be most grateful and we'll take this matter no further."

Ted grabbed Amy's arm and pulled her out of the reception area and out into the car park. Amy was so shocked; she couldn't believe that she'd allowed him to take her outside, she felt emotionally drained and extremely frightened. She was starting to fear for her own life and needed to buy time.

"I'm sorry," she said gently. "I didn't know what I was saying."

"We'll talk about it when we get home. You're not well Amy. You need to go back to the doctors and get more antidepressants, you should never have come off them," he said leading her to his taxi. Amy felt a familiar crying pain returning in the pit of her stomach, one of frustration and despair. She remembered how down she'd felt a year into their relationship and how depressed she'd become. Antidepressants had aided her initially and had eventually helped her to see the wood for the trees. It didn't take her long to realise that Ted was a complete arse and that she didn't need pills.

He held the passenger door open and waited for her to get in but Amy pulled her arm away from his and tried to turn and run. Immediately he caught her again and pulling her close to him, he whispered in her ear. "Don't try anything stupid," he spat out the words. "Be a good girl or you'll be sorry!" He fully expected her to obey him but she wasn't willing to be bullied and responded by stamping hard down on his toes with her heel; Ted yelled and let go of her arm.

She ran as fast as she could towards her car and searched desperately through her bag to find her key; it wasn't in its usual place. She found it in her pocket, pressed the fob hard and was glad when she heard the central locking system open. Nervously, she looked over at Ted; she swung the door open and jumped into the car, slammed the door shut and then with a shaking hand tried to get the key in the ignition. Panic stricken, she looked back at Ted, he'd recovered and was running towards her. The car made a choking noise and then sprung in to life. Amy forced the gear stick in reverse and without looking sped backwards and then moved into first and tore off leaving Ted standing alone in the car park; he looked furious.

Amy tried to control her breathing; she was almost hyperventilating with fear. The road was clear and she turned left and tried to think where the ambulance might have taken Sarah; she hadn't thought to ask. She didn't know why, she hoped it was her psychic ability helping her but her instincts were telling her to go to north.

As she drove; she thought about the spirit that had helped her find Sarah. She was surprised that she could see her at all as she'd gone back in time and she didn't have any psychic ability until 2013. Things hadn't gone well at the police station and she wondered why her mission to stop Ted from murdering woman was proving so difficult. She was sure that if someone was reporting a murder at a police station then they would take notice. There was something very strange going on; she no longer felt that she was in control of her destiny.

Amy looked in her rear view mirror to see if she could see Ted following her; he wasn't behind her. She remembered what had happened in the car park with Ted and angry tears spilled out of her eyes; she was annoyed with herself for saying sorry to him. He was a diabolical person and he'd humiliated her in front of the police officer, made her look like a mad woman and made anything she said worthless. Amy turned on the radio to take her mind off things for a moment, there was a talk show playing but she couldn't concentrate on what they were saying. She turned off from the main road and decided that she would go through Crawley to get to Redhill. She just followed the signs and hoped she would see one for the hospital as she hadn't been there before.

The hospital car park was quite busy and she had to wait for a parking space. She looked in her bag and felt her pockets; she would have to pay for parking but didn't have any change. She hoped the parking machine would take a debit card but had no idea how much was in her account - there was probably very little.

Amy stopped by a notice board showing a plan of the hospital and she looked for the accident and emergency department. The wind was cold and she shivered and decided to zip her coat up. She thought about Sarah's night in the boot and wasn't surprised that she'd become so ill, she was lucky not to have died of hypothermia. She began to walk a little more urgently; she felt cold and wanted to get inside. As she passed an alleyway between two buildings something made her stop and look down it; a familiar figure appeared at the end of the alley; it was the spirit of the girl that Ted had killed. She looked at Amy with apologetic eyes. She knew she was trying to tell her something and wondered why she was there. She thought that she might have died at the hospital. The girl's face changed and she looked as if she was screaming. Amy walked towards her to get a better look and to help her. From nowhere, someone's arm went across her throat and dragged her further into the alley and into the shadows.

She struggled with her attacker and tried to scream but a hand went over her mouth and stifled her cries for help; she cursed herself for not running when she'd seen the girl; she should have known that Ted would be nearby. The grip around her throat loosened and she thought for a moment that he was going to let her go but this didn't happen. She saw out of the corner of her eye a kitchen knife in his hand and then felt the cold steel blade go into her stomach. Ted drew her into him as if he wanted the blade to go through himself too; she could feel that he was erect and she felt sickened by the fact that he was getting some sexual satisfaction from hurting her. He released her and it was only when he drew out the knife did she feel an excruciating pain rip through her body. She felt faint and knew that she was bleeding; her legs felt wobbly and threatened to buckle. She managed to walk a few steps away from him but then her legs gave way and she fell to her knees and then slumped over. Ted said nothing and kicked her violently in the head as if it were a football; she shut her eyes and prayed that he would leave her in peace.

When she opened her eyes again he'd gone. From the cold concrete floor she could see a patch of grass, the car park beyond and the sky. She wondered if this would be the last thing she would see before she died. Tears of despair ran down her cheeks not from pain but from disappointment as she wouldn't be able to stop him from committing more murders. She almost laughed, it was ironic, she'd become his next victim and her miserable spirit would be linked to his for eternity.

She could feel no pain now, just a coldness creeping through her body. Her vision became blurry and she wondered how long it would be before the sky would turn black. She sensed that she wouldn't die alone, she felt warm hands on her body, people calling to each other to get help and she felt hopeful that there might be someone out there that could save her. The most striking and intriguing sentence that stood out from all the rest was that they would catch the bastard as they had him on camera; someone had seen Ted running off and had videoed him on their mobile phone. Amy smiled. If she was going to die, she wasn't going to die in vain, there was a witness and Ted would be captured.

The last thing she saw before she drifted out of consciousness was the spirit of Ted's first victim. She was standing at the entrance of the alleyway and was smiling at her, reassuring her that she would live. Amy allowed herself to close her eyes and sleep.

34

Thousands of snowflakes swirled down from the night sky; large white flakes like feathers, some almost as big as saucers twirled down onto a thick white carpet of snow. Relieved to be breathing again, Tom blinked away the snowflakes that lay on his eyelashes and tried to make sense of his new surroundings. He didn't know how he'd got to be lying on the ground looking up at the heavens. The pain in his head had gone and he wondered if he might have died and become a ghost of a fox. He couldn't hear the chickens clucking or the cows mooing and he couldn't hear the wind whistling in the hills; the familiar sounds of the farmyard had gone. He wondered why it was snowing in the summer and why the world around him felt still and void of any life.

The snow was beginning to build up on his face and without thinking he brought up a paw to clear it from his cheeks and then stared hard at his paw only to find it was a gloved hand - a human hand. Triumphant, he lifted his other hand to verify that his eyes were not deceiving him and that he really was a person again. He sat up quickly to check that the rest of his body had transformed and looked down at his legs and his feet; he recognised his black wellington boots. Carefully, he got to his feet. He felt incredibly tall and the ground seemed a long way away. He looked around him and knew where he was immediately and he smiled as he recognised his front garden covered in snow and his beloved sports car parked on the road. There was a spade at his feet and it looked as if he'd been clearing the path and perhaps fallen over because of the ice. He wondered why he'd bothered to come out and clear the path at all as the snow looked set to fall through the night and all his efforts would have been in vain. He picked up the spade and carefully walked up the partly cleared path to his front door. He laid the spade against the wall and then seeing that the door was open went inside. There was a candle burning on the side table and it lit up the hallway making him feel welcome.

Tom took off his boots and looked at his feet, it was taking him time to get used to having a human body again; he felt like he'd been a fox for a life time. As he hung his coat up, he looked at a photo of his daughter Ruth, hanging on the wall, When the photo had been taken she'd been about six years old, she was wearing a fairy costume and was smiling at him. She'd always liked dressing up and he felt a surge of happiness run through him at the thought of seeing her again. He patted his pockets to see if he could find his mobile phone and with a sigh of relief found it and took it out to make sure it was really there; he put it back in his pocket and decided that after he'd made a cup of tea, he would give her a ring.

He walked past the stairs and made his way to the kitchen and turned on the light. The kitchen wasn't quite as he remembered it to be - there was something missing or out of place - but he wasn't sure what it was. He made himself a cup of tea and took two ginger nuts from the biscuit barrel and walked through to the sitting room, hoping to find Barney in his basket. He looked around the room but there was no basket and no dog. Tom sighed; he missed him and felt guilty that he hadn't held on to him when the Chanctonbury Ring had exploded.

He sat down and stared at the fire, it needed another log so he took one out of the basket and threw it on to the fire. The log spat as the flames engulfed it. He leant back in his arm chair and looked around the room. Apart from the absence of Barney, the front room looked the same. The lamp on the mahogany sewing cabinet with its tasselled lampshade was just as he remembered and everything else in the room was positioned correctly; unlike the kitchen which looked as if it was in need of decoration again. Tom looked up at the time on the dusty clock on the mantelpiece and it surprised him how late it was, it was ten past twelve - too late to ring Ruth.

It was good to be home and he hoped that his life would get back to normal and he would walk a dog, look after his sports car and visit the Frankland Arms for his lunch. He decided that past events had been hallucinations; he'd obviously knocked himself out when he slipped on the garden path and had given himself concussion. He smiled at the thought of establishing his weekly routine again.

The clock's ticking echoed in the silence and gradually, his smile faded as he realised that his life would never be the same again. He still had the same grieving feeling inside his chest, the feeling of loss and loneliness but it was stronger than it used to be and this puzzled him. He thought of Martha and although he missed her terribly, the reason he was feeling so miserable was because Evie wasn't there with him.

Losing her was too painful to endure and he didn't know how he would cope without her; he just wanted to find her and start living again.

On the side table next to Tom, was a newspaper, he picked it up and read the headlines and then looked at the date and sighed, it was 5th April 2008. Wearily, he flicked through the newspaper to reacquaint himself with the news and then became irritated by the old news and flung it down. He couldn't understand why he'd gone back in time by about five years but then again, he couldn't understand why he'd gone back to the war years and then turned in to a fox. Something sinister and peculiar had happened to him up at the Chanctonbury Ring. Then a thought caught his breath, shocking him right through to his core and with a mixture or anxiety and trepidation, he stared up towards the ceiling and wondered if his wife might be up there.

***

Martha's eyes snapped open and through them Evie could see a bedroom with black beams protruding from a whitewashed ceiling. The walls were covered in floral wallpaper and through the window; she saw snow falling outside from the night sky. She didn't recognise this room and thought that she might be dreaming and still in a coma. The room was lit by a bedside lamp and she could hear music but wasn't sure where it was coming from. She could feel herself moving, a foot shifted and a head moved but it wasn't her initiating this, she was in someone else's body and she felt trapped like a spider under a glass. She couldn't speak; she couldn't escape from this body and could do nothing but lie there.

Only moments ago, she'd been hugging Edward and crying about the death of a fox and then, in a blink of an eye, she'd been transported to become a prisoner in someone else's body.

She took a deep breath in and was pleased that she could still breathe and was glad that she could remember everything that had happened to her. She couldn't understand why she'd been shunted from one time to another. There had however, been a lesson or a wish granted each time but she'd suffered terribly too. She felt cross that her life was being engineered and she'd become nothing more than a puppet.

She regretted not going up to the Chanctonbury Ring with Tom. She smiled as she thought of him and hoped that he was ok; she didn't like to think of him alone and she knew she must find him again. Now things had been settled with Albert, she could move on and not feel guilty about loving Tom. Evie sighed, there was very little she could do at the moment and hoped that her lesson would be over quickly; life was becoming very tiresome. The sound of footsteps approaching stopped her thinking and she listened; she could hear someone coming towards the room. Uneasily, she waited for a stranger to appear in the doorway.

Tom stopped near the top of the stairs and stared at Martha's bedroom door, he didn't know if he could continue and open it. He was afraid of what he might see, afraid of seeing Martha in pain and dying. If it was the 5th April then that was three days before her death and if she was in the bedroom then she would be suffering; motor neuron disease wasn't a pleasant disease to die from. She wouldn't be able to speak to him and would need him to wash, feed and care for her. He didn't like to leave her alone for too long and when he was with her, he couldn't bear to see her as just a shell of what she'd once been. He hoped that this door would lead him to somewhere else and to Evie.

He didn't want to see Martha again; the memories of her last few days still haunted him in his dreams. Reluctantly, he took another step and he knew that he'd no choice and would have to go into her bedroom but he was afraid. Slowly, he climbed the last few steps and walked across the landing to her bedroom. He opened the door hoping that a white light would engulf him and drag him away and into Evie's arms.

Tom stepped into the bedroom and he waited but nothing had changed. He could hear the radio playing classical music in the background and could smell something familiar; there was a smell of illness in the air. At first he couldn't bear to look at the bed but after taking a deep breath, he looked over and forced a smile. He wasn't sure what he was expecting, he half expected to find a mummified corpse or a zombie ready to fly up from the bed and attack him. The sad scene in front of him was exactly as he remembered, it was, just Martha lying there, looking straight at him with miserable watery eyes. Resigned to the fact that he was expected to look after her; he went over to the chair by her bed and reached out to hold her hand. He'd spent many hours this way, hoping that somewhere in her dying brain, his tenderness would register.

***

Evie was overjoyed, Tom was right by her, he looked like his old self, a little tired perhaps but was almost as she remembered him when she met him in the Frankland Arms. With excitement, she called out his name but he didn't hear her and then she remembered that she was in someone else's body. It was so infuriating, she could see that he was holding hands with the body she was in but she couldn't feel his fingers or the warmth from his hand; it was maddening.

She could hear his voice, he was talking to someone with soothing calming words but he looked sad and lost. Sadly, she realised that his words were not meant for her and she felt as if she was intruding and was tempted to block her ears if she could but then she heard the name Martha; she was shocked and appalled that she was trapped in Tom's late wife's body. She tried to make sense of what was happening and guessed that Martha must be gravely ill as she hadn't spoken to Tom and had moved very little. Evie tried to hear what he was saying, he was speaking softly and it felt like he was in another room.

***

"... There's been so much I wished I could have said to you, my poor darling; it's been a long time since we were together. I hate to see you like this; I feel so helpless. I don't know if you are hungry, thirsty or in pain. You can't tell me and that's so hard to bear. I did my best for you and I hope you realised this and if you are here again to tell me that my best wasn't good enough then I am truly sorry. I think I did a good job and know I shouldn't torture myself. I remember the happy times too we had together; that always makes me feel better.

That caravan we had, I wonder where it is now? We towed that thing all over the country and had wonderful holidays in it with our little Ruth. She liked to sleep in that battered tin can even when we were at home. You should see her now Martha, she's doing so well. Did you know she got that promotion she was after and earns more than Dave does? I was going to ring her but it's gone midnight and she'll have gone to bed. She should drop in to see you soon on her way back from work tomorrow. I shouldn't say this really but she said I should put you in a hospice. I kept to my word Martha, didn't I?" Tom turned the radio down a little.

Do you see the snow? It's April and by rights, it should be getting warmer, not snowing - that's just crazy. Talking of crazy, the strangest things have been going on; you will not believe what I'm going to tell you. For the past few months, perhaps the last year, I'm not quite sure how long it was, but I became a fox. What do you think of that? You're probably laughing and think that I've lost my marbles, sometimes I think I have but it's true. I'm not sure I like being a human, life's a lot simpler as a fox ... Although it was difficult to communicate, that was a downside and going back to the war years, that wasn't easy either. I'm going to give you a drink Martha and turn you, I'd better get back in to the old routine, I don't know how long you've been lying here, I've only just arrived. You need to sleep, it's getting late."

***

Evie was speechless, she should have known that the fox she'd cried over was, in fact, Tom; it all made sense now. She felt guilty that she hadn't stopped Milly from shooting him and now understood why she'd cried so much. Again she felt infuriated that she couldn't reach out to him and tell him that she was sorry and loved him with all her heart. She tried to will Martha to move but instead Martha's eyelids began to close as she fell asleep. Evie felt wide awake and didn't like being plunged into darkness. Tom had stopped talking and all she could feel was Martha's head being lifted to sip water, then her being turned onto her side. She heard the floorboards creaking as Tom left the room and she knew she had to be patient and wait for morning to arrive.

***

As Tom climbed into his bed he looked at the space next to him where Martha used to sleep. He'd never quite got used to sleeping alone and that was one of the reasons he'd got Barney and had allowed him to sleep on the bed next to him. He missed having a dog too and forgave him for snoring so loudly at night. It occurred to him that as he'd gone back to 2008, then Barney might be available for adoption. When the snow cleared he would visit the farm where he'd picked him up and see if he was there. The thought of getting his dog back cheered him up; he would be able to cope better if his old friend was with him. Tom pushed his pillow in to shape and then sank back, he was exhausted but he knew he wouldn't be able to sleep properly; there were too many thoughts churning in his head to let him rest

He tried to think about what was worrying him most: there was one concern that was surfacing, he'd done his best to bury it for more than five years but now there was no getting away from it; he had to face the fact that he'd done something terrible in 2008 and he knew that he'd been brought to this time in his life to address and perhaps amend his mistake. It was Martha's fault really, she'd always been wary of strangers and had refused any nursing assistance and begged him not to put her in a home. He'd taken full time care of her and when she'd become too weak to walk, he'd muddled through the best he could. He'd pushed her in her wheelchair around Washington and had taken her to Ferring so she could see the sea.

Motor neurone disease was unforgiving, every day there was something new and when one day she was unable to speak, he realised that he'd already lost his wife and his best friend - it was heart-breaking. Eventually, she became so frail that she preferred to stay in bed rather than be hauled into a chair. He'd managed by himself for almost a year and a half, keeping Martha clean and fed, administrating her medication, keeping her company and reading to her but he knew he couldn't cope for much longer as he was becoming exhausted.

Two nights after the snow had cleared; he'd been sitting by Martha talking about his day when he found himself breaking down in tears. That day had been particularly difficult as Martha had a stomach virus and he had to change her several times that day and had been unable to feed her properly as her ability to swallow had diminished overnight. He tried not to let her see his tears and wiped them on his sleeve, he was pretty sure that she didn't know that he was distressed. Her eyes had a wild lost look and he thought that mentally she must be in pain too. She'd no quality of life and he couldn't see any point in her living. If she was an animal, he would have taken her to the vet and put her out of her misery long ago. It then seemed the logical thing to do, to end Martha's suffering and to let her go. If it was the other way round, he would have wanted Martha to pull the plug; he wouldn't have liked to have been a burden. They'd never spoken about euthanasia and realised that this is what he was considering. Shocked by his thoughts, he'd gone out of the bedroom and had gone downstairs for a cup of tea and to think things over; he didn't want to end her life on a whim.

All those years ago, he'd made a plan to end Martha's life. He hadn't slept much that night and had dreamt that his mother was trying to lock him in a cupboard. As the birds began to sing, he'd finalised in his mind what he would do. So that Ruth could see her mother for the last time, he planned to call her and ask her to drop by on her way to work. He knew that she would be concerned as Martha was looking so ill and knew that she would beg him again to call the hospice. He would say that he would ring them and then when he could, whilst Martha was sleeping, he would summon up the courage, creep into her room and place a pillow over her face until she stopped breathing.

In the morning, after a cup of tea, he'd made the call to Ruth and trying not to make her too alarmed, asked her to drop in, on her way to work. When she saw her mother, she'd tried to ring the hospice herself but Tom had stopped her and had promised he would call them. After Ruth had gone to work, he'd paced up and down in the kitchen until it was almost four o'clock, waiting for Martha to go to sleep. He'd taken a spare pillow out of the airing cupboard and tiptoed into her room; she looked so peaceful asleep and for a moment he faltered and questioned what he was doing. When he eventually got to her bedside she'd woken up just as he'd raised the pillow up ready to do the deed and she'd looked at him with confusion and bewilderment. He'd then forced the pillow over her face with more force than he'd intended and it was the look in her eyes that had haunted him afterwards. He held the pillow in place for five whole minutes and then lifted it cautiously. Martha's eyes were open but lifeless; he felt her wrist for a pulse to make sure that she'd gone and was relieved to find nothing.

Tom had sat down next to her in shock and it was then that he realised that he'd made a terrible mistake; he shouldn't have done it, he should have let his daughter ring the hospice. Tom had cried bitterly. He stayed with her until she was cold and then, after burning the pillow had rung the doctor. Tom didn't consider what he'd done to be murder but knew if anyone found out about what he'd done then that is exactly what they would call it.

The years had passed and he'd finally managed to convince himself that he'd done the right thing and then the pain inside him had subsided. He hoped that Martha had forgiven him. Tom turned off his bedside light and lay back down and hoped that he would fall asleep but all he could think of was that his poor wife in the next room was needlessly suffering. He knew he was being tested; someone wanted to see if he would make the same mistake twice. It was a cruel joke if that was the case and he wondered who was laughing at him.

35

Michael waited nervously for the Devil to reply but there was only silence. All he could do was hope that Sarah and the baby had survived but he suspected foul play and he dared not think about them. He felt so alone; he feared for his life and was sure that what he was experiencing was real and not a figment of his imagination. This was his day of reckoning and there was very little room for negotiation; really, he was at the Devil's mercy. All he could do was his upmost to save his life, the lives of his friends and the people he loved; he had to figure out a way to achieve this.

His skin felt like it was on fire and he was starting to feel claustrophobic; the walls around him looked as if they might close in at any moment and crush the life out of him. He didn't like being trapped under the Chanctonbury Ring; it would be a terrible place to die. He feared that he would have to listen to the wails and cries of the lost souls left to wander in the vaults beneath him for eternity and God help him, he might be forced to join them.

From the corner of the room, he heard the clip of claws against the stone floor as Barney trotted over to him, his tail wagged feebly as he looked up at him, he seemed to be saying sorry for not trusting him earlier and that he accepted him as an ally. "So you want to be friends now?" Barney wagged his tail and looked towards the far end of the room and growled as a door opened wide. Michael hadn't noticed a door being there before. Hoping this was a way out; he walked to the end of the room with Barney following but didn't go into the next room as it was in darkness. As he approached, a cinema screen lit up and revealed rows of seats. Michael stood in the doorway and looked at the spectacle before him; the seats were full of people, moaning and screaming out in agony; their cries hurt his ears. Neither he nor Barney wished to go into the theatre as the odour coming from the room was disgusting; he could smell burnt flesh, car fumes and alcohol.

"Who are these people? Why do you want me to go into this room?" Michael called out.

"Oh ignore them; I do," the Devil replied. "I'm saddled with them, they are just suicide victims, not worthy of your pity; they don't count. I lock them in here as they have nowhere else to go. They will do you no harm; they are chained to their seats and they are what you would call the living dead. Take a seat Michael, I need you to see what your so called friends have been up to and see if you think they still deserve saving. Be quick, I have much to do, it's Halloween. I haven't got all night"

Reluctantly, he sat down in a seat next to an old man in ragged clothes who was holding a knife in his right hand and was staring at his cut wrists. Thankfully, his arms were chained to the arms of the chairs. With desperation in his eyes, he turned to Michael. "My wrists won't stop bleeding, I'm going to die. I thought they'd find me but it's too late. I don't want to die."

Michael didn't know what to say, the man didn't know that he was already dead. "I'm sorry," is all Michael could think of. Fortunately, he didn't persist, he turned to a woman with a plastic bag over her head that was sat next to him and repeated what he'd just said. She sympathised with him but her voice couldn't be heard properly as the bag had no air left in it and covered her mouth tightly.

Michael's attention turned to the screen and the cries for help subsided as the film started. He saw the Chanctonbury Ring appear on the screen in front of him; it was silhouetted against a sickly yellow sky. Michael was determined not to watch the film, he felt as if he was being treated like a child and didn't like being told what to do. The film began just before the tsunami hit the South Downs and he couldn't help but look, it was so strange seeing himself on the screen and he was surprised how worn down and desperate he looked; he realised that if he'd stayed a week longer on the run then he might not have survived.

He watched Nabeel try to take Sarah back down the hill and saw himself fight with him. He watched the wall of water hit the hill and then saw how shocked they'd all looked when they'd realised that although they'd survived the tsunami; their lives had been ripped apart.

Later on when everyone had been sat around the fire, lost in thought, he heard again what everyone had said about him after Nabeel had died and he remembered the pain he'd felt when some had turned against him. Seeing Nabeel's death confirmed that there was no way he could have thrown him through the air and onto the tree stump - dark forces had been to blame.

He watched the hill split in two and then saw how they'd climbed down into the ravine and found the doors that had taken the others away from him and he watched himself in a wretched state, contemplating death, alone on the island.

One by one, each of the survivors' tragic experiences were played out. Michael wasn't comfortable being asked to judge them. He shouldn't have to decide whether they were worthy of finding peace and resolution. Their stories seemed tragic and yes they should have followed a different course at times and been stronger but then like him, they were only human. He didn't consider them all to be bad people, just weak willed.

Michael was horrified with Sarah's treatment as she'd been dragged into the lunacy and didn't deserve to be treated so cruelly, she'd done nothing wrong and perhaps needed therapy to help her get over her kidnapping ordeal. Surely it wasn't a crime to be a victim. He couldn't believe what Ted had done to her but was relieved that she was alive and in hospital. He longed to go and see her, hold her and tell her that it was all going to be all right and she would be free. "She did nothing you bastard, nothing," he blurted out. All he could hear was laughter from those around him as if he'd said something funny.

He felt outraged that Amy had been stabbed by Ted, she didn't deserve that. It wasn't her fault that he was a murderer; a devious fiend that covered his tracks well. Even though she suspected him of murder, there was very little she could have done as she didn't have any hard evidence. A ghost wouldn't have been able to make a statement and stand up in court. She had, much to his relief, saved Sarah's life and had in the process, nearly lost her own life. Amy had suffered enough and he would always be grateful to her - he would save her if he could.

Michael wondered if the Devil was tapping into his mind and listening to what he was thinking, he suspected that he was. Evie's face suddenly appeared on the screen as if he was being prompted to judge her. Her only crime was to hang on to a tin of ashes that she imagined belonged to the father of her child. It was a tragedy that she'd spent her whole life grieving. She was a lost soul and was just looking for love; she shouldn't be punished. He'd seen that she was trapped in the body of Tom's wife and urged in his mind for the Devil to release her. He also thought that she shouldn't waste any more time on Tom; he wasn't to be trusted. When Nabeel had been impaled on the tree stump, Tom had accused him of murder. He'd been judged by him without knowing the full truth. He frowned as he thought of Tom; if he decided to smother his wife a second time then he wasn't worth saving; he could burn in Hell.

"You should burn in Hell too Michael, you're a killer aren't you? Are you sure you didn't kill Nabeel? You took the life of an innocent child; strangled him with your bare hands. You deserve to die," spat the Devil as the credits rolled on the screen.

"I do not," yelled Michael. "It was trickery. You set me up and sent Aaron after me. If anyone died, then that was your doing. I'm a good man, I wouldn't hurt a child. Even when I was sick and could hear the bombs falling and hear the children and grown men scream for mercy, I know that I wouldn't have hurt or have killed a child. To murder is not in me. I am not a monster. I don't need to see any more, I have made my decision. You must end this and set us free, no more deception, our dearest wishes, whether we wanted them granted or not have been fulfilled. It is time to stop playing games and restore our lives. Where is my son, he should be with me and Sarah? What have you done with him?"

"Do you have a son? I wonder...? You were only with Sarah for a day or two. How could you have made a child in that time? Was he yours Michael?" the Devil asked and he made Michael's blood boil with fury.

"You know he is mine. You give him back to us your bastard! This all has to end. Do you hear me?"

"I'm weary of you all and there are others that as we speak, are walking around the ring of trees eager to receive soup or have their dearest wish granted. I wonder what they will get? We shall see. Yes you must leave, your so called friends will be set free too, go before I change my mind. There will be however, a price to pay and you will find out soon enough."

Michael didn't argue, he jumped up from his seat and noticed a green exit sign by the screen on the left of the room light up. He was sweating and longed to breathe in fresh air and escape the revolting smells that were all around. Barney followed close to his heels, frightened by the crazy people yelling and jeering at them, displeased by their lucky escape.

The exit door was closed and he pulled down the handle and pushed against the door with his shoulder expecting it to be locked but it opened easily. He fell out into a brightly lit passageway and the door began to close slowly behind him. Michael looked around his feet to see if Barney was with him but he wasn't and was stood in the doorway too frightened to enter. "Come on, quickly before the door closes, you daft thing," he called but the dog stood still. Reluctantly Michael walked back to the door and grabbed the edge of it to stop it from closing completely but it was burning hot and he pulled his hand away. "Come on boy, quickly. It's fine out here, come on." Barney looked behind him for a moment; Michael thought he was going to return to the putrid room and wondered why he would want to. Just before the door closed, he fled out into the passage as if he were being chased by something.

Relieved, Michael followed him and pushed open swing doors at the end of the passage, let Barney through and walked out into a brightly lit gallery; the walls were festooned with paintings from local secondary schools. The building had a glass front and he noticed that it was dark outside. There was no one else in the gallery. Michael sat down on a seat in the middle of the room and breathed in the cool air and Barney sat on the floor next to him - they were both shaking.

"I didn't think it would be that easy, we've come out of this in one piece. I've no idea where we are but we're alive," he said to Barney. He wanted to pat him but he wasn't sure if the dog trusted him enough to allow that. Michael looked down at the dog's neck; it looked sore and in need of bathing. Even though he was probably in pain, he could tell that he was pleased to have escaped from Hell. "I need to get a lead for you and take you back to Tom. I'm not sure if you would stay with me if we went outside without one. I don't know where he lives or if he's at home. I don't even know what year it is. If the bargain has been kept then it should be 2013."

"It's 2008 and you are far too early to see the next show and oh my, you've brought a dog in with you. I'm sorry but we only allow guide dogs in here."

Michael looked up to see a lady standing next to him. She was dressed in a black uniform and was holding a bunch of keys; she looked puzzled but smiled kindly at him. Michael couldn't believe his ears, he'd been taken back to 2008 and immediately, he felt let down. He scowled, he wasn't sure if the Devil was playing games again – the idea horrified him. His mind was whirling; he hoped that Sarah was in the same era as him. A sudden thought shot through his head, if the Devil had released him and sent him back to 2008 then that would be a good thing. He would have just left the army and he would be staying with his sister and best of all Aaron would be alive and well. He needed a moment to take in this new information and he hoped that the woman would leave him in peace.

"Your dog needs to see a vet - what's happened to him? And what's happened to you? Why are your clothes all charred and ripped, have you been in a fire?" asked the woman.

"Something like that," replied Michael not quite sure how to reply. "The dog isn't mine, it belongs to someone I know. He needs medical attention."

The woman, kneeled down and stroked Barney who responded by licking the lady's face. Michael could clearly see that he liked her. "You poor old thing," she said to him. "My dad keeps greyhounds. Your friend shouldn't be allowed to keep a dog; he's obviously had a collar on that was too tight. Seriously though, this dog needs help."

Michael agreed, Barney needed a vet to look at his neck but he'd no idea where one was and had no money on him. "I'd take him but I'm homeless," said

Michael despondently trying to win her sympathy. He was hoping that the woman would take Barney off him.

"Look, I'm finishing in five minutes, I'll take the dog to my dad and he'll take care of him. Tell your friend that you lost him. I really couldn't live with myself if he went back to a life of abuse."

"I think that would be best, he's a great dog and he likes you. His name is Barney." Michael stood up to go; he didn't want the woman to have second thoughts.

Without looking back, he ran down the stairs following the exit signs. He would find out where he was then head off for the hospital, where he hoped he would find Sarah. As he walked through the glass entrance hall, he looked around for clues to see what town he was in but saw nothing of significance. As he left the building through revolving doors, he walked down the stairs to the pavement below and he was surprised to find that there was snow on the ground; he shivered the air was cold and it was a stark contrast to the heat in the Devil's theatre. He turned right and started to walk, the road was busy with cars and he felt a bit guilty that he'd left Barney behind but knew he would be in good hands. When he reached the top of the road he found he was at Horsham station.

Michael didn't know Horsham and wasn't sure how far it was from Redhill but after studying a rail map, he was relieved to find that he was only a few stations away. The station was busy with commuters returning from London and they poured through an open barrier. Michael noticed an old ticket on the floor that had been discarded. Discreetly, he picked this up and then when a guard was preoccupied, he slipped through the gate and up the stairs to find the north bound platform.

When he reached the platform, he noticed people were staring at him. He wasn't sure why at first and thought that they might recognise him from wanted posters and then he laughed out loud at his own stupidity, if it was 2008 then he wasn't a wanted man – he'd done nothing wrong. He looked down at himself and realised that his clothes were in a terrible state. There were holes in his shirt and trousers and the flesh that was exposed was red and sore thanks to Aaron's fiery hands.

He wasn't sure if he wanted to see his nephew again, he couldn't imagine him being a normal boy. Although he feared seeing him he couldn't help but feel euphoric; all he wanted to do was to begin his life again with Sarah and knew that he was no longer mentally ill. All he had to do when he got to his sister's house was to make sure that there were no fire hazards to ensure that Aaron didn't die in a house fire and then come after him.

As the train pulled into the station, he noticed an overcoat draped over the back of a seat, the owner of the coat had his back to him and was talking on a mobile phone. Without hesitating, Michael picked up the coat and then climbed into the train. The man didn't notice and continued with his conversation; he felt bad as the wind was icy but the man he'd taken it from had been wearing a thick jumper and wouldn't suffer too much. Michael however, was freezing and needed to cover up his clothes to stop people staring at him. He slipped the coat on and sat down - he smelt like he'd been barbecued.

He travelled to Redhill without his ticket being inspected and managed to get through the barrier and leave the station without being stopped. The station's car park was just as busy as Horsham's with people making their way home from work. In his coat pocket, he found six pound coins and a few silver coins; he hoped that would be enough to get him to the hospital by bus. He got directions to the bus station and then caught the 100 to the hospital. Sitting on the bus, he stared out of the window, watching the street lights race by and thought how illuminated the streets looked covered in snow. The thought of seeing Sarah again excited him, she'd looked so much younger in the film and he just hoped that she would remember him.

His attention turned to a boy sat on the opposite seat to him; he was very like Jawid and his black hair was almost identical to his. Sarah didn't know that Jawid had been shot; he wasn't looking forward to telling her that. He thought about his own son, he longed to see him and hold him; he'd only seen him on the film and had no idea what had become of him. He dared not think about it but there was a possibility that the baby wasn't real and was just part of one of the Devil's elaborate film sets. That thought was too awful to contemplate and he wasn't sure how he would tell her that either.

The bus driver called out to him when they stopped near the hospital and as he got off the bus, he wished him good luck. Michael looked at the bus as it drove off and wondered why the driver would say such a random thing; he must look like he needed a bit of moral support. Eagerly, he walked towards the hospital's main entrance, he needed all the luck he could get; finding Sarah and Amy wouldn't be easy as he didn't know Amy's surname or what day they'd been brought into the hospital but he was sure that someone would remember a stabbing in the hospital grounds.

The receptionist wasn't too helpful at first but after telling her the he was Amy's brother and Sarah's boyfriend; he won her round and she made a few calls, told him where to find them and then directed him to Sarah's ward. He was overjoyed that he'd found her again but then doubt set in and he knew that he had to keep an open mind until he saw her in case the woman he was going to see wasn't his Sarah. Michael stopped for a moment to check his appearance in a window, he didn't look too bad, his neck and back were very sore but his face wasn't injured, just a bit grubby and his eyebrows looked singed; his coat covered anything unsightly He did up another button and then headed towards the building where he hoped he would find her. He didn't notice that someone had come out of the shadows and was following him.

36

The morning hadn't come quick enough so Tom had gone out into the snowy streets to walk and try and clear his head. There was nobody around, just him and his thoughts. He'd considered walking up to the Chanctonbury Ring to see if it was still split in two but it was a long way to walk and he didn't like to be too far away from Martha. The snow had a calming effect and the first rays of morning sunshine glistened on its crystalline surface; he was pleased to be out of his house.

It was quite a blow to have to take care of Martha again and although he wasn't exhausted at the moment, he knew that it wouldn't be long before he would become too tired to cope. The answer was so simple, he would go home and ring the hospice and ask them to take her in. As he reached his house, he felt as if a great weight had lifted from his shoulders and couldn't understand why he'd not done that before. Although he would have broken a promise, it would have been for her own good. He realised that he couldn't have been in his right mind and at the end of his tether when he smothered her. Surely it would have been much easier to live with the thought that he'd let Martha down by not allowing her to die in her own home than living with the fact that he committed murder.

As Tom brewed a pot of tea, he rinsed out beakers and made up some thin porridge for her and some milky tea. He added a little syrup to the porridge and took the two beakers and some tea and toast upstairs. He would have a final breakfast with her and then ring the hospice. He wouldn't need to ring his daughter; she would be overjoyed that he'd made that decision. As he reached the top two stairs his mouth fell open with surprise and he dropped the tray; Evie was stood on the landing – she'd a sheet wrapped around her from Martha's bed.

"Oh my God... What on earth? How? Evie? How did you get here? Where's Martha?

"I don't know Tom, I just woke up and I just stepped out of her. Yesterday, I was trapped in her body and I heard you talking to her. She's gone now, it's just me I'm afraid and I'm freezing, do you have a blanket I could put around me? I'm sorry about your wife."

Tom thought he might be having heart failure; he was almost speechless with the shock of it all. Her grey curls framed her face; she'd a golden glow around her and looked like an angel.

"Martha's gone and you're here, standing in my house in 2008, the snow is still here so the date's not changed. I can't believe my eyes, I have dreamed about this day, when I would see you again. But not like this, not before Martha died, how she can be gone, I just don't know - I don't understand."

"I know Tom, look for yourself - 2008? Am I old again? Are you pleased to see me then? When you were a fox you brought me flowers and an egg." Evie was starting to feel distressed; she hadn't spoken to him since he disappeared from the flat in Brighton and although he said that he'd dreamed about this day, it didn't feel like it. "I'd better go back to London; I guess I have a flat there still. Although..."

She didn't finish her sentence as Tom was there in front of her with his arms around her, hugging her tightly.

"You are my life, my reason for breathing and why I have been getting through each day, always hoping that I would find you again." Tom kissed her with the same passion as he had when they were together in Brighton. Evie didn't resist. It felt right, she didn't know how long she would have with him and wished that moment would never end.

"You're ice cold, Evie," Tom said pulling away from her. "It's snowing outside and you're stood here in just thin cotton," he said taking his dressing gown off the back of his bedroom door. "And these socks," he said, rummaging through a chest of drawers. He picked up some red thermal socks that he'd been given as a Christmas present but had never worn and passed them to her. "Come downstairs with me, the kitchen is much warmer. I'll make you a cup of tea, with two sugars and some toast."

Tom led Evie to the kitchen, he dared not let go of her hand in case she disappeared in a puff of smoke. He was distressed that she'd thought that he might not be pleased to see her again. She must have been so confused when she'd gone back to their room in Brighton and found that he'd gone. Whoever had messed with their lives had really given them a hard time and had a lot to answer for. "Do you think this is it, now we are together again and that we will be left in peace? Do you think we can get on with the rest of our lives without worrying?" he asked her as she sipped a large mug of tea.

Evie didn't reply immediately; her head was spinning. She felt like she was floating. She didn't know whether it was the sweet tea or the fact that she was so excited that she was with him again. There was no doubt in her mind that they should be together now for the rest of their lives. "Don't you feel like something has changed? This feels real, we are old again and although we are younger than when we first met, positively spring chickens now, I feel like this will be permanent? No more surprises, we've both endured enough. I've closed a book where Albert is concerned and I think you have ended something too - a ghost has been put to bed hasn't it? Tell me the truth Tom, I don't want there to be any secrets between us."

Tom could feel his hands shaking. She'd a right to know and it was true he'd been tested and had chosen this time to ring the hospice and not to euthanize Martha. He knew Evie cared for him but he wasn't sure if she would stay with him if he told her what had happened in the past. He couldn't bear to lose her again but then he couldn't lie to her.

He went in to great detail about how he'd been on the verge of a breakdown before he smothered Martha and then given a second chance, had chosen to ring the hospice. The whole time he spoke, he held Evie's hand and feared she might pull her hand away but she didn't until the very end of his story. Tom stared anxiously at her face to see if there was any sign of condemnation or disapproval. He couldn't read what she was thinking as she was staring down at the table and then noticed her shake her head and he feared the worst.

"What you did was awful, Tom, but you were not yourself and you regretted your actions," she replied. "I know that the guilt you have felt has been a burden and will probably haunt you until you die. I can't forgive you for what you did but I understand why it happened and I do not hate you for it. When you were talking to Martha yesterday I felt that you loved her. Tom you are a good man I do not think badly of you. We are not perfect. Look at me; got myself pregnant before marriage and carried around a bag of ashes from the grate for sixty years and then when I had a chance to put it all right, made a hash of everything - at least Edward got to see his father. ...I love you Tom and I always will."

Tom sipped his tea thoughtfully. He felt encouraged by Evie's words and thankful that she'd not stormed out of the house - she was a remarkable person. He was just thinking about finding some more clothes for her, when he heard the front door open and someone come into the house.

"It's only me dad. Are you in the kitchen?" It was Ruth, his mind began to race. How would he explain the sudden disappearance of Martha and the arrival of Evie? He could feel himself going red. Ruth appeared in the kitchen doorway and looked concerned when she saw her dad's face. "Are you all right dad? You look dreadful! It's not mum, is it? I was just passing and I thought I'd drop in. It is isn't it? She didn't look good when I last saw her. I know she didn't want to go into a hospice but it's not fair on you dad. Look at you, you're worn out." Ruth then looked at Evie. "Who's this?" she said nodding towards Evie. "Why is she wearing your dressing gown?" Ruth's mouth then dropped open and she looked shocked as if she believed that her father had been up to no good whilst his wife was dying in the next room.

"It's not what it looks like, don't get upset. I've known Evie for a long time and she's lost all her clothes and so I helped her out with mine."

"What do you mean? How can anyone lose all their clothes? Even the ones she was standing in? Dad!"

Ruth stormed off and they heard her feet thumping on the stairs as she climbed them on her way to see her mother.

"Oh my," groaned Tom putting his head in his hands. How am I going to explain where Martha's gone, I'll have to say that the hospice have taken her. That will give me time to think of something."

"You won't have to," replied Evie patting his hand. She's still up there in her bed. When I said that she'd gone, I meant that she'd passed away. I think that's how I was able to step out of her body. Ruth will go up there and find her and will come down shocked. You will then call the doctor and I had better leave. I can't believe she would think that I spent the night with you with Martha here. It wouldn't be right Tom. Please could you call me a taxi? I'd better go back to London. My neighbour has a key and I have some money indoors to pay the driver. It's not right me being here."

They both heard Ruth scream and then heard her run down the stairs and she appeared in the kitchen doorway in tears. "Dad, she's dead, did you know this?"

"Yes poppet, I was going to ring you "She didn't have anything to eat last night and I didn't think she had long - I was going to ring the hospice today. Come and sit down and have some tea, I'll go up in a minute to see her and then call the doctor. Don't be upset, your mum's got her wish; she died at home just as she wanted. She's at peace now."

Ruth sat down as far away as she could from Evie and after wiping her eyes with a tissue Tom had given her, she had her tea. Tom went upstairs to say goodbye to Martha leaving Evie and Ruth alone together. Evie felt very uncomfortable. She felt that any words of comfort would be thrown back at her but by not saying anything seemed to make her look guilty.

"I knew your dad during the war, before he met your mother," she began, which was true but knew that she wasn't being sympathetic enough. "I'm sorry for your loss; both my parents died during the Blitz. I promise you that your father and I are just good friends. We bumped into each other recently and the reason, I'm wearing his clothes is that I was in a car crash and the hospital had to cut me out of my clothes. Amazingly, I sustained no injury and have walked away with only a bump on my head and a bit of bruising. I had no other clothes with me. Your father is a decent man, he collected me from Worthing hospital and when he comes back downstairs, he's going to order me a taxi so I can go back to my home in London." She looked at Ruth with false confidence, hoping that she'd bought in to her complicated lie.

"I'm sorry," sniffled Ruth, "I was just a bit surprised at seeing you with just a dressing gown on and socks. I didn't know. I'm really sorry. You can't go back to London in a dressing gown, I've got a clean gym kit in the boot of my car and you're more than welcome to wear that." Ruth offered kindly. Evie smiled, she'd won her over.

"That's really kind of you. I'm sure that will be much better than these clothes as they will only get the neighbours talking."

Tom had protested when Evie insisted that he call her a taxi but finally, he'd agreed. She'd managed to tell him, when Ruth had gone to the toilet, her story about how she'd come to lose her clothes. Tom had laughed and had then held her hand briefly as if he'd almost believed it to be true.

The taxi had arrived half an hour late and had made it with difficulty, through the snow to Tom's house. She'd got into it wearing Ruth's gym kit and a thick winter jumper with a reindeer on the front that Tom had found for her. He'd begged her to stay but Evie knew that this was her chance to continue with her life in a respectable manner. When she'd stepped out of Martha's body it was almost as if she'd been reborn.

Evie had looked back in the rear view window and had seen Tom's anxious face and wanted so much to go back and hug him and tell him that everything was going to be all right. The car slithered its way to the main road and then picked up speed on the dual carriage way. She felt light hearted and was happy to chat with the driver, who she found out had lived most of his life in Turkey with his wife but had lost their land and had come as refugees to England. He was also very keen to find out where she'd got her jumper from as he hadn't seen another like it. Evie wasn't sure if she was flattered or if he was making fun of her.

As they approached London, her thoughts turned to Tom and how wonderful it would be to be his wife and she could then spend the rest of her life as a respectable married woman. An odd thought entered her mind, what if she got sick and didn't have the chance to tell him that she didn't wish to be euthanized? What if, one night, he had enough of her and decided to suffocate her? What then? Was Tom, beneath his calm exterior really a beast? Then, as a song came onto the radio by Madonna, she realised that it was 2008 and that history was being rewritten. This time around, Martha had in fact died naturally and Tom hadn't actually committed any felony. She thought back to when he'd told her what he'd done and she knew that he was truly sorry for what had happened.

Yes, thought Evie, she would wait until Martha had been buried and two weeks after the service, she would contact him and they would marry. She then changed her mind as Ruth might think this too soon and improper; she didn't want to annoy her. Tom and her would go on dates for six months and then marry and she thought it might be wise to draft a prenuptial wedding agreement which would include arrangements that should be carried out should any party get sick and not be able to express their requirements.

The taxi turned into Callow Street and she looked at a young girl sat by an illuminated flower barrow. Despite the warm glow of the light bulbs, the girl looked cold and the flowers in danger of petrifying. Evie was glad to be going back to her cosy flat and hoped that her neighbour would be in. Daisy was much older than her and only went out occasionally to shop. They were good friends and she visited her twice a week to keep her company as she'd no family.

The taxi cab driver had waited patiently whilst Evie had got her key from her neighbour and she was glad to find enough money hidden under her bed to pay for her fare. She was surprised how much it had cost to get to London, even at 2008 prices.

Evie had promised to ring Tom to tell him that she was home and then sighed; she'd left the piece of paper with Tom's number on the seat of the Taxi. She would have put it in her pocket but she didn't have any. Eventually, she found Tom's number using directory enquires and when she got through, it was good to hear his voice; they'd only been separated a few hours and that seemed to be far too long. Her request for them not to have contact for two weeks had not been well received but she'd convinced him that it was the right thing to do, out of respect for Martha. As they put down the receivers, they both knew that the next couple of weeks would be almost impossible to endure.

37

When Sarah came round, the first thing she heard was the sound of birds as they fought for roosting space in the fir tree outside but she couldn't see them, which indicated that the bird's dispute was at the centre of the tree. She could see the dusky sky and snow topped trees from her hospital bed. She thought it odd that so many birds needed to share the same area and wondered what they were arguing about; they were clearly not happy to be together. Did they all stay together because there was safety in numbers? Surely she thought, there were enough trees and shrubbery for every pair of birds to have their own place to roost.

She heard someone in the ward cry in pain and her attention turned to an old woman in a bed opposite to hers. A nurse was trying to fit a cannula into the back of her hand. Sarah looked down at her own hand and realised that she too had a needle in the back of it and there was a long tube connected to a drip full of clear fluid; she wondered why she needed it. She looked out of the window again and tried to remember how she'd ended up in hospital. The last thing she remembered was being in a police station and feeling ill; she remembered nothing else. With her free hand, she felt her jaw and was pleased to find that the swelling had gone down dramatically but it felt sore and she could barely open her mouth. There was a glass of water on a table next to her and someone had kindly left her a straw. She sat up picked up the glass and tried to suck the water up, this was difficult and she discovered that the process of swallowing was also quite painful. She put the cup back on the table and laid back on the pillows, she felt a lot better and she could tell that her temperature was normal again.

After the nurse had finished attending to the old woman, she came over to Sarah "You're looking a lot better today. How are you feeling? I'll take the drip away in about half an hour; we just wanted to get antibiotics into you as you had a blood infection. I'll give you some painkillers for your jaw too as it must feel very sore at the moment."

"Thanks," said Sarah trying not to open her mouth too wide. "What day is it?" she asked.

"It's Sunday 6th April," she said looking concerned.

"And the year?"

"2008. You mustn't worry, you'll probably feel a little bit confused for a while but it will soon pass. You've been on very strong medication. I'll get the doctor to see you."

The nurse left the ward and Sarah tried to make sense of what she'd been told. If it was 2008, then she was only eighteen and was doing her A' Levels and could choose to have any career she wanted. She doubted whether she would do a degree and train to be a teacher and her future most definitely didn't include going to Afghanistan and getting kidnapped. Then she thought about her mother, there had been no tsunami, she would be alive and she could see her again; this made her feel so happy and she held her jaw as it hurt too much to smile. She couldn't wait to phone her and hear her voice; she was probably wondering where she was. Sarah didn't know how long she'd left in 2008 but as soon as the drip was removed she would ask to use the phone; she couldn't wait.

Time ticked by so slowly, she'd no watch to go by and had asked the old lady opposite if she knew the time but her request had been met with silence and a disapproving look. When the doctor came to see her, she'd asked him and found out that it was just before seven. As her drip was being removed, she asked if she could use the phone and the nurse told her where the nearest public phone was. She'd no money and was too embarrassed to say. She found her muddy clothes in a plastic bag next to her bed and checked the pockets for change or for her mobile phone but they were empty.

Sarah decided that she would go to the toilet; it was good to be up and about; she didn't have to worry about being attached to a drip. As she passed the old woman she saw a paper lying on the end of the bed. It was the headline and photo that caught her attention. 'Woman Stabbed in Hospital Grounds." The photo was of Amy.

"Oh no!" Sarah said out loud picking up the paper. "I know her, she saved my life. Have you read this?" she asked.

"Yes, you can have it," she replied which surprised her as she hadn't responded to her earlier; she thought that she must be hard of hearing. She took the paper back to her bed and sat on the edge and read the report anxiously, hoping that Amy had survived. She was relieved to find that she had, although she was in a critical condition. After asking the old lady what hospital they were in, she discovered that Amy was in the same one as her. She saw a photo of Ted and this made her shiver. The police were looking for him and were asking for people to come forward if they had seen anything suspicious. She could tell the police a lot but first she wanted to find Amy and see how she was doing.

Sarah looked down at herself, all she was wearing was a hospital gown that gaped open at the back and she felt very self-conscious. As she put on her trainers she wished that she had a long cardigan or dressing gown to wear. The old lady had gone to sleep and she noticed that she had a lime green silky dressing gown folded neatly in the cabinet next to her bed. She didn't want to wake her and hoped she wouldn't mind if she borrowed it for half an hour. She tiptoed across the room and pulled the dressing gown out of the cabinet and then slipped it on. The old lady murmured something in her sleep but didn't wake. She felt guilty borrowing it without her permission.

Sarah didn't see any nurses as she left the ward and she wondered if she should have asked permission to leave. She felt so much better and there was no sign of any infection raging through her body, so she guessed it would be fine to walk through the hospital without contaminating anyone. After passing through several corridors, she stopped to study a map of the hospital to see which way she should go to get to the intensive care department. She did her best to try and memorise how to get there and then continued on her way.

At first, she didn't recognise him, he looked much younger and his clothes were not familiar but it was his eyes that caught her attention and it was only when they walked a few paces past each other, did they stop and look back to check that they weren't seeing things.

"Michael," Sarah called out jubilantly. "It's you! Tell me you know me. I know we hadn't met in 2008 but I remember everything, the Chanctonbury Ring and Kabul. Why did you stop and then look back at me? It wasn't just a coincidence was it?" The people around them listened with bemused expressions on their faces.

Michael didn't smile and she thought it might be her worst nightmare, to be thrown back together and for him not to recognise her. She hoped that she didn't look too much different from the last time he'd seen her but then she'd been heavily pregnant and was now a slim eighteen year old with a swollen jaw. She held her breath as she waited for him to reply and watched with relief as a broad smile spread across his face.

"Sarah," he called out as he ran back to her. "Sarah, thank God you're here, I wasn't sure, it could have been the wrong year; it wasn't clear what year it was in the film. I can't believe it, I've finally found you," he said flinging his arms around her and then hugged her tightly.

Sarah clung to him and couldn't stop the tears spilling from her eyes. "I've lost Jawid and the baby, I gave birth to him but he's gone, there was nothing I could do."

Michael pulled her away and held her hands and then wiped away her tears with his fingers and shook his head. "You did nothing wrong Sarah. I'm beginning to think that there was no baby; I think it was all make believe. I will explain everything, he drew her to him again and hugged and kissed the top of her head. "You're alive and that what matters the most, we've the rest of our lives together. You're shaking, let's have a coffee, I just passed a cafe a moment ago and I think I've got enough money. The foolishness is over. No more horror stories; no more games. We can be ourselves. Come and sit down and I'll tell you what happened."

***

Sarah's boyfriend had become a problem, no doubt she would give him the full story and if that was the case then he would have to be taken care of too. He cursed himself for not punching her harder in the face and finishing her off as then he wouldn't have had to shave off his hair and deal with so many loose ends. Ted rubbed his head with frustration, not liking the prickly feeling of new hair growing. He'd been unlucky and had fully expected Amy to keel over and die when he stabbed her in the stomach and was annoyed that she was still breathing. He wished he'd strangled her like the other girl then at least he would have had the satisfaction of seeing her die in his hands. He shivered as he thought about his first victim and tried not to think about her stinking mummifying body. He wished he'd built his cabin in the woods before his first act of cleansing and then he could have buried her nearby and not had to put up with a bad smell.

Tonight, after he'd sorted out his problems and for a few night after that, he would have to stay in his cabin with Sarah and then when all the fuss had died down, he would bury her body, go and visit a friend in Ireland and make a life for himself over there; he'd read the headlines and knew that he was a wanted man. He'd laughed at the state of security in the hospital and had been up to the intensive care unit several times, trying to pick a moment to go in without being questioned. He smiled sadistically to himself as in the pocket of the white coat he'd found; he fingered a syringe full of drain clearing liquid ready for Amy, his ungrateful bitch of a girlfriend. It would only take a second to inject it into her vein and they would just think she'd just passed away.

He had almost yelled out when he saw Sarah in the corridor and had slipped into the nearest room in case she recognised him; he didn't expect her to be up and about yet. It was going to make her abduction more difficult. He'd thought about injecting her too but had decided that he'd unfinished business with her and he would take her to his cabin and finish her there; in his own special way. Sarah's boyfriend appearing on the scene had complicated things and he wasn't sure what he would do about him. In frustration, he smacked the wall and held his head; things were getting out of control. People in the waiting room he was in stared uneasily at him and he knew he was drawing unwanted attention to himself.

***

Sarah sipped a hot chocolate with her hands wrapped around the cup to try and warm them. She was still shaking with the shock of finding Michael. She tried to take in everything he was saying. He told her about his encounter with the Devil beneath the Chanctonbury Ring and the bizarre film he'd been shown. She didn't question anything because she knew he was telling the truth. He knew every detail of her escape from Ted and what he'd done in the past, he knew about the girl he'd killed before he stabbed Amy as he'd seen her ghost in the film. She cried when she heard that Jawid had been shot and couldn't accept that her two years with Michael, Jawid and then giving birth to a baby hadn't been real. She remembered everything vividly, she could even remember the smell of the dust on their clothes and the pleasure she felt when she hugged Jawid or the feeling of her baby moving inside her. That wasn't all fantasy, an illusion - it was all real to her.

"Why do you think that the Devil has set us free, why would he do that?" Sarah asked him; she felt angry that he could be so naive.

"When I saw the Devil it was Halloween and I offered to do a deal with him. At first I didn't think we would have a chance but by some miracle, he announced that he'd tired of us all and wanted to move on to others. He had his fun at our expense and is probably now tormenting a group of students I bumped into when I was walking up the hill to see him. He thinks he has in some way taught us lessons by granting us our dearest wishes, whether we asked for them to be granted or not."

Sarah frowned as she put down her cup, "I don't think I've had any wish granted or learnt anything of value. It's all been a nightmare."

"That's true. He did say you were just unlucky but I suppose we wouldn't have got to know each other," Michael said taking her hand. "I'm so glad I met you."

Sarah smiled, his hand felt warm and she felt reassured that he was there for her. "Me too, let's hope this is forever," she replied.

Michael sighed with relief and noticed that she was looking at someone chatting on her mobile.

"I need to ring my mother and the police to tell them about Ted attacking me and about the girl he murdered. I also want to go and see Amy too. I don't know what to do first. It's so annoying, I've got no money and no clean clothes, and I feel lost without my mobile. What about you? You don't have any money left as we spent it on drinks and chocolate. If I ring mum, I'm sure she'll drive over and pick us up. I can't bear to think of her worrying about me."

"I don't think you're well enough to go home tonight Sarah. Your jaw still looks inflamed and you might need an operation. After you've seen Amy, you can ring 999 for free and then when you've told them about Ted, they'll probably let your mum know you're safe. I'm here with you now, you mustn't worry."

Sarah nodded, "Please, I don't want you to leave my side; it gives me the creeps thinking Ted is out there still. He could be looking for me. What if he decides to come after me again? I can't bear the thought of it Michael - he's depraved."

As they walked to the intensive care ward, Michael couldn't help thinking how lucky Sarah was to be alive. He would make sure they locked Ted up and then threw away the key. He wouldn't let him or anyone else hurt her ever again.

Visiting time was nearly over and the ward was busy with anxious relatives grouped around their seriously ill loved ones. Michael and Sarah waited at the reception desk to find out which bed Amy was in. The receptionist pointed to a bed in the corner with curtains around it. "She's in the bed in the far corner. I think there's a doctor in there with her at the moment," she said waving goodbye to some visitors leaving the ward. "If you wouldn't mind waiting until he's done, he shouldn't be long."

Sarah and Michael waited and after a few minutes they saw the curtains move and the doctor appear. "It's not a doctor," Sarah whispered. "It's Ted!" As soon as she said that, he started to walk briskly towards them; he'd seen them and looked as if he was intent on doing them harm. Sarah, didn't have time to run, she just slipped behind Michael hoping that he would be able to defend her.

"Call security," Michael shouted to the receptionist, she looked puzzled. "That's not a doctor, that's the man that stabbed Amy. The receptionist picked up the phone to call them.

"Oh my God," Sarah said under her breath. "He's really is after me."

Michael was ready for him and blocked his first punch but wasn't that quick with the second punch as he didn't want to move away from Sarah and leave her exposed. Ted's punch caught him squarely in the stomach, knocking the air out of him. Sarah squealed as Michael bent over and then she ran behind the receptionist desk as Ted tried to grab hold of her.

Annoyed with himself for being so foolish, Michael stood up again and tried his best to breathe, he was recovering quickly and wasting no time, lunged at Ted who was still trying to get at Sarah. She was now standing with her back against the wall with the receptionist looking for a way out. Michael pulled, Ted around and swept him to the ground, turning him over, he twisted his arm behind his back and said firmly. "I will break your arm if you try anything." Ted tried to move so Michael applied more pressure to his arm so that it caused intense pain. He cried out and decided that it was better to stay still.

"Have you called security?" Michael asked the receptionist and she just nodded and looked frightened.

Confident that Michael had control of Ted; Sarah came out from behind the reception desk and looked down the corridor towards the entrance, hoping that security would arrive.

"You're hurting me," snarled Ted fidgeting. "Why did you attack me? This is a violation of human rights, I'm innocent."

"Then what's this," asked Michael picking up an empty syringe that had fallen out of his pocket. "What was in it? What have you injected Amy with? Sarah go and check on her. As he spoke a warning signal started ringing from the monitor behind the receptionist signifying to the nursing staff that Amy was in need of urgent medical attention. Sarah ran to Amy's bed and drew back the curtains and was horrified by what she saw. Amy's eyes were wide open but she wasn't focusing properly and her body convulsed as if she was having a fit. Ignoring Ted, nurses ran to assist and called out to the receptionist to call the crash team. Sarah looked at Amy's pale sweating face and realised that she was slipping out of consciousness, she felt helpless; she looked as if she was going to die.

The security team arrived and after Michael explained what had happened, they put handcuffs on Ted and got him to his feet. Ted snarled at them as if he was being mishandled. Michael couldn't understand why he was saying he was innocent. Ted was smiling to himself as he watched the nurses and doctors try and revive Amy. The security guards called for police back up.

"I don't hold out much hope for the bitch," snarled Ted as they waited. "Right waste of time she was - fucking tart!"

Michael was shocked how insensitive he was being; he wasn't remorseful. He seemed to be living in a parallel universe where the loss of human life meant nothing to him, he believed that he was a victim and he was the one that was suffering. He was standing there waiting for the police as if nothing had happened and everyone around him were irritants and unworthy to be stood next to him.

"So you like raping little girls do you? Makes you feel big does it?" Michael shouted, sickened by his presence.

Ted just ignored him. Michael got a bit closer to him so he wouldn't miss what he was saying. "I've seen what you're capable of, I've seen the spirit of that girl you raped and killed; she was just a child, you bastard. You tried to get Sarah too but she was too smart for you and got away, she's going to tell the police what happened and after everything you've done, they'll lock you up and throw away the key. You're just a pathetic excuse for a man; you'll get what you deserve when you're inside. I hope you're mother's proud of you."

The last comment seemed to trigger a reaction and Ted catching the security guard unaware barged into Michael knocking him flying. Michael flew back and hit a partition between the reception area and the ward, he smashed through the glass, lost his footing, slid downwards and screamed out as a large shard of glass cut through his coat and under his right arm slicing into his flesh. A security guard caught hold of Ted and dragged him out into the corridor so that he couldn't attack anyone else. He didn't fight the security guard and stood staring at Michael with a condescending look on his face. Michael looked down at himself and saw blood splattering on to the floor; he'd never seen so much blood. He could feel the blood pouring out of his body and thought that he must have cut an artery.

38

The snow had melted away and two weeks had passed since the funeral. Tom looked out on to his garden with pride. He hadn't felt like gardening recently but none the less, the tulips were now in full bloom, standing majestically above the dying daffodils.

Martha had always loved pruning, weeding and growing seedlings; he couldn't think why he'd chosen to have her cremated as she would have much preferred a burial and to be planted in the earth. A sudden guilty thought entered his head and he realised that the reason he had her cremated was to hide any incriminating evidence - he felt ashamed of himself. To rectify things, for her second funeral, he'd decided that he would bury her at St Mary's. He also didn't want to go to the Chanctonbury Ring again to scatter her ashes – the thought of going up there again made him tremble.

The day had gone well and everyone that knew her had attended but he'd felt stressed and the effort he made, pretending to be grieving, had been horrendous. He would have felt a lot better if Evie had been by his side but he knew that this would have been improper.

Ruth had been so helpful over the past few weeks and had called in on him regularly to make sure he wasn't wasting away; she brought him leftovers and sweets and he could see that she was worried about him. He let her believe that he was missing her mother but the reality was that he'd barely thought about her. All he could think about was Evie but he couldn't tell her that; she would be appalled that he was pining for someone other than her mother so soon after her death.

Tom frowned and walked through the house to the front window to watch out for Evie, he'd not heard from her and with every day that passed, he was becoming increasingly distressed. The last time they'd spoken was over two and half weeks ago, when she'd got back to her flat. They'd only spoken for a few minutes as Ruth was there and it would have been rude to chat for too long. He was annoyed with himself for not taking down her phone number and he couldn't remember her surname but was thankful that he remembered where she lived and he decided that if she didn't ring him by the weekend then he would travel up to London and call on her.

Tom thought back to when they'd been reunited; she'd kissed him as if he meant something to her. Yet, as the days ticked by, doubt spread like a virus through his mind and he became more and more unsure. He wished he'd not told her about ending Martha's life, he felt like he'd tainted their relationship in some way. Another disquieting thought bothered him, Evie might have been taken off somewhere, perhaps to another year or to another life and he would never see her again. To save himself from a complete breakdown, he knew that he had to stay optimistic and believe that Evie still loved him and was just waiting for him to make the next move.

As the days passed, he found that he was sitting more frequently by the window in the front room, hoping that she would suddenly walk up the path and that thought alone kept him going. He'd tried to keep himself occupied, by cleaning the car and reading the newspapers and he'd laughed at the naivety of the economists and the complacency of the government as he read all the news stories. He knew the economic future was grim and he seriously thought about selling his house whilst the property prices were at their peak.

He had one bit of good fortune that cheered him up, he'd gone to visit a friend that kept greyhounds, looking to adopt one. It was around the time he'd been before and he'd hoped that Barney might be there. His friend lived on a farm and as he'd stepped out onto the courtyard, he'd almost been knocked over. Barney had recognised the sound of his owner's car and had charged out of the farm house to greet him, almost sending him flying as he leaped up at him for attention. Tom's friend found it curious that the dog his daughter had brought to him, that had obviously been abused, had taken to him so much and was more than happy for Tom to take him home.

Barney lay on the floor next to his chair and he followed him everywhere. He stroked his head and ears tenderly; it was good to have his dog back. After the wounds on his neck had healed, he couldn't imagine how that had happened; he would like to meet the blighter that had done that to him - they'd gone out every day for long walks together. The fresh air and the lighter evenings were a tonic and this had helped him stay positive.

When the weekend finally arrived Tom got up early and after walking Barney, he set off in his car to visit Evie. He couldn't bear to wait any longer. He didn't know what to expect, whether she would welcome him with open arms or shut the door in his face. Either way, he needed to know. He couldn't sleep and he didn't feel like eating and knew that if he carried on like this then he would lose his mind.

His car purred as it sped along the motorways, he loved driving her and thought that she was worth every penny but most of all it was good to be doing something to help his tortured soul.

It took him longer than he expected to drive to London, he was surprised at the volume of traffic on the roads for a weekend and it was lunch time when he turned into Callow Street. He drove slowly along the road past the smart town houses and then finding a gap between two cars, reversed his car into the space. He fed the meter and then walked along the street looking for Evie's house.

As he stood outside the blue shiny front door, he realised that there were several flats within the building and he wasn't sure which was Evie's. He put on his reading glasses and stared hard at the labels by the bells. Finally, he found a label for Evie and noted that her surname was Merryweather. He smiled, he hadn't expected her surname to be that and found it quite unusual. He wondered if she would like being, plain and simple Evie Barns. With a mounting sense of apprehension, Tom pressed firmly on the bell and waited. After a few moments he tried again in case he hadn't pressed the bell properly.

"Hello, who's there?" asked an elderly woman. It wasn't Evie's voice and he realised that the second time he'd pressed Daisy Trent's bell by mistake.

"I'm sorry, I was calling for Evie Merryweather, I pressed the wrong bell," he felt guilty that he'd made someone so old get up to answer the door.

"She's gone to catch a train," replied Daisy. "You've only just missed her."

"Which station would she have gone to?" asked Tom, not sure whether she would reply as she didn't know him.

"South Kensington, I think dear,"

The intercom went dead; Tom turned around and felt confused, he wasn't sure what to do next. In the end he started to walk to the station to see if he could find her, he had to try and see her otherwise he thought he might die in the night of a broken heart. Briskly, after asking the way, he headed towards the station, checking to see if he could see her ahead of him.

When he walked into the ticket hall, he noticed a woman with grey hair passing through a turn style on her way to the trains and he knew immediately that it was her. He wanted to call out to her but she'd disappeared into the crowds. As quickly as he could he bought a ticket for the next station and then looked for a sign for eastbound trains, he thought it unlikely that Evie would be going westbound as he hoped that she was heading to Victoria to get a train to see him. He walked quickly through the crowds and then he saw her again. He managed to keep her in sight although it was difficult as it was busy and he got caught behind a group of Japanese students with pull along suitcases.

The platform was even busier but he could still see her at the far end. As he worked his way up the platform a train pulled in and he saw her get on to it and he did the same. It was quite full and he apologised as he squeezed past the other passengers as he made his way through the carriage; this was made more difficult as the train began to move. He was pretty sure that she was in the same part of the train and he eventually found her sat on the very last set of seats; she had her back to him. The seat next to her appeared to be free. As he reached her, he noticed that the seat was taken up by a shopping bag and within it he could see a large battered biscuit tin with picture of a steam train on the front. He stopped still for moment gathering his thoughts, he remembered Evie telling him that she'd kept Albert's ashes in a similar tin. He couldn't understand why she would have them with her, when she'd admitted to him that they were only ashes from the fire. He wondered if she'd lost her mind.

They would soon arrive at the next station and if they continued on then his ticket would no longer be valid. "Evie," he announced gently, picking up the shopping bag and putting it on the floor between his legs so he could sit down. "We need to talk." She looked surprised to see him and then her face turned from looking shocked to looking cross.

"Oh Tom," she cried. "You shouldn't have come looking for me."

"What's the matter Evie, why didn't you call me again? What's happened?" he asked realising that everyone was listening to them as they pulled into Sloane Square station. "We really need to talk but not here, please get off the train with me and we'll have a coffee. You know how I feel about you, you owe me that much."

Embarrassed that everyone was staring, she nodded and followed him onto the platform. As the train left the station she turned to him "Where's my shopping bag Tom, I saw you holding it?"

"I left it on the train Evie; you really don't need it any more," he replied trying not to sound patronising.

"I do, you don't understand, I found Albert's ashes in my flat when I got home and I was going to find a place to sprinkle them somewhere."

"But Evie, you know they're not his; you're doing this out of habit; it's meaningless. You know that he died somewhere in Africa and you really don't have to carry that old biscuit tin around with you any longer. You need to let it go and move on. I'm sorry if you think I've been cruel but it's for your own good. You look so pale! I'm really sorry, Evie."

They found a cafe near to the station and Tom ordered tea for two and they sat in the window. He watched her as she poured the tea into the cups; she looked tense. She was wearing a pale grey suit and her floral shirt was buttoned all the way to the top making her look very formal. She seemed so distant and her manner was cold. After a sip of tea Tom summoned the strength to speak but Evie sensing he was about to say something, spoke first. "Tom, I've had time to think. You shouldn't have come, don't you see, we can never be together. The moment we relax, something terrible will happen and we will be ripped apart. If we had found ourselves back at the Chanctonbury Ring in 2013 when we first met, then I might have believed that we had hope but this is not the case is it Tom? We're in 2008 and I think we should continue with our lives as we were in 2008 until these episodes are over. You shouldn't have left the ashes on the train; that was a terrible thing to do."

Tom felt relieved he wasn't being rejected for euthanizing Martha but he was puzzled by Evie's decision. "I know you care for me," he said, watching her reaction. She was trying to stay in control but he could see that her hard shell was beginning to dissolve. Encouraged, he continued. “You know I love you Evie. What if this is it and our lives are left to run their course and we do nothing about it. What if we spend the rest of our lives waiting for something terrible to happen and all we do is grow old and then die alone. How sad would that be?” Tom placed his hand on hers, she tried to move it away but he hung on to it, if he let her go now he knew that he would never see her again and he couldn’t live with that thought. He could feel her iciness melting and then he saw her face soften and a tear drop down her cheek. She looked around, hoping no one would see her crying.

“I don’t know Tom, I’m frightened, I’ve spent my whole life grieving over lost love and now I don’t know if I am able to... to...” she didn’t know how to finish the sentence, she couldn’t bear to see the pain and sadness in Tom’s face any longer.

“We can try and enjoy each day we’re given. We don’t know how much time each of us has but we should make each day count. I could be struck down tomorrow, hit by a bus but I wouldn’t care if I knew that I had spent today with you knowing you loved me.”

“Oh Tom, don’t say that,” replied Evie holding his hand with both of hers.” I do you love you, you know I do.”

Tom smiled and jumped to his feet, his heart felt as light as a feather and he felt like shouting out to the world that she loved him. His hand knocked his tea cup and it went flying, landing in a pot plant next to her and tea splashed up the wall. He retrieved the cup and looked around him to see if anyone had noticed and realised that everyone was looking at him with amused expressions. "Is there any more left in the pot?" he asked as he sat back down trying to make out nothing had happened. He noticed some earth on the side of the cup, brushed it off and set it back down in the saucer. He felt self-conscious but, it didn't matter as Evie was laughing. "You do realise if you marry me, you may be cleaning tea off the wall several times a week. I can be a bit accident prone."

"Marry you?" questioned Evie surprised.

"Yes Evie, I would have married you in Brighton if I'd got the chance. Evie Merryweather, I want you to marry me. I can't live without you. Please say yes."

Evie gazed enchanted into Tom's blue eyes and couldn't believe what she was hearing. "Yes," she replied, feeling a rush of emotions course through her body and then she realised what she'd said. Her response had been automatic; she didn't even have to think about it. She didn't regret saying yes; he made everything sound so straight-forward and uncomplicated.

When she was by herself, her life ran limply along and she thought back to the past three weeks. She'd spent them in isolation, thinking and rethinking how she would spend the rest of her life. She'd been frightened to go to sleep in case she woke up in an alien place and had decided that she needed to follow a routine and try and restore her life to how it had been. She'd fallen in to her old ways and found herself going on trips once or twice a week to find a place to scatter the ashes. She knew it was irrational but out of respect for Albert, she felt she had to find a suitable spot but hadn't been able to let them go - she didn't know why. She'd been thoroughly miserable but she thought that if she carried on with her life as it had been before then she might feel better emotionally.

That day, she'd been on her way to the Chanctonbury Ring and was determined to leave the ashes there. When she'd realised that Tom had left them on the train, she'd been furious but thinking about it now, it really didn't matter any more and it made her smile to think of them travelling on a never ending journey on the Circle Line.

"It's a beautiful day, let's go for a walk and plan our future together. You've made me very happy Evie Merryweather."

After finishing their tea they walked hand in hand around Sloane Square, talking about their past and their future. They both decided that it would be best to sell their houses and live as far away from the Chanctonbury Ring as possible and talked of moving to Wales or the Peak District so they wouldn't get washed away in the 2013 tsunami. They found a bench to sit on in a public garden and just held hands as they admired the spring flowers. Evie unbuttoned her top button of her blouse and Tom thought she looked radiant in the sunshine - he'd never felt happier.

39

Amy sat in her car outside her flat and with trepidation stared up at the top window; the flat was empty and Ted had been locked up awaiting trial but it didn't make going back in there any easier. It was good to be out of hospital and she knew that she could have quite easily become his second victim. Fortunately, he'd not managed to find her vein when he'd injected the drain fluid into her and the nurses and doctors had been able to save her. He was a complete stranger to her now and she felt uncomfortable with the fact that once she had feelings for him.

The police had told her that the flat had been turned over when they were looking for the knife that he'd used to stab her with and for evidence that would support Amy's claim that Ted had killed a girl. She wished she could have given them a name and she'd sat for several hours, looking into the police files of girls that had gone missing in the area but couldn't find her. She'd been shocked at how many girls did go missing every year that nobody ever heard about. It upset her to think that the girl that Ted had killed didn't mean enough to someone to actually report her as missing. Every day, Amy's psychic ability was improving and she found this strange as in 2008 her powers were non-existent. She'd introduced herself to Inspector Brandon and asked him to contact her if anyone went missing and told him that she would do her best to give them an idea where to look or details of the abductor. She knew that he was open minded and would call her and eventually he would see that she would be able to save lives.

The thought of going into the flat was making her feel sick; she wished that she had someone with her. Sarah was at school, her mother was at work and Michael was still in hospital. He'd lost the use of his arm, having cut all the nerves on the broken glass. She wasn't going to stay long in the flat, just collect her things and then go back to Sarah's mother's house. They had insisted that she stayed with them until she was well enough to find a job and pay rent on another flat. When she'd been in hospital, Sarah had been up to see her nearly every day, sometimes with her mother who was very kind and had been very supportive.

During her three week stay in hospital she found that she'd lost a lot of weight; mainly due to the hospital food but also because she'd lost her appetite; she didn't know why and the clothes Sarah's mother had given her, hung on her. The doctors had prescribed anti-depressants but she hadn't taken the tablets as she really didn't feel depressed just a little shaken - who wouldn't after what she'd been through?

She walked up the stairs to the flat and she tried to remember what Sarah had told her when she was in the hospital whilst poor Michael was having surgery. She'd said that they were all free to carry on their lives. He'd negotiated their freedom with the Devil and the price he'd paid was losing the use of his right arm. Amy didn't know if this was true but a month had passed without incident and her life was starting to take shape.

She opened the front door slowly and, after hesitating for a moment, walked into the lounge. The flat was in a terrible state and was a lot worse than she expected. To get through, she had to step over the contents of drawers and cupboards spread across the carpet. The sofa had been turned upside down and the underside slit open. She looked briefly into the kitchen and again it was a scene of devastation but she didn't need anything from there. Leaning against the skirting board in the lounge, she saw a photo of herself and Ted on holiday together in Tenerife. She remembered that day well, they'd gone to a bar that evening and Ted had accused her of looking at another man. She'd pleaded with him that she didn't know who he was talking about. That night Amy had spent the night on the patio crying whilst Ted had slept alone. When the morning came he'd insisted that they have sex as if he needed to mark his territory but at the time she was just grateful that he was no longer cross with her; she shuddered as she thought back to that day.

She found a suitcase and wheeled it through to the bedroom and as she opened the door she saw the spirit of the girl that Ted had killed standing by the chest of drawers. Amy's heart stopped beating for a moment; usually Ted was nearby when she saw her and she spun around to see if he was behind her and she was reassured to find that she was alone. The spirit looked miserable and seemed not to see Amy standing in the room. She began to fade, then floated upwards and slipped through a panel in the ceiling. Amy hadn't noticed the panel before and walked beneath it to inspect the edges; they were crudely cut and seemed to give access to a space above; Ted had never mentioned that there was storage space in the roof.

As she stared up at the ceiling images of the girl filled her head and she was able to see what had happened to her, just before her death. The girl had been walking home from school; her uniform was second hand and was worn out, her cuffs of her sweatshirt were ragged and her skirt too short. The rain was falling hard and she'd no coat on and she was soaked through. From the desperation in her eyes, she sensed that her mother was a drug addict and wasn't there for her and she had to look after herself. She had an extremely low opinion of herself and had no friends. She kept out of trouble at school and didn't want anyone knowing her business. Nobody cared for her, nobody spoke to her, she survived as best she could from money earned from a paper round and didn't care much for living.

Amy sat down on the bed. She could see in her mind Ted curb crawling in his taxi, his predatory instinct was driving him to search for young women with no morals. She saw the girl crossing the road in front of him and she could feel Ted's excitement as he pulled up by his victim and offered her a lift. She refused at first and Amy screamed out to her to run but Ted managed to persuade her to climb into his taxi out of the rain.

Amy jumped up from the bed. The next scene had taken place in their bedroom and on their bed; she felt revolted that he'd brought the girl back to their flat. She could see him on top of her trying to rape her. The girl couldn't scream, she had tape over her mouth and she was too malnourished to fight him off for much longer.

He slapped her around the face and she then just lay their limply as Ted violated her.

He'd left her tied to the bed and then later, she noticed by the light in the room that it was evening, she saw him raping her a second time; the girl didn't fight him, he seemed enraged that she wasn't enjoying their love making and saw his hands around the girl's neck as he raped her and she could see that he was killing her, she couldn't breathe properly through the tape and gasped to get air. She could hear him grunting as he forced himself into her and it sickened her stomach to see it. She'd seen enough and tried to switch of these horrendous visions. The last thing she saw was Ted pushing the girl's body wrapped in some carpet through a hole in the ceiling and then replacing the panel he'd created; he looked pleased with himself.

There was obviously a space big enough between the ceiling and the flat roof to store a body and she'd been up there ever since. Amy wondered where she was when this murder had taken place as she was usually at home after midday. She thought back to her vision and realised that there were none of her belongings in the room; the murder must have happened before her and Ted had met but it still disturbed her to think that she'd spent night after night in the same bed.

Amy wished she could have prevented the murder from happening but there was nothing she could have done. She was surprised that she hadn't noticed the girl's presence before and she looked up at the ceiling to see if she could see any signs of her but suspected that she had issues and didn't believe that she was worthy of being helped. Some spirits preferred to remain hidden and she wondered why Emma Mills had decided to show herself after all this time. Amy smiled as her name had just popped into her head and she knew that she was slowly feeding her information so she could help her to free her spirit from Ted's dark soul.

Amy rang the police on the home phone as Ted had smashed her mobile and then told them where they would find Emma's body. As quickly as she could, she packed her suitcase with all her belongings and then realised how little she had. As she walked through the lounge she was glad to be leaving the flat. All she had to do was get through Ted's trial and then she could start a new chapter in her life.

The police came and broke open the access panel and found Emma's body. Amy didn't stay to see her being removed but knew that she'd found peace and wouldn't have to follow Ted around for eternity. She felt elated as she drove away from Findon to Horsham; it felt like this was the beginning of her new life. She turned the radio on to listen to some music which she hadn't done in a while as Ted had always mocked her song choice. She felt guilty, doing exactly as she wished and knew that it would take some time to find herself again.

The sun was shining as Amy parked in Denne Road car park and the warmth from the sun made her feel so much better; her life the last few months had been dark and winter like. She locked the car and then walked up the hill and around the corner to the Job Centre to look for work and to sign on.

As she looked through the lists of jobs available, she noticed with some amusement that there was a vacancy at Treadmill Marketing and she was sure it was for the job that she used to do. She considered applying for it as she'd left the company on good terms. She thought about her future friendship with Vicki and welcomed this but then remembered that in the future the boss' nephew would be taking over the company and she couldn't ever contemplate working for him as he was insufferable at the 'Who Done It' weekend and if she ever saw him again she would probably punch him. Apart from working at Treadmill Marketing, she was willing to do anything and decided to ask about a vacancy she'd seen for a carer in a nursing home.

Amy walked back to the car and felt quite down hearted as the woman she'd spoken to had treated her with contempt. She'd insinuated that by leaving Treadmill Marketing to become a housewife and not attempting to find employment for over a year made her an unemployable freak that was likely to terminate her employment on a whim. Amy didn't have the inclination or the energy to explain that she'd been living with a jealous serial murderer that had pressurised her to give up work as he couldn't handle her having contact with other men and had then nearly killed her. Later that week she'd another appointment to sign on but wouldn't receive any financial support for several weeks which was worrying as she only had a few pounds left in her bank account.

She stopped for a moment in the entrance of the car park as she was beginning to feel really tired; she'd only been out of hospital for a few days and had limited energy levels. She was feeling hungry which surprised her as she'd not felt like eating for weeks. She walked back up the hill and treated herself to a sausage roll from a sandwich bar and then feeling a bit stronger after eating, went to her bank and emptied her account; she'd a twenty pound note and a few coins. She would have to give some money to Sarah's mum as she'd insisted on cooking evening meals for her and with the remaining money she would go to a supermarket and buy herself some bread, spread and cheese and that would have to last her until she got some money through.

She walked from the Carfax and through an alleyway back to the car park and was looking forward to getting in her car as she was feeling really tired. As she approached the car she saw someone she recognised; it was James. Amy could feel herself blushing but then she remembered that it was 2008 and he wouldn't recognise her. He was stood by a ticket machine and he was having difficulty finding the right change to get a ticket. Amy couldn't resist assisting him and she walked over and digging into her purse pulled out her change.

"Hi Jam..." she almost said his name but stopped herself as he would be surprised that she knew it. "Do you need any change?"

He looked at her curiously for a moment. "Yes, I need to change ten pence worth of bronze for a ten pence piece. Do I know you? You nearly said my name?"

Amy felt herself blush again, she couldn't help herself as they'd slept together and it was then that she realised that she'd feelings for him. She didn't know what to say without making herself sound ridiculous. "I thought you were someone else, she said, I know someone who looks like you. His name is James" she said.

He smiled. "That's a coincidence, my name is James too."

Amy sorted through her change and found James a ten pence piece. As she passed it to him, his phone began to ring. He pulled it out of the inner pocket of his jacket and looked at the screen, frowned and cancelled the call.

"Sorry," he said replacing the phone back in his pocket. "That's the fifth call from my wife in the last hour – she's really getting on my nerves!"

"Oh dear," replied Amy, surprised that he was informing her about something personal about his relationship with his wife. It was a bit of a disappointment to find out that he was married as when she'd met him before, he'd been divorced.

James gave her coppers back and then she knew she should go but she didn't want to. "Your mobile looks smart and I like your ring tone," she said trying desperately to continue talking. "I need a new one, where did you get it?"

James inserted the ten pence piece into the machine and waited for the ticket to drop down. Nothing came out and all his coins fell through the machine into the collection tray. "Not my day today is it?" he said collecting the coins. Smiling, he then opened his briefcase and handed Amy his business card. "I can do you a good deal on a mobile phone; I own a chain of shops. If you go into the one in Horsham and show them my card they will give you a discount. It's the least I can do after you helped me. I'll have to try another ticket machine."

Amy thanked him and as she walked back to her car she looked at the business card, it had his number on. She decided that when she got a new phone she would send him a text and say if he ever found himself single again then he should call her. She knew she might have to wait a few years for him to become single again but he was worth waiting for.

40

Six months after Martha's death, Tom and Evie were married in St Mary's church, in Washington. It had been a glorious hot summer's day with not a cloud in the sky. Tom thought Evie had looked beautiful in her knee length ivory dress as she walked up the isle to him, holding onto the arm of her son Edward.

There hadn't been that many guests at the church or the reception which was a shame as many had promised to attend. Tom didn't like to tell Evie but he suspected that this was because of the rumours that were circulating around Washington village. He'd heard from a reliable source that some of the villagers believed that he'd been seeing Evie behind Martha's back as she lay dying in her bed and some said far worse and he could hardly bear to think about it. Ironically there was talk that Evie had strangled Martha so that she could wed Tom and take all of his money. He knew what was being said were lies and he didn't have the heart to repeat such ugly gossip to Evie and ruin what should be the happiest day of her life.

Edward and his flat mate Jon had travelled down from Cambridge to be at the wedding and had both cried as Evie and Tom had taken their vows. On Tom's side of the church were a few of his close friends from the

Frankland Arms, his daughter Ruth and her husband. Tom thought about his Ruth. It had been a difficult time when he'd told her that he wanted to marry Evie. She'd been very shocked and disappointed and thought it to be immoral to want to marry so soon after her mum's death. He could tell from the look on her face as she stood singing 'All Things Bright and Beautiful' during the wedding service that she didn't approve of the marriage. At the reception, she'd said that she was pleased that he'd got over his grief and was happy but had gone on to say that she didn't particularly trust Evie, she couldn't say why but there was something odd about their first meeting when she'd found Evie in her dad's dressing gown.

"Oh I do like going to go for a drive," announced Evie as they climbed into Tom's car. "It's such a lovely day; shall we go down to the sea?"

"Yes, why don't we? We'll have a little drive, have lunch and then stop off by the cove and have a walk," replied Tom as he helped Evie with her seat belt; after five years together she still couldn't quite work out how to click the metal end into the slot. Tom turned on the engine and was pleased that it had started as lately he'd not been able to attend to his car's needs as much he would have liked to. As they pulled away, he looked in the rear view mirror at their bungalow and wondered if he would ever see it again.

After the wedding, they'd both sold their house and flat just as the house prices peaked and had bought a house as far away from the south coast as possible to avoid being washed away in flood water. It had taken them a while to get used to living in Wales and he did miss the cottage that he'd grown up in. The bungalow was situated at the top of the hill and there were some wonderful views across the Welsh countryside from their back garden. Tom had wanted his daughter to move away from the south too but she'd laughed when he told her why. Sadly, his relationship with Ruth had deteriorated over the past few years and he wished he could make things better.

"I do love to see the sheep out in the fields, they look so happy eating the grass with the sun on their backs. Wouldn't you like to be a sheep too Albert?" she asked.

"It's Tom, not Albert, Evie. No, I don't think I'd like to be one, they've got no sense sheep and their coat is too thick. I'd like to be a greyhound, just like Barney, they're intelligent dogs... Poor thing, he's not got long Evie, he's very old and not looking himself these days."

"I like dogs" replied Evie looking at the road ahead. "One day we'll get one."

Tom sighed silently and edged his way out on to the motorway. He didn't know how long they'd be gone and he'd arranged for the neighbour to look after Barney, should they not return for a while. He over took a motor home and admired it; he'd always fancied living in one and thought that travelling around the country and Europe might be something to think of doing in the future. They'd tried their best to make the most of each day and had been very happy for the past four years but as the autumn of 2013 had arrived Tom had become nervous and was worried that they'd become too complacent and at any moment they could be transported off to another time or annihilated by a freak flood or hurricane and of course there was Evie's problem that needed to be sorted.

"Where are we going?" asked Evie. "Will we be on the motorway for much longer?"

"No not for much longer," lied Tom. "Are you hungry?"

"Oh yes, I'm always hungry," replied Evie. "It's a shame I didn't have breakfast."

"There's some wine gums in the glove box; have one."

"Oh, thank you Albert," replied Evie as she helped herself.

Tom smiled as he watched Evie select a green one; at least she hadn't forgotten that the lime ones were her favourite; she'd however forgotten that she'd eaten a full English breakfast that morning.

Evie's mental decline had been gradual; he'd first noticed that she was forgetting things in 2010, it was just the odd thing and he'd not really taken much notice. At the beginning of 2012 she'd gone into town to get her hair done and come back to the car in tears as she hadn't made an appointment. Tom looked at the appointment card and then at the name of the hairdressers she'd come out of and realised that they didn't match. He pointed to a different hairdresser further down the street and asked Evie if that was the one she used and she'd laughed at herself as she'd gone to the wrong one and couldn't understand why she'd do such a thing.

After several more memory loss incidents, which included her not being able to find her way home after walking around the corner to post a letter, Tom encouraged Evie to go to see a doctor and she was diagnosed with having Alzheimer's disease. Despite taking various tablets, Evie's memory was fading rapidly and Tom knew that it wouldn't be long before she would be unable to recognise him which he couldn't bear. More often than not, she called him Albert, he knew he shouldn't be upset but this he found most hurtful.

"Where are we going?" asked Evie.

"We're going for a long drive, it's a lovely day. We might drop in and see Ruth."

"Whose Ruth, do I know her?"

"She's my daughter, she came to our wedding."

"Oh how lovely, I remember getting married in St Mary's. It was on a day just like this."

"It was a wonderful day," Tom said sadly. Sometimes he wondered if he might be losing his mind. Evie had remembered their wedding day and sounded so normal talking about it that people might think that she was well. It wasn't always like that, some days were better than others. He was finding that it was taking her longer and longer for her to get dressed. She was still a very private person and didn't like him trying to help her but if he didn't then she would forget what she was doing and appear wearing her day clothes over her night clothes or not be wearing what he'd laid out for her and be looking for an item of clothing that had been thrown out. He felt weary from looking after her and was convinced that the Chanctonbury Ring had something to do with her illness.

Today was the anniversary of the day they'd first met in 2013 and he hoped that if he took her up to the Ring then there was a chance that her mind might be healed and they could spend the last few years of their lives together as they had when they were first married. He hated the place but it was his last hope; he didn't know what he would do if this didn't work.

As they drove into West Sussex, he thought about his daughter and hoped that she'd gone to visit her friend up north as she'd done on the day of the flood. He decided that he would stop at her house and make sure she hadn't changed her plans and stayed at home. He couldn't be sure if the tsunami would hit the south coast but so far, everything news worthy had happened as it had done before.

"I'm hungry, could we stop and get a bite to eat please," Evie asked as they passed a services sign.

"Of course we can," he replied as he signalled to leave the motorway. It was lovely to see her smiling and happy and not anxious and confused. Tom looked at the clock it was almost midday; he really needed to get up to the Chanctonbury Ring before the wave hit the hill and he realised that he didn't have time to see if Ruth was at home. "I've got a picnic in the back; we're going to have our lunch at the top of a hill. There will be a beautiful view."

"Oh how lovely, you are kind Albert, to take me out. Are we going to have lunch soon?"

Tom drove his car up the chalky path towards the Chanctonbury Ring, he knew he shouldn't but he couldn't let his beloved car get washed away in the flood if history were to repeat itself. As they approached the Ring, Evie looked at him with concern.

"Oh dear," she said. "Why are we here, I don't want to have lunch up here, don't you remember that this is an awful place?"

"Do you really, remember the Chanctonbury Ring and what happened here?

"Of course I do, silly, I don't want to be here," she was starting to panic.

"We won't stay long; we'll just have our lunch and go home. I'm hoping that you will be cured if you spend some time up here."

"Is someone ill?"

"Yes Evie, you're getting very forgetful these days. You know this is a magical place and I thought it might help. You don't want to go into a home do you?"

"Are you mad Albert? I'm not forgetful. I might forget the odd thing but talking about a home, that's horrid."

"Don't worry about that, we'll just have a sandwich or two and some cake, the one with the cherries in you like so much and get a bit of fresh air."

"Oh I love cake. Is it home made?"

"Yes, I got it from the farm shop."

Tom stopped the car on the side of the hill furthest from the sea, so that when the tidal wave hit the hill, his precious car wouldn't get salt water over it. He opened the boot and pulled out a blanket to sit on and a rucksack with their food in. Behind the seats he'd stowed a two man dinghy with oars and in the boot, he'd a cool box with some supplies, two warm coats as although it was a warm autumn day the evening was likely to be cold. The remainder of his boot was filled with tins of biscuits, this was part of Evie's collection and he planned to dump them somewhere but hadn't had the chance to do this.

Soon after they had married, Evie had started to collect decorative biscuit tins. At first Tom found this to be an unusual past time but as the months went by the collection had become so extensive that Tom found the piles that were displayed around their house to be an eyesore. Knowing that there was a link between the tins and Albert, when he'd asked Evie about it, she'd always looked sad that he was questioning her motives and he found that he couldn't continue with the conversation. Now she was losing her memory and unable to go shopping; he'd decided that he would get rid of as many of them as he could. So far, he'd managed to reduce her collection by half - she hadn't noticed.

Silently, they sat on the rug looking out at the landscape around them, deep in thought. Evie smiled at Tom. "I do love you, you know?" she announced picking up a large piece of cherry cake. "The countryside is so beautiful, if only those trees weren't there," she said looking over her shoulder at the beech trees behind her.

Tom smiled sadly back at her, he wondered if she was talking about himself or Albert; the latter was more likely. Tom looked at his watch, they'd been at the Chanctonbury Ring for nearly two hours and there'd been no sign of a flood or the hurricane strength wind they'd experienced when the tragedy had happened. He was becoming increasingly uneasy and although he'd been repeating over and over in his head for Evie to be given the gift of a healthy mind, nothing miraculous had yet happened. Tom stood up, there was nothing for it, they'd have to walk seven times anti clockwise around the beech trees and then he would ask for Evie to be restored back to her old self. "Come on, let's go for a walk, we've had our lunch and we should walk some of it off.

"I'm tired," replied Evie, you go, I'll be fine. I might shut my eyes for a moment or two."

When Tom was sure that Evie was asleep he began his walk and realised how desperate he'd become; he didn't want to lose Evie again. If his friends could have seen him they would have said that he was on the verge of a breakdown but none of them knew what he'd been through and what a wonderful person Evie had been. When he finished walking around the trees and after checking that nobody was around, he called out to what he believed to be a spirit in the hill; he dared not believe that the Devil lurked there. "Please, it was you that started all this," he yelled. "You must make my Evie better, we've been through enough, and she doesn't deserve to lose her mind. Please, I beg this of you. I will do anything."

When Tom returned to Evie, she was still sleeping, he still thought she looked beautiful when she slept and then it occurred to him that if she spent the night on the enchanted hill, then the magic would work and he could collect her in the morning and they would return to their home in Wales and continue as if nothing had happened. Tom left her some food, covered her with both coats and believing that she was in a trance like sleep, drove away.

When she woke, it was dark and she was alarmed to find herself outside. She'd been dreaming such bizarre dreams. She remembered seeing a hill on fire; she didn't like what she'd seen and had moved her dream on to find herself sitting on the side of a road as if she was waiting for someone to pick her up. She wasn't sure who was coming or where she was going, she just had the feeling that whoever was meant to come for her had forgotten about her and she'd felt so alone and helpless. Her worst dream that had woken her up was that she'd miscarried and lost Edward. It had been a relief to wake up and know that this wasn't true as she could remember him as a child asking for a biscuit and then as a man. She tutted out loud as she couldn't remember where he lived. She would have to look in her address book and find out; she didn't like to forget such important things.

She pulled off the coats that were on top of her and was puzzled how they'd got there; she didn't remember covering herself with them. The night air was cold and she decided it was too cold to be in the garden and she really should go inside and make herself a cup of tea. She would ask Albert to bring in the blanket and coats later and was a little cross with him for leaving her out so long. She stood up, the kitchen light was out and she would have to feel her way back into the house. When she found him she would give him a piece of her mind. She tried to see if she could make out the shape of the building but all she could see were the outline of trees in front of her. They were familiar and she remembered them from somewhere.

Blindly, she walked on and thought that she might be at the foot of the garden; she would walk towards the trees and hoped that she would find the back door. She felt cold and shivered, the wind was picking up and she could hear a rumble of thunder in the distance; she didn't want to get caught in a storm.

Tom rang his daughter and then waited for her to pick up. He'd waited outside her house confused and worried that he might have done the wrong thing by leaving Evie up at the Chanctonbury Ring. In the darkness, he could hear thunder rumbling in the distance and wondered, as a storm was approaching, if the tsunami would come during the night; there was a good chance that things might have altered. There were some things in 2013 that were not exactly as they had been,

Evie for instance had been fine when he first met her and Barney hadn't been so fragile.

He was glad that Ruth and her husband were not at home. He'd hoped to sleep at her house as he still had a key but he didn't like to go into it without permission. Tom looked up at the sky as another flash of lightning lit the sky and was followed by a rumble of thunder; he didn't feel safe where he was.

"Hi Dad, are you ok? I haven't heard from you for a while."

"Well I'm not having one of my best days. You know Evie's not been that well lately... I know this sounds a little crazy but the day I met Evie and took her up to the Chanctonbury Ring something very odd happened; something out of this world and I am convinced that is why Evie got ill. I'm glad you're not here and the flood won't get you, it didn't come earlier but I think it might tonight. I thought that if I left her up there for the night then she might be cured; it's her last chance," he replied and waited patiently for a reply, not knowing what his daughter would say. He hoped that she would understand what he was trying to do.

"Dad, not that flood story again? Are you completely mad? As much as I don't like the woman, please don't tell me you've left her up there all alone in the dark, she's probably frightened to death by now. You're really starting to worry me; why didn't you ring me before you did this?"

"She'll be fine, she was asleep when I left her, I know it sound's mad but I'm sure it will work. You don't know how bad she's got; I don't know what else to do."

"You've got to go back and get her. I'll get her some more help. There must be a doctor out there with a new drug. Please Dad go and get her before it's too late. I've got to go now, the taxi's just arrived. No, I'll come home, go and get Evie and I'll get the train back, you're not right Dad, I think caring for Evie has made you ill.

"No Ruth, I'm fine, don't come back, I'll go and get her, I promise. I'll ring you later. You mustn't worry. Bye love, I'm sorry to have worried you."

Tom cancelled the call before Ruth could reply, he was surprised by her extreme reaction, she didn't understand about the Chanctonbury Ring.

Tom looked up at the sky, the storm was heading towards them and this he considered to be a good sign; his plan was beginning to work and he knew that whatever hid inside the hill had heard him and his prayers would be answered. He looked over at Ruth's house and decided it wasn't a good place to stay as it wasn't far enough away from The Chanctonbury Ring and he suspected that the flood water might reach as far as Dorking. He started his engine and would look for a bed and breakfast on the North Downs but then that might not be any good, his only chance of surviving the tsunami was to go back to the Ring and hope that he wouldn't affect Evie's transformation.

Evie shivered. The night air was cold and she rubbed her hands together to try and warm them up. She'd started to walk down the hill away from the trees that she disliked so much but wasn't sure where she should go. She could hear the rumble of thunder and she knew that the storm was approaching and although she didn't want to go back, she thought that the trees might give her shelter should it start to rain. She frowned, she could remember being in this very place once and it had rained heavily but she couldn't remember when that was.

She turned around, looked at the black silhouette of the trees against the night sky and thought how terrifying they seemed. Her attention was drawn to a shadowy figure of a woman standing by one of the beech trees and she thought it curious that she seemed to be sparkling and had a pale white light around her. She thought that this woman might be able to tell her the way back home; she hoped that her mother would be up and wouldn't be cross that she was back so late.

As Evie approached the woman, she noticed how young she was; she was a teenager perhaps and she smiled as Evie approached. Her skin was so pale and the clothes she wore were unusual. Evie blinked, trying to adjust her eyes. There was something quite surreal about this woman but she seemed friendly enough and she put her hand out to take Evie's hand.

"Come with me Evie, I will look after you and protect you from harm. You will be safe with me. I have seen you before, do not be afraid, you are lost to all those that love you but soon you will be free of your pain," said Cornelia, the spirit from the Roman temple.

"I wouldn't say I was in pain exactly, I just need directions to Cambridge. No not there, mother doesn't live there. Give me a moment and I will remember." Evie took Cornelia's hand, she couldn't help herself and as she felt her cool skin touch hers, her head began to spin. She felt as if she'd been drinking too much champagne and for a moment she was looking down on herself and her new friend as if she was watching herself on film. She wanted to fly up higher and soar through the air and fly across the Downs like a bird and she knew that the girl wanted that too but there was something stopping her - someone. Slowly, she allowed herself to drift back in her body as if she was entering a shell of herself. She let go of the girl's hand, she looked so sad - so lost.

She gasped with surprise, it was like a bank of fog had lifted from her mind; she could remember everything, every detail of her life. She remembered what had happened up at the Chanctonbury Ring all those years ago and she knew every element of that day. The girl had cured her and she knew that her home was in Wales with her beloved Tom and not with her dreadful mother. She wondered what she was doing up on the hill at night and wondered where Tom might be. She looked out across the Downs at the twinkling lights and then at the spirit who was smiling at her.

"I too am trying to go home. I have been trying to leave this hill for a very long time. We will find a way out of here together."

"Yes," replied Evie. "Thank you for helping me, I need to find Tom; he'll be very worried about me." She could feel herself shivering. She felt sleepy and so very cold. She looked back at the girl for guidance but she'd gone.

The rain began to fall and the lightning exploded in the sky, sending a jagged fork onto the Downs and was followed by a loud clap of thunder. Tom parked his car in the same place, found his torch and then with urgency ran up to the top of the hill, through the rain to find Evie; he'd been a fool, maybe Ruth had been right, perhaps he'd become ill looking after his sick wife and had lost his mind too. What was he thinking of leaving her alone on the hill; he knew he'd made a dreadful mistake.

He found the picnic rug and was alarmed to find that she wasn't sleeping under the coats where he'd left her. He called out her name but she didn't reply. He picked up the coats, put his on and continued his search. Eventually he found her, at the foot of one of the beech trees; she was sat up leaning against it and appeared to be asleep. Gently he crouched down next to her to wake her, his heart thumped in his chest from anxiety.

"Evie it's time to wake up. I'm sorry I've been so long," he took up her hand and then gasped - it was as cold as ice. "Evie it's raining you need to put your coat on." Tom looked at her with despair; he couldn't see her chest rising, he couldn't tell if she was breathing. He stood up again and looked around for help; he was on his own. He knew that he should try and resuscitate her; he'd never attempted to do this before. He could feel himself crying, he hadn't cried since he was a boy; he bent down to move her away from the tree and to lie her down so he could try and restart her heart. He didn't know if he was too late but he had to try.

"Tom, is that you?"

"Yes, you're alive," he touched her cheek, tenderly, brushing away the rain and his tears; he was still crying. "You must put this coat on or you will freeze to death, please love, it's raining. I'm so sorry, I did something terrible. I'm a terrible person"

Tom, I know why you left me here, I understand. I am better now and love you dearly. Can we go back to our home in Wales? I really don't like it here."

"Yes Evie, my darling, let's go home."

They sat in the car, talking, while they waited for the storm to pass and they were relieved to find that there was no tsunami. Storm clouds passed over them innocently and the sky began to clear.

In the early hours of the morning as they drove back to their home in Wales, Tom realised how lucky he'd been; he'd saved Evie from the brink of death and somehow, her mind had been restored. Although he felt elated and the luckiest man in the world, it did occur to him that he'd asked a favour from the Devil and that there may be a price to pay - perhaps he would go to Hell. Evie swore that she would never visit the Chanctonbury Ring again.

41

Amy smiled, if you'd asked her if she would be where she was now, this time last year, she would have laughed hysterically at the very idea. She looked up at the flickering strip lighting and wished it would stop flashing; she was tempted to turn it off but then there were no windows in the room and she would be plunged into darkness. The cream suit she'd borrowed from Sarah's mother pinched her at the waist so she stood up to undo the button; cross that her attempt to diet had failed - since she'd left hospital she'd gone up two dress sizes. Amy clutched her flowers a little more tightly, she felt excited and nervous all at the same time. She wished she could open a window and let some fresh air into the room; she felt too hot, was starting to sweat and was becoming intoxicated by the smell of the freesias and an orange flower that she couldn't identify at the centre of her posy. Anxiously, she looked down at her wrist watch it was just before 10am - just ten more minutes and then she would be married.

She sat back down and placed her flowers on a table next to her chair. There were several magazines left there to read, they looked as if they had been there a good few years and had been read many times as the corners were curled with age; not one was issued in the current year 2010. Amy looked around the room at the pictures on the walls; they were of sailing ships - mostly steam ships which she found odd. She wished there was a friend in the room to talk to.

Amy's phone beeped, she hoped it would be a text message congratulating her. Eagerly she looked into her bag for her mobile and then frowned when she saw who the message was from - it was from James. She unlocked her phone, it was nothing like the one she had in 2016 and then pressed the message icon to read the text.

"Call me, we need to talk."

Amy was annoyed, he really did have a nerve to text her on her special day and she wondered if he'd found out that she was getting married. She wondered what he wanted to talk about.

A lot had happened since she'd been given her life back in 2008. In the last two years she'd managed to get herself a good job in a marketing department in Crawley; a rival to Treadmill Marketing. She'd excelled there and now managed some impressive customer portfolios. She'd bought herself a show home in Horsham and had rescued a black cat and although her name was Ruby, had renamed her Molly - she didn't seem to mind. At weekends and in the evenings she couldn't help herself and she found herself trawling through the papers looking for people that had gone missing so she could help trace their bodies or find them alive which pleased her more. Her psychic skills were now finely tuned and she was able to give Inspector Brandon precise crime scene locations.

The servant girl and baby she'd discovered in 2016 at Oakwood House had puzzled her. She'd tried to concentrate and seek her out to see if she was still in the clutches of Lord Grey and had even driven to the house to see if she could feel her presence to make sure that she'd actually helped her. The girl didn't come forward and she hoped that this was a good sign and that she and her baby were at peace. Whilst she was there, she could sense the malignant spirit of Lord Grey and hadn't stayed for a moment more than she needed to. As she'd sped along the drive in her car, away from the house, she was almost sure she'd seen him looking out of the downstairs hall window - his face twisted with disgust.

Amy thought back to the day she'd appeared in court. That had been a difficult and distressing time and as she gave evidence, she'd keep reminding herself that if Ted walked out that court room, then he would continue to murder innocent women. Sarah had chosen to give evidence via video conference as she couldn't face Ted again. The jury found Ted guilty of murder, attempted murder and grievous bodily harm; he was given a life sentence of twenty five years. Sarah was incensed that they hadn't thrown away the key and even more enraged that there was a possibility that he could be let out perhaps after only serving fifteen years. Ted had cried when his sentence had been read out and Amy had stared at him with contempt as he was taken away.

When Amy had returned home, she'd sat in her front room, found a bottle of wine and had then sobbed. She'd slept badly that night and couldn't understand why she was so miserable. She thought that when Ted had been locked away in prison she might feel a weight lift of her shoulders. She was surprised to find that she felt guilty that he'd been imprisoned and felt somehow responsible for turning him in to a monster; she wondered if she'd been more loving that it might have made a difference. This thought she dispelled, he'd killed a school girl before he'd met her and she told herself off for thinking such preposterous thoughts.

Amy looked at her watch, she'd five more minutes before the service started and she wondered if she'd time to ring James; her finger hovered over the call button, they'd not spoken in six months. She was still smarting from the shock when he told her that their relationship had ended and that he was going back to his wife. She thought they had been happy, she thought that they had a future together. After he'd gone, she'd blamed herself for their break up as it had been her that had made him leave his wife in the first place.

She thought back to the day she'd summoned up the courage to talk to him. She found his mobile number on his business card and rang him on the pretext that she wanted to buy a mobile phone. She'd arranged to meet him in his mobile phone shop in Horsham. He could have quite easily asked one of his staff to look after her as he'd suggested before but after chatting for over half an hour about her incompetence with technical devices, she'd managed to persuade him to meet her in person. When she'd been talking to him she could tell that he was attracted to her and she thought that it was really quite strange that she knew so much about him already. She knew that he would build a kit car and she knew what it was like to sleep with him when all he could remember was a chance meeting with her in a car park.

The first time they went out together, James had taken her to a restaurant in Burgess Hill as he was sure that he knew no one there that might tell his wife that he was two timing. Amy hadn't minded the cloak and dagger relationship and was sure that James would leave his wife for her within weeks of going out together as his marriage was in trouble anyway. James's wife transpired to be a hypochondriac and was extremely paranoid.

Amy soon discovered that their secret liaisons were constantly interrupted as James' wife kept calling him with various concerns. Her calls eventually became too much for Amy and she begged him to leave her. He'd promised and had kept to his word but constantly worried that his wife might take her life or that his daughter would be suffering without him. He stayed with Amy for eight weeks and then went back to his wife for the sake of his daughter.

Amy was inconsolable as she knew when she'd met James in 2016 he'd been divorced and had been able to have a relationship with her without feeling guilty. In hindsight, if Amy had waited until that year to contact James, then things might have worked out for them.

One evening alone again in her new house, she'd been watching a documentary about life inside a high security prison and it suddenly dawned on her that Ted was in a similar one. Conditions inside were grim and it occurred to her that he would be suffering, he'd never liked being cooped up and he must feel so alone; she knew the pain of solitude well. She looked at her glass of red wine and thought she might be going soft in the head to be concerned about his wellbeing. It was his punishment for murder and for almost killing her; she rubbed the scar where the knife went in, it still hurt her.

The following night Amy got out a notepad and with Molly lying on the table next to her, she started to write to him; she wanted to understand why he'd wanted to kill her and what went through his mind. As she wrote she realised that she was seeking closure. She needed to know what had gone wrong; she wanted to know what was wrong with her. She didn't expect to receive a reply.

A week later as she was leaving the house for work the postman handed her some mail. She'd already closed the front door and not wanting to open the door again and let Molly out, she opened her handbag to put the letters into it and then noticed a hand written envelope - it was from Ted. She wasn't sure if she wanted to open it; in many ways she felt revolted by its very presence. She put the other letters in her bag and then placed Ted's letter on the car seat next to her and then into the foot well as she felt uncomfortable having it so close to her. She imagined the letter opening itself and exploding with expletives, mocking her and running her down so that she felt small, worthless and pathetic. Amy was cross with herself for writing to him in the first place - she obviously had a death wish.

Whilst Amy put together a mail shot on her computer, all she could think about was the letter. She would read it at lunch time and if it was horrific she would tear it in to shreds and throw it away so she wouldn't be tempted to read it again and take note of his words. She was a lot stronger these days and knew that she must not allow him to break her down and become a shell of a person as she'd been before.

At 12:02, tentatively, Amy tore open the letter, took out a wad of paper and unfolded it; she was surprised by the number of pages he'd written. It took her a full forty five minutes to read through his letter and she was speechless and confused. There wasn't a bad word said against her, it was a tender, apologetic and a repentant letter. Ted revealed at the end of the letter that he'd turned to God and said that he was a changed man. He knew that he deserved to be in prison for what he'd done and prayed every day for God's forgiveness. Most surprising of all he declared his love for her and although he knew that she might not be able to love him again after what he'd done to her, he hoped that she would forgive him and begged that she keep in contact and they could at least be friends. Amy had been so shocked by his letter that she'd asked her boss if she could go home as she wasn't feeling very well.

Over the next few months, they exchanged letters and finally she believed Ted to be a changed man. He was devoted to God, was in therapy and was taking medication for depression and anxiety. He told Amy that he'd not been in his right mind when he'd committed murder and swore that he could never carry out such a terrible crime again. He praised Amy for her courage and told her that she was a wonderful person. His letters were gushing, loving and sometimes desperate and he begged her not to stop writing as he couldn't continue his life without her. Amy found that she was looking forward to his letters and then in the thirteenth letter from Ted she remembered almost passing out when she read the words 'will you marry me' jump from the page. She hadn't expected that and she felt a strange sense of relief that his past conduct wasn't her fault. He said that she was the best thing that had ever happened to him and he considered her perfect enough to marry.

Sarah and Michael were very shocked when she told them that she was going to marry Ted but she didn't expect them to understand. Sarah's mum had patted her hand sympathetically and told her that she should follow her heart but should be cautious.

It was now two minutes to ten, Amy stood up again and did up her button on her skirt and then checked her suit over for fluff. She looked nervously at the locked door, she hadn't seen Ted for a long time, not since the trial and at ten o'clock she would marry him in the prison's chapel in the next room. She was sure that Ted would approve of her outfit; he liked women to wear skirts. The door leading to the cells didn't open until one minute past ten and Ted was led into the room by two prison officers who were going to be witnesses when they took their marriage vowels.

"Oh, I'm so glad you're here, you look wonderful, you've had your hair done too; it suits you," said Ted smiling.

"Thank you," replied Amy looking at Ted's suit she'd sent him. It didn't fit properly and hung off his shoulders; he'd lost a lot of weight. A prison officer took off his handcuffs whilst the other office locked the door behind them. The waiting room door on the other side of the room was opened and the wedding party moved through to the chapel. There was no one waiting for them, no congregation just empty pews. Amy shivered, she could sense deceased inmates in this room trying to fight their way out of the prison; unable to leave its walls.

Silently, they stood in front of the altar and waited for the vicar to arrive, he was nearly ten minutes late. Amy's phone began to ring; she'd forgotten to turn it off. Embarrassed, she fumbled through her bag to cancel the call, she could see it was James and a wave of guilt flushed through her body; she'd not told Ted about him, she didn't think he could emotionally take her having a relationship with someone else. Amy cancelled the call apologised and put her phone on silent

"Who was it," whispered Ted.

"Just a friend from work wishing me well," replied Amy but she knew she didn't sound convincing. Ted gave her a weary smile and was going to ask something else but saw the vicar enter the chapel.

"I'm sorry I'm late," he announced. "I've had a difficult morning." Instantly Amy knew that he'd just read the last rites to an inmate and he'd died as his translucent figure was stood in the vicar's shadow. The spirit looked confused as if he wasn't sure where he was or where he was meant to go. He looked over at Amy for help and she knew instinctively that if she didn't act quickly then his soul would be trapped in the prison for ever, walking the corridors lost in a world where nobody heard your bewildered cries for help.

"John, you're dead," Amy called. "Your cell mate poisoned you and you have died. You must go from here. You know what happened now; you can join your mother in heaven and leave this place. You're free now." The spirit nodded and faded away.

"How did you know..." asked the vicar but he couldn't finish his sentence as Ted cut in.

"What on earth are you saying Amy, who's John?"

"He was a spirit Ted, I told you that I have psychic ability and I've been helping West Sussex Police with murder investigations."

"Yes, you did but I'd never imagined you would be calling out men's names in public. People might think you're possessed."

"I'm sorry Ted, it won't happen again." Amy looked at Ted's bitter face and knew that he'd not finished with her; she was disappointed that he wasn't proud of her. She remembered how he'd worn her down when he was displeased. Amy's phone vibrated loudly in her handbag and she knew it was James trying to call her again.

"Who is that who keeps calling you? Don't they know you are getting married today?"

Amy felt that she'd nothing to lose, James was a friend and she should be allowed to have male friends without worrying. "He's just a friend. It was James..."

"I thought as much. You've been having an affair with him haven't you? You bitch!"

Amy's mouth fell open in amazement; Ted hadn't changed one bit! He might regret murder and write that he loved her but he didn't trust her; his jealous streak was incurable. She laughed at herself as she thought that by marrying him that he would see that she wasn't interested in other men. Ted had proved that this wasn't the case. She could feel anger building; she couldn't allow him to think of her as a bad person. "How dare you, you bastard! He's a friend and I don't need to explain myself. If you think I would marry a jealous creep like you then you've got another think coming." Amy gasped, what she'd said had been the absolute truth and she was pleased that she'd said it.

"No, Amy, we can get through this, you need medication, you can't help yourself and I can help you. God can help us both."

Amy had heard him call her a fucking bitch as she was let out of the chapel and she'd cried. She didn't feel let down or upset that she'd walked out on him but just relieved that she'd escaped a fate worse than death. She was annoyed with herself for being so naive; she should have listened to Sarah and Michael. The one good thing that had come out of this was that she realised that she didn't need help or medication; she was just a normal person. Perhaps a little lonely but normal none the less - she would have to work on coping better at being by herself.

When she got in the car, she looked in her bag for a tissue to wipe away the mascara that had run down her face, she could see herself in the mirror in the visor and she looked a state. Her phone vibrated in her bag and she took it out and decided to take James' call, she felt fragile and hoped he wasn't going to hurl abuse at her too.

"Hi James, why are you calling?" she asked, wiping the last of her mascara away.

"Thank goodness you've answered; I just had to talk to you. Amy, I shouldn't have gone back to Brenda, she's left me, taken Pippa and gone to live with her mother. Amy, I can't live without you, I'm so sorry for putting you through so much. Please say you'll have me back, I've been such a fool."

Amy cancelled the call but then after a few moments felt guilty and rang back. "I've been a fool too." she began.

42

Sarah pulled her car up in front of Michael's sister house and looked anxiously at him. "You look so pale, are you sure you're ready to face him?"

"Yes, I've got to get this over with, he's just a boy. I don't know why I'm so worried. Anyway I've got to accept he's human and I need to stay with my sister for a while until I'm certain that her house is as fire proof as it can be."

Sarah felt miserable, if he stayed with Helen then they wouldn't be able to see each other during the week; they'd only be able to meet up at weekends as he couldn't drive. She wanted him to live with her in her mother's house but she knew that wasn't possible. Her mother, although she seemed to like Michael, was alarmed that she'd a boyfriend nearly twice her age and she sensed that she disapproved. The only way they could live together would be for her to finish her A 'Levels, find a job, and then earn enough money to pay rent. She was sure her mother would come around eventually but it did make her sad that she was upset with her. It had been a wonderful moment seeing her again, she'd hugged and kissed her and hadn't let go for at least five minutes as she was so pleased to see her alive and well.

"Come on then, let's go. I have to keep reminding myself that my sister thinks that I've just been released from the army and have some psychological issues. The thing is, I've actually never felt better mentally. It's a shame I've lost the use of my arm but at least we're still alive and I've got you. I'm not sure what we should tell Helen about how we met. Perhaps we could say we met at the hospital, which is true and that after saving you from an evil maniac we fell hopelessly in love with each other. What do you think?"

"Ok," said Sarah getting out of the car. "Just don't talk about me doing A 'Levels or she'll think that you're some sort of pervert." Michael smiled, "I'm a lucky boy aren't I?"

When Helen opened the door, she flung her arms around them both as she was so happy that Ted hadn't killed them. She'd read all the papers in great detail and had been horrified; the only thing that she couldn't understand is why Michael had been in the hospital in the first place. After a pause and some quick thinking, Michael explained that he'd been visiting a friend that was recovering from being caught in a bomb blast and had seen Ted loitering in the reception and just had a hunch that he was up to no good and had followed him. Helen didn't question their story and seemed more interested in his injured arm.

Michael was relieved to find that Aaron and Brighton had gone to the park with their friends next door and wouldn't be back for a couple of hours. When Michael asked if he could stay with Helen, until he found employment, she'd said yes immediately. He was pleased to hear that he'd a home but wasn't sure he was doing the right thing. By staying with Helen then perhaps, he would be repeating what he'd done before and the fire would still happen regardless.

All too soon, the front door bell rang and when the door was opened his nephew and niece ran into the front room to greet their uncle. "They're a little bigger than you remember them, not babies any more," Helen said proudly.

Michael was a bit confused when he heard that but then he remembered that it was 2008. "You were both in prams when I last saw you," he said looking anxiously at Aaron to see if there was any malice in his eyes. They said hello and then rushed off to the kitchen to get some crisps but were turned away as they would be having lunch soon. As Helen made some coffee, he did his best not to stare too hard at Aaron; he didn't want to make him feel uncomfortable. "He's just a small boy," whispered Sarah.

After they'd finished their coffees, Helen went with the children to the kitchen to get some lunch and his niece and nephew returned with a sandwich each and asked to watch the television. They'd seemed to have accepted Michael and just ate their sandwiches sat on the floor as they watched a cartoon as if he wasn't there. He couldn't help staring at Aaron's blond curls. When he'd died in the fire he'd been eight years old; he was a lot smaller than he remembered perhaps no older than five and his hair was much shorter but there was something about the boy that made him shiver.

Whilst Helen got their lunch, Michael went upstairs to the bathroom and as he passed the smoke detector, he pressed the red button to test it and see if it was working. The alarm went off making him jump and he hoped the alarm would stop soon as it was so loud. He felt satisfied that if there were a fire then everyone would be able to hear it and get out of the house in time. When he came back downstairs, his sister looked at him curiously and he wasn't sure but he thought that he caught Aaron's eyes and saw them narrow for a moment.

"Your smoke detector is working just fine," announced Michael, trying to make light of his investigation.

"I nearly dropped a plate," laughed Helen. "I didn't know we had a smoke detector."

Michael looked at her in disbelief. "You really do have one and one day it could save your life. We'll need to check it regularly, at least once a month," sighed Michael. "Please."

"Yes I will. I hope you're not going to turn in to a bossy brother when you stay?"

"No, I won't" replied Michael. "I've been thinking, it's very kind of you to allow me to stay," he glanced at Aaron who was now staring at him and then turned to Sarah. "I know this is quite early in our relationship to ask this but I think, I could afford to support you while you finish..." he nearly said exams but he'd promised not to, "your course but I think we should move in together straight away. I've got a bit of money saved and I'm sure I could get some kind of work. What do you think?"

Sarah could have done back flips in celebration but she needed to show Helen that she was a responsible adult and not just a wild teenager. "Yes that'll be great; you just know when something is right. We'll need to tell Mum and she's bound to want to talk about it. I am sure I can persuade her, I am an adult. Yes Michael I'd love to live with you."

They both looked at Helen who looked bemused and then smiled, "You look good together," she said finally.

As they drove home, Sarah couldn't help beaming at Michael. "What? Why are you smiling?" he asked.

"I knew the moment Aaron walked into the room, you weren't going to stay; I can read you like a book. He's not normal, he's alive but there's something about his eyes, they pierce right through you."

"Believe me the fiend version of Aaron would make your blood curdle. I'm surprised I sleep at night. Just remind me to get Helen to check the smoke detector every month."

"So Mr McGrath, where are we going to live? I would be happy with just a room, as long as we're together. I'll get a part time job to help of course. Do you mind staying in Horsham; I'd quite like to be near my mother."

Michael laughed, she was so excited to be with him and he was glad that he didn't have to stay with Helen. He stroked Sarah's hand on the gear stick affectionately. "I would be happy to live in Horsham," he replied.

As they travelled home, Michael watched the fields and trees fly by and he could feel himself drifting off to sleep, he'd taken painkillers for his arm and they were making him feel very relaxed. He slipped into sleep without any nightmares and started a dream about being on a ship. It had big white sales and was cutting through the waves at great speed. He'd the feeling he was in a race, they were doing well and the finishing line was in sight. A mobile phone rang and he heard Sarah reply, he awoke to hear her having a conversation with her mother on the loud speaker.

"Calm down," he heard Sarah say. "Explain to me what's happened."

"I've brought him in and he's here in the lounge with me. Who would leave something so small on our doorstep? It makes me want to cry. He was in a carrier bag - he could have suffocated. How terrible, such an awful thing to do. Who would have done such a thing? Why us? Should I call the police or an ambulance?"

"Mum," Sarah said firmly. "What have you found? You're not making any sense."

"A baby Sarah! That's what I've found. "A poor little baby boy, with no clothes and lying in a carrier bag in the freezing cold. It's a good job I was leaving the house and found him; he could have perished."

The baby began to cry, Sarah could barely contain herself and had to stop herself from speeding, they were on the edge of Horsham and it would only be minutes before they were home.

"It's ours," said Sarah confidently. "I just know it is; I know his cry."

Michael looked at Sarah anxiously; she could be jumping to conclusions. "It might not be ours. Why would we get him back? There's no reason. Although when I bargained with the Devil, he was on my list."

"What are you talking about?" Sarah's mum asked. Michael had forgotten that he was on loud speaker. "We'll be back in a moment. Don't ring anyone, we're hoping that we know who the baby's parents are," he replied wondering what she might be thinking.

Sarah didn't park properly; she didn't have a moment to lose. Michael followed her and when they burst into the lounge and found her mother sat on the sofa, holding a baby wrapped in a towel; she seemed to be in shock. The baby was crying pitifully, he was desperate for milk and to be cared for. Sarah took him from her mother and while she rocked him to sooth him, she stared at his puckered face, he looked as if he'd just been born. She could feel tears of joy falling and she stood up to show Michael his son.

"This is our baby Michael, he is perfect, he has your eyes and my hair; he is amazing."

Michael hoped that Sarah was telling the truth and hadn't slipped into a psychotic state; her grief being so great, causing her to believe that the baby was hers. Michael stroked the baby's hair on his head, he was all he'd imagined him to be and instinctively he knew that they were the parents – he'd not been this happy in a long time.

Michael looked over to Sarah's mother who was looking anxiously at them both; it was going to be difficult to explain to her how they'd managed to have a baby and why it had arrived in a carrier bag. "He's ours," he said to Sarah's mother. She'd looked at her daughter and then back at him with a startled and confused expression. "I'll explain what has happened when I get back. This baby needs milk, nappies and clothes. Where's the nearest chemist?" Sarah's mother just nodded; she was speechless.

Sarah knew what he was saying was right; she was unable to feed their baby herself. "There's a chemist at the end of the road. Do you want me to go? You're not strong enough; you've only just come out of hospital?"

When Michael returned, he was hot and out of breath. He had with him a bag full of supplies for a new born baby, his mind was racing with possible stories that they could tell Sarah's mother and in the end he could think of nothing but to tell her the truth. It was very unlikely that she would believe them but if they both told the story then there was a chance that she would at least accept that they had known each other for a while and would explain how Sarah had become a mother overnight. Sarah was reluctant to tell her at first but as she began to ask questions she agreed.

As their baby sucked eagerly on a bottle of warm milk, they told her what had happened and she didn't say a word. When they'd finished, she didn't question them, she just looked concerned. "We should move," she said. "I don't want to be here when the tsunami hits. I'm not having my grandson washed away."

Sarah and Michael watched their baby as he drifted off to sleep; he was a little miracle plucked out of an insane world and they would do everything they could to protect him from harm.

***

In South London, a small boy with golden curls stared out of the window. He had in his hand a box of matches, which he knew he shouldn't have. His mother would scold him if she found him with them. He did his best to obey his mother and his teacher but there was a voice in his head telling him to do bad things. He tried not to listen but he feared that he may be in trouble if he didn't do as he was told. Just recently, he'd heard the same message over and over. He could hear it in his dreams and if he stood by the window that faced south, he could hear a voice in the wind calling him, telling him that he must start a fire soon. Carefully Aaron hid the matches away in the far corner of his cupboard until it was time.

***

From within the Chanctonbury Ring:

I do not sleep easily in the sea of blood that runs so freely,
Night and day makes no difference to the pain I feel inside.
I do not take the hearts of the undeserving; they come to me.
The day of reckoning will come and so will those that lied.
Until that day, I wait and watch; my tears a swollen tide.

If you have enjoyed Chanctonbury, you may be interested in reading my first novel

3004

London, a thousand years from now. The capital sprawls across the whole of England and every last bit of land is taken up by human habitation. The capitals are protected from terrorist and criminal infiltration, by an invisible shield and the people live under constant surveillance. Everyone, though, is happy – or seems to be. Law breakers are cast out of the shield, into the wilderness and are left there to fend for themselves.

Somewhere in the French wilderness, two sixteen-year-old Londoners are about to embark on the task that every boy their age must pass. They couldn't be more different: Kayleb is clever but puny; Rowan is strong and obstinate. They've never been friends – far from it – but they quickly realise that, if they are going to survive the bloody dangers ahead of them, they are going to have to learn to trust each other – and fast!

A thrilling, powerfully imagined sci-fi adventure that will keep readers guessing until the very last page.

To get your copy of 3004 or Chanctonbury go to Amazon or my 3004 Book Shop at http://www.freewebstore.org/3004-Book-Shop

Also available as e-books online at the 3004 Book Shop, Amazon and all other major online booksellers.

If you are interested in writing and would like advice or would like to read about my writing and marketing journey please visit my website www.nmurray.moonfruit.co.uk

PLEASE LEAVE ME A REVIEW ON AMAZON OR GOODREADS ☺